Saving Summer

by Olivia Linder

To everyone who made it,

and in memory of those who didn't

You are not alone.

If you are experiencing thoughts of suicide, please use the
following numbers:

988

or

1-800-273-8255

(National Suicide Prevention Lifeline)

1

Nolan

NO STUDENT, and I mean *no* student should be expected to wake up before ten in the morning during summer vacation. Save me all your crap about summer jobs, camps, activities, whatever—this is the one time a year when kids are allowed to be kids, or in my case, teenagers are allowed to be teenagers. No deadlines, homework, study sessions, or anything holding us back—unless, of course, you want to go on a thirty-five day excursion to Europe the summer before your senior year, and then the program decides you need to meet every weekday from nine to two-thirty for three entire weeks.

"If you're going to receive school credit for this trip, then you'd better believe you're going to have a thorough cultural education about every country we're visiting," the program coordinator had told us.

But this was the last of those three weeks. The last Monday I had to be awake at this hour. And come Friday evening, I'd be on a plane to Barcelona, and all of this would be worth it.

I shut off my alarm, jumped in the shower, threw on some khaki shorts and a T-shirt, and hopped in my truck. It was sunny today, bright and beautiful like a summer day should be. The past few days had been rainy and gross, which was rare for California in general but even rarer in June. It was nice to have the weather back the way it should be: warm enough to drive with the windows down, resting my arm against the side of the blue Chevy.

I pulled through the Starbucks drive-through for a double-shot espresso, parked in the community center's visitor lot, and headed into the auditorium with my drink in hand. There were no windows in the auditorium, but the fluorescent lights overhead cast a sickly, flickering glare over the seats, which was as close to that natural California sunlight as we were going to get in here.

Seated up near the front was Katie, my soon-to-be girlfriend, and one of the only people here I actually liked spending time with. We were already texting almost every night, so I'd probably be able to work some magic on the trip. I took the seat next to her and set my black schoolbag on the ground.

"Morning," I said. "How was your weekend?"

"Fine," she said to her phone. Her long, thick, golden-blonde hair was held back in braids today. I liked it better down, but she had swim meets right after these meetings on Mondays, Wednesdays, and Fridays, so she typically came at least halfway ready for that.

"How was your swim meet Friday?" I asked, since she'd skipped over that question in our last text conversation.

"We won two of the events," she said, clicking her phone off and finally turning to face me. "It was a tough team, though. One of the best in the county. How about you? What'd you do this weekend?"

"Chores around the house," I said with a shrug. "Saw a movie with the guys; it was alright."

I much preferred hanging out with my actual friends than almost everyone here, but I was friendly to them since we were, after all, going to be in Europe together and had to put up with each other. Most of them were friendly to me, too, but to be honest I missed my real friends and found most of the other people on the trip annoying—especially some of the girls who tried to flirt with me; I'd be glad once Katie and I labeled things and they'd leave me alone.

"What movie did you see?" Katie asked.

Before I could answer, the program coordinator, Tim, cleared his throat, meaning it was time to put our phones away and pay attention. He usually came in clapping and talking loudly; today he was so quiet I wouldn't have noticed he was onstage if I hadn't been sitting closer than usual. The lights on the stage made his pale skin blend in with the white sheet hung across the back wall.

"Everyone, listen up." Tim was serious, more serious than I'd heard him before. Usually the guy was so loud and full of energy we had to wonder what he was on to be so *awake* on a weekday morning during the summer. And then I realized it was 9:14; the meeting was supposed to start at nine. Tim was late, and he was *never* late. "Everyone, eyes and ears up here." His raspy voice shook like he was afraid of something; like he had seen a ghost. Due to the lower-than-usual volume, it took longer for everyone to quiet down.

A couple rows in front of me, a girl from my school named Marta was seated by herself, her reddish-blonde curls up in a ponytail. Marta wasn't the worst person here, but she still reeked of desperation, and I didn't enjoy interacting with her. My bigger issue was with her best friend, Summer—but then I realized Marta was sitting alone.

If she was sitting alone, that probably meant Summer wasn't here at all; Summer and Marta always sat together. I couldn't help but be thankful; Summer was irritating. Clingy. Not the kind of girl I wanted to be stuck in Europe with for thirty-five days. But I supposed she had just as much right to sign up for the trip as I did.

"Everyone, I..." Tim was really struggling today. I almost felt bad for the guy. "I don't know how to say this, but it's very serious, so I need everyone to *really* listen this morning, okay?"

The last few chatterers took the hint, and as their whispers faded out, an eerie silence fell over the room.

"I—truly regret to inform you all... Summer Madison passed away over the weekend."

Shock—that was the only way to describe it. For a moment, I was physically frozen. Seventeen-year-old girls didn't just "pass away over the weekend," did they? I saw her on Friday. I *talked to her* on Friday before we left—grudgingly, sure, but I didn't just imagine that encounter. She wasn't sick or anything like that.

I didn't think anyone believed Tim, but he continued.

"It's not up to me to discuss the details of her death," he said, "but due to the circumstances, I've hired a few grief counselors that will be available to talk to you over this next week. Emails are being sent to your parents, and if you no longer feel like you can participate in this trip, partial refunds will be available. I cannot stress enough the importance of reaching out for help if you feel like you need it."

I had *just* spoken to Summer on Friday. She couldn't have just *died*. I could still see her standing at that bus stop outside Starbucks; there was no way.

"Today's cultural enrichment has been cancelled," Tim said, "and instead the counselors will be meeting with anyone who would like to speak with them. In the meantime, you all are free to talk to each other, but *please* do not speculate about Summer's death. Be respectful."

"*What* is happening?" Katie whispered to me. "Summer's... just dead?"

"That can't be right," I said. "This can't be—"

I didn't know how to finish my sentence.

"You talked to her on Friday, right? Did she say anything? Do you know what—?"

"No!" I hissed, and Katie recoiled. I must have come across as defensive. Maybe I was—how dare Katie ask me if I knew anything about Summer's death? I never asked to be a part of Summer's life in the first place. She was nothing to me, just someone I knew. Someone I passed in the hallways at school. Why would *I* know anything?

* * *

MARTA STORMED across the courtyard like she was trying to lose the crowd following her. They were all asking her about Summer. That made sense, though—Marta was Summer's best friend. She was probably one of the first people to find out—then again, if she'd known, I doubt she would have come in today. I wouldn't have.

"Get *away* from me!" she snapped. "I don't know anything!"

"But she was your best friend, wasn't she?" someone asked.

"I said go away!"

I watched from a patch of grass outside the auditorium as Marta disappeared into the bathroom. I wondered if Tim would try to break up the crowd. Katie went to talk to one of the counselors, which I thought was a bit dramatic seeing as she'd probably talked to Summer all of twice, but I knew better than to tell her that.

"Hey."

I looked up and recognized Esme leaning over me, her long black hair falling forward. She tended to float between friend groups here; she was friendly with Summer sometimes. I used to think she was into me, but apparently she was gay. She'd never talked to me much, so I wasn't sure why she was talking to me now.

"What's up?" I asked her.

She took a seat on the grass beside me, took a deep breath, and said, "Just trying to make sense of it. Tim wouldn't say what happened to her."

"I don't think he's allowed to."

"I guess not, but... what are we supposed to think?" She hugged her legs to her chest. "She was a healthy—well, physically healthy—young girl."

"I think we're not supposed to think about it," I said. "Didn't Tim say not to speculate?"

"You don't sound like you're upset about this," she said with an accusing tone.

"It's not like she was my friend."

Esme took another deep breath. "She told me you gave her a ride home on Friday. I texted her that evening to make sure she got home alright in the rain. I wanted to give her a ride, but it was so far out of my way... She said you took her home."

"And?"

Her voice rose. "And I just want to know what happened!" She stared at the grass. "I'm sorry. I just... You might have been the last person to talk to her in person, besides maybe her mom." Another breath. "How did she die? Why can't Tim tell us that? My grandma has been a high school principal for forty years, and there's only one reason she wouldn't disclose a student's cause of death."

"So you've probably solved your puzzle," I said. "Whatever that is, it's probably the reason."

She stared at me. "Do you know what that is, Nolan? Do you have any guesses?"

"No." It occurred to me that I didn't *want* to know the reason. I wanted to know as little as possible. "Look, you're obviously taking this hard—"

"It's suicide."

My heart pounded at the word, and heat rushed through every inch of my body. I suppose a part of me had known that was what she was going to say, and now I couldn't unhear it. Esme stared at me like she was waiting for me to make some kind of connection, but I was done talking about this.

"Tim said not to speculate."

She pulled at the grass. "You weren't exactly nice to her, you know."

Anger surged at her implication. "What are you saying?"

She didn't answer me at first, but then she turned to face me. "Don't you at least feel a little bad? Or *sad*, even? Summer's *dead*, Nolan. She died, and you don't even seem upset about it. Maybe she wasn't your friend, but she didn't deserve to die at seventeen."

I couldn't hold myself back. "What the hell am I supposed to feel?" I shouted. "Just because I'm not handling this the same way as you, you think I had something to do with it? Do you even hear yourself? We don't even know how she died! All you have is a theory, and we're not supposed to speculate! Don't you *dare* try to make me feel like this is my fault!"

Esme didn't respond. She stood up, then glanced back at me like one of us was supposed to say something more. But neither of us did, and she walked away. It wasn't worth going after her to keep defending myself.

It was such a beautiful day out. The sun, the warm breeze, the smell of fresh-cut grass... but now everyone was upset. Summer had to go and ruin the first beautiful day we'd had in almost a week.

I walked back into the auditorium, this time to the backstage area. I was hoping to catch Tim, maybe ask him what he knew so I could prove Esme's theory was bull. But he wasn't there. I decided to go to his office—I couldn't find him there, either, but the door was open, so I figured I'd sit and wait for him to come back. Not like I had anything better to do with everything canceled.

His desk was, understandably, a gigantic mess of papers, sticky notes, stray pens, checks, and pamphlets. Out of respect for his privacy, I let my eyes wander to the garbage can on the floor, then the large orange bin next to it labeled "lost n found" with a faded black marker.

Right smack on top was a purple spiral-bound notebook covered in stickers. My heart started pounding when I noticed a big sticker on the top corner that read "SUMMER" in yellow bubble letters.

Summer is also a season, I reasoned. *Clearly this is just someone's "summer" travel notebook, or... isn't there a summer school program that meets here?*

To prove that I was being ridiculous, I opened up the notebook to see what was on the first page.

September 7ᵗʰ—

First day of junior year. I know a couple people in my A-Day classes, we'll see how tomorrow goes I guess. I saw Jonah today. I wish he'd move on. We broke up months ago.

Well, Summer *did* have a boyfriend named Jonah last year. I didn't have a clue what her handwriting looked like, but there was a pretty good chance this was her journal after all. Maybe if I kept reading...

I don't know why I let him talk to me, maybe I'm just worried I'll never do any better, or be able to get anyone else to like me. I mean, I tried to talk to Nolan today—

I felt my heart hitting my chest—even if I knew this was Summer's journal, I didn't expect to see my own name in it, much less on the first page.

—and he said "hey" or whatever but we didn't talk. I don't know why we can't just be friends. Maybe I'm not good enough.

What was this, some kind of manifesto about how I didn't give her enough attention? Did she leave this behind on purpose? I flipped to the last page that had writing on it.

June 24th—

I don't know what to do. I can tell nobody else on the trip wants me there, even the few who are actually nice to me sometimes. And Marta… she's got her new, better friends now and doesn't need me. She never needed me. This fight was just a way out for her.

Something's wrong with me but I don't know what. I guess I've never written that out before, but I've always known. My mom won't let me see a psychiatrist, she says I don't need one and it's a waste of money. But there has to be something wrong with me.

Do I even want to go on this Europe trip anymore? Is it worth it? It's too late to pull out of the trip, though. I guess I screwed everything up. I could've saved everyone so much trouble. All of this is my fault, I'll never learn how to just be normal.

I couldn't read any more. I wasn't sure *why*, since the last entry didn't mention me at all, but I couldn't shake some sense of... guilt. But why? What did I have to be guilty for?

I remember she was writing in a notebook when I came back here to look for Katie on Friday. I was going to give Katie a ride to her swim meet, but Summer told me she'd already left with one of her friends. She said *she* didn't have a ride home, though, and she'd buy me a coffee if I helped her out. I pointed out that her house was out of the way... She made it into a bigger deal than it needed to be and somehow guilted me into giving her a ride. Well, part of the way.

Staying here was pointless. I wasn't going to talk to a grief counselor because I felt no grief, and I wasn't going to talk to anyone else because I didn't want to talk about Summer, and that's all anyone else wanted to talk about. I left Tim's office and got back in my car before realizing I was still holding Summer's stupid notebook. I shoved it under a bunch of crap in my glove box and headed home.

My parents were still at work. They'd never know I came home early today; they always got home after me anyway. I sat back on the living room couch, turned on the TV, and tried to get my mind off this whole Summer thing. Even though I *knew* I had nothing to do with it, a part of me couldn't shake that small degree of guilt—did Esme have a point?

The last time I'd talked to Summer was on Friday. She freaked out at me because I said something wrong, according to her. I was always saying the wrong thing to her because the girl could never just be happy; she was never satisfied no matter what I told her. She wouldn't even let me drive her the whole way home. All I told her was the truth: we're not friends, and she needs to understand that.

I never asked for her to talk to me. I never wanted anything to do with her. She forced her way into my life, and now I was supposed to believe she killed herself because of something *I* did? Fat chance.

My phone rang—it was my father.

"Are you at your meeting?" he asked. "I'm looking at an email from Tim—"

"Yeah, I know about that."

"Summer... Was she one of your friends? Her name sounds familiar, but I don't remember you bringing her over or talking about her."

"She's not my friend," I assured him. "Uh, well, she *wasn't* my friend." The tense correction left a taste in my mouth that I didn't like. Why couldn't *anyone* talk about something besides Summer? "I hardly knew her, anyway. I'm fine; you don't have to worry about me."

"Are you sure? Even if you hardly knew her, it can be hard to process—"

"There's nothing to process because I didn't know her," I insisted.

"Alright." He sighed. "Look... I still want to send her family a card and maybe bring over some food tomorrow. Tim left her mother's contact information in the email. On your way home, can you pick up a card?"

"Why?"

"What do you mean, 'why?'" he asked. "Lose that tone. Someone's daughter just died, Nolan. You might not have known her *well*, but you knew her enough that I got an email about it."

"Everyone got that email! There's seventy kids on the trip, Dad. It's not like I ever talked to her!"

I know she died. Stop reminding me.

"*Lose* the tone." A pause, and I heard him take a breath. "Pick up a card on the way home; you can use the credit card if you don't want to pay for it. I'd expect a little more empathy from you, though; the way you're acting is shameful and I suggest you rethink your attitude before we go drop off the card tomorrow."

"Whatever."

"Pick up a sympathy card. We'll discuss this later."

I rolled my eyes but told him I would and ended the call. I'd go get one later; I had time. I didn't even want to think about psyching myself up to see

Summer's parents yet.

Why was I so... *afraid* to see them? It's not like Summer would be there. No one was going to ask me to share all my favorite memories of her or anything like that. I just had to say I didn't know her. Truthfully, I didn't *have* many memories of her, good or bad.

I had nothing to be afraid of as far as seeing Summer's parents. To admit fear in this case would mean admitting some sort of guilt or responsibility. Whatever happened to Summer had nothing to do with me, no matter what anyone said.

Grudgingly, I turned the TV off, grabbed my wallet, and got back in my truck. For a while, I just drove. I wanted to drive until I could stop thinking about her. But it was no use, so I pulled up in front of a Walgreens, parking next to a fountain and meandering to the card section. I found a section of cheap ones labeled "sympathy," grabbed the first one I saw, and headed to check out.

"Hey, man," I said, placing the card on the counter.

"How's it going?" the cashier replied. "Find everything you need?"

"Yep, thanks."

"That'll be $1.71."

I handed him two dollars, and he gave me back some change. One of the coins slipped out of his hand and hit the floor before I could catch it.

"Sorry," he said.

"It's fine, I got it." I held up the penny. "Heads up."

"Wow," he replied. "Today must be your lucky day."

I picked the sympathy card up off the counter. "I guess so. Have a good one, man."

My lucky day. Sure. I'm sure in a couple moments of annoyance over the last few weeks, I might have passively wished that Summer wouldn't go on the trip and I wouldn't be stuck in Europe with her, but I'd always imagined some issue with timing or her chickening out. Never *this*.

How did she die? Why couldn't Tim tell us? I was being ridiculous; obviously it was out of respect for her family. Even so, say Esme was right and it was suicide—that didn't mean it was because of anything I did.

What was the last thing I said to her? All I could remember was watching her get on that bus… Maybe it was a bus crash? No, that would have been in the news, and Esme said she'd talked to Summer later that night after she got home.

On my way out of the store, I bumped into someone, causing her to drop her wallet. I immediately bent down with her and helped her pick up the change.

"I am so sorry, ma'am," I said to her. When our eyes met, the dark-skinned woman appeared familiar to me, but I couldn't figure out where I knew her from. "You look familiar."

"Leah Browning," she said, straightening up.

Browning, Browning… Ah, yes. Leah Browning led an assembly back in February. It was some generic "bullying: knock it off" garbage that got everyone hyped up for a couple days before they went back to using slurs in casual conversations. Everyone got a free wristband that read "be kind;" I forgot what I did with mine.

"Nolan." I shook Leah's hand. "Well, I should get going. Sorry again."

"No worries," she said. "Remember to be kind."

I wondered if she ended all her conversations that way.

Before I got back in my car, I took another look at the fountain. Rolling my eyes, I reached into my pocket for that "lucky" penny.

Alright, God, I thought. *You want me to believe I had anything to do with this? Fine. Send me back in time and I'll undo it. Oh, wait, that's impossible? There's literally nothing I can do about it? Exactly. So leave me alone. Summer's Your headache now.*

I tossed the penny into the fountain and headed home. I set the stupid sympathy card down on the entryway table with my keys, then went back to the couch, laid back, and closed my eyes, because what I really needed now was a nap.

* * *

WHEN I opened my eyes, I wasn't on the couch. I was in my bed and my alarm was blaring at me. It was seven a.m.

I had not woken up where I'd gone to sleep. So yesterday must have just been a dream. Just to scare me, make me think twice about being "rude" to Summer when I saw her at the meeting today. Well, I didn't need to be awake until eight, so I shut the alarm off—guess I'd set the wrong one last night—and closed my eyes to enjoy that last hour of sleep.

"Nolan!" my mother shouted. "Nolan, wake up! You're going to be late for school!"

"Good one," I said, turning over and snuggling into my pillow. "Look, it only takes me like ten minutes to get to the community center, fifteen if I stop for coffee. I can sleep until eight."

"What are you talking about?"

"For the Europe trip meeting?"

She gave an exasperated sigh. "Look, you've made it to junior year without any tardies on your record, and I'd prefer if you kept it that way. Get up; we don't have time to argue."

I glanced at the clock again. In the corner, it read *09/07*. What the hell? September? *No, no, it's June! It's June!* I picked up the clock, thinking maybe if I stared hard enough, the *09/07* date would go away. But it didn't.

I set the clock down and picked up my phone to double-check. It was my old phone with an old picture of me and my buddies Jake and Liam as the wallpaper, rather than a picture Katie had sent me of a turtle she saw at the beach, and the date read *Tuesday, September 7.*

September 7. Then... it was the first day of junior year.

My room looked mostly the same, but there were things on my nightstand that shouldn't be there, and there weren't things in the corner that should have been there, and there were orange leaves dangling from the tree outside my window, and I was wearing pajamas I hadn't worn in months. I glanced at the door. My mother's hair was shorter, like it was last fall.

Was it *all* just a dream?

And then I remembered the fountain. *There's no way.*

"It's... the first day of junior year," I said, trying not to make it sound like a question as my heart pounded against my chest.

My mother rolled her eyes. "What did you think it was? I'll say it again: you don't have time to waste. Get up!"

"But—it was just..." Didn't she realize there was something wrong? "It was June. I fell asleep on the couch, and it was June. It can't be September again!"

"What can I say? Summer vacation flies by." She scoffed. "Get out of bed."

I sat up, still trying to figure out if I was going crazy or if it was all just some vivid dream. "I'm getting out of bed. Happy?"

"Thrilled. Hurry up and get ready."

This can't be real.

* * *

STANDING IN front of the school, I didn't get it. The first day of junior year? I forget most of my dreams shortly after I wake up, but I could still vividly remember so many things that were supposed to happen between now and June.

It couldn't have been the fountain. First off, I've wished for several things in fountains over the years, and if that was how wishes worked, I would've been living with the San Jose Sharks, or at least seeing free hockey games for the last six years.

Second, if this was about Summer, I only would have had to go back to Friday. Friday afternoon, after the meeting, when she asked for a ride home. I wouldn't have gone all the way back to the start of junior year. But... why else would I be here? And how was I supposed to get out of it?

I couldn't just stay in whatever weird timeline this was and pretend nine whole months of my life hadn't happened! I had to get back to that fountain.

"Hey, Nolan!"

I looked up to see who was talking to me, and speak of the devil, it was Summer. Summer, who not even a day ago was supposed to be dead. But here she was, in the flesh, walking to school as usual, dressed in this white tank top and a floral, ruffly skirt like a lot of girls wore. Her hair was down, straight, plain like always. There wasn't a thing out of the ordinary about her, and yet her presence was the least ordinary part of this whole time-warp situation. It felt like I was looking at a ghost.

"Hey, Summer," I said to the ground. If she annoyed me before, it was near impossible to look at her now knowing she could be the reason I was doing junior year over. I wanted to walk away, but then I remembered that if this *was* all about her, then the whole point of being back here was to be nicer to her.

Her greeting was normal; she always said hi to me in the halls. She'd always acted like just because we'd been in the same classes since elementary school, she was someone I cared about. But at no point during all that time were we ever friends.

I took a deep breath and tried to smile as we walked inside together.

"How was your summer, Summer?" I asked.

She smiled. Her lips were chapped and she didn't wear makeup. "It was great. I went to the beach with Marta's family for the fourth of July, and down to Los Angeles for a week, where I got this outfit." She moved her hands as if to show me, like I cared. "I love back-to-school shopping. Oh, but mostly, I just worked at the theater."

A memory hit me, one I didn't realize I had—Summer sold concessions at the downtown conservatory theater over summer break. She'd invited me to see one of the plays, since she got one free guest per show. I think I told her I was busy. Seems like something I'd do.

"How about you?" she asked. "What'd you do this summer?"

What *had* I done last summer? "Went to my family's beach house in Newport," I said. I was pretty sure that was right.

"Did you have a summer job?" she asked.

I shook my head. "No, vacation is a vacation. But I do help out at my dad's law firm sometimes, just assistant stuff that'll boost my application for Pepperdine. For their law school."

"Oh, wow." There was shock in her voice. "That sounds expensive."

I supposed I should show some interest in her, too. "Do you know where you want to go?"

"I haven't thought about it too much, but I'll probably go to a state school," she said. "I have to do well this year, though. I'm already retaking geometry, which means I'll have to take an extra math class senior year or over the summer. And I *really* want to go on this Europe trip over the summer... Have you heard about it?"

Oh, right, it *was* Summer who'd told me about the trip in the first place. I think she'd brought it up in whatever class it was we had together this year.

"No, not yet." I checked the time on my phone. "Well, I have to get going to trig."

"Wait, you know your schedule already?" she asked.

Right. We got our schedules in homeroom on the first day.

"Homeroom," I said. "I meant homeroom. I'm just thinking about trig, I guess, 'cause I hate it already."

She laughed. "Well, I'll see you around."

I sighed. "Yeah. I guess so."

This was so weird. I watched her fade into the crowd.

"Hey, man!" A hand clapped me on the back. It was Jake, with his hair buzzed like at the beginning of every school year and a smile that clearly said, *"I have no idea I have gym first period."*

"Oh, hey." I returned the handshake-hug he offered and noticed the smile fade from his face.

"You good?" he asked.

"Yeah," I lied, realizing I probably should've been way more excited to see him. He spent last summer... somewhere. Doing something. And Liam and I didn't see him until the first day of school.

"Alright." He shrugged. "Well, grandpa's farm sucked, so I'm ready to spend my days with people who aren't over the age of sixty or livestock." He shuddered. "Homeroom?"

"Yep, sounds like a plan."

Summer

I SAT down in homeroom, and I couldn't stop smiling. I couldn't believe I actually had a pretty good conversation with Nolan Alden. He'd always been in my classes, but over the years he became popular and I... didn't. He was always nice to everyone, though, and I didn't think his popularity would stop us from being friendly. I always tried to talk to him like a friend, because we *should* be friends. We'd known each other for years, but I guess it was true that we traveled in separate groups and never really talked. I guess I just assumed he'd be friendly to me since we'd known each other so long.

And of course, I'd basically had a crush on him since third grade; I'd had crushes on other guys over the years and even had a boyfriend last year, but my feelings for Nolan always seemed to come back eventually. It was like a celebrity crush, where I knew nothing would ever happen. But with the way he talked to me this morning, I had to wonder if maybe he did at least see me as a friend.

I didn't have a lot of guy friends. Well, I didn't have *any* guy friends. I didn't even have that many friends. I tried to be nice to everyone, but they weren't always nice back. Nolan was for a while, but the more I'd said hi over the years, the less receptive he'd become. He started sounding annoyed when I talked to him, and I didn't know why. I figured I should just keep being nice and hope for the best.

I didn't think I was overwhelming. I just waved to him in the halls, and sometimes he acknowledged me. We didn't often have actual conversations, but today... It was nice. Maybe he really would start seeing me as a friend, which could eventually lead to something more...

Through the doorway, I caught a glimpse of a short, fit boy dressed in a loose brown T-shirt and baggy, ripped jeans, his cropped black hair gelled back so much I could see the shine from my desk: Jonah Strauss, my ex from last year. I tried to hide my face with my hair—I wondered if maybe he'd finally gotten over me this summer.

A voice in the back of my head told me I shouldn't give up on him so easily. I should've tried harder to make our relationship work, even though I wasn't feeling it. He might be the only person I could ever make it work with, the only one who would like me that way. Sometimes I believed that, sometimes I didn't. The fact that Nolan was so *nice* to me this morning could be a sign that I shouldn't stoop down to forcing a relationship with Jonah again.

I didn't want to think about it anymore, though, so I stared at the date on the whiteboard until it blurred into a big blue smudge. It didn't always help, but one of the ways I could get myself to clear my head and stop overthinking was to stare at something familiar—like the whiteboard in homeroom—and think about the pleasant things it reminded me of, like my first day of freshman year when I sat in this exact seat and thought about all the possibilities of how high school would go.

Which ended up being nothing like the way it really went, and now high school's halfway over, and oh, no, I'm thinking too much again.

I'd had a suspicion for a long time that there was something wrong with me. I didn't know what it was, I just knew it was something. My whole life, I'd felt like everyone around me naturally fit into some secret world that I couldn't be part of. It was like I had something blocking me from having a "normal" social life, from having friends who wanted to do stuff after school like go to the mall and hang out, a group of friends to take candid pictures with, or even multiple friends who got along with each other.

It blocked me from having guy friends—or even just guys who treated me like… like they treated pretty girls. From having people be nice to me, more than just a quick wave in the hall. From knowing what to say when people *did* talk to me. From being invited to parties and knowing what to do at a party if I *were* to be invited…

It's like normal life was behind some kind of paywall and I had no way to pay. Every year, I thought, "Maybe this year will be different—maybe this year will be my year," but it was the same old story each time, and I never knew what to do to change that.

When the schedules were passed out, I stared down at mine, looking for some indication that this year would be different:

Madison, Summer Iris — Gd. 11 (SID#512999)

A-Day

Per. 1: Gym — Ashton (GYM)

Per. 2: US History — Johnson (55)

Per. 3: French III — Carp (37)

B-Day

Per. 4: Chemistry — Mior (4)

Per. 5: Geometry — Admiral (12)

Per. 6: English 3H — Harris (30)

I beamed at my sixth period; I wasn't sure they were going to let me take honors this year when I'd barely passed on-level English last year, but my teacher must have seen something in me. I'd had Ms. Harris since freshman year, and she'd told me she knew I was capable of more than what my marks were showing. I guess I showed enough improvement in the last couple months of sophomore year.

When the bell rang to go to first period, I thought about what had made Nolan pay attention to me today. Was it my new clothes? Were my clothes really that important? I felt weird wearing such a short skirt to school without any leggings or tights underneath, but this was what the other girls wore, and I was hoping to fit in better. I guess it was working.

This year was going to be great, I thought. Maybe it really would be this time.

Nolan

FIRST-PERIOD TRIGONOMETRY. The course I'd almost failed. I'd had *multiple* parent–teacher conferences over this class, pounded my textbook through the drywall in my room *twice* while doing homework, and ceremoniously burned all my work at the end of the year. If this was a dream, now would be a great time for me to wake up back on the couch in June.

I was *four days* from being in Europe, but I guess Summer had to overreact to some stupid thing I said and now my conscience had sent me back nine months to fix it. Why did I have to be such a hero? I could've just gone to Europe and let her be dead, but no, I had to wish for the chance to undo it. No, it wasn't worth it.

Alright, God, You've made Your point: I should've been nicer to Summer. Can I please go back to the normal timeline now?

After school today, I had to go back to that fountain. I had to figure out where it was and go back.

"We're going to start with a warm-up quiz," Mr. Sands announced at the beginning of trig. "I don't expect anyone to pass it; you'll retake it at the end of the year and your percentage of improvement will help curve your final grade. All I ask is that you show your work."

"What if we *do* pass it?" asked Lucia Torres, the Ivy-bound showoff who had an emotional breakdown if she ever got below a ninety-four on any assignment.

She might have been the only person more annoying than Summer.

Mr. Sands just laughed. "If you pass this quiz on the first day of class? Yeah, right. Don't worry, it won't be entered into the gradebook. It's just to assess your improvement in nine months."

Someone laughed—Grant Hayward, one of the special education students; a few of 'em always ended up in the "normal" classes. "It's okay, Lucia," he said. "It won't affect your grade. But I still plan to get a higher average than you."

"But there should be a reward if anyone *does* pass it, right?" Lucia asked, ignoring Grant—most of us did.

Mr. Sands sighed. "Alright, smarty. Since you're so confident, how's this? Anyone who gets above ninety percent on this quiz will be exempt from all unit tests for the year. But you have to get above a ninety, which I guarantee *none* of you will today."

The class cheered as Mr. Sands passed out the quiz. I rolled my eyes and started filling it out. I thought about writing a bunch of joke answers. What if going back to the fountain and wishing my way out of this do-over didn't work? In case I was stuck here, maybe I could purposely get a ton of questions wrong and curve my grade up at the end of the year.

Once the quiz was over, Mr. Sands gave us some notes to copy down while he graded them. The bell rang, and we all got up to head to our first break of the day.

"Could I speak to a Mr. Nolan Alden after class?" Mr. Sands asked.

Great, it's already starting. What did I do this time? I didn't remember him getting on my case *this* early. The only assignment I'd turned in was the quiz, which wasn't even officially graded!

"What'd I do?" I asked once everyone had left.

"Mr. Alden... you answered every question wrong on the quiz—"

"Doesn't the quiz not count?"

"—but your work... your *work* is flawless. In fact, if I were to take the answers from where you showed your work and not count the answer you circled, you would have a ninety-two percent on the quiz," he said. "I don't believe you could have cheated because there was nobody else you could've cheated off of—the second-highest was Miss Torres at an eighty-eight—and so I have to ask… is this your first time taking this class?"

"Yeah." Technically no, but telling him the real answer would probably result in my parents getting an uncomfortable phone call.

"I'd like you to retake the quiz after school," he said, "with my close supervision. If you pass again, I will keep my word about your exemption from unit tests. I might even recommend you skip trigonometry and move right up to calculus or statistics."

Hmm… if I could get out of trig, or at least the unit tests, maybe redoing this whole school year wouldn't be that bad. I mean, I was going to have to take calculus or statistics next year, anyway. Why not take it now and have an extra elective or a free period as a senior?

Summer

As FAR as first days of school go, today was actually pretty good. Not just because Nolan talked to me, but I enjoyed the classes I had so far. Well, mostly. We'd gotten a new French teacher, and the only reason I'd taken a third year— besides my mother making me because it'd look good on college applications— was because I enjoyed the teacher. I didn't know anyone in my class this year. I mean, there were some people from my French II class, but no one I talked to.

A girl named Daisy who I'd known since elementary school was in my gym class, so at least I had her to talk to. We were friends, but she didn't really get along with my best friend Marta, so we didn't talk much anymore outside of the classes we had together. Other than that, I didn't really know anyone in my classes that well.

It was fine, though. All I needed to do this year was pass everything. If I didn't have to repeat any more classes, then I could go on the Europe trip that the community center was sponsoring. If I *did* have to repeat classes, not only would I be in school over the summer to make sure I earned the credits I needed to graduate next year, but I'd also be working until every last cent of the deposit for the trip was paid back to my mother—we had to send the final deposit in by March, when the informational meetings would start.

I should be fine. I turned the front door key and set today's mail on the table in the entryway. After setting my backpack down in the living room, I started my frozen French bread pizza in the toaster oven and went back to the couch to watch reruns of *That '70s Show* until it was ready. Since it was only the first day of classes, I didn't have any homework today.

I took my phone out and started scrolling through my social media feed. I "liked" all the pictures of the popular girls reuniting with their friends, all wearing such cute outfits. Maybe I should've done something more with mine, like a necklace or a cardigan, or cuter shoes than my plain white flats. They weren't even dressy; they didn't go with my skirt. And maybe I should've worn makeup...

Then again, Nolan Alden did talk to me today. He never really talked to me, not like that. Something I'd done was working. If it was my outfit, then that meant I needed to get a cute look together for tomorrow, too. I wasn't sure how long I could stretch my back-to-school wardrobe, and aside from the handful of new pieces I'd gotten over break, I didn't have that many cute clothes. I still wore some things from eighth grade, because I couldn't really afford to replenish my wardrobe that often.

Since I was feeling so good about our conversation, I decided to do something... kind of bold. I'd sent Nolan a friend request when I first set up my social media profile, but he'd never accepted it. I figured maybe he got a lot of them and couldn't keep up with them all, or... any excuse I could think of besides *"he doesn't even like you enough to scroll past your posts or let you see his posts even though adding each other online isn't a big deal to anyone else,"* so the request had just kind of sat there unanswered for a couple years. Maybe he wouldn't notice if I canceled the request and sent another one. If he *did* notice, I would look more desperate and pathetic than ever, but if not... maybe he'd accept it this time.

As I went to get my pizza from the toaster oven, I thought about our actual conversation. I never knew Nolan wanted to be a lawyer. I'd known him since elementary school, and today was the first time I'd heard him mention law school. He didn't seem worried about how he'd pay for it, especially on such a fancy private school campus. It must be nice to not have to worry about that kind of thing.

I pulled a purple spiral-bound notebook out of my backpack. I kept a journal every year, so this one was brand-new. I wrote a little bit about every day and used it to track my mental health. My mother didn't really believe in mental illnesses, so I had never been to a psychiatrist, but I knew something was wrong with me. When I got to college, I'd finally be able to start seeing a psychiatrist, so I thought it'd be helpful to have a general record of how I was feeling over the years and where my biggest struggles were.

September 7th—

First day of junior year. I know a couple people in my A-Day classes, we'll see how tomorrow goes I guess. I saw Jonah today, and a part of me wanted to talk to him but I didn't. I think it's because Nolan talked to me today. I used to wonder if anyone but Jonah would ever pay attention to me, and even if Nolan's just being nice to me, at least I know I'm worth another guy's time in some way. We did have a really nice conversation, though: we talked more than we ever have before. I don't want to jinx myself, but I feel hopeful that this might actually be a good year.

Nolan

"HOW WAS the first day of school?" my mother asked, handing me my dinner plate as we joined my father at the dining room table.

"It was good," I said, savoring the smell of pot roast and garlic mashed potatoes. "Uh, I passed this pre-test for trig, so now I don't have to take exams for the whole year."

"That's fantastic." She poured herself a glass of red wine. "You'd better get an A, then. You still need to bring up your average from the B- you got in AP Bio."

"Well, it was weighted as an A-, anyway," I reminded her, "but yeah, this should help."

I was actually feeling so optimistic once Mr. Sands told me I'd passed the after-school pre-test that I'd decided to hold off on going back to that fountain. At least until tomorrow, just to see what else I could get out of this. It wasn't like junior year was a *bad* school year, just that I'd rather be in Europe than in trigonometry.

We all talked about schoolwork over dinner, how I needed to really start applying myself this year. SAT prep courses, extracurriculars...

"I, uh, heard something about a Europe trip," I said. "For school credit. Cultural enhancement. It's over the summer and sponsored by the community center."

"Do you have a flyer?" my father asked. "Or any more details?"

"I'll get them," I said.

It wasn't until about a month into the school year that Summer had brought it up in the normal timeline; I remembered now. We both happened to be in a chemistry tutorial period, and she was talking about it with her friend Marta. She turned to me and said I should come, that I'd like it. She gave me the website on a sticky note.

I didn't want to go on the trip for Summer, obviously. I wanted to go because it was a trip to Europe that I could get school credit for. Have a blast and boost my college applications. Summer being there was just... inconvenient. If I had to stay in this do-over, a part of me wanted to convince her not to go after all, so I could go without worrying about her, but that wasn't the point of this reset.

Whatever. At least there was something in it for me: no exams in trig.

I'd probably pull a higher score this time.

After dinner, I went up to my room, and my phone vibrated. I read the caller ID:

NIAMH RYAN

Niamh. I hadn't spoken to her in—

Well, days, I guess. Niamh was my... not *girlfriend*, but we were hooking up exclusively at this point in the year. We'd met at some party over the summer; she went to school across town. We broke it off a few weeks into the school year and I hadn't spoken to her since. I didn't even remember why we broke it off; maybe we got bored. I had to answer the call, though, because as of now we were still a thing.

"Hey," I said, hoping it didn't come across as uncomfortable.

"Hey, how was your first day?" she asked.

"It was fine. Uh... how was your... third Tuesday?" Her school started at the end of August.

She laughed. "It was good. I'm finally getting used to my schedule. You should come over tomorrow while my parents are at work."

Ah, yes, I got to get some action in this new timeline. Niamh and I broke things off in September, I got shot down for homecoming by a pretty girl in my English class, and I'd hooked up with a girl on the volleyball team for a couple months after winter break, but that was it until I'd met Katie.

Hm, I wonder what Katie's doing now... Now that I thought about it, maybe I could redo my dating life, too, and nab Katie a little earlier. *Thanks, Summer!*

"Tomorrow sounds great," I told Niamh. "What're you doing tonight?"

"My friend Rob is coming over to study for our APUSH exam."

Oh, right, that's why we broke it off. She was lying about us being exclusive. I was the sidepiece.

But I didn't want to argue now. I still wanted to come over tomorrow. "Have fun."

"I'm sure we will," she said sarcastically. "See you tomorrow. Pick me up from school?"

"Yeah, sure. See you."

When we hung up, I had a friend request from Summer. I didn't even know she had any social media; she'd never tried to add me in the normal timeline... had she? I guess I had to accept it, right? I did, then scrolled through her recent posts:

September 7, 7:14 a.m.: First day of junior year! So excited!

September 6, 9:43 p.m.: Back to school tomorrow :(

September 5, 10:10 a.m.: Strawberry pop tarts are life

September 5, 9:08 a.m.: I might be going to Europe next summer!! :O

September 4, 11:17 p.m.: So not ready to go back to school :(

Nothing interesting, as I could have predicted. Summer was boring; she was just Summer. But now I had to be extra nice to her, I guess.

Summer

"DO YOU think he'll talk to you again?" Marta asked, using my locker mirror to fix the clips in her strawberry blonde curls.

I shrugged, closing the locker door. "I don't know. Yesterday was the first time..."

"You're not still thinking of inviting him on the Europe trip, are you?" she asked. "You don't even know if you're going yet."

"How could he pass it up, though? Even if he doesn't like *me*, it's a trip to Europe. And we're bound to grow closer spending that much time together. It's worth a shot, isn't it?"

A familiar basil cologne filled my nostrils, making me cough. I turned around, and sure enough, Jonah was standing behind me in his typical ripped jeans and leather jacket, his hair gelled back.

"Can I help you?" I asked. He shouldn't still be talking to me. We'd broken up in April.

"Just saying hi," he said. "How was your summer?"

"It was fine. What do you want?"

"Geez, Summer." He rolled his eyes. "Just trying to be friendly."

He sulked away, and I turned back to Marta. "Any tips on getting rid of an ex?"

She laughed. "Hate to break it to you, but Sutton and I are never breaking up."

"Whatever. Even if you did, he doesn't even go to our school."

"You and Nolan are welcome to double-date with us," she said. Her wink told me she wasn't that optimistic.

I sighed. "At this rate, it'll be me and Jonah."

"You're not really thinking of getting back with him, are you?"

"No, but... what if he's the only one who'll ever—?"

"You'll find someone. Trust me." She pushed her curls out of her face. "I did."

I rolled my eyes. Marta barely even saw Sutton; they'd met lifeguarding over the summer, and he went to the all boys' prep school in the rich part of town. He played water polo and was probably cheating on her with one of the girls who always showed up in his tagged photos. I hadn't even met him, but based on social media alone, I got a bad vibe.

I used to have a list of all the things I wanted in a boyfriend, but eventually I realized that a girl like me just had to settle for what she could get—like Jonah. I'd probably end up going back to him eventually.

Nolan

WHEN I woke up and it was still September, I wondered if the whole year really had just been a dream. Maybe I didn't need to be involved with Summer; maybe I'd imagined everything. The only thing that didn't add up was passing the trig pre-test.

The school day was pretty boring. I had lunch with my friends, and just like yesterday I had to pretend I didn't know that Liam's crush on Darcy would fizzle out after homecoming or that Jake wouldn't be able to go to the concert he'd bought us tickets for because he'd have to attend a family reunion.

I knew I had to at least *try* to get out of this timeline, but I had plans with Niamh after school and I wasn't going to miss that. In reality, the last time I'd even made out with a girl was months ago. Katie and I had *kissed* but we hadn't *made out*.

Just as I was heading to the parking lot after school, I heard that stupid, stupid voice.

"Hey, Nolan!" Summer called cheerfully. Grudgingly, I turned to face her.

"Hey, Summer." I sighed. "How was your first B-Day?"

"It was great. I really like my English class. I'm in honors this year."

"Wow, congratulations." I looked at my phone. Niamh's school got out half an hour after ours, and it took about fifteen minutes to drive there.

Summer blushed. "Thanks."

Another guy came up to us, Jonah Strauss. I was sure the two of them had dated once. I wish they hadn't broken up; he took up all her attention, and they were good together. They *fit* together. If she was still with him, maybe she'd leave me alone.

"Who's this?" Jonah asked, looking at me. He knew damn well who I was; we'd all been in the same grade since freshman year. The question he was asking Summer was more like, *"What are you two?"*

"My friend, and none of your business," Summer replied. "Run along. We're still over."

Jonah rolled his eyes but did as she said.

I started to shuffle away. "Well, I should get going."

"Wait." Summer took a deep breath, like she was nervous. "Do you want to get smoothies?"

I stared at her. I absolutely did not want to get smoothies, and either way, I already had plans. But... this do-over had been pretty good to me; maybe I owed Summer a small something.

"I have plans," I said.

"Oh." She deflated. "Alright. That's fine. I mean, I don't usually make plans so last-minute anyway. I just was thinking—"

"But if we're quick…" I knew it was rude to interrupt her, but I didn't have all day.

Her face lit up. "Okay! Yeah, it won't take long! It's just across the street."

She smiled so big I realized she had braces, with dark pink bands. How long had she had *braces*? She was seventeen! Or—was she still sixteen? Was *I* still sixteen? No, my birthday was in August, and it was September. When was Summer's birthday?

"Let's go," I told her.

* * *

SUMMER LOVED to talk. She told me practically every detail about her classes: how her chem teacher kept calling her "Madison," thinking it was her first name instead of her last name; how geometry had a long-term sub so she'd thought she was in the wrong class; how Jonah was in geometry with her but she didn't want to talk about him; how her English honors class was so great and Ms. Harris always encouraged her… and then she asked if she was talking too much, and of course I had to say, "No, you're fine," lest she take the truth the wrong way.

The good news was I had to get going. I had to meet Niamh for one last roll in the backseat of my truck before I busted her for using me. Maybe I could make it a little more fun this time around, humiliate her instead of accidentally calling her at midnight on a Saturday and having Rob answer.

When I pulled into the parking lot, I realized Niamh had never said where to meet. I got out of the car and wandered the parking lot, trying to remember if there was somewhere we'd normally meet.

"Are you looking for someone?" someone asked.

I turned around and found my almost-girlfriend watching me. "Katie?"

She nodded, confused, twirling her short blonde hair around her fingers. Her bag had the same plush turtle keychain that it did during the trip meetings. "Do I know you?"

"Uh... you just look like a girl from my school named Katie," I said. "Weird coincidence. Uh, I'm looking for Niamh Ryan."

"She just left," Katie replied. "Her boyfriend gives her rides home; they left like five minutes ago 'cause his cross-country meet got canceled or something."

"Rob?" I guessed.

Katie nodded. "Why are you looking for her?"

"That's not important."

She laughed. "You're one of her side-dudes."

"*One* of?"

"It's okay." She put a hand on my shoulder. "There are way better girls out there."

I rolled my eyes. It wasn't like I was even emotionally invested in Niamh at this point. I just wanted a little bit of action. But then I realized...

"Girls like you, you mean?"

Katie smirked. "I have a group project today, but you can text me sometime. I'll give you my number."

Well, well. Maybe this timeline really was shaping up to be better for everyone.

Summer

WAS I being pranked? Was a guy like Nolan really being this nice to me all of a sudden?

I looked at my reflection in the mirror: I'd left my hair down today, and I wore a cute, simple sundress. I wasn't wearing any makeup; I couldn't get the hang of it. I guess I looked okay. But I wasn't sure what was so *different* that had gotten Nolan to pay attention to me.

Maybe I was just reading into things. I was nervous, though, because the homecoming dance was next weekend. I'd never been asked; Jonah and I hadn't started dating until later in the year. I wanted to go with someone. I wanted that high school experience. But I didn't think Nolan would ask me. I wasn't going to be that optimistic.

Then again, it was the twenty-first century. Maybe I could ask him. But what if he said no? Wouldn't that be humiliating? I wasn't sure I was up for the risk. I would have asked Marta, but she only cared about Sutton and how great things were going for them. No time to consider that maybe her best friend was having issues.

Maybe if I got back together with Jonah, she'd see that I needed help. But I wasn't going to stoop that low.

Not yet.

Nolan

I BLOCKED Niamh's number once I got back in my car. I wasn't going to give her the satisfaction of an explanation when I was merely *one* of the guys she was cheating on Rob with.

Tapping my finger against the back of my phone, I considered. Before I could chicken out, I typed "Walgreens" into my maps app to see if I could figure out where that fountain was. Sure, I had no trig exams and an earlier shot with Katie in this timeline, but undoing my wish would put me past trig, close to dating Katie anyway, and mere days from Europe.

But Summer would be dead. Why did I have to remember that detail? I shook the thought from my head; maybe I could wish to go back to Friday instead of Monday and see if there was anything I could do to stop her from dying.

I zoomed in on the satellite images of every Walgreens within a seventy-five mile radius, but not one of them had a fountain. *How far did I drive?* I switched to the browser and searched "Walgreens shopping center fountain Bay Area California."

Sure enough, there was a news article from last month:

COMING THIS MAY! A new shopping center is under development in the Bay Area, just off Peach Avenue. Once a vacant field, by May 12, the Peach Avenue Shopping Center will be home to a California Pizza Kitchen, Kohl's, JOANN, Walgreens, Burger King, BevMo!, and Supercuts. The family of Anita Prunell has also donated funds for the Anita Prunell Memorial Fountain to be constructed in the parking lot. The funds for this shopping center were allocated from a budget passed in February that stated...

I couldn't read any more. I locked my phone and threw it at the floor mat. The fountain I'd used to make this stupid wish didn't exist yet, and it wouldn't until *May*! By the time I was able to undo the wish, it would be so close to June anyway that it wouldn't even matter!

I groaned. Maybe this timeline wasn't going anywhere. Maybe this really was my life now: back to junior year, redoing everything to save Summer. But that didn't mean I wasn't going to get a few things out of it, too.

I guess I'm stuck in this do-over timeline, so I might as well make the best of it.

2

Summer

SITTING AT the kitchen table before school, I couldn't figure out what I wanted to write. My notebook sat open and blank in front of me. I felt like I wanted to write *something*.

Then it hit me: a list of goals for junior year. Goals would give me something to look forward to and something to work towards. The most important thing was passing all my classes so I could go on the Europe trip, but I went on and wrote more:

1. Pass all of my classes

2. Make honor roll?

3. Make a new friend

4. Go to a school dance

5. Go to a school dance with a date (not Jonah)

6. Stop talking to Jonah

7. Get a boyfriend (not Jonah)

8. Kiss Nolan

I debated crossing out the last one. It was such a ridiculous, unachievable goal. Maybe I could get a boyfriend who wasn't Jonah, but Nolan still seemed like such a reach.

I closed the notebook, shoved it in my backpack, and set off for school. When I got to my locker, Jonah was waiting.

"What do you want?" I asked him. "Your locker isn't around here."

"I just want to talk, Summer," he said. "I don't like how we ended things last year."

"Well, I'm just fine with it," I said. "I don't have feelings for you, and there's no point in being in a relationship with one-sided feelings."

"I can make you feel things, though. We could try."

"I said no."

"You really think you can do better than me?" he asked. "You think that Nolan guy's gonna fall for someone like you? Dream on, Summer. I'm the best you'll ever have."

"Go away. I need to get to class."

He rolled his eyes but left me alone. Just as I shut my locker, I turned to see Nolan behind me.

"Oh, hey," I said, startled.

"Good morning." He seemed to be in a good mood. "Ready for A-Day classes again?"

"Yeah, I think we actually dress out in gym today. How were your plans yesterday?"

"Oh, better than expected," he said. "Broke things off with this chick I was seeing, but this other girl gave me her number out of pity, so it worked out."

So he had a girlfriend? But he didn't anymore? But now he was talking to a new girl.

"Wow, were you two together long?" I asked, trying to piece it all together. I guess I should've expected someone like him to have a girlfriend, but none of his social media had indicated that. Maybe he was just a more private person.

"No, just a couple months, if that." He shrugged. "I was kind of expecting it, too."

"Well, I hope she leaves you alone. Some exes never do."

"Oh?"

"My ex, Jonah, he keeps trying to get back with me," I said. "He claims I can't do any better. But I don't even have feelings for him anymore. What am I supposed to do?"

"Honestly, I thought you two were good together," Nolan said. "What happened?"

I shrugged. "I just didn't have the right feelings for him, I guess." I didn't want to get *too* much into the details with Nolan. I just... wanted him to know I was available if he was interested. "It felt wrong being with him. Icky, even. Like he's not the right person for me, you know?" I didn't mention that Jonah pressuring me for sex was also a big part of it.

"Well, sometimes you don't think someone's right for you, but things can change," Nolan replied. "You could probably make it work if you just talk."

Was he trying to convince me to give Jonah another chance? Were they friends? I'd never seen them hang out, and Jonah had never talked about Nolan. Yesterday Jonah acted like he'd never even met Nolan.

And if he's pushing me back to Jonah, that must mean... he doesn't...

"But I don't have feelings for him," I reiterated. "Plus he's kind of become an even bigger jerk after the breakup. He thinks that by insulting me and following me around, he'll wear me down. Yeah, right."

"I'm just saying, don't write him off so hastily," Nolan said. "Relationships are rough, but they're not so bad in the grand scheme of it all."

"Thanks for the advice, I guess."

Yeah, there's no way he likes me.

Nolan

SUMMER HAD definitely seemed put-off by my advice about Jonah. As I walked to class, I thought about whether or not I really wanted to push her to date him. Having her out of *my* hair sounded great, but was Jonah the way to go? What if he just made things worse for her?

Maybe I could set her up with someone else. Then again, who did I know who'd want to date Summer? Jonah was already bottom of the barrel. Summer was clingy and awkward and exhausting. I didn't dislike any of my friends enough to set them up with her.

I didn't want to slack off in trig. Even though I wasn't taking the unit tests, I knew if I got too cocky, I'd end up falling behind again. I took probably the best notes in my life, then took out my phone during break to text Katie. I figured I'd start with something short and sweet.

NOLAN: Hey, thinking of u ;)

KATIE: who r u?

Right, she gave me her number, but I never gave her mine.

NOLAN: it's Nolan from yesterday

KATIE: oh ok

Hm, she didn't seem too thrilled. On my way to my locker, I passed Jonah standing by Summer's locker again. The way he was always hovering around waiting for her was kind of sweet, but I had to admit it would be unnerving for a girl he used to date. Summer probably felt the way I'd feel if *she* were always hovering by *my* locker—someone I had no interest in talking to invading my personal space. Not so charming when I thought about it that way.

Maybe I should get rid of Jonah for her. Maybe that would help.

"You waiting for Summer?" I asked.

"Who are you?"

"Nolan. Don't worry, we're not talking or anything."

"Right, you're the guy she thinks she has a shot with." He laughed. "Yeah, I knew she was on something when she said that."

So she *did* like me. And she'd told Jonah? If she hated him so much, why would she gossip with him? Or maybe... *Did she tell him we were dating to get rid of him?* I hoped not. There'd been a point in sixth grade when people thought Summer and I were dating because of something *she* did; I didn't want that happening again.

"She told you she thinks she has a shot with me?" I asked.

"Nah, I overheard her talking to that annoying friend of hers. Look, Summer's cute and all, but you're one of those rich kids, yeah?"

"Uh, I guess." I wasn't really sure how to label my social circle. Jake's mother was a doctor, Liam's parents both worked in tech, my father was a lawyer, and my mother did something on a corporate level, so I guess we were probably the "rich kids" to some people.

"Yeah, you're out of her league for sure. She could barely get a guy like me."

"Well, if she's so revolting, why do you want to get back together with her so bad?" I just didn't get it. There had to be *something* redeemable about her for him to be this obsessed. "Is she amazing in bed or something?"

"Nah, Summer doesn't even put out." Jonah laughed. "Look, she's easy to manipulate because she knows she can't do better. I figure I can get more from her in a few weeks. You gotta take it slow to get the payoff sometimes."

"So you're after her on the off chance that you might convince her to sleep with you, rather than going for someone actually hot who would do it willingly?" Then again, there was probably a shortage of attractive girls willing to sleep with Jonah.

"It's all about being in control. I like a challenge." He winked, which creeped me out. "Summer just makes a guy feel so... in charge. Dominant."

No wonder she was so turned off by this guy. The last thing I needed was a mental picture of Jonah being *dominant*.

"Come on, man," I said quietly, glancing around the hall to make sure nobody else was listening to this. "That's creepy, and she's not even that hot. Just go find a chick who'll put out for you and leave her alone."

"Why do you care? Are you looking to fuck her?"

I shuddered at the thought. "No, thank you. All I'm saying is, you could probably find another girl who actually wants to sleep with you. You don't need to keep harassing Summer. Date a freshman; they'll do anything to be with someone who has a car and can take 'em to prom in the spring."

Jonah smirked. "I think someone has a crush on Summer." His confidence wasn't faltering; he was seriously reading this as me being into her. "You're just not ballsy enough to admit it. Summer knows you're out of her league. She knows she'll never do better than me. She's not good enough to do better."

What an ass. No matter how much I disliked Summer, this guy was out there. Why wasn't *he* the one sent back in time to fix things with her? He was saying way worse stuff about her out loud than I'd probably ever thought.

"If I wanted to date Summer, I'd be dating her," I said to him. "She's not my favorite person, but she sure as shit can do better than some creepy stalker who's only interested in weird BDSM games."

Jonah snorted. "You're pathetic."

"You say that like I wouldn't sleep with her just to spite you," I said, quieter. I did *not* need anyone overhearing that, with or without context. "You know she'd let *me* boss her around before she'd ever go back to you."

"Alright, rich boy, how much is she worth to you?"

"Excuse me?"

"If you want me to leave Summer alone so bad, how much would you pay to make that happen?"

"You're asking for *money* to respect a girl's boundaries?"

Before he could answer, the bell rang. I glared at Jonah to let him know he had about five seconds to leave without any money, and he glared back before he finally left, scoffing.

I needed to go to class, too, but I was shaken by how *weird* that guy was. Summer was right: I felt *icky* after talking to him.

"Nolan?"

I turned to find Summer walking up to me. That's right, I'd been by her locker all this time. Wait... did it look like I was waiting for her at her locker? I didn't want that.

"Uh, thanks for standing up for me," she said. She looked embarrassed. "I stopped to listen... You don't have to pay him to leave me alone."

I wasn't going to, I wanted to say. "When did you walk by?"

"He asked you how much money I was worth."

"Oh, okay." I guess he *was* louder than I was. "Well, I'm not giving that dick any money; he'd probably just spend it on weird BDSM porn or something."

She giggled uncomfortably. "Just hours ago, you were practically begging me to date him again."

Yes, before I actually talked to him. If I was dating someone like Jonah, I'd probably rather be dead, too. I had to say something to her.

"You can do better than him, Summer. I hope you realize that."

And I hope you realize I don't mean me *when I say that.*

Summer

I PUT the mail on the table, set my bag in the living room, put my French bread pizza in the toaster oven, and turned the TV on to the usual *That '70s Show* reruns. Nolan had confused me today. He wanted me to give Jonah another chance, and then he didn't. Suddenly he said I can do better than Jonah. *Does he mean himself?* No, he wouldn't.

But the way he'd stood up for me...

Nolan was such an enigma. *But I think I want to figure him out.*

Nolan

WHEN I finished my trig homework, I opened up a new page in my notebook—I wanted to come up with a plan rather than keep throwing things at a wall to see if they stuck, like this afternoon with Jonah.

OPERATION SAVE SUMMER

I cringed as I stared at the line. It felt too cheesy, like when I was a kid and I used to play spy games with my friends. I crossed it out and wrote instead:

SAVING SUMMER

Underneath that, I wrote down everything I knew:

- Summer died between June 24th (late afternoon) and June 27th (early morning)

- I talked to her on June 24th before we left the community center

- She wrote some stuff down in a journal about how I don't give her enough attention

I tried to remember what else was in that journal. Maybe I should have read more of it, but it was too late for that now. I kept thinking about the facts.

- Esme said I was an asshole to Summer

- Esme thought Summer died by suicide because Tim wouldn't say why

- Summer got home on Friday and talked to Esme

- I think her journal mentioned something happening with her friend Marta?

- She used to date Jonah who is a weird pervert and manipulates her into stuff

I tried to remember more, but my memories from the normal timeline—or, I guess the *old* timeline—were getting fuzzier.

I listed Summer's friends on the back of the page: Marta, as far as I knew. But I couldn't think of anyone else; there was Esme, but I didn't think they'd met until the trip meetings. I also made a list of people she didn't like—just Jonah for now. What else did I know about her? She wasn't sure if she could afford college. Jonah called me a "rich kid."

I wrote: Summer struggles with money?

Then: Summer struggles with school. Except English. I think. Just math?

I pulled out my phone and scrolled through her social media to see if I could figure anything else out. She didn't say much online, but she did post some vaguely unhappy things amidst being excited about things like school starting. I wrote: Summer is moody.

If I was going to figure this out, I was going to need to get to know her better. Ugh. I needed to actually be friends with her, didn't I?

I tried to remember more from the old timeline, but it was getting harder to distinguish what were real memories. It was still sinking in: I was almost an entire year from where I'd been. So many songs, movies, episodes of shows that hadn't been released yet...

But there was the fact that I could bet my friends money on what would happen in certain shows or games, and I knew which concerts were actually worth going to. It wouldn't be so bad.

I turned back to my notebook, trying to see if anything else came to mind. Esme seemed to think I was a jackass to Summer. I'd never said anything *that* mean to Summer; I just wanted her to leave me alone and respect the fact that we weren't friends.

Summer and I had that fight in the Starbucks parking lot, but Esme wasn't around for that. And it wasn't like I'd said anything horrible to her. From what I remembered, Summer had started it and kept pushing it even after I apologized. Then she stormed off and got on a bus instead of letting me take her home, which she'd begged me to do in the first place. Esme couldn't have been referring to that fight... unless Summer told her about it?

Maybe the reason I kept thinking of that afternoon was because it was the last time I'd seen Summer before she died. But if she told Esme about the argument, then Esme was the last person she'd talked to. Or maybe her parents. But none of them were the ones sent back in time.

Somewhere in the process of trying to figure it out, it hit me how bizarre this whole situation was. Summer had died. She'd *died*, and I hadn't processed it at all because I'd woken up nine months earlier and she was still here. She could have been gone, but she wasn't.

I had the chance to stop it. I could save someone's life, and I was stuck dwelling on how it was someone I found annoying. I had no concern at all for the family or friends she would've left behind, or the people whose lives she would've affected after high school. What would it have been like if I hadn't been sent back?

I closed my eyes and tried to think back to that moment when Tim told us the news. I thought of sitting outside with Esme. But I felt nothing. Frustrated, I went to the living room and sat back on the couch, exactly as I had been when I'd fallen asleep that day. I tried to pretend it was that morning again. I had just gotten home, and Summer was dead.

What if life had just gone on from there? With no chance of seeing her again? Would we still have gone to Europe knowing that someone in our travel group was dead?

I tried, but I didn't feel anything. Knowing that I was going to see Summer tomorrow, it was hard to picture a timeline where she was dead. That timeline was gone.

What if the same thing happened now? What if I got to school tomorrow and the teachers called an assembly and announced that Summer was dead? What would that feel like?

Maybe I could think about when someone else I knew had died. My grandparents were all still alive. But my friend Liam's neighbor had died when we were in fifth grade, from cancer or something like that. I remembered him telling me about it at school.

"She wasn't old or anything. She didn't have any kids, so I didn't go over to her house to play, but we did say hi to each other when she'd get the mail. And when I was first allowed to cross the street, I remember asking my dad if I could bring her and her husband some leftover cookies

we made since her house was right across from ours. She was nice. We brought her husband some casserole last night. He's always seemed nice. Like, he didn't deserve to lose his wife or anything. And she obviously didn't deserve to die. Well, I mean, maybe she was secretly evil or something but I don't think she was. And even though I never talked to her much, it's freaky to think I'm never gonna see her again. Things are gonna be different, and it's weird. Like, I didn't know her well enough to miss her, but it's still freaky to think she's gone."

And then, a few years ago, we'd found out our kindergarten teacher had passed away. I didn't cry about it—Jake did, but he'd kick my ass if I ever told anyone—but I'd still felt *sad.* I'd felt something. I remembered her daughter had had a baby around Christmastime and brought her to class so we could meet her first grandson. My first thoughts after the shock wore off had been about them and how they were taking it.

Liam was a kid who'd barely even known his neighbor, and he'd still felt her loss when she died. I'd felt the loss of my teacher years after the last time I'd seen her. I *knew* Summer—I'd had classes with her for years— and I was being an asshole about her death. She was annoying and clingy, but that didn't change the fact that she was still a person. Somebody's daughter, somebody's friend, somebody's future pediatrician or librarian or mail carrier or whatever she wanted to be. Just because I didn't want to be involved in her life didn't mean I could push her away now, not when I'd been tasked with saving her.

Whether or not I had anything to do with Summer's death, I needed to put aside my issues with her. I had to help her now. I'd been given this chance for a reason, and if I wasn't careful, then she could just as well end up dead again.

And it was at that moment that I knew I would feel different if she did. If I woke up tomorrow and we all had to meet in the multipurpose room for the principal to announce that Summer had passed away last night, everything would feel *wrong*. That couldn't happen. I couldn't let that happen. Summer Madison *could not* die.

Summer

I WAS hoping I'd see Nolan at school in the morning again; starting my mornings talking to him had really been boosting my energy. I waited at my locker a little longer before heading to class, and finally, there he was, heading towards his own locker. I approached him.

"Morning," I said, trying to sound casual.

He glanced up at me but didn't say anything at first.

"Hey, Summer." He was quiet, like he'd seen a ghost or something.

"Everything okay?" I asked.

"Yeah." He sighed. "Yeah." Another pause. "You're here."

Before I could ask what he meant by that, he pulled me into a hug. I hugged him back, but this felt like way more than a friendly hug. He held me tight and squeezed my shoulder in his hand like he was looking for proof I wasn't a hologram. I think he even sniffed my hair.

"I'm sorry," he whispered, just before pulling away.

"Sorry for what?" I asked.

He shook his head. "I should get to class. Uh... see you around?"

I nodded, and then he was gone, and the bell rang. I felt so confused, but I wasn't going to complain about that hug even if it seemed weird. That was *not* just a friendly hug. There was something else there. What it was exactly, I wanted to find out.

3

Summer

HOMECOMING WEEK came as it did every year, and as usual, every day of the week had a "theme." I usually tried to participate, but sometimes it was something like "sports fan day"—I could tell you what the Sharks or the Giants played, but that was about it. I watched sitcoms, not sports. So today I didn't even try to try. Marta, on the other hand, refusing to be left out of anything, wore a jersey from some team her boyfriend liked.

"Are you going to homecoming?" she asked me, adjusting a hair barrette in her locker's mirror. She should have known I wasn't going; I'd never gone. She'd gone by herself freshman year but claimed to have the flu last year. I think she just hadn't wanted to go by herself again when nobody asked her.

"What do you think?" I asked.

"I think you should ask Nolan."

"I don't know." I crossed my arms. "I don't know if he'd even want to go with me."

Marta turned to face me. "He's not going to ask *you*, but if you ask him you might have a shot."

I shut my locker door. "If he doesn't want to go with me, why would I ask him?"

"He *does*; he just doesn't know it yet. So you need to show him," she explained. "You know you want to go with him."

"Maybe I just won't go again. And it's not like you and Sutton will even be there." He was a senior, so they were going to *his* last homecoming at his school on the same night. I'd still have one more chance to go next year, anyway.

"No, you're going, and you're going to ask Nolan."

"What makes you so confident in me all of a sudden?" I asked. Marta didn't usually encourage me like this. Any other time I'd mentioned having a crush on Nolan since elementary school, she'd laughed and treated it like a celebrity crush—the way I usually looked at it.

She smiled. "I know feelings when I see them, Summer, and based on everything he said to you last week... it's there, trust me."

I sighed, and we parted ways. I was halfway to class when I realized Jonah was following me.

"What now?" I demanded.

He smiled big like he was excited to show me something. "You know, homecoming's on Saturday..."

"And I'd rather sit at home watching reruns than go with you, so don't even think about it."

He shrugged. "You'll come around. Not like anyone else is gonna ask you."

I didn't even dignify him with a response; how could he think he still had a shot with me? I just had to remember what Nolan said: I could do better. And maybe, just maybe, that was a hint.

Nolan

"HEY, MAN," Liam said, sliding into his seat at our lunch table. "Could I get a ride home today?"

"Sure." He was going to get a car for his seventeenth birthday, but that hadn't happened yet in this timeline. "Just meet me in the parking lot; I'll run the air while I wait."

"Oh, it could be a while," he said. "You know Darcy, the girl I was telling you about yesterday?"

Yesterday when Liam and Jake came over to go swimming—one last time before we closed up the pool for the fall—he spent the whole time talking about this sophomore he'd met in student council who he wanted to ask to homecoming. I had to pretend I hadn't heard everything he was saying before, and that I had no idea how little he would care about her after their lackluster night at the dance.

"Yeah, I remember," I told him as Jake took a seat beside us.

"Did you ask Darcy yet?" he asked Liam. "I saw her with a flower in the hallway."

Liam scoffed. "Do I look like a flower kind of guy?" It was true; his most romantic gesture was probably switching seats with some girl in third grade so she had a better view of the movie we were watching. "That's from her mom; she got hired at Home Depot, so her mom sent her a flower to celebrate."

Jake raised an eyebrow. "Home Depot? That's... quite a job for a lady."

"She's so cool." Liam grinned. "Wouldn't know it to look at her, but she knows her way around a hardware store. Her dad—"

I zoned out while Liam droned on about Darcy's dad making sure his daughters knew the same kinds of things his sons knew, and vice versa, and all the shit I'd already heard. I wouldn't be as annoyed if anything had happened with them after homecoming, but *all this* for one date that didn't even go well? God really was punishing me.

Liam turned back to me. "Anyway, I have to wait for her to finish tennis practice, and then I'm gonna ask her. So can you give me a ride after that? She should be done by four."

As boring as it would be, I'd done it before, so I could do it again. Who knew how long it'd take him to get over her if she got asked to homecoming by someone else?

"I got you, man," I said.

"Sweet, thanks, bro."

"Do you have a poster or anything?" Jake asked. "I'm making a poster for

Viv. Girls kind of expect that sort of thing, you know."

"I don't need a poster," Liam insisted.

"Yeah, you keep telling yourself that's *not* why Thuy turned you down last year."

Liam rolled his eyes. "It's not. Thuy was out of my league."

"Why not both?" I asked.

After the final bell rang, I sat on one of those crusty metal benches in front of the school to wait. I was playing a game on my phone when Summer sat next to me. She didn't even say hello. She was dressed in a big T-shirt from Sarasota, Florida that covered most of her shorts.

I wasn't getting any more used to having her around like this. Especially when she showed up unannounced.

"Waiting for someone?" I asked.

When she turned to face me, I could tell she was nervous about something from the panic in her eyes and the way her mouth gaped just slightly. "I just... saw you and thought I'd sit next to you while I... figure out what I'm going to do."

"About what?"

"I just have to decide something," she said. "How about you? Don't you drive?"

"Yeah, my friend Liam's waiting for someone and then I'm giving him a ride. Do you walk home?"

She nodded. "I live really close. Like, three or four songs."

"You tell time with songs?"

"Sometimes." She seemed embarrassed.

"That's actually cute," I said, and she blushed. "What's your favorite song?"

"Well, it's kind of old," she said. "My mom loves Fleetwood Mac, and she'd always play their *Rumours* album when I was younger, and I really like this song called 'Never Going Back Again.'"

"No way; I love them! That was the first CD I ever played in my car." All these years I'd thought Summer and I had next to nothing in common.

This was something, at least.

"Cool." She smiled, then looked out into the parking lot again. But she was still *here*. She must have had something more to say if she wasn't leaving. Or maybe she assumed we were hanging out now that she was sitting here. And… screw it, talking to Summer would make the time pass faster than swiping at virtual fruit on my phone.

"What other kinds of music do you like?" I asked, shoving my phone into my pocket.

"Well, I'm into popular stuff, like from the radio. I don't really have favorite artists or anything; I just change the station until I hear something I like."

"Well, what's the best concert you've ever been to?"

"I've never been to a concert."

I shook my head. "You've got to go to one. Concerts are amazing."

"Well, what about you? What other kinds of music do you like?"

"Country and rock, mostly; classic rock, too."

"How many concerts have you been to?"

"Only a few."

She stared at me like she wasn't sure what to say next, but there was a look in her eyes like she knew what she wanted to say and she just wasn't sure if she should say it. And then she did.

"Would you maybe want to go to homecoming with me?"

The way she cringed after she said it, it was like she immediately felt she'd made a mistake she couldn't take back. I almost felt bad for her.

It wasn't like I had anyone else to go with, or anyone else in mind, even—in the old timeline, I'd gone alone. But going to the dance was like going on a date. Sure, it was only one night, but I knew she liked me and she'd want it to be more.

"It doesn't have to be super serious," she said, backpedaling after I didn't respond. "Just, like, casual. See where things go."

"Uh, I guess, sure." I barely had a chance to think. Saying no felt so mean. I knew I didn't sound very enthused, but truthfully, I wasn't. It was fine hanging out with Summer just now, but now she wanted to go on a date. "Like, just casually, right?"

"Right." She nodded. "Casual. Super casual." She was saying "casual" so much, it was obvious she wanted it to be more than that.

"Yeah. Sure. We can go to homecoming and... see how it goes."

"You don't have to, if you don't want to," she said.

I shook my head. "No, I—let's see where things go. It's worth a shot." All things I'm sure a girl loves to hear.

"Are you sure?"

"Yes, Summer. Homecoming sounds great." It was like she needed me to spell it out.

She blushed and smiled, but it was like she was trying to hide it. I still couldn't get over the fact that she had those neon braces. "Okay. Um, thank you. I—I guess we'll talk about details later?"

"Details?"

"Like, pictures before, or if you want dinner, or like, where we'll meet... Do you need to know what color my dress is?"

"I'll have dinner at home before," I said, not wanting to make this into any more of a date than it needed to be. "We can take pictures at your"—*Isn't she insecure about money or something?*—"in front of the school; some people do that. And we can just both meet here, if that's okay. Uh, do you care if my tie matches your dress?"

"That sounds good," she said, "and do *you* care?"

"Not really."

"Then I don't, either."

"Great. See you tomorrow, I guess."

She grinned as she headed towards the parking lot, punching the air once she probably figured she was out of sight. I couldn't believe I was really doing this. What was this going to accomplish?

But it was too late to change my mind.

Summer

IT WAS a good thing Nolan didn't need to know what color my dress was, because I wasn't even sure what I was going to wear. I hadn't been to a school dance since middle school, and we'd never dressed up for those.

Truthfully, I was still in shock that he even agreed to go with me. He didn't sound very enthusiastic, but he *did* say yes, even when I asked again to make sure. This all felt so fragile, like one wrong move could make him change his mind, so I decided it was best to just work with the information he'd given me and not press any further.

As an episode of *That '70s Show* started to end, I realized it was five, which meant my mother would be home in about twenty minutes, which meant I should take the chicken out of the freezer like she'd wanted me to do hours ago when I got home. I tossed it in the microwave on "defrost" for ten minutes, figuring that would make up for the three hours it should've been defrosting in the sink.

Once I set it in the sink, I heard the garage door open. I scrambled back to the couch and took out my geometry textbook, grabbed my pencil, and opened to a random page in my notebook. By the time I heard footsteps in the laundry room, I figured it looked natural enough.

"Did you finish your homework?" my mother asked, setting some work down on the table. She pulled down the sleeves of her purple sweatshirt and reclasped the clip holding up her light brown hair.

"I'm working on it still," I said.

"Then why is the TV on?"

"Background noise," I said. "We've been over this. It helps me concentrate."

"Yes, but you're retaking tenth grade math, so it obviously didn't help you concentrate last year. Did you at least remember to take the chicken out of the freezer when you got home?"

"It's in the sink."

"Great." She went into the kitchen to check.

"I got a date to homecoming," I offered.

"Oh, are you getting back together with Jonah?"

"No, it's, well, it's Nolan Alden. You might remember him."

"Really? He asked you?"

"No, I asked him, but—"

"Summer, I thought I told you that you can't do stuff like that. If a guy wants to date you, *he'll* ask you. Asking him just makes him feel pressured to say yes."

"Well, he seemed excited about it," I lied. "He, uh, wanted to know what color my dress was so his tie wouldn't clash. I told him I didn't have one yet."

"Look through your closet," she told me, taking a frying pan out from the cabinet. "You should have something that'll work. What about your graduation dress?"

"From eighth grade?" I cringed thinking of the poofy purple dress with its butterfly pattern. "I don't think that'll still fit."

"Well, if we buy a new dress, it has to last," she said. "I'm assuming you're going to want a prom dress in the spring, so this will affect the budget for that."

"That's fine," I said. "I don't even know if I'm going to prom."

"Okay. When's the dance?"

"Saturday night."

"We'll go shopping in the afternoon, then."

Nolan

SUMMER SEEMED to avoid me for the rest of the week. When Liam and Jake planned to ask their dates to watch the football game with them Friday night, I told them Summer had work. I didn't even know if she had a job during the school year.

The guys did, however, thwart my plans to meet Summer at the dance. They decided all six of us should have dinner at the Cheesecake Factory at the mall and then take pictures at the park nearby before going to the dance. This decision was made after school on Friday, and I realized I didn't have Summer's phone number to let her know.

I messaged her online and asked for her number, and when I woke up Saturday morning, she'd replied. I gave her a call, figuring it was easier than texting.

"Hello?" she answered.

"Hey, it's Nolan," I said. "Uh, about tonight…"

"You're canceling? Now?" she asked, panic in her voice.

"No. What? No, I didn't say that."

"Oh, sorry."

"I just wanted to let you know that, uh, the guys want to have dinner at the Cheesecake Factory and take pictures at the park before the dance. So…"

"Oh. Um… thank you, but… the Cheesecake Factory is kind of expensive for me."

I took a deep breath to stay patient. "I'll pay for yours."

"Oh. Well, um, thank you, then. Yeah, that sounds great. Wow. Thank you."

"Sure thing. Pick you up at four-thirty?"

"Four-thirty?"

"If we want to have dinner and pictures in time."

"Oh, uh, yeah, that works."

"Wait, one more question." I realized how awkward it would look if Summer and I were the only ones in the pictures who didn't match. "What color's your dress?"

She got quiet. I thought maybe she'd hung up, but I could still hear her breathing. "Pink."

"What kind of pink?"

"Dark pink. Magenta. Like my braces."

Right, her stupid pink braces. "Great, thanks."

Summer

NOT ONLY did I have to find a dress under fifty dollars, but now it had to be magenta, and I had to be done in time to be ready by four-thirty. We had already exhausted the sparse selections at T.J.Maxx and Ross.

I browsed through the Target clearance rack one more time before giving up and heading to the cosmetic section to find my mom, who was putting some stuff in a basket.

"What's all that?" I asked.

"Here." She took out a couple bottles of skin-colored liquid. "Let me see if I can tell which shade is right... This one." She put one of the bottles back in the basket and the other on the shelf. "I thought you might want some makeup for tonight. I'll show you how to do it."

"Oh. Thank you. Um... there's been a change of plans, though."

"He canceled on you? Well, at least we didn't buy anything yet."

"No, we're still on!" I assured her. "He just wants to meet earlier, for dinner and pictures. He wants to pick me up at four-thirty."

"Well, if we can be done by two-thirty then that should give me enough time to do your hair and makeup. Does that sound like a plan?"

"Okay. I'll try a different store for the dress; there's nothing here."

Nolan

SUMMER TEXTED me her address, and when I pulled into the driveway, I thought it didn't look *that* bad. The yard could use some work, sure, but it looked like a perfectly fine single-story house. She was waiting on the porch with her mother, who looked how I'd imagine Summer would in a couple decades: plain greying hair clipped out of her face, dressed in a baggy T-shirt and jeans.

Summer actually seemed to have put some effort into her appearance. When I got closer, I could see some pink eyeshadow that matched her outfit. The dress itself was tight in the chest, but the skirt part was loose and hit about mid-thigh, longer than most homecoming dresses. It had thin straps that did little to conceal her skin-colored bra straps. She had a pair of plain silver flats that looked fairly worn.

The biggest difference was her hair; it had a bit of a curl to it and was tied up in a ponytail with a dark pink ribbon tied around it. I could see her face better than usual. Her ears stuck out just a bit, and her brown eyes sat a little wide above her narrow nose—things that her hair overshadowed when it fell in her face all the time.

"Hey," she said nervously. "Um, thanks again for dinner. I'll order something cheap."

"It's fine," I assured her. "You look nice." I knew I was supposed to say it, and she *did* look better than usual, even if that wasn't difficult.

She grinned. "You, too. I'm glad the tie color situation worked out."

I held up the last-minute magenta tie with a smile. It did look nice over my black button-up and dress pants. But my eyes wandered back to her shoes. Girls didn't usually wear flats to dances, not since middle school. Did she think I was too short for her to wear heels? I was a few inches taller than her, so it wasn't like she *had* to wear low shoes.

I wondered what she'd think when we got to pictures and the other girls were wearing six-inch heels, or if it would look weird in the pictures. I wasn't a stickler for that kind of thing, but the other girls would probably say something to Liam or Jake about how *my* date made their pictures look weird, and I didn't need another situation like when Jake's eighth-grade girlfriend told him he couldn't hang out with us anymore because Liam ruined her Valentine's dance pictures by eating a cookie in the background, and now she couldn't post them, and Liam wouldn't apologize, and Jake wanted to get to second base so he ignored us for a month until she broke up with him for something equally stupid.

Liam and I smacked him over the head for choosing a stupid girl over us. That month without him in the friend group was rough. We had to do our rocket project with Jimmy Vogel, one of the special education kids, and he talked *so much* about some stupid video game that we almost told him to let us do the project and we'd put his name on it. But he was the smartest of the three of us, so we put up with him to get the A.

I decided not to say anything about the shoes. I shook hands with Summer's mother and assured her Summer would be home by eleven.

"Nice car," Summer said, getting into my truck. "Is it yours?"

"Sixteenth birthday present. You've been in it before, haven't you?"

"No."

I realized the only time she'd been in my car was when I gave her that ride to Starbucks, which apparently had never happened.

"Oh, well, welcome, I guess." I wasn't sure how to talk to her. "So, uh, we're just meeting up with Jake and Liam. You know them, right?"

"I've had classes with them, yeah."

"Great. Liam's taking a sophomore from student council, and Jake's going with Vivian."

"I think I've had a class with her."

Being in the car with Summer wasn't weird until I started thinking about how the only other time she'd been in my car was right before she died. Well, maybe not *right* before. There was a whole weekend in between... possibly.

"Do you listen to music in the car?" Summer asked.

"Sometimes," I said. "Not for short trips, though; the mall's just down this road."

"I know. I've been there." She smiled like she was trying to be funny.

"Never would've guessed." I tried to sound funny in return.

"Maybe you'll think this is funny," she said, "but I was actually just there earlier today to get my dress."

"Wait, really? You just got it today?"

She nodded. "My mom has work during the week, so this was the only day we could go."

"What do your parents do?"

"My mom works at the university downtown," she replied.

"And your dad?"

"He lives in Florida."

"Oh." I wasn't sure where to go from there.

"It's fine; he left a while ago," she said. "I still see him once a year, usually, and he calls on holidays. But, like, I'm fine."

"Alright. Well, it's a good dress for last minute," I told her. "I'm surprised you were able to find one."

"Me, too. I was actually still looking for one when you called to ask what color," she said. "I just panicked and said magenta, and fortunately I was able to find this."

"Wait, so you could've said any color and you went with magenta?" I asked. As annoying as it was to have to buy a new tie, I could see some humor in her picking a color at random and coming up with the one I didn't already have. "Summer! Magenta?"

"It was the first color that came to mind. I'm sorry!" She laughed. "I'm just glad you *had* a magenta tie or else I would've felt really awkward."

"I bought this today," I told her, "at the menswear store near my house. Is magenta your favorite color or something?"

"Yeah, kind of," she said. "I don't know if I have a *favorite* color, but I like it. It's the color my braces have been for the last few months. I'm sorry.

I didn't mean to make you buy a new tie."

I pulled into a parking space. "It's fine, it's fine. I'm sure I'll find another occasion to wear it. How long have you had your braces?"

"Close to six months," she said. "I get them off in July if all goes well."

"Sixteen is pretty late for braces."

"Well, my mom had to save up," she said. "Plus the dentist didn't recommend them until, like, right after my fifteenth birthday."

When we walked into the restaurant, Liam and his date had already gotten us a table.

"Hey," I said, sliding into the booth. "You both know Summer, right?"

"Yeah. Hey, guys," Liam said. "This is Darcy. She's a sophomore."

Darcy was dressed in a very tight, strapless blue dress, and her long golden hair was curled with her bangs pinned back. She wore blue glitter around her eyes that matched the dress, and I think she had fake eyelashes—she looked way hotter than Summer. It was weird to see Liam and Darcy together, since I knew—at least in the old timeline—that they'd hardly spoken after homecoming.

"Summer, I love your eyeshadow!" Darcy said. "It goes perfectly with that dress."

Summer blushed. "Oh, thank you. My mom helped me; I don't really wear makeup."

The way Summer was sitting in the booth was awkward. She seemed so stiff and reserved, like she was afraid to fully commit to sitting there.

"Where do you work, Summer?" Liam asked.

"Oh, I don't have a job right now," she said, "but over the summer I sold tickets at the conservatory theater downtown."

"Didn't you have work last night, though?" he asked her.

"What?"

"Nolan said you couldn't come to the game with us because you had work."

"The homecoming game? No, I didn't know you all were going..." She looked at me, confused.

"I didn't have your number," I reminded her quietly.

"Well, I don't really like to watch sports, anyway," she said. "Sorry for the miscommunication—"

Before the conversation could get any more awkward, Jake and Vivian showed up. Vivian also looked a lot hotter than Summer, with her black hair in some intricate braid and her bright red lipstick popping against her golden-brown skin, matching her short strapless dress that looked kind of like it was wrapped around in front like a towel.

"Hey, guys!" Jake called. "What'd we miss?"

"You know Summer, right?" I asked.

Vivian smiled, her small brown eyes lighting up. "Of course! You look so pretty, Summer!"

"Thank you," Summer said with another blush. "I like your dress."

I supposed it was good that all the girls got along so well, because that meant the three of them would do most of the talking and I wouldn't have to interact with Summer much during dinner.

A waitress brought out a couple appetizers that Liam had ordered, and the six of us browsed the menus for our main courses. I noticed Summer was scanning the appetizer section.

"We have appetizers," I reminded her. "You're welcome to eat them; Liam's parents are paying for those."

"Oh, I know. I just didn't want to spend that much on dinner, since you're paying," she said.

"Summer, it's fine," I said, resisting the urge to roll my eyes. "Get an actual entrée; it's not a big deal."

Summer

I FELT so bad ordering an eighteen-dollar pasta dish, but Nolan insisted it was okay. I did enjoy getting to know the other girls, but I couldn't help but feel like Nolan didn't particularly want me there—the whole misunderstanding about the homecoming game rubbed me the wrong way, even if I wouldn't have wanted to go anyway.

When we got to the park to take pictures, I couldn't help but notice I was the only girl wearing flats. Vivian had on these strappy black stiletto heels, and Darcy had tall silver sparkly pumps. I was wearing my shoes from eighth grade graduation, which still fit but were a little snugger than they were three years ago.

I also had to remember that I was wearing makeup and couldn't touch my face. How did other girls do this every single day? How did Vivian and Darcy manage with *even more* makeup than this? I watched them touch up their lipstick, wishing I'd thought to bring mine. I was also certain my hair wasn't staying curled, even though my mom had used hairspray on it. It felt stiff when I touched it—but I was also careful not to touch it too much and ruin whatever curl it still had. I hated the crispy feeling from the hairspray, anyway; touching it or even remembering what my hair felt like right now made me cringe.

Nolan put his arm around me for the first picture, the way the other couples were standing, but he felt stiff, like he didn't particularly want to touch me. We did another pose where I was supposed to stand in front of him and he put both arms around my waist. The other two guys had to stand a bit to the side because of the girls' shoes, but Nolan was taller than me and I had flats on, so it wasn't an issue for us.

There were some photos with us squatting in front of the guys, some with just the guys, and some with just us girls—Vivian and Darcy showed me some cute poses they wanted to do. They assured me I looked good and the pictures would be cute. Then each couple took some photos on their own; some cute and some funny. I asked Nolan what he wanted to do.

"Just a couple normal ones, I guess," he said offhandedly, as if the thought of having pictures with just me was unpleasant.

"Well, we don't have to take them if you don't want; we got some cute group ones."

"It's fine," he insisted. "We're going to the dance together, so we take pictures together. It's fine, Summer."

Finally, we stopped with the pictures and went to the actual dance. The gym was decorated for this year's homecoming theme, which was Pixar movies—each grade had been assigned a different movie as their own theme, but I didn't pay too much attention to the theme days or pep rallies. I dressed up for the easy ones, like pajama day or "class color" day, but I never went all out. Maybe I should have, if I wanted to fit in more and have a genuine high school experience... but it was already so late for that.

"Did you want to check your shoes?" Nolan asked.

I looked down. "What's wrong with them?"

"Most girls leave their shoes at coat check," he said. "I mean, I guess you're wearing flats, so they won't be too uncomfortable, right?"

"Yeah. I wouldn't want to be barefoot in the gym anyway."

"That's pretty smart," he said. "Well, should we dance, I guess?"

"I don't really know how to dance to fast songs," I said. At middle school dances, my friends and I had usually just talked outside; we didn't spend much time on the dance floor. Daisy stopped going to dances altogether after middle school, and Marta took them so seriously now it was a little overwhelming. Our other friend, Bella, had moved away, but I doubt she'd go to "serious" dances like homecoming; she'd never taken anything seriously.

I blanched at Nolan's next words: "You know how to grind, right? That's usually what people do."

"No," I blurted out.

"Here, come over here," he said. He led me over to a circle of people from our grade and stood behind me, placing his hands lightly over my hips. My arms erupted in goosebumps at the touch, and I looked around to see that this was what everyone else was doing. Paired off, each girl was rubbing up against a guy's crotch while each guy rested his hands on the girl's waist. And everyone was just... talking casually, like they didn't even care what they were doing.

I glanced back at Nolan. "Is that... is that what you want me to do?"

"Yeah, it's just grinding," he said. "It's easy."

"Are you sure?" It seemed like it would be so uncomfortable, but everyone else in the circle appeared to be just fine.

"Yes, Summer." He was obviously getting annoyed with me.

I didn't want to make this night any worse than it probably already was for him, so I reluctantly obliged. Sometimes people talked, and sometimes it was silent. We were just standing there "grinding" and occasionally letting more people into the circle. This lasted for a few songs and didn't get any less awkward, and then a slow song came on and couples started breaking off.

"Are we supposed to slow-dance now?" I asked Nolan.

"If you want," he said. "We could sit and talk somewhere, too."

"No, I—I think I'd like to dance with you," I said. "If you want to, of course."

"Let's dance."

He put his hands on my waist and I draped mine over his shoulders. That was how most people seemed to be doing it. We didn't move much, just swayed gently back and forth.

"I'm sorry I'm so annoying," I told him. "This is... It's my first high school dance."

"Jonah never took you to a dance?"

I shook my head.

"Well, it's easy. Don't read too much into it. You grind to the fast songs, and you can slow-dance like this or hang outside. They're not as big a deal as some girls make them seem."

"Did you really want to come here with me?" I asked. "It's okay if you didn't. You can be honest. I mean, I get it."

"I said I'd go with you, Summer. I'm having fun, really."

"Okay, I just... You didn't invite me to the game—"

"I didn't have your number."

"Right... just..."

"Didn't I say not to read too much into this?" he asked. It was like he was trying to smile, but it wasn't quite there. I didn't want to annoy him anymore.

"Okay. Sorry."

"You'll be fine," he said. "Just have fun."

Nolan

I SHOULDN'T have told Summer I'd go with her. I thought it was the right thing to do, but she wasn't even having a good time. She was so worried that I didn't want to be here, and I could only lie so well. Obviously I didn't want to be on a date with her, especially not something like this that had turned into a bigger deal than it needed to be, with dinner and pictures and it being her first high school dance.

She did seem to relax after I told her not to read into things. After grinding through a couple more songs, I asked if she wanted to talk outside for a while and she said yes, so we stepped outside the gym and sat together on a concrete platform. She instantly seemed more comfortable, though she was obviously still nervous, no matter how much she was trying to hide it.

I could tell she wasn't into the grinding thing; she was so awkward the whole time, and, like, it wasn't like I *loved* grinding with Summer, but it was what my friends and I did with our dates at dances. Nobody cool was out on the actual dance floor unless there was a slow song.

Neither of us spoke, and I tried to think of something I could ask.

"Is Marta here tonight?" I asked, realizing she'd never come up in regards to dinner or pictures.

"Her boyfriend's homecoming is tonight, and she said she was going to his instead of ours. But she said since I was going with you, I'd probably be fine without her. He's a senior, so it's his last homecoming."

"Oh, nice. Who else do you hang out with? I don't usually see you with anyone else."

"Well, I'm friends with Daisy Cabedo if you know her; we talk in gym, but we don't hang out as often as we used to."

"Yeah, I've seen her around." Daisy Cabedo... She hung around with the group of honor students who never dressed nicer than jeans and big T-shirts or went to any school events. Perfectionist, tattletale, generally annoying... Yeah, I could see someone like her being nice to someone like Summer.

"I don't think she's here; she doesn't really go to dances," Summer explained. "I'm glad your friends are here, so we have more people to talk to."

"Yeah."

We went back inside and danced for a few more songs, some slow and most not. When the night was coming to an end, we said goodbye to the other couples and headed towards my truck. I wasn't sure if it was her speed, but I figured Summer might want to make out a little before I took her back to her place, and even if I wasn't attracted to her it'd be nice to get *something* out of the date. She'd probably take it the wrong way if I turned her down, anyway, since she took everything the wrong way.

"Alright," I said, "we can drive around for a little bit if you want; we've got an hour 'til you need to be home, right?"

"I guess, but I live super close," she said. "We could just stay in the parking lot and talk, if you wanted to."

"Talk?"

"Didn't you want to drive around and talk?"

"No, I meant drive somewhere with less light and no adult chaperones."

"...Why?"

"To... you know." She really had never been to a dance.

Her eyes widened. "I—we—it's our first date and you want to do that?"

"Didn't you and Jonah ever do anything?" I knew they hadn't had sex, but they had to have done *something* for a guy like Jonah to stick around so long *trying* to get there.

"Well... we kissed some, but we'd been together for a while," she said. "You—I—I don't want to do anything like that tonight. I just don't... I just don't."

I tried not to roll my eyes in front of her. It wasn't like I *wanted* to do anything with her, but wasn't *she* the one who'd asked *me* to homecoming? And now she was freaking out over the prospect of even kissing? It felt like I couldn't do anything right with her; I just didn't want to seem rude by not offering.

"I'm sorry," she said. "I—I didn't even think you'd want to. You hardly seem like you like me anyway. I had no idea. I really didn't."

"Whatever, Summer." I shook my head. "Let's get you home."

"We can still talk," she said. "I'm sorry."

"I'll take you home."

I didn't know what to do now. She was the one who'd begged me to take her to the dance. And now she wasn't even into me?

When I got to the driveway, she jumped out of the car, thanked me, slammed the door, and ran up to the house. She got out so fast it was like she was worried I'd try to jump her if she lingered even a second. Please; she was hardly so irresistible.

As I was heading back home, I pulled to the side of the road before taking out my phone to text Katie. Summer was a dead end, so I might as well try and get with someone I *did* have feelings for.

NOLAN: Hey

Her response was almost immediate.

KATIE: Hey

NOLAN: Do u remember me?

KATIE: Yeah lol

NOLAN: What're u doing tonight?

KATIE: Studying.

NOLAN: Wanna hang out?

It was after ten, so it was kind of a risky hour—since I was texting this late, she might assume I only wanted to fool around. I kept forgetting that Katie didn't really know me. In the old timeline, asking her to hang out this late wouldn't be such a big deal, whether or not we ended up fooling around—but now, I was practically a stranger to her. Which was why her next message surprised me:

KATIE: We could hook up if u want

I had to rub my eyes to make sure I'd read her message right. Katie had never been so forward, especially not about sex. Then again, I *was* a guy she barely knew texting her at ten-thirty. But if she was offering... I supposed I might as well get *some* action tonight.

NOLAN: Ok, if u want. But I'd be ok to just hang out.

KATIE: Nah I'm dtf. Here's my address

Perfect.

Summer

I WAS so stupid; how could I think tonight would be anything but awkward? I should've known by his voice that Nolan didn't really want to go with me. He just felt bad for me. I hated pity; it was worse than flat-out rejection. I wished people would just be honest with me instead of telling me what they thought I wanted to hear.

My mother was waiting in the living room. "He didn't walk you to the door?"

"No," I said. "I figured you'd be waiting up, so we said goodbye in the car."

"Well? Did you have a good time?"

"Yeah." Truly, I did, until the end. "He was very nice. He introduced me to his friends, and we took some pictures... I guess he'll send them. We slow-danced a few times. It seemed like he had fun."

"Did he kiss you?"

"No," I said. "I—there was never a good moment."

"Hm." She nodded. "Well, at least he didn't try to jump you."

"Are guys supposed to do that on dates?" I asked. "Like, if I agree to go out with a boy, should I expect that even if it's our first date and we haven't kissed, we're supposed to do something?"

"Most boys will try that," she said, "but if you don't want to do something, you need to be firm with them. They'll probably try to guilt you into it, or think that if they keep asking you'll give in. Did he try anything like that?"

I shook my head quickly. "No, I just... Marta said—"

"Marta has had *one* boyfriend; she doesn't know what she's talking about."

"Okay. Well, goodnight."

I walked down the hallway to my room and changed into my pajamas. I realized I'd need to take my makeup off; my mom had bought me some makeup wipes since all I'd had was regular face soap. I sat on my bed and took my makeup off. I took my hair out of its ponytail and tried to finger-comb it, but it was still stiff from the hairspray. I wanted to wash it tonight, but it was already so late. I hated going to bed with wet hair, and I hated the feeling of hot air blowing in my face from the hair dryer, so I'd have to make do.

How could I have been so stupid to believe Nolan might actually like me? That a guy like him would ever like me, that I'd ever be able to do better than Jonah?

When my mom was in high school, boys loved her. She loved to tell stories about all the boys fighting over who got to take her to prom or throwing rocks at her bedroom window at night... Sometimes it felt like she was disappointed that I didn't have the same experiences, that I wasn't the kind of girl guys would buy a dozen roses for. That I was the kind of girl who had to beg a guy to take me to homecoming.

And even my mom, who'd had plenty of eligible bachelors to choose from, ended up divorced from her college sweetheart and hadn't been on a date since. Even if I *could* be the kind of girl she was, spending all my time with guys trying to get in my pants, I still just came home right after school every day and watched reruns of the same show. Maybe sometimes I hung out with one of my two friends, and sometimes I actually did something with them, like see a movie, but never anything interesting like going to a concert or a party or even a school dance. I'd play video games in Daisy's living room or act out Marta's favorite episodes of *Glee*, nothing more.

I wouldn't blame my mom for being disappointed in me. She couldn't even relive her teen years through me because my life was more depressing than hers had ever been, then or now. She was divorced, but maybe trading with her wouldn't be so bad. At least I'd have a daughter I could give love to. And... maybe I wouldn't shit on anything exciting she told me, and I wouldn't ground her for failing geometry because I'd understand how hard it was, and I wouldn't do anything to make her think I was disappointed in her for not being "normal."

The lump grew in my throat. My mom was disappointed in me. Nolan pitied me. Jonah was the only one who wanted me. When I went into the bathroom to brush my teeth, I opened up the bottom cabinet and took out one of my pink plastic disposable razors before heading back to my room. I broke off one edge of the plastic surrounding the two razorblades, just like my friend Bella had shown me in seventh grade when I was sleeping over at her house.

"You don't do it too deep, though," she'd said. *"Just a little bit, like a papercut."*

"But why?" I had asked.

"There's two reasons: the first is that when you're doing it, you forget about everything that's wrong—with yourself and with life in general."

"And the second?"

"Someone might see it," she said. *"They might ask you if you're okay."*

"Are you *okay?"*

"That's for you to decide," she said. *"It's being asked that's nice. It makes you feel like someone actually cares."*

I decided that I *was* okay, but tonight I wanted to forget about everything that was wrong with me and with life in general. Just like how, a few days after Bella showed me how to break a disposable razor or unscrew a pencil sharpener, I'd decided that I was okay, but I wanted to forget that one of my best friends was hurting herself and I had no idea what to do about it. Or how Bella had moved to Reno at the end of eighth grade and I hadn't heard from her since, so sometimes I wasn't even sure she was still alive, and I liked to forget about that possibility.

Tonight, I wanted to forget that I was an awkward idiot who nobody sane wanted to date and how I didn't even know *how* to date normal guys and I'd never learn because I'd be lucky if I ever got the chance.

And maybe—just maybe—I wanted someone to ask me if I was okay.

Nolan

KATIE SNUCK out her back door and I met her a little way down the road from her house. I drove us to the parking lot behind the mall that almost nobody used since its remodel a few years ago. She was in pajamas: a blue tank top and black cotton shorts, no shoes. Her hair was in braids like it was for swim practice, and it was wet like she'd showered recently. I could smell some kind of fruity soap when she got in the car. She didn't say anything about my formal attire. I forgot I was even dressed for homecoming until I started to undress.

Fortunately, I had already cleaned out the space behind the seats in case Summer had wanted to do anything, so other than the always-awkward climb into the back and grabbing a condom from the box I kept back there, it was nice and smooth.

It was weird, because I felt like I'd known Katie much longer, but really we'd only talked once before tonight. She didn't know *me*, and that meant she was just magically okay with a random hookup. I didn't see her as that type; the Katie I'd talked to at those trip meetings was sweet and wanted to get to know me first. We'd kissed once in my car, but when I tried to make out with her, she said she wasn't ready for anything serious. But tonight, she'd agreed to a random hookup—she'd *offered*.

"How long 'til your parents notice you're gone?" I asked her.

"They won't," she said, pulling her tank top over her head to reveal she wasn't wearing a bra underneath. "They don't notice anything I do anymore, not since the divorce."

Ah, yes. Baggage. "...Did you want to talk about that?"

It was weird; I knew her parents were divorced because she'd mention *"my mom's house"* or *"my dad's new boyfriend,"* but I'd just assumed they'd been divorced for a while. It never occurred to me that it'd happened recently. She'd seemed so chill about it before.

"I talk enough in family counseling," she said. "That's not really what guys like you are for."

"Guys like me?"

"Guys who want to hook up on a Saturday night. That's what you're here for. If I wanted to talk to you about my parents' divorce, I'd make you ask me on a date first."

"Alright, then."

We'd been on a couple dates in the old timeline. Well, drive-throughs and one actual sit-down lunch. We'd only known each other for a couple months, if even that, and we'd only been *talking* for a couple of weeks. I guess she saw me differently because I'd been trying to date her then, not just hook up.

I wondered if this was a mistake, if after this she'd just see me as some guy she hooked up with to spite her parents, but I figured I could convince her to let me take her on a date later. Chicks probably loved that: a guy they thought was a hookup actually wanting to get to know them after. I'd only been with a few girls, but Jake gave good advice in that department.

I guess I really did have to thank Summer; my guilt over her had sent me back in time, and now I got to fix all kinds of stuff I was doing wrong. Things were going to be just fine.

"Hey, careful, it's cramped back here," she whispered. "You're pushing my head into the side."

"Sorry, Summer."

"What?"

"I said sorry."

"Did... you call me Summer?"

I suppose I did. Why was I thinking about her right now?

"I—it's a long story."

"No, that's fine," she said. "I just wanted to make sure I heard right. I can be Summer, if you need me to be."

"...Uh...I really don't," I said. "It's just been a long night."

"Suit yourself."

This wasn't Katie. It couldn't be. This wasn't the same Katie who had that plush turtle keychain, who carried reusable straws, who told everyone her favorite movie was *Mean Girls* when it was secretly *Back to the Future*, who wanted to be an Olympic swimmer more than anything in the world. Who the hell was this girl? And what was I doing with her?

We were quick. I dropped Katie off a couple houses down and watched to make sure she got back through the gate before I drove home.

This wasn't great. No, it was bad. Straight up, it was terrible. Katie didn't even seem like herself. The Katie I'd spent all those weeks talking to at the trip meetings wouldn't use a guy she barely knew for a hookup to cope with her parents' divorce. The further I got from her house, the more I felt like maybe I shouldn't have hooked up with her. I should have just waited until I "met" her at the community center during the trip meetings in the spring and gone about this the way I had before—but that was *such* a long time from now.

Something didn't feel right about tonight. But why wouldn't it? I got what I wanted. I got rid of Summer and I hooked up with Katie. But all the way home, I couldn't stop thinking about how awkward Summer was. How she didn't know anything about high school dances... but why would she? Why would I expect that she'd gone with a guy to a dance before?

And why was it such a big deal that she didn't want to fool around? I wasn't even into her, and anything we had done would've just made her clingier than she already was.

Summer was different than the girls I usually talked to: more awkward, less attractive, more annoying and naive...

"You're home late."

My mother's voice startled me. She and my father were waiting on the living room couch.

"I had to drop Summer off," I explained. "She was... chatty."

"Well, I hope you were at least using protection for your 'chatting,'" she said.

"Gross, no." I shook my head. "We didn't—I'm not into her. It was a pity date."

"Well, you remember curfew is midnight, right?"

I checked the time on my phone—12:28. "Sorry."

"Just because you have your own car doesn't mean you can stay out past curfew," my father said. "Consider this a warning."

"I will. I'm going to go to bed now."

"Wait—how was the dance?" my mother asked.

"I told you, it was a pity date," I said. "Summer's... awkward."

"You two looked cute in the pictures Jake's parents sent," she replied. "I hope you had a nice time. I'll forward you the pictures tomorrow so you can send them to Summer."

"Thanks."

After getting into bed, I scrolled through social media to look at everyone else's pictures. Jake had already posted his photos, including the group ones. He hadn't tagged anyone; he never did.

It was weird looking at the pictures—it felt like Summer had been photoshopped into them. They were *so* similar to the photos I remembered from the old timeline, but now she was there, too.

Summer didn't look terrible. She was plainer and definitely less hot than Darcy and Vivian, but my mother was right: we did look kind of cute together. In Jake's pictures, Summer actually looked ecstatic. *So* happy to be there. It made her seem kind of cute, in some way. I thought of how bizarre this all was. This date with Summer was one of the most awkward and uncomfortable nights I could remember. So why was I still thinking about her?

Maybe tonight sucked because I didn't really give it a shot. Maybe I needed to give Summer a real chance. We *were* having fun talking on the bench before she'd asked me to homecoming. Maybe a casual hangout wouldn't be *so* bad—as long as it wasn't a whole big thing like homecoming. Or maybe we just needed to try being friends for a while first.

Summer

"SUMMER, YOUR friend's here!" my mother called.

"Coming!" I shut my laptop and jumped out of bed. I didn't remember having plans with Marta today. And the last thing I needed was to hear about how amazing her night with Sutton was when mine...

I went into the hallway, and there stood Nolan Alden at our front door. I immediately regretted coming to the door in pajamas, even if they were cute—a red tank top and pink shorts—and my hair all tangled from not having showered yet today, plus the hairspray residue and the indents from where my ponytail had been. He was only wearing a T-shirt and jeans, but I was a total mess.

"Hey," he said.

"Hey," I managed. "Um..."

"Can we talk?" he asked.

I nodded, and we sat down on the front step of the porch. This was where Jonah had kissed me for the first time; every time I looked out at my driveway, I remembered that. Maybe Nolan would kiss me... but did I even want that? Knowing he was ready to do more than that last night?

Dream on, Summer; you know that's not what he's here for.

"I'm sorry about last night," he said. "I'm just used to... Well, I don't know what you... I'm sorry."

"It's fine," I said, looking down at my hands. "I—I've only ever had one boyfriend, and he waited a few weeks just to kiss me. I like taking things slow. I don't think I'm ready for anything sexual right now, and I don't know when I will be. And you also didn't even seem like you were having a good time, so I was just really confused."

"That's okay. I don't want to pressure you," he said. "I'm sorry about last night. I guess I was expecting... I don't know what I was expecting. I didn't realize you'd never been to a dance before, for one. But after I dropped you off... I felt like maybe we rushed into things, and we just need to try hanging out as friends for a while."

He wanted to hang out? With the *possibility* that it could lead somewhere? I wondered if he could hear my heart pounding—he could probably smell the rush of warmth under my arms that made me remember I hadn't showered since before the dance.

He sighed. "I just wanted to apologize," he said, "and... maybe we could hang out again sometime. Like, try again, to see if it goes any better."

I froze.

"Well... as long as you know I'm not... ready for anything, like, physical."

"I know," he said. He half-smiled. "You bolted out of the car before I could even kiss you goodnight."

My heart pounded faster. "You were going to kiss me?"

"Well, no. But you didn't even give me the chance."

"I think we should take things slow," I said.

"Cool."

"So... did you want to hang out again, as friends this time?" I wanted to be completely sure, in case my mother asked what we'd talked about. It would be nice to have something exciting to tell her.

He laughed. "You aren't gonna make this easy, are you?"

"Probably not."

"Well, lucky for you, I like a little challenge."

He looked at me, and I looked back at him. It seemed like the moment we should kiss, but we'd *just* talked about taking things slow and being friends first.

"I should go back inside," I said. "Uh... homework."

"I'll see you at school tomorrow, then?"

"Yeah."

We stood up, and he gave me another lingering look. I gave him a half-hearted wave before rushing back through the front door, and then I felt like such an idiot, an immature sixteen-year-old girl who had no idea how to talk to a guy she really liked. I only hoped he meant what he'd said about not minding a challenge.

4

Nolan

I COULDN'T believe it. I actually drove to Summer's house to ask her to hang out *again*. I don't even know why I thought trying to hang out with her again would be a good idea, but it wasn't like this do-over came with a manual. I guess I just figured I owed her a better chance at seeing if we even *could* spend time together since homecoming was so awkward—this would be a *real* test to see if we got along, in a way.

She thanked me for sending her the pictures, and she posted them later, but we didn't talk Sunday. She didn't even come to my locker Monday morning. I did hear Marta talking to her by her locker, though.

"Sutton was such a gentleman," Marta said. "He didn't even try to hook up. Did Nolan try anything with you?"

"No—well—it was messy," Summer replied. "But he did say he wanted to hang out again sometime."

"Well, good! Maybe we can double sometime. Your pictures looked cute, by the way."

The bell rang, and I wondered what I was supposed to do next. Maybe actually make plans to hang out with her?

At lunch, I sat with the guys like usual.

"How was your night?" Liam asked in that saucy voice that meant *"did you get any?"*

"Summer likes to take things slow," I said, "but I got an offer from that girl I met at Niamh's school, so at least I got some action."

"Oh, the one who told you about Niamh's boyfriend?" Jake asked. "Do you have a picture?"

I shook my head. "She wasn't that good, anyway. Oh, but don't mention it to Summer; I didn't tell her I went and hooked up with another girl after our date."

"Mmhmm, so you *like* Summer, then?" Liam raised an eyebrow.

I rolled my eyes. "I do not *like* Summer. I just don't want to hurt her feelings."

I felt weird about what I did with Katie. She was so different; I wasn't sure I would hook up with her like that again. Regardless, it would hurt Summer's feelings if she knew anything like that had happened, and in the interest of not screwing up my do-over, I wanted to avoid that as much as possible.

"If you don't like her, rip the bandage off; don't lead her on," Jake said.

"How was *your* night?" I asked, changing the subject.

"Oh, Viv's alright," he replied. "She had to be home by eleven-thirty, so we were pretty rushed, though."

"Darcy only let me get to second," Liam said, "and once we were alone, she didn't seem very interested. I don't know if we'll go out again."

"Hey, at least she let you do *something*," I said.

"Shut up, you still got laid; it just wasn't by your date."

"My pity date," I corrected. "That was for the best, trust me."

After school, I noticed Summer on the way to the parking lot. She was wearing jeans and a plain purple T-shirt, and her hair was up in a ponytail. I called out, but she had her earbuds in. I caught up to her.

"Hey."

She jumped, then took an earbud out. "Oh, hey."

"What're you listening to?" I asked. Up close, I noticed she had makeup on her eyelashes.

She showed me her screen; she was listening to a Paramore song. What I noticed more, however, was how cracked her screen was—how did she live like that?

"Oh, nice," I said. Paramore wasn't really my thing. "You should get your screen fixed, though."

She blushed. "My mom says I can have a new phone if I pass all my classes; it'll be better to have when going to Europe, anyway."

"Oh, right, that Europe trip. Do you know where I can get a flyer for that?" I asked. "It sounded interesting."

"Yeah! They've got them at the community center, and there's info on their website."

"Cool, thanks. And... do you want to see a movie on Friday, after school?"

"Oh, um, sure." She smiled. I was getting less annoyed by her braces. Maybe I was just getting used to them. "Yes. Thank you."

"Great."

Summer

WHEN NOLAN said he might want to hang out again, I didn't think he was serious—but then he asked me to see a movie. I almost couldn't believe it. Was it because I started wearing makeup to school? It was just mascara and tinted lip balm, but still, maybe it made him see me as more... like the girls he usually talked to, even just as friends.

Not only that, but he was interested in the Europe trip. *This could really happen! We could end up going on the trip together!* I had to pass all my classes, of course, and I was already struggling in geometry for the second time.

I tried not to think about the negatives, though. I focused on the positives: we had plans for Friday. My mom even told me I could borrow her eyeshadow palette since it had more neutral colors than the pink quad she'd bought me for the dance.

Since the plan was to leave right from school, I showed up on Friday dressed as if this were a date, even though I knew it wasn't: a cute brown striped sweater to wear with my jeans and a pair of knee-high black slouchy boots from the mall—they weren't great quality, but they were ten dollars and they looked nice enough. My mom had done my makeup before she left for work, and my hair was tied back in a ponytail.

In geometry, the girl who sat in front of me, Jess Romano, spun around in her seat. "Summer, are you wearing makeup?"

"Yeah," I said.

We didn't usually talk, but knowing another junior was retaking this class—besides Jonah—was comforting, so I enjoyed seeing her and the two other non-psychotic juniors around in class.

"You look so pretty!" she told me. "You should wear your makeup like that every day."

I blushed. "Oh. Thank you. I'm not very good at makeup, though; my mom had to help me."

"It looks good," she said again, touching my arm. "Hey, I saw you went to homecoming with Nolan. How'd that go?"

"Oh, um, it was fun," I said. "We're hanging out again today after school, actually."

She grinned. "Ah, so *that's* why you're wearing makeup."

I was surprised that someone like Jess would talk to me like that. She wasn't "popular," so to speak, but she was up there; she seemed to get along with all the more popular kids in our English class, and I usually saw her hanging around people I knew were in student council.

When the final bell rang, I met Nolan by his locker.

"Hey, Summer," he said. "I'm almost ready."

"Cool. Um, what movie are we seeing?"

"I thought we could see that, uh… What's that girly movie everyone's talking about?"

"You want to watch a girly movie?"

"Well, this way, you get to enjoy the plot, and I get to enjoy the hot actresses," he said. "Unless there's something you'd rather see?"

"No, that's fine," I said.

"Cool. And we'll get some dinner after, at the food court."

"Okay."

The ride to the mall was quiet, but I wasn't sure why. When I'd gotten into the passenger seat of his truck, Nolan had stared at me for a second too long. As we drove, it seemed like he was deep in thought, and I wasn't sure how to ask what he was thinking about.

"I have money. For my ticket," I said. It was the only thing I could think to say. "I wasn't sure what the arrangement was going to be, so I brought some."

"How about I get the tickets and you get the popcorn?" he asked.

"Okay." I smiled. "Um... how are your classes?"

"They're alright." He looked at me for a second. "You ever feel like... you have a flashback to something that never happened?"

I laughed. "How could you have a flashback to something if it never happened?"

"I don't know; do you ever have a memory that feels so real, but it can't be real because it just... doesn't add up with reality?"

"You're weird, Nolan," I said, hoping it came off playful.

He stared at me again, quickly as the light changed.

"I guess I am."

Nolan

SEEING A movie was a much better idea than a dance, it seemed. We barely had to talk to each other. We shared a large popcorn, we'd check each other's reactions at certain parts of the movie, and at one point I put my arm around her—just to see how it felt. She leaned into my shoulder, but we only stayed like that for a minute because the theater seats didn't make it very comfortable.

But then there was dinner at the food court, and I still wasn't sure what to talk to her about. I didn't want to talk about anything that deep. In the car, I'd wanted to find a way to talk about the whole timeline issue in a way that would make sense... but it *didn't* make sense. I couldn't have a flashback to something that had never happened, even if every damn time Summer sat in the passenger seat of that truck, I thought about giving her that ride to Starbucks. I still couldn't remember what I'd said or done that day. But I couldn't just ask her.

After talking about the movie, our conversation lulled. "How are your classes?" I asked. What was I, her mother?

"I'm doing well in English," she said, taking a bite of her pizza. "And I'm doing okay in history. Not so much in geometry; it's my second time taking it, and I'm still so lost."

"I got an A in geometry freshman year," I said, poking my pasta with a plastic fork. "I could help you out."

"You took geometry freshman year? Wow, you really are good at math." She sighed.

"I'll help you, and you'll pass," I said. Maybe her grades were a big factor in all of this. Then again, she must have passed geometry in the old timeline, because she was able to go on the trip with us.

"Are you sure you'd want to help me?" she asked. "I know you hate trig, so I wouldn't want to make you do any extra math."

"Please, I'm doing so much better in trig than I thought I would," I said. "If you wanted to do something in return, you could proofread my stuff for English."

Her face lit up. "Okay! I'd love to help."

"You like helping people, do you?"

She nodded. "I love being able to help."

"Do you want to do something with that after high school?" I asked.

"Oh, I'm not sure what I would do. I used to have this idea for, like, a network for teenagers like—well, teenagers who need help." She trailed off for a second. "But I don't know what, exactly. I mean, there are already counselors and support groups and hotlines. I guess I just want people our age to be able to access those things, even if their parents don't believe in that stuff."

"That sounds like a great idea," I told her. But the concept was so... dark, knowing what might have happened to her before. "Do you—is that something you think *you* need?"

I tried to gauge her reaction, but she seemed perfectly calm—she was looking down at the table, but she hadn't been making a lot of eye contact all evening anyway. She shrugged, kind of slow, like she wasn't sure it was the right action.

"I don't know. I mean, sometimes I just *know* there's something wrong with me, but I can't figure out what."

"Are you depressed?"

What kind of person just asks that? I was gonna blow this.

"I don't know. I don't really have a reason to be," she said to the table. "My life isn't bad or anything."

"That doesn't really have anything to do with it, though," I said. "Didn't you take health freshman year? It's all about brain chemistry, not whether you have a 'bad life.'"

"Well, it's not something I'll ever figure out. At least not until I'm on my own health insurance," she said. "My mother doesn't believe in that kind of thing, so she thinks getting help for a problem I can't even put into words is a waste of money."

"It's not a waste if you know there's a problem," I said. "Doctors could put it into words for you. It's better to get help now than, well..." Was I really going to ask her? "Do you ever, like, think about..."

"Suicide?"

To hear her say it... I felt for a moment that maybe none of this was real. Maybe it was all a dream produced by my guilty conscience: a long, elaborate dream that I couldn't seem to wake up from. Maybe the old timeline was real and Summer was really—

"No," she said, snapping me back into the moment. "Don't worry."

"You've never thought about it?"

"No. Have you?"

"Of course not."

"Well, good."

I tried to smile at her, but I was still a little shaken. "Yeah. Good."

The drive back to her place was silent; I just couldn't shake the memory of the only time she'd been in my car before this whole do-over. *What* did I say to her that afternoon?

She lingered in the car for a moment when I pulled up in her driveway.

"Did you have fun?" she asked.

I had to think for a second—before that conversation, wasn't I having fun with her? "Yeah. I did. Did you?"

"Yeah," she said. "Thank you."

"Well... goodnight," I said.

"Goodnight."

I watched to make sure she got inside okay before driving home.

Summer

I FELT weird about my "hangout" with Nolan... It kind of felt like a date, but I knew it wasn't one. He wanted to take things slow and just hang out. Two friends could go see a movie. Marta and I saw movies all the time. But... the way he'd put his arm around me...

Before I got out of his car, I wondered if he would try to kiss me, which was stupid because we weren't on a date. I didn't even feel ready to kiss him, if he was going to try to tonight.

I guess I wanted it to be real. I didn't want to kiss him until we were...

unless we ever were officially dating. I was old-fashioned. I'd only ever kissed one person and it was a big deal to me.

Jonah and I hadn't even been going out for a month when he'd kissed me for the first time. He'd never tried before. We were sitting on my porch talking, and before I even realized what was happening, he was kissing me. I didn't kiss him back at first, but I felt awkward doing *nothing*, so I went ahead. It wasn't very good, but I couldn't just *not* kiss my own boyfriend after that; he would expect me to.

I also felt guilty lying to Nolan when he'd asked if I ever thought about suicide. It wasn't like it was something I *actively* thought about, but I'd be lying if I said it had never crossed my mind. But I didn't want to get into that on our second date. Maybe it was my fault for bringing up mental health resources, but I wanted to have a deeper conversation with him; we'd mostly only talked about surface-level things. I wanted to get to know him more. Despite having "known" him since elementary school, I'd realized how little I actually knew about him.

My mom would probably tell me how stupid I was if I told her I'd even *hinted* at the concept of mental health on a date; she'd say I was going to scare him off. The thing was, my mom didn't even know any of that about me. I didn't think she *wanted* to know, with the way she brushed off any mention I made of my mental health.

But sometimes we'd be watching a show together, and a character would bring up their mental health struggles with a partner or a close friend, and she'd say something like, *"Oh, no! You're gonna scare them off if they think you have mental issues. Nobody wants to deal with that."*

Maybe she was right. I had to be more careful about what I said to Nolan. The only friend I'd ever talked with about mental health was Bella, and she'd initiated that. It didn't scare me, but I was evidently not normal.

If I brought it up with Marta, she'd change the subject, and I didn't know how Daisy would react because we'd never talked about that kind of thing.

At the very least, Nolan asked questions, making him seem interested in the conversation. Interested in me.

Maybe that was something.

* * *

"SUMMER, YOU need to get over your stupid 'kissing is a big deal' shtick," Marta told me on Monday, fluffing her curls in my locker mirror as always. "Sutton and I kissed on our first date. If it seems like a good moment to kiss and he's not going for it, you can go for it."

I glanced away. "I just think this could be something special, and I don't want to rush it. It wasn't even a date!"

"He's going to think you don't even like him!" she insisted. "You have to give him a little something to keep him interested, you know? I'm not saying you have to have sex, just... At least kiss him, Summer! He's a *guy*; he needs *something*."

"But I don't want to scare him if he's not ready to take things to that level! I just want the moment to be right," I said. "It wasn't right with Jonah. I think everyone deserves a magical first kiss at least once in their life."

"Who says Nolan's the only guy you're ever going to kiss from now until you die?" she asked. "Even if you go out with him now, you're bound to meet someone in college or something."

"If I can even go to college." Which reminded me that Nolan had offered to help me with math, and I'd help him with English... which would mean spending time together.

She rolled her eyes. "You'll go to college. It's not that hard. Just go to West Valley like Sutton and I."

I smiled, deciding it wasn't worth the *"I still have to pass my classes to go to a community college like West Valley or DeAnza"* conversation.

Nolan

"Two dates and you haven't kissed her?" Jake asked.

I shrugged. "It wasn't a date."

"It was the two of you seeing a movie. A chick flick at that. It was a date."

"We've seen movies together!" I reminded him. "What, have we been on a date?"

"Well, if we have, it wasn't a very good one since you didn't kiss me at the end." Jake smirked.

"Yeah, keep talking and kissing's the farthest you'll be *able* to go on a date." He rolled his eyes, but I continued. "I *hung out* with Summer. It was not a date. At best... I feel bad that she doesn't have a lot of friends, I guess."

Liam shook his head. "Bro, *one date* is a pity date. You're hanging out with her again? Seeing a movie only she's gonna like? That's a date. A *second* date. There's gotta be something there."

"Not if she won't even kiss him," Jake replied. "Nolan, don't waste your time chasing after Summer. I could find you a hotter girl in, like, seconds."

"I'm not chasing after Summer," I said. "I'm just being nice. She's... sensitive."

"Aww, she's *sensitive!*" Liam cooed.

"Shut up. I just meant she takes things the wrong way," I said. "I don't want to hurt her feelings."

"Well, if you keep leading her on, you're only going to hurt her more," Jake said. "So either admit you like her, or quit playing."

I rolled my eyes. Whether or not he had a point, I didn't want to think about it.

Summer

I was starting to get used to wearing makeup, at least eyeshadow and mascara. Sometimes I would get compliments, but I still wasn't very good. And I had to remember not to rub my eyes.

Wednesday after school, Nolan asked if I wanted to study at the school library. I didn't like making last-minute plans or missing out on my after-school routine of French bread pizza and *That '70s Show* reruns, but he wanted to help me with geometry, and I didn't want him to think I was blowing him off.

"Do your grades stress you out a lot?" he asked, looking at the test I was supposed to do corrections for.

"Yeah," I said. "If I can't pass geometry, then I can't go to college, so I'll be stuck at home forever working minimum wage jobs. I mean, it's not like I could move out on a retail salary; it's California."

"You could move somewhere else," he said, glancing at my test and making a note on some graph paper. "I think it'd be nice to live somewhere different for a while."

"I like it here," I said. "I know where everything is. I can walk most places or get around by public transportation."

"You're sixteen, right?" he asked.

I nodded. "I turn seventeen in April."

"How come you don't drive?"

"I don't need to, really. I feel like adding Drivers Ed to the list of stuff I have to do would be more stressful than it's worth. Maybe I'll learn over the summer, or after high school."

"I could help teach you if you got a permit," he said. "Not legally, but still. Having a license makes you feel free; you can drive anywhere you want, practically." He turned his notebook so I could see what he'd written, but asked: "If you could drive anywhere right now, where would you want to go?"

I picked up the notebook and tried to make sense of his explanation for whatever I'd done wrong on the test. "If I could drive anywhere right now, I'd drive off a cliff."

"What?" He stared intently at me. "Why?"

"Because I hate stupid geometry." I stuck my tongue out at him.

"Oh, so you're not serious." The relief in his voice was evident. I didn't realize my joke would worry him so much.

"No, I wasn't." Not this time, at least. "Sorry. I forget not everyone likes dark jokes." Damn, I really did need to be more careful.

"Let's just focus on geometry," he said. "Do you see what you did wrong on this problem?"

"I... added something wrong?"

"No." He pointed to what he'd drawn on the graph paper. "It's an irregular polygon. To find the area, you need to put it on the graph, like this. See?"

He talked me through the problem, and while I still didn't fully understand it, I was eventually able to come up with the right answer. He said he'd look at the rest of my test if I looked at his essay on themes in *The Great Gatsby*.

"Do you know how to use a semicolon?" I asked him. "It's not just a fancy comma, you know."

"I know," he said. "What'd I do wrong?"

I read: "'When we think of the green light, it represents hope; looking forward to the future.' You can't use a semicolon to separate a dependent clause. It has to separate two *independent* clauses, and 'looking forward to the future' can't be a sentence on its own. You'd be better off using a regular colon or the word 'and.'"

"I thought just the first half had to be a full sentence," he said.

"A common mistake," I said. "It goes back to that 'a semicolon is where the author *could* have ended a sentence but didn't' thing. But for that to work, the author would have to continue the sentence with another independent clause."

"Where have I heard that quote before? That sounds familiar."

"It's about suicide prevention," I explained, hoping I sounded casual because now I had accidentally brought up mental health *again*. "A person could kill themselves—semicolon—a person could also keep on living."

"Are you *sure* you've never thought about it before?" he asked. "You seem to know a lot about... that."

I rolled my eyes. "You don't have to worry. Driving off a cliff was a joke about how much I hate math."

"Okay. But you know, if you ever *do* think about that, you can talk to me, right? We're friends."

"I know."

And that was all we would ever hope to be if I ruined things by scaring him off.

Nolan

I COULDN'T tell if Summer was into me. She was so hot-and-cold about it; she was closed off when we talked, but there was still something about the way she looked at me. But why did that matter to me? I didn't like her that way. I was *just* getting used to the idea of being friends with her.

I did notice she was always wearing her hair up nowadays. That, and she was wearing a little more makeup. It seemed like she was putting in some effort, and I was starting to realize that Summer wasn't too bad-looking. Actually, she was kind of cute. Not *hot* like the other girls I'd been with, but she was cute when she tried.

Working on homework with her was fun, too. I didn't think homework could be fun, but I liked talking to her while we studied in the library. Summer was in the middle of explaining an essay prompt to me when I brought up seeing another movie together.

"We should go to the nice theater, the one across town," I said. "They've got an arcade. I used to go there all the time as a kid. Birthday parties there were the best."

"I think I went to a few there," she said. "Wait—did *you* have your party there in third grade?"

"Yeah."

She beamed. "I was there! I think that was the only party you invited me to."

"Well, my parents said if I wanted to have a party somewhere besides our house, I had to invite the whole class," I said. Then, I remembered something. "Didn't we hang out there?"

She nodded. "I remember that day. You showed me how to play that one game with the wheels, where we raced each other. And then you won this ugly pink thing from the skill crane, which you said I could have because I was standing right there and I was a girl, and it was pink."

"You remember all that?" I asked her.

"I don't have a lot of great memories from elementary school, so I have to stick to the ones I do have," she admitted. I still couldn't get used to her saying dark stuff like that and then insisting she was fine. Who's fine and talks like that? "You'll probably think this is super weird, but I still have that pink thing at my house somewhere. I never got rid of it."

"Huh." All this time I thought Summer had been into me, but maybe she was just associating me with one of her "few good memories." I wondered if I'd gotten it all wrong.

"I can show you if you ever come over for dinner," she said. "I mean, if we keep hanging out, I'm sure my mom will want to actually meet you and get to know you and stuff, besides saying hello at homecoming."

"Uh, yeah." She wanted me to meet her mother. Was I supposed to introduce her to my parents? How would that even go? She wasn't like any other girl I'd brought home, friend or otherwise.

Have I even brought a female friend home to meet my parents before?

Maybe I *was* wrong about her feelings for me, but it sure felt like she was trying to lead things in that direction. Meeting her mother would also make this a whole big deal. It'd feel less like a friendship and more like we were going out. I was getting used to being friends with her, but *dating* her... Then again, there wasn't really anyone I was interested in right now. Anyone I'd gone out with or hooked up with in the old timeline seemed stale now, like even though I technically *hadn't* been with those girls, I knew I had.

"Does your mom ask to meet all your friends, or just the extremely handsome ones?" I asked her with a smile so it would come off like a joke instead of me clarifying that she wasn't trying to drive this friendship into something else.

"My mom just likes to know who I'm hanging out with." A pause. "Especially if said friends are people she knows I've been on a date with before, even if that date was a disaster and we're just trying to be friends. She's… protective of me, I guess. Don't your parents want to know who their kid is with?"

"They trust me," I told her. "I don't know. I get it, though, like it makes sense that your mom wants you to be safe. And, I mean, she's right that we *did* go on a date before, so I can see why she'd be suspicious."

"Do you—?" She hesitated, then shook her head, indicating she wasn't going to finish the question. "Never mind." I was certain she wanted to ask if I saw us going on a date again but didn't want to rush things. I didn't want to rush things, either. Being friends was going well for us. Why take that next step now?

Would it be *so* bad dating Summer, though? After all, the whole reason I was back here was to help her. Maybe that *was* part of it… but if we started dating, I'd have to be serious about it. I definitely couldn't hurt her in this do-over. Was I ready to commit like that?

Summer

WAS IT pathetic of me to climb through the storage room to find that stupid pink stuffed *whatever it was supposed to be* that Nolan gave me all those years ago? I set it on my pillow and stared at it.

I'd been skeptical to even go to his birthday party, because he didn't usually talk to me in class, but this was back in third grade when everyone in your class went to everyone else's birthday parties and it wasn't a big deal. It was only the first week of school, and my mom thought going to someone's birthday party would give me a chance to get to know more of the kids. Even back then, I only ever talked to Marta and Daisy, and they'd never gotten along, so I hung out separately with each of them.

Marta was also more possessive of me back then, meaning I only got to hang out with Daisy on the days she was absent, and then I'd hope she didn't ask me who I'd hung out with at recess because I cracked like a twig under pressure. One time she made me a list of "approved" people I could talk to while she was absent. The teacher found it and talked to my mom about it, and they told me if Marta called and asked who I'd hung out with, I wasn't allowed to answer. I had to say, *"That's none of your business,"* but it always came out like, *"My mom says that's none of your business, sorry."* Eventually she outgrew it.

But I still remembered leaving Nolan's birthday party with that stupid pink thing in my hand, thinking that day could be a turning point. I could have a friend who was a boy—a boy who was popular, to whatever degree someone *could* be popular in third grade. When my mom picked me up, I showed her the ugly pink *is it a cat?* and told her all about how Nolan won it for me. And for a few weeks, I talked about my new crush Nolan and how I was almost certain he liked me back—even though we had next to no interactions after his birthday.

Months passed and I made no efforts to talk to him, nor he to me, but I'd smile at him across the playground. We gave each other valentines, though that was back when you gave the same thing to the entire class, so it wasn't a big deal. But I still kept his valentine in my nightstand drawer for years, fawning over *"To Summer, From Nolan"* next to some generic Power Rangers caption. I kept the equally generic ones he gave me in fourth and fifth grade, too, but sometime in middle school I rearranged the drawer and put the cards in the storage room with the rest of my elementary school stuff.

A couple weeks after that Valentine's Day in third grade, everyone was staying late to finish working on our mammal reports, and my mom came to pick me up. Feeling bold—but not too bold—I pointed out Nolan and told her she could tell him that I liked him. She must have thought I was joking, but I insisted, saying I was too scared to do it myself. So as we were all leaving, she said, *"Nolan, Summer wants me to tell you that she likes you."* She said it in a way that I could have played off as a joke if I wanted, but I just blushed and avoided his glance.

The next day, he was so nice to me. He got some animal crackers for me so I wouldn't have to get up and get my own when the teacher was handing them out. He sat next to me at lunch, though we didn't talk. He clapped first when I finished presenting my mammal project. And when he was in front of me at the water fountain, he waited until we were both done to go back to his desk.

However, the next day, he didn't really interact with me. I sat next to him at lunch—I initiated this time—and then when we were walking to the playground after lunch, he said, *"Summer, can you leave me alone, please?"*

I wasn't sure what was wrong, but I obliged. Over time, I found new boys to chase after on the playground or stare at from behind my locker in middle school, but my feelings for Nolan always resurfaced. It was weird to think he might actually be interested in me now... Could it even be real?

I pushed the pink *maybe it's a bird?* off the side of my bed with the rest of my stuffed animals, and I looked at the time on my phone: 2:19 a.m.

Tomorrow was Saturday, and Nolan would pick me up and take me to the movie theater across town where he'd had that birthday party. Maybe he would meet my mom if he came to the door. If he didn't, I bet she'd ask me why he didn't like me enough to come to the door, and if we still didn't kiss or even label our "hangout" as a date, then she'd probably say, *"Well, he must not really like you."*

I didn't want to think about the what-ifs.

I am okay, I said to myself, opening up my nightstand drawer.

I am happy with my life right now, I reminded myself as I picked up the broken razor, sandwiched between a *Precious Moments* book of Bible stories and a box of change.

I am fine. I just don't want to think about everything that might not be.

It was stupid to be doing this now when everything was going so well. But it was addicting, in a way. It was how I knew something much deeper was wrong with me: normal people *didn't* cut, especially not when they were happy. Not even just once, just one prick, before putting the razor back and trying to fall asleep.

Once every few months, I'd decide I was quitting—*for real this time*, every time—and throw out whatever broken razor or pencil sharpener blade I was using, but I always went back. From Bella's bedroom in seventh grade until now, I think maybe I'd had a record stretch of eight months clean. Something always triggered me sooner or later, no matter how "good" things were going for me.

It's hard to say what triggered me into starting up again. It was something I hoped a psychiatrist would be able to explain to me one day. I just had to wait.

Nolan

WHEN I knocked on Summer's door, her mother answered. She was dressed in sweatpants and a big T-shirt with her hair clipped back like before.

"Summer's almost ready," she said. "Come in and sit down."

So here it was. I was going to meet Summer's mother.

"What movie are you going to see?" she asked as I took a seat on their burgundy loveseat.

"We haven't decided," I said. "Uh, nice living room."

Nice living room—something that was natural to say when meeting a girl's parents, but probably *not* the right thing to say about a blue room with a loveseat, tray table, TV and fireplace, exercise ball, sparse china cabinet, and a single framed photo of Summer at a very young age.

"Oh, thank you. It's a work in progress," her mother replied. "We're having work done."

I nodded, wishing Summer would hurry up. What if her mother asked me something like—?

"I'm here." Summer stepped into the living room, dressed in a grey sweater and jeans tucked into that pair of black boots she wore all the time. Her hair was down and a little wet.

"Summer, didn't I tell you to dry your hair?" her mother asked quietly.

"I don't like drying it," she said. "I hate the hair dryer."

"Okay, but now you're going on your date with wet hair."

Date. Did Summer tell her mother this was a date, or did she assume?

"I think it looks fine," I said. I just wanted to get out of this conversation with her mother and talk to *my friend* Summer alone.

"We'll be back before dinner," Summer told her mother.

"It was nice meeting you... again," I said on the way out the door.

Not a second after the front door shut, Summer said, "I'm so sorry that was awkward. I didn't tell her it was a date, I swear—"

"It's fine."

Her nerves seemed to ease up. Once we were in my car, Summer giggled and reached into her purse and pulled out something pink and fuzzy and ultimately indiscernible.

"What *is* that?" I asked.

"I still don't know." She laughed. "It's the hideous pink thing you won from the skill crane. I found it last night and wanted to show you."

"Oh."

"Do you remember a few weeks after that, when we were working on our mammal reports, and my mom told you that I liked you?"

I thought for a minute. Third grade... yes. Summer's mother had told me that Summer liked me. I didn't know what to say, so when I was hanging out at Liam's house later that evening, I asked him, *"What do I do if a girl likes me?"*

"That means you're her boyfriend," he said. *"You have to do nice things for her and sit with her at lunch."*

"Do I have to invite her to play soccer with us?"

"No. Girls don't like sports."

It was stupid, but I was nine. I took his advice and started doing nice things for Summer in class. When my other friend Sahas asked me why I was being so nice to Summer all of a sudden, I explained the whole situation, and he told me—and Liam—that a girl was only my girlfriend if I liked her *too*, and even back then I knew I wasn't into Summer. So I asked her nicely to leave me alone, and she backed off.

I put some music on for the drive. It was just the radio, but Summer's face lit up.

"I love this song!" she said. "Don't change it!"

Her excitement was kind of cute, and I turned it up for her. I could smell her shampoo, something fruity.

"What shampoo do you use?" I asked.

She blushed. "Oh, um, just strawberry from this cheap brand my mom gets. Sometimes she gets this ocean scent but I like the strawberry best."

"It smells nice." I didn't know enough about girls' hair products to know what a "cheap" shampoo did differently from the regular kind. Maybe it had something to do with her hair always looking so dull, but since she'd been wearing it up more, I hadn't really noticed.

"Thank you," she said. "I hate the feeling of the blow-dryer; it's like I can't breathe with all the hot air in my face. I've never been able to use one."

She went to push her hair behind her ear, and the sleeve of her sweater dropped down. We were at a red light, so when my eye caught on the red line and all the faded scratches on her wrist, I stared for a few seconds until the car behind us honked at me.

"Do you... have a cat?" I asked, stepping on the gas pedal.

"No," she said. "We used to, when I was, like, three."

"Oh." *How do I ask her about this?* "It just looked like cat scratches on your arm there."

She pulled her sleeve down. "It's just a shaving cut."

"You shave your arms?" I knew some girls did, but Summer never struck me as the type.

"No, I was shaving my legs and I slipped," she said. She laughed as if recalling a funny memory. "It was a whole slippery shower mishap. Nothing to be worried about."

I wasn't sure I believed her, but she didn't seem to want to dwell on it. "Alright, clumsy," I said. "Guess that's something I've never had to deal with."

We were quiet until I pulled into the parking lot. I bought us both some lunch, even though she insisted she had money. I didn't want to patronize her or make her feel awkward about her money situation, but I didn't mind spending an extra five dollars on a slice of pizza, and *"I know you don't have as much money as I do so I'm not going to make you spend what little your mom gave you on overpriced low-quality pizza"* wasn't exactly something I could say to her.

"I got an A on my stupid *Gatsby* essay because of you," I said, handing her a slice of pizza. "Consider this a thank you."

She was quiet again while we were eating.

"Do you know what movie you want to see?" I asked her.

"Honestly... I kind of want to hang out in the arcade today."

"Done."

Once we got to the arcade, her face lit up again like it did in the car with that song. We had fun challenging each other in multiplayer games and cheering each other on through single-player games... and then on the way out, we passed the skill crane.

"So... this is where it all began, huh?" I asked.

"What do you mean?" She shrugged. "It's not like we were friends after that."

"But this is where you realized you liked me."

"In *third grade.* I got over you when you told me to leave you alone."

"So you don't still like me?" I asked with a playful smile.

She blushed. "I never said that."

I put a token into the crane. I was always good at these. I wasn't sure what I was going to get, but it only seemed right to get her something. I watched the crane drop a neon green dolphin into the prize slot, which I grabbed and held out for her.

"For you," I said.

She smiled and took it. "And we actually know what it is this time."

I put an arm around her as we walked back to the car. It felt like an instinct, and I started to feel something... warm. Something nice.

"Nolan?" she asked, breaking away.

"Yeah?"

She took a deep breath. "Do *you* like *me*?"

I froze. "I—" What was I supposed to say to her?

She sighed and looked at the ground. "You don't have to answer that. I'm sorry."

The ride home was quiet again. She didn't get excited about any more songs. When I parked in her driveway, she hesitated.

"Here." She handed me the ugly pink thing from her purse. "You should have this."

"Why? I won it for you, remember?"

"Yeah, but you won me this now." She held up the dolphin. "I want you to have the pink thing. Maybe you'll figure out what it's supposed to be."

"Uh, thanks." I wasn't sure where to put it, so I just held on to it while she got out of the car.

"I had fun," she said. "Thanks for today."

"Of course. See you at school."

I watched her get inside her house before driving away.

5

Summer

I WASN'T a fan of gym class, especially on days when we had to run the mile, but Daisy and I typically ran the mile together—we were both pretty slow—and we got to talk. She was telling me about something she did this weekend with Ben, her boyfriend from summer camp, so I told her about my arcade hangout with Nolan.

"He hasn't asked you on an actual date yet?" she asked.

"Not since the homecoming trash fire."

I hadn't given Daisy a lot of details about my dating life; I guess I was afraid she'd react like Marta, even though she'd always been excited for me when I'd shared good news over the years. Anyway, we usually had better things to talk about than boys—she'd tell me about her online multiplayer games, and I'd... listen. And she'd ask me questions about me and offer to show me how to play the games she liked. But I liked my boring life of watching TV and reading.

"Did he try to kiss you or anything?" she asked.

"Have you and Ben kissed?" I asked her.

"Summer!"

I wasn't sure if that was *"obviously, yes"* or *"obviously, no,"* so I just said, "Sorry."

"It's fine," she said. "I just thought Nolan would have kissed you by now if he likes you. I mean, he doesn't seem like the kind of guy to take it slow."

"No, but I told him I like to take things slow, and he said that was okay. He wants to work on our friendship before we try dating."

"Well, I guess he's a good guy, then," Daisy said.

It was nice having someone supportive. Marta just shook her head when I told her about the not-date. Must be nice dating Sutton, who was apparently perfect in every way even if I'd never actually met him. I'd only seen pictures of him online, and in most of those pictures he was just a little too close to girls who weren't Marta, but I guess I just didn't know the ins and outs of their "complex, mature" relationship.

I'd actually known Daisy longer than Marta, but I spent more time with Marta outside of class. It wasn't like Daisy and I weren't close; she was just always so busy with extracurriculars, studying for AP classes, or LARPing. Marta was less concerned about college and didn't have many hobbies outside of being with Sutton and rewatching *Glee*, so she was more available.

"I don't know if he even likes me," I said to Daisy. I was surprised I'd admitted it, but I felt more comfortable confiding in her than in Marta or my mom, and I *needed* to talk about it with someone. "He wouldn't say it."

"Well, you *have* hung out just the two of you a few times. I know that doesn't mean anything if he doesn't want to call them dates, but I think if he liked you that way, he'd at least *try* something. Or hint at it. My parents always told me guys would try to go for... *you know* by the third date."

"Sex?"

She nodded.

"Do you think he's using me to get sex?" I asked. "Like, in the long run? I mean, he's been okay about taking it slow, but... so was Jonah, in the beginning."

He'd started pressuring me for sex towards the end of our relationship, but it was so subtle that I hadn't realized what he was doing at first. I tended to catch on better when people were direct, and I think he knew that.

"I don't think he'd play the long game just to use you for sex. Just be careful," Daisy warned.

Nolan

"ARE THERE any good Halloween parties you've heard about?" Liam asked. "I was gonna see if I could throw one this year, but there's no chance of my parents being away two nights in a row."

Liam's birthday was on Friday, so his parents had told him he could have a small party on Saturday with a handful of close friends—me, Jake, and some guys from student council, and probably some girl he liked and a couple of her friends so it wasn't obvious—but Halloween was on Sunday, and despite having school the next day, most of us were still trying to find a party to go to. I tried to remember what we did in the old timeline.

"I heard Jada Martin talking about hosting one," I said. "Didn't we go to a party she hosted freshman year?"

"She does have a pool," Jake pointed out.

"Would anyone go swimming this late in the year?" I asked. My parents had already closed our pool up for the season.

"I miss Sahas," Liam said. "He had a pool *and* a movie room. Why'd he have to move to Gilroy? His parties probably would've been the best."

I chuckled. "You think *his* parents would be naive enough to leave the house long enough for him to have a party? His mom made him wear a life vest in the pool when he was thirteen."

"Doesn't Jada have a basement?" Liam asked. "At the party freshman year, I was talking to some sophomore who asked if I wanted to move things to the basement."

"I love a good make out basement," Jake said with a smile. "I've got fifth period with her tomorrow. I'll ask if we can go."

Liam turned to me. "Speaking of make out basements, you never told us about your date. Did you finally get some?"

I rolled my eyes. "No. Same as before." I'd given up trying to convince them it wasn't a date. They weren't buying it, so it was easier not to argue.

"Three dates, and no action?" Jake shook his head. "Look, man, either drop her or admit you actually like her. I've heard of playing the long game, but if she hasn't even *kissed* you?"

"I do *not* 'like' Summer," I insisted. "She's just fun to hang out with. As a friend."

"You don't go on three dates with a friend," Liam said.

"It's okay if you like her," Jake said. "I mean, she's nice and all. I went out with Carla freshman year; I'm not one to judge."

"Yeah, man, just admit it," Liam replied. "If you like her, you like her, and that's fine. Otherwise stop going on 'pity friend dates' with her, because that's weird."

I shrugged. "You don't get it, and I can't explain it."

How *was* I supposed to explain? I could hardly wrap my own head around it. I liked hanging out with Summer. She said she liked me, but she still acted so closed off around me most of the time. I didn't want to hurt her feelings by saying I wasn't interested, but I was confused as to whether or not *she* was.

And... a part of me would feel let down if she wasn't, I guess.

But I was positive that wasn't about liking her back, just... I don't know, the idea of Summer thinking she was too good for me? *No, that makes me sound like an ass.* It was something, but it wasn't a crush, that was for sure. I didn't—I *couldn't*—like Summer Madison that way.

"What's there to get? You like Summer," Liam said.

I inhaled deeply. "I don't *dislike* Summer."

"Getting warmer." Jake laughed. "Whatever, man. Hey, you know what you can do, though?"

"What?"

"Give her my Bruno Mars ticket."

Right. Jake had scored us three tickets to the Bruno Mars concert in November, then found out he had a family reunion that week. In the old timeline, he'd sold his ticket. But now... what if I *did* invite Summer?

I saw her at her locker after school, so I tapped her on the shoulder. Her makeup was a little smudged, but I thought she had gym today, which would explain it. Her clothes were more casual than normal.

"Hey," I said.

"Hey." She seemed... distant.

"Uh, what're you doing for Halloween?"

She shrugged. "Hanging out with Marta. You?"

"Going to Liam's birthday party," I said. "Maybe another party on Sunday. If you want to come—"

"No, thanks."

What was up with her today? "Well... I have something for you, if you're interested."

"Oh?"

"Yeah, Liam, Jake, and I were going to see Bruno Mars next month, but Jake can't go and so we have an extra ticket," I said. "I was wondering—I was *hoping* you'd come with us. Um, with me."

She stared at me like she was waiting for some kind of catch.

"What day is it?" she finally asked.

"The sixteenth."

"I'll ask my mom. How much is the ticket?"

"It's free, Summer; we had an extra. Plus, you'd be my—"

"Date?"

There was hope in her voice, but it was like she was trying to hide it. She couldn't hide it enough, though. And before I gave myself too much time to think about it, I found myself saying:

"Yeah."

I expected her to smile, but her face remained neutral. She almost looked upset by my offer. Was I actually wrong about her feelings for me, even after she'd admitted she liked me at the arcade?

"Nolan, I'm not comfortable with you spending money on me like this," she said slowly. "It makes me feel like... you're going to think I owe you something."

"You don't owe me anything, Summer," I said. "Besides, I didn't pay for the ticket. Jake did."

"Well... okay. I'll ask if I can go."

Summer

I WISHED I could tell my mom good news without her asking a bunch of questions to make it not fun anymore. Like, *"You've 'hung out' a few times; do you think he'll kiss you soon? Why hasn't he asked you to be his girlfriend? He must not really like you. Are you doing something to make him feel pressured into spending time with you?"*

Marta and I sat at the picnic table in her backyard with a pile of candy in front of us. Her younger brother was a great trick-or-treater and ended up getting enough candy that her parents made him share with us. I was grateful, since my mom told me I was too old to go trick-or-treating.

Marta and I still wore costumes, though. She was dressed as a witch, and I was reusing old costume pieces—some wings from eighth grade, along with my dress and silver flats from homecoming.

"A concert is a good date," she told me. "Besides, his friends will be there, so it's not like he can try to hook up with you. Assuming you're still not ready."

"Right." I sighed. I didn't want to ask her how Sutton was doing, because we'd gone a few hours without talking about him and I thought it was nice. Marta and I hadn't hung out without mentioning him in ages.

I missed elementary school, when we could talk about dolls and shows and movies. We used to talk about music, because we both liked the same stuff back then. We'd gossip about teachers and other kids in our class. Now it seemed like she only wanted to talk about boys. She'd been that way since middle school, and it had only gotten worse. I remember in sixth grade when I asked if she'd seen the new American Girl doll—the very dolls we'd bonded over on "bring your doll or stuffed animal to school day" in kindergarten where we'd met—she reamed me for bringing up something so childish. Gradually over that year, I'd boxed up all my dolls and stopped playing with them at all.

"You want to know a secret?" Marta asked.

"What?"

"Sutton actually didn't kiss me until homecoming."

"What? I thought you two kissed over the summer—"

"I lied, because I thought it would make me seem pathetic if we hadn't kissed yet," she said. "But I don't want you to feel like whatever's going on with Nolan isn't real."

"What if it's not, though?"

"Guys are a different breed," she said. "I still don't fully understand them. But he wouldn't let things go on this long just to use you."

"Jonah did."

"Nolan isn't Jonah."

I wanted to believe her. We ate some more candy from the pile, and I glanced at my fully exposed wrist. Marta and I have been friends for years, and she never seemed to notice that I cut. Nolan was the first person to ever say anything about it, and I was so caught off-guard that I didn't know how to talk about it. Ever since Bella had first shown me how, I would imagine all the different scenarios where someone would notice and what I'd say and how they'd respond... but after a long time of nobody asking, I kind of stopped.

I hoped Nolan had bought my stupid shower excuse. He didn't seem freaked out by my scars... but I couldn't be too sure. And either way, I wasn't ready to talk about that with him when I'd never even talked about it with my best friend.

"Do you remember Bella?" I asked.

"Bella…?"

"Bella Montes."

"Didn't she move to Reno?"

I nodded. "Have you heard from her recently?"

"No," she said. "I wasn't that close with her, anyway. But you were, right?"

"I just… wonder if she's even still alive sometimes."

Marta shrugged. "Some people just don't have social media. How would she have died, anyway?"

"She could have killed herself."

"Okay, that's dark. Are you trying to be scary 'cause it's Halloween?"

"No, I mean she might have," I said. "She was a cutter—"

"Okay, can we *not* talk about that?" she said, shuddering.

"She showed me how to do it, you know."

Marta didn't say anything.

"I—used to."

Still nothing.

"Sometimes I still think about it." *Sometimes I still do it.*

Nothing.

"Do you want to talk about something else?" I asked.

"Yes, please."

I nodded. "How's Sutton?"

When I got home that night, I changed out of my pointless "costume" and climbed into bed. I reached into my nightstand drawer and took out my broken razor.

I am okay, I said to myself. *I just wish my best friend would care if I wasn't.*

Maybe Marta wasn't supposed to care. Maybe it *was* too weird for me to be doing this, and nobody was going to actually care if I was okay or not. They were just going to see me as weird and unstable.

Instead of putting the razor back in the drawer when I was done, I threw it in the garbage—under some crumpled tissues so it wouldn't stick out too obviously.

I am okay, I said, heading into the bathroom to wash my hands. *I need to start acting like it.*

Nolan

WHEN I saw Summer at school on Monday, she was dressed in a green striped shirt and those black boots that went up to her knees.

"Hey, Sum," I greeted her. When did I start calling her that?

She glanced at me, then back at her locker. "Oh, hey."

"How was your weekend?"

"Fine," she said. "How was your party?"

"Boring," I told her. "You should be glad you didn't go." I don't even think Liam's seventeenth birthday was all that fun the *first* time. Jada's was okay, but just as unmemorable as before. "Excited for the concert?" I tried when Summer didn't respond.

"Yeah."

She clearly wasn't in the mood to talk. "Well, see you around."

"See you."

When I sat down in chemistry, Liam turned around in his seat to face me.

"So, you ready to admit you like her?" he asked.

"You ready to stop being a dick?" I asked.

"Touché."

Summer

I FELT weird around Nolan, unsure of what he really wanted from me or what this concert would mean. I tried to keep up small talk with him, but even our study sessions were just talking about homework now.

To give credit where credit was due, I did get a B- on my last geometry quiz, first try. And he did seem excited about the concert, but that could be more of a Bruno Mars thing than a Summer Madison thing.

I flipped to the page in my notebook where I'd started a list of things to look forward to—with each thing crossed off as it happened. Things like homecoming, seeing Marta on Halloween, or even *"Mom said she'd make my favorite soup the first day it rains."* Stupid things sometimes, but all things to look forward to. Way, way at the bottom of the next page—assuming I'd have enough stuff to fill two pages—was *"Europe trip (?)."* With Nolan's help with geometry, it really was starting to seem feasible.

After *"Marta's birthday party,"* I wrote *"Bruno Mars concert."* After all, my first concert was something to look forward to regardless of what Nolan's intentions may be.

On Saturday, I did my makeup for Marta's party. I'd be meeting her friends from her summer job, including Sutton, so I had to make a good first impression.

"Hey, Summer!" she cried when I arrived. I was hardly the first one there. I could see a couple girls standing by the snack table, and then Sutton: tall, tan, muscular, with a mop of shaggy black hair. "Sutton!" Marta called. "This is Summer."

He waved, but it didn't seem like he wanted to spend much time talking to me. It was hard to tell what his first impression of me was. When the last guest arrived, we began the party activities. Marta was mostly talking to the other guests, so I stepped away for a minute to call Nolan. I wasn't having much fun and thought maybe he'd want to talk, but he didn't answer. Figures.

Nolan

I HATED visiting my aunt and uncle in Stockton; it always took all day and it was never interesting. By the time we got home, it was already eight. According to my phone, I had a missed call from Summer four hours ago. I called her back.

"Hey," she said, sounding unenthused.

"Hey, Sum," I said. "Sorry I missed your call; family thing."

"It's fine," she said.

"So... what did you want to talk about?"

"Oh, nothing," she said. "I was just bored. But I have homework to do now."

"Oh, okay. You sure you don't want to talk?"

"Yeah. Thanks anyway, though."

We hung up, and I felt weird. I went up to my room and took out my notebook, opening it to the page with notes about Summer and writing down today's tidbit: Answer the phone when Summer calls, just in case.

I stared at the notebook. If I did what it took to stop her from dying, would I just wake up in June with everything back to normal? I supposed it made sense that even if I fixed whatever I was supposed to fix, I'd stay in this timeline and play it out. It would be weird to return to the other timeline where Summer and I barely spoke, let alone... whatever this was.

Either way, I'd realized spending time with Summer was kind of fun. I liked how she'd get nervous when she thought she'd said the wrong thing, and it was cute when she crinkled her brows concentrating on math homework. I liked the warm feeling when I put my arm around her sometimes, and how she kept that stupid pink animal that was now living under my bed because it reminded her of my birthday party, and how she remembered things like that so well. She could remember details from third grade when I could barely remember the old timeline that I'd lived in just months ago.

Oh, no.

Now that I was alone, and there wasn't any banter from Liam or Jake, or questions from Summer, and it was just me and my thoughts, those thoughts all seemed to lead to something I never thought I'd say, even to myself.

I liked spending time with Summer. I liked talking to Summer. I was disappointed when she didn't want to talk. I was nervous that she didn't really want to go to this concert and that she didn't even like me that way, or that I'd said something to make her *not* like me that way.

There it was: *I like Summer*. Who would've known that this whole time, if I had just talked to her, I would have liked her? But now *I* knew. And now… I liked her.

But what did I do with that?

Summer

THE WEEK leading up to the concert was awkward, to say the least. I tried to make small talk with Nolan, I really did, but I was just so nervous around him. I couldn't tell if he liked me or not, and I didn't want to waste my time if he didn't. But I kept telling myself to just go to the concert and see what happened. That was the advice my mom gave me, too, as she helped me pick out an outfit.

"It'll probably get hot in the concert hall, so I'd recommend short sleeves," she told me. "Do you have something black, or white?"

I found a white graphic T-shirt, which was a few years old but still fit fine. I put my hair in a ponytail, and my mom helped me put on makeup that was just a little darker than usual, with eyeliner.

Nolan came to the door, and my mother waved as we left—this time, he held my hand on the way to the car. I blushed.

"You've been quiet lately," he said. "Did I do something wrong?"

I shook my head. "I've just been… I don't know. I'm not always sure what's real anymore."

"What do you mean?"

"Like… you. You've been really nice to me since school started, and I don't know why."

"We're friends, aren't we?" he asked.

"But we weren't before."

"Sure we were. Well, friendly. We've known each other for years."

"I just sometimes don't believe a guy like you would be nice to someone like me."

"What does that mean?"

"You're... popular, and I'm... me."

"Popular?" he asked.

"Like, you can walk into a room and most people know who you are. And people besides your close friends talk to you all the time."

"Yeah, but I don't have, like, a ton of friends; I usually just hang with Liam and Jake."

"But you *could* have a lot of friends. People like you."

"That's not all it's cracked up to be," he said, and as if he were trying to make a joke, he added, "Sometimes I'd honestly want to trade places with you, like if it meant Grant Hayward didn't think we were close enough friends to drone on about Minecraft when the teacher pairs us together."

"Well, he does that to me, too." Grant was one of the better-known special education students. "Honestly, I'd say Grant is popular. Everyone knows him and Jimmy. Didn't he get nominated for homecoming prince?"

"Out of pity," Nolan said, looking a little surprised. "Grant and Jimmy being 'popular' isn't exactly, uh, for a good reason. They probably don't like all the attention they get, anyway; some of the girls will talk to them like, 'Wow, you're eating a sandwich with your own hands? You walked to school *all by yourself* from across the damn street? How brave and inspirational of you!' Like, yeah, they're... special ed, but they can still, like, talk to us and do normal things. They're just awkward, socially."

I looked away. "Yeah."

"And I promise you, unfortunately, not everyone 'loves' them like you think."

"No, I know." I'd overheard what people called them. "Well, either way, *you're* popular in a *good* way. People know you. You're cool without having to try."

He looked thoughtful. "I never thought of it like that. I mean, Jake, Liam, and I just kind of... float through school without worrying about that stuff. I've always tried to be nice to everyone, and they're nice back." A word came to my mind: *charismatic.* Nolan had no problems talking to anyone. "You probably have a point. I guess we can pretty much go to any party we want, and most of the time girls we like will at least go on one date with us. It's probably not the same for you, is it?"

"Not even a little bit the same," I said. *Girls we like...* Did he like other girls? If he liked me, was there a possibility of him liking other girls at the same time?

"You should really stop reading so much into things," he said. "Honestly, people will like you if you don't try so hard."

"I don't know how to stop."

When we got to Liam's house, we piled into his sedan. To my surprise, Nolan sat in the back with me, though he talked more to Liam than to me. They were talking about sports, and they did try to include me, but I'm sure I came off as uncomfortable because I didn't have much to contribute. I knew the Sharks played hockey, but I couldn't name a single player. It was the longest drive to San Francisco I'd ever taken.

Once we were in the venue, though, I felt better. More comfortable.

"This is your first concert, right?" Nolan asked me, and I nodded. "Well, I'm honored to be a part of it."

He slung an arm around my waist. I blushed, feeling nervous again. The opening act was some rap thing I couldn't really get into, but Nolan and Liam seemed to like it. Nolan kept his arm around me as if he was afraid I'd run off... or maybe it was out of affection.

Bruno Mars came out, and during this slow song, "Count On Me," Nolan stood behind me and put his arms around my waist, swaying back and forth. I went along with it, trying to follow his lead. This was a cute song... about friendship.

During "Nothin' On You," I decided to be bold and ask.

"Nolan?"

"Yeah?"

"Do you like me?"

He stared at me like I'd asked an uncomfortable question, which wasn't a good sign. Why did I decide to ask *now*, when it was so loud and crowded, and in the middle of a hit song?

"Why do you have to ask that, Summer?"

"Because you never answer it."

"Why would I go on this date with you if I didn't like you?"

"What do you see in me, then?" I asked. "Can you tell me that?"

"Summer, I—I care about you," he said. "You're not so bad, you know. Stop doubting yourself."

He cared about me... but he still wouldn't say that he liked me.

"I think I need some air," I said. "It's crowded in here."

He looked around, probably wondering how we were going to get back inside if we stepped out *now*. He turned to Liam.

"We'll be right back," he said.

"What?" Liam asked. "What do you mean? How are you going to get back up here?"

"We'll figure it out later. Summer needs air."

I felt so bad making him walk out with me, but I needed to get somewhere less crowded if I was going to talk to him about this.

"Are you okay?" he asked me outside the brick building. The colored lights on nearby venue signs illuminated the area around us. The cold air helped me feel less overwhelmed, but I was still so nervous to talk to him about this.

"You care about me," I said, "but you still can't say that you like me, or why you care about me."

"I'm sorry," he said. "I don't know how to do this, okay? I never thought I'd *like* you like that, Summer, but I do. For years I thought you were just annoying and awkward, but getting to know you these past months, I see you differently, and it's true: I like you. This whole thing is just weird for me. I can't explain it fully, but—well, sometimes you end up in situations you thought were impossible, but you're there."

"You think *liking me* is impossible?"

"No—caring this much about you," he said. "Wanting to be there for you. Wanting to be *with* you. Missing you when we don't talk. Thinking you look beautiful tonight, and wondering if you like me or not because you're always so closed off, and being disappointed at the thought that you might *not* like me."

"I've liked you for a long time," I said. "I never believed you'd like me back. That's why I needed to hear you say it. Before I—before I can... give myself to you."

"Give—did you think we were going to hook up tonight?"

"No. Well, I thought maybe *you* would want to, but I meant more like... the reason I haven't tried to kiss you." It sounded so stupid once I said it.

We could hear "Just the Way You Are" playing from inside. I couldn't believe my stupid insecurity had caused us to miss the most anticipated song of the whole concert.

"I'm sorry," I told him. "I ruined tonight, didn't I? Like I ruin everything."

"You didn't ruin anything," he said. "Listen..."

He was leaning towards me. I backed away.

"Nolan, can you... just say it one more time?"

I was worried he'd be annoyed, but he smiled.

"I like you, Summer," he said. "Do you want to be my girlfriend?"

I gasped. Was this real?

"I—uh—well—yes."

He smiled again and leaned in closer. I didn't back away this time. I waited and finally felt our lips touch. I wrapped my arms around his shoulders as he placed his on my lower back, pulling me close to him, as our mouths opened and closed against each other. When he pulled away, I smiled, and he kept an arm around me as he prepared to fight our way back through the venue.

Whether or not this was real, it was the best I'd felt in ages.

6

Nolan

SO THERE it was: Summer was my girlfriend. I was dating Summer Madison, officially. We held hands in the hallways and kissed when faculty weren't looking. Summer was my girlfriend... and it felt good.

It was still so nerve-wracking to be with her. I didn't know why she'd died before, so I didn't know if what I was doing was right or helpful or what, but I did know that since getting to know Summer, I liked her, and I liked being with her like this.

She spent most lunches with me and the guys, and they were nice to her, but I couldn't tell if they actually thought she was cool or if they were just putting up with her for my sake. I told Summer she was always welcome to hang out with Marta or one of her other friends, but she insisted that she was fine.

On the day before Thanksgiving break, I saw her talking to her friend Daisy Cabedo by her locker.

Daisy spotted me. "Nolan!" she called. "We were just talking about you."

"Daisy's birthday party is next Saturday," Summer said, "and she says I can invite you."

"I think I can go." Next Friday was the Black & White winter dance, but I didn't have anything planned for the day after. "Hey, by the way, did you want to go Black Friday shopping?"

"Oh, I never go to those," Summer replied. "But thank you."

"Come on. It'll be fun," I insisted.

"When else is your boyfriend going to invite you to go shopping?" Daisy snickered.

"You can get your dress for Black & White," I reminded her.

"Oh. Um, I actually can't go," she said carefully. "There's... family things."

"What kind of family things?"

"Don't worry about it," she said. "Maybe next year."

I wondered if Summer and I would still be going out in a year. I didn't see why not, but I also didn't like to think that far ahead with girls. But the fact that she'd mentioned something a year from now—a date she never would've gotten to in the old timeline—was a good sign, as far as "saving Summer" business went.

Summer

WHY DID I still feel like I needed to lie to Nolan? Why couldn't I tell my own boyfriend, *"I can't go to the dance because I can't afford another new dress?"* What if he offered to buy me one? He already spent more money on me than I could justify spending on myself.

When he'd first brought it up, I thought, *"Of course I'll go to the dance with my boyfriend,"* but when I was about to tell my mom the news, I realized I would need something to wear. I knew she'd start about the dress and how I would have to wear an old one, so I never even told her about the dance. I'd heard the "Black & White" moniker didn't mean we had to dress in black and white, but nothing in my wardrobe was suitable.

Thanksgiving was a more relaxed holiday for my mom and me. Because what little family she was in touch with wasn't local, it was always just the two of us. My father would call, and we'd make small talk, and I'd lie about how school was going—but this year I didn't have to lie as much, because Nolan was really helping me with math. I was at a steady C-, which I would need to improve, but at this point in the semester last year I'd had a thirty-eight percent in the class. I was proud I could tell my dad all about Nolan, too. My father had "liked" our relationship status online and probably wanted some details—though not enough to ask at any point between then and now.

After the phone call, I helped my mom cook dinner: roast chicken—which was a more reasonable size for two people than an entire turkey—stuffing, mashed potatoes with gravy, sweet potato casserole, green beans, dinner rolls from one of those twisty cardboard containers, real cranberry sauce, a green salad, cornbread, and pumpkin pie. It was a lot of food, but with the portion sizes scaled down, it worked and gave us great leftovers. Sometimes we brought some over to one of our neighbors who always *seemed* like she lived alone but we didn't know her well enough to invite her over.

Cooking Thanksgiving dinner with my mom was one of the nicer activities we got to do together. We usually didn't get into arguments, and we often reminisced about my childhood, or she'd tell stories about when she was younger. It reminded me of when I was a kid and we'd bake a loaf of bread together every Monday afternoon while my dad was at work. We hadn't really had the chance to keep up that tradition since she'd gone back to work and I'd started kindergarten. Occasionally we would find time to make some together, but it was never like before.

"Nolan wants me to go Black Friday shopping with him tomorrow," I said, pouring stuffing mix into a pan. "I don't think I would buy anything, but it might be fun to look around."

"If you see any good deals, you could get something," she said. "I'll give you some cash. I'm assuming his parents will be there?"

He didn't say. "Yeah."

"Will they be picking you up, or would I need to drop you off?"

"I'll ask him tonight."

"Has he tried to have sex with you yet?" she asked.

I almost dropped my measuring cup. "No! I—ew, of course not!"

"Well, he's a high school boy; he's probably going to try sooner or later."

"Our relationship isn't like that," I said. "I—he knows I'm not ready for sex. We haven't even gotten to second base yet."

"Well, you know you won't be having sex *here*," she said. "I'll know if you do."

"Mom! I don't want to have sex!" I shuddered. "I don't want to see his... *thing*."

"Well, if you can't use the actual word, you're definitely not ready for sex," she said. "And don't think I'll be paying for any kind of birth control, either. He seems like he can afford condoms."

"We're *not* going to have sex," I said again.

"I just want you to be aware of—"

"I know. No sex in high school, STDs, pregnancy, emotions, et cetera."

"Alright. Now, have you seen the measuring spoons?"

I wondered if next year I could invite Nolan over to spend Thanksgiving with us. I still hadn't met his parents. I doubted my mom would let me invite them over; the "we're having work done on the house and that's why it looks like this" excuse only worked for so long. We'd been "having work done" since we'd moved in.

Nolan

THE GOOD news about having a million extended family members in the same house was that nobody would notice if I snuck away to call Summer.

"Hey," she answered right away.

"Hey, Sum," I replied. "How was your Thanksgiving?"

"It was good," she said. "My mom just went to take some leftovers to one of our neighbors. How about you?"

"It's been alright," I said. "We're at my aunt's house in Stockton. I've probably only got a few minutes to talk, but I wanted to make sure I called you."

"Oh, that's nice of you. Um, speaking of, what are the plans for tomorrow?"

"I can pick you up at four-thirty," I said. "Is that okay?"

She didn't answer right away. "Four-thirty as in a.m.?"

I chuckled. "Yeah. It's Black Friday, Summer."

"Right, yeah, um, I can be ready. Is it just us, or are your parents coming?"

"Just us. Maybe we'll meet up with Jake or Liam."

"Okay. Just checking. I'll try to be awake."

Summer

SOME NIGHTS when I couldn't sleep—or in this case, when it seemed better to just pull an all-nighter—I'd stare up at the ceiling and get lost in my thoughts. And sometimes my mind went to... not-so-great places.

The first time I thought about dying, I was eleven. It was sixth grade. I never fit in, and while I wasn't popular, I wasn't *unpopular* enough for anyone to single me out and bully me. I was grateful for that, even as I watched it happen to people I cared about. I felt bad, but I never did anything—at least I can say I didn't join in, but as I learned soon enough, being a bystander wasn't much better.

It wasn't like I would've known what to do; I'd freeze up in awkward situations and feel like I *couldn't* do anything. My aunt took my mom and I to Disneyland last summer and my cousin tripped and fell, and I just froze because I wasn't sure what to do, even though the answer was obvious: help him up. My mom yelled at me right there in the park. *"You can't just stand there, Summer! Help him, for the love of God! Are you just retarded?"*

My mom used that word a lot. Sometimes I started to think—*was* there something wrong with me, mentally? I knew I wasn't normal, but... I guess that couldn't be it. I'd seen the special education students at school, and we were very different. Even the "high-functioning" ones, as the teachers said, like Grant Hayward and Jimmy Vogel... Whatever was wrong with me had to be different than that. I knew my mother wasn't calling me the r-slur because she thought I was mentally challenged. She'd just grown up in a time when it was synonymous with "stupid."

One night, I found myself lying in my daybed, staring at the ceiling while Top 40 songs played softly on my radio. During the commercials, I started to think about how easy it would be for me to just disappear. If I didn't show up to school one day, would anyone notice besides my friends? Maybe when the teacher called roll and got to *"Summer Madison"* and nobody responded, someone would wonder where I was. Maybe after a few class periods of that, they would be curious. When the teacher asked, *"Does anyone know where Summer Madison is?"* would anyone even know *who* I was?

It wasn't that I hated my life or that I was miserable. I'd just realized how easy it would be if I disappeared. Maybe not *died*, but disappeared. If anyone at my elementary school had been absent for more than a few days, it was custom for everyone in their class to sign a "get well" card. I used to hope I'd get sick so I'd be absent long enough to get one, but I never did. There was one summer when everyone at my day camp had strep throat at one point, and I was the only one who never got it.

Then, in eighth grade, a girl in our class got hit by a car on the way to school. She didn't die, but she was in the hospital for a while, wheelchair-bound for weeks, and then booted at the start of freshman year. I didn't know her very well, but in the few interactions I had with her, she wasn't nice to me. She wasn't necessarily mean, but her friends were—to me, to Daisy, to Bella—and she didn't say anything to stop them.

The point is, this girl got hurt and *everyone* in our grade acted like she'd died. Classes were basically canceled for the eighth graders that day. The teachers told us we could do whatever we wanted, so I put my earbuds in and wrote in my notebook while everyone else mourned this girl who was still alive and fully conscious with a leg injury. I still remember what I wrote:

Why should I feel bad for someone if they've never been nice to me? If someone has made fun of you and your friends for years, what gives them the right to your sympathy? I feel like I'm the only one who isn't sad today. Even my teachers gave us special privileges. Even Daisy is acting upset, and she HATES this person.

Marta is acting like this girl died, like they were the best of friends. When I broke my toe in gym last year, Marta told me I was being dramatic and stepped on my foot to show me it was fine. I wish Bella was here today. She'd probably feel like I do. I don't know what it is, but I can't get myself to be sad about this even if I wanted to.

Someone in my grade was hit by a car. Supposedly she only broke her leg. She didn't even come close to dying. It would be one thing if she'd died or was in a coma or something, but multiple teachers have assured us she's fine and going to make a full recovery. So why is everyone acting like she's dead?

Would all these people be crying if I got hit by a car? If I died? Probably not. Nobody would miss me. And so I don't feel bad about not feeling bad today.

At the time, I felt the amount of attention this girl was getting was absurd.

Looking back, it did suck, what happened to her. I wouldn't wish that on anyone. I still thought our classmates were being dramatic, but I understood better than I had then. The thought still haunted me that at thirteen years old I'd honestly been wondering if anyone would care if something happened to me. Even now at sixteen, it was too young for someone to be having thoughts like that. I was just a kid.

Some days, I still felt like nobody would miss me if something were to happen. Even my friends. Marta had Sutton; with him, she'd get over it soon enough. Daisy had a whole group without me. She'd be sad, sure, but she'd move on. Nolan could easily get another girlfriend, one who was prettier and easier to deal with. He'd miss me a little in the beginning, but we hadn't even been close until this year. And my mom would be free of her disappointing daughter. She could spend her money on herself again. That's the only effect I would really have: people would be sad for a little while, but they'd move on and forget about me. I'd never been significant enough to anyone for my absence to cause a real disturbance in their lives.

And so sometimes I'd have nights like this—nights where I wondered what would happen if I just closed my eyes and never opened them again. If I just died, suddenly, for no specific reason. Or if maybe I went into the kitchen and took some random things from the medicine cabinet. Maybe I went for a walk in the middle of the road at night. Maybe I cut a little too deep with my razor—by accident. Maybe I drowned in the lake, or laid on some train tracks, or found a high enough surface to...

I closed my eyes and imagined different scenarios, as I usually did. I imagined how people would react. Maybe someone out there would think they'd taken me for granted. Maybe they'd think they should've done something differently... Or maybe nobody thought about that at all. Maybe I just became an empty desk that a new student would fill, a vacant locker that someone would trade for because it was in a better location, an empty bedroom that could be converted into an office or a storage room, one less expense for my parents to worry about... but maybe someone out there cared.

Nolan

I HAD to call Summer at 4:45 when she hadn't come out to the driveway yet. Apparently she was planning to pull an all-nighter but fell asleep anyway without an alarm set. When she finally got to the car, she was dressed in a sweatshirt and jeans and her hair was up in a messy ponytail. She smelled strongly of some floral body spray.

"You could've worn pajamas," I told her, pointing out my gym sweats. "It's not a fashion show."

"I wasn't sure; I've never done this," she said. "I'm sorry. I really tried to time everything—"

"You're fine, Summer. Don't worry. Oh, and if you see something you like, it's on me."

"You don't have to do that," she insisted. "My mom gave me fifty dollars. She

124

said I can't spend *all* of it, but it should be more than enough."

"Alright, well, my offer stands if you change your mind," I said. "Where do you want to go first?"

"Um... what's a good place to start?"

"I'm hoping to get a couple things at Target," I said. "I'm sure Sephora's got some good deals for you, too."

"I get my makeup from Target," she said. "Well, the makeup I have."

"We could look at some while we're there."

"I don't know." She sighed. "I don't know much about makeup, and I don't like wearing it all that much. I think I'm fine with what I have now."

"You look really pretty with it," I told her. "I never noticed how beautiful you were before you started wearing it."

"Don't you think I'm beautiful without it, though?" she asked.

"Of course," I lied, not wanting to upset her, but it was five in the morning and she looked like she'd barely slept. Did she think she was going to look half as good without makeup? "It's just easier to see when you *are* wearing it."

She nodded. "I guess that makes sense. Well, I don't know. Maybe I'll pick up a couple of things."

"I'll take you to Sephora," I told her. "I bet they've got some good deals, and you can get something nice. You can look around there; I'll run to Target and meet back up with you."

"Oh, okay. Um, I just figured we'd be shopping together."

"I guarantee I'm not gonna be much fun at the makeup store," I said, hoping she'd laugh.

She managed half a smile. "You probably know more about makeup than I do."

"Knowing how little you know about it, I still doubt that," I assured her. "I just know where the girls at school like to buy it."

I dropped her off at Sephora, which was reasonably crowded but not nearly as bad as Target. I wasn't sure I'd get the stuff I wanted before she was done, but when I texted her, she said she was still there, so I headed back.

"You find anything?" I asked her.

She shook her head. "All of this stuff is, like, *really* expensive, and for not-that-big amounts of stuff. Also... a *lot* of the makeup here is named after sex stuff."

"What do you mean?"

She walked me over to a display. "These ones I was looking at are the worst."

I assumed they were blushes because they were pink and sparkly, but sure enough, they had names like "deep throat" and "sex appeal" and "super orgasm."

"Well, they're just blushes, I think. Just 'cause they have sex names doesn't mean they wouldn't look good on you."

"Yeah, I just can't imagine telling my mom I spent thirty dollars on a tiny thing of blush named 'super orgasm,' could you?"

"I think if I told my mom I spent thirty dollars on blush, we'd be having a much different conversation."

"Your parents wouldn't let you wear makeup, if you wanted to?" she asked.

"I'm sure they'd *let* me; we'd just have to have an awkward conversation about it first."

"Fair enough." She sighed. "Well, I don't know what I want. There's some eyeshadow palette everyone's obsessed with, but it's fifty dollars—thirty with the sale—and the shades look pretty basic. I really don't think makeup is my thing."

I didn't want to push the issue and upset her. "Okay. Well, I just thought, you know, you look pretty with it so you might want to look at some nicer stuff, but I'm not gonna make you buy anything you don't want."

As we were heading out, her eye caught on something, and I followed her to the window of a boutique where she seemed to be looking at a sparkly white dress.

"That's pretty," I said. "Are you thinking of buying it?"

"There's no way it's in my price range; besides, where would I wear it?" she asked.

"You could wear it to Black & White."

She glanced away. "I told you, I can't go."

"Because you can't afford a dress?"

She didn't say anything.

"What if you could?" I offered.

She shook her head quickly. "No, Nolan, you can't buy me a dress like that."

"Don't think of it as me doing something for you," I said. "I, selfishly, want to go to the dance with my girlfriend. I also, selfishly, want to see you in that dress."

She couldn't hide her blush. "I can't let you do that," she said. "Even if I didn't feel weird about it, my mom would want to know where the dress came from, and there's *no way* she would be okay with you buying me a dress like that."

"How much *could* I spend on a dress for you?"

She shook her head. "Just... don't, okay? Maybe next year."

"Alright," I said, "but you owe me a school dance. We have to make up for how awkward we were about homecoming."

"Okay. The next dance, we'll go."

"You should also come to Jake's after-party," I said. "Everyone will be in their nice clothes, but I'll wear a T-shirt and jeans if you come."

"A party?" She had a panicked look in her eyes, like I'd asked her to join me for an afternoon of reckless driving. "I've—never been to a real party. Just, like, birthday parties for my friends."

"Well, you'll have me to show you the ropes."

"Like homecoming?"

I reached for her hand and tried to meet her gaze, but she wouldn't look up. "Better than homecoming, I promise."

"What do I tell my mom?"

"That we're hanging out. It won't go past midnight; the dance ends at ten anyway."

"Okay. We'll see."

I could tell she was nervous about the idea, but I was going to make sure she had a good time. It was the least I could do.

Summer

OUR WEEK back at school was uneventful, but the looming date of this party was making me anxious. Daisy even had to remind me that hers was the next day; I'd almost forgotten until she'd said, *"See you tomorrow"* as I left school on Friday.

My mother had bought my explanation that Nolan wanted to hang out with a group of friends, but my curfew was eleven-thirty, meaning we probably wouldn't spend too much time at the party. Not that I minded that much; I felt very underdressed in my sweater and jeans, even when Nolan showed up looking even more casual than I did.

"You look nice," he said as I got in the car. "Your makeup's different."

"Thanks," I said. I'd tried to go a little heavier on the eyes since he'd said he liked when I wore makeup, but I wasn't so sure I'd done it right. "Um, are you sure this is fine for the party?"

"Yeah; they all know we're not coming from the dance," he said.

"How many people are gonna be there?"

"Probably not more than twenty."

That didn't sound too bad. I felt better knowing he'd be with me the whole night—at least I hoped he would.

We got some dinner first, since the dance was still going on, and when we pulled up to Jake's driveway, right away I could tell his family was rich. This was the nice part of town. The two-story grey brick house sat comfortably with its double garage doors and its red brick steps up to the front porch, the small fountain, the glossy oak door, the iron porch swing... all things I was sure my mother would love to have if we could afford it.

Inside, music was playing and everyone was standing around talking in their dressy outfits. Nolan slung his arm around me and led me to the kitchen, where Jake was opening some bags of chips.

"Hey, man, you made it!" He greeted Nolan with some handshake-meets-hug gesture and then waved politely at me. I tried to smile back.

"How was the dance?" Nolan asked.

"It was just a dance; the usual," Jake said. "I'm actually about to meet Caeley upstairs, but the guest bedroom's all yours in half an hour if you'd like it."

Nolan glanced at me, a worried expression on his face to tell me... what? Did he think we were going to have sex tonight? At the party?

He turned back to Jake. "We'll see."

Now I was uncomfortable. When Jake left, Nolan looked at me.

"Don't worry about what he said," he told me. "That's not why I brought you here."

"Then why did you?" I asked.

"So we could hang out," he said. "Here, let's get you something to lighten up a little; you seem nervous."

I am nervous, I wanted to tell him, but I was tired of being a square. He handed me a cup of punch. I took a sip, but there was something off about it.

I took another sip. It was burning my throat a little. "What flavor is this?"

"I don't know," he said. "I'll ask Jake next time I see him." He was glancing around, maybe looking for some friends or a spot to sit.

"I think I'm allergic to it," I said. "It's burning my mouth."

"You don't have to finish it," he said. "I just thought a drink would help you relax."

"I'm not very thirsty right now, anyway," I said. "Did you want the rest?" I realized he didn't have his own cup.

"Nah, I have to drive you home later," he said. "We could go somewhere and talk."

I was a little confused as to what him driving me home had to do with having punch, and then it hit me. "There's alcohol in this."

He raised an eyebrow. "Is... that a problem?"

"I—I've never had any before."

I was staring at the ground, but when I looked back up at him, he had an apologetic expression on his face. "I guess I should've put two and two together when you said you'd never been to a party. I just thought... you might figure, since... Well, you don't have to have any if you don't want."

I was sure it wasn't a good idea, but I wanted to be more like him and his friends. "I'll just finish this."

Nolan

SUMMER WAS on the skinny side and had never had alcohol before, which was a basic recipe for a lightweight. I wasn't sure exactly what Jake put in the punch, but that one cup sure made her less tense.

And when Summer wasn't tense, she was talkative. Difficult to understand, as her words slurred just a bit, but it wasn't so bad that I couldn't figure out what she was saying—even if some of it didn't make sense.

"I just never really thought I was the type to go to parties," she said. "I never got invited to one. I wasn't even sure I was interested in going to one, but I don't want to drag you down and all because I know this is what you like. I don't know if I like parties. I think I like parties. What am I supposed to do at a party? I don't really know."

I laughed. "This is fine, Sum. We can talk like this, maybe make out later when you're less... talkative."

"Am I talking too much?" She frowned. "Oh, no. I knew I was doing something wrong. I'm always doing something wrong."

"No, no, that's not what I meant!" I assured her. "I was trying to say it nicely, but... you're kind of drunk."

"I'm not drunk," she said. "I only had a little bit of alcohol. What alcohol was it? I didn't have that much. I can't be drunk. My mom would kill me."

"You won't be when I drop you off," I assured her. "Hey, let's have some water and probably some food. I'll make you a sandwich."

She smiled and followed me to the kitchen, poking at Jake's fridge door while I got ingredients out.

"This is a nice fridge," she said. "My mom wants a fridge like this, but it's so expensive. She always points at them in the store and says how pretty they are. But she needs money for my college if I can get into college so we have a boring old fridge."

I'd never thought there was anything special about the fridge. It was a stainless steel two-door model with the water dispenser in the door; my family had the same one. But I suppose it was nice. I couldn't remember what Summer's fridge looked like, or if I'd even seen it.

"What do you like on your sandwiches?" I asked her.

"I'm okay with anything," she said. "Wait, I don't like mayonnaise."

"Who does?" I spread some mustard on a slice of bread. "Just turkey okay, then?"

"Yeah," she said. "Whatever's easiest. I don't want to inconvenience you."

"Relax; I practically live here, too," I said.

She took her sandwich back to the couch and I watched her practically shove it into her mouth. It was amusing watching drunk people eat; sometimes the entertainment value made not drinking at parties worth it. The first time Jake got drunk, I watched him put his entire face into a bowl of popcorn.

"You act like you've never had a sandwich before," I teased. "Or like you'll never see another one."

"It's a good sandwich," she said. "You're good at making sandwiches. I'm probably good at sandwiches. I'm not sure what else, though. I usually make frozen pizzas after school."

"Maybe I could take you to get a real pizza after school on Monday."

"That's okay," she said. "I like my routine." A pause. "Oh, wait, you're asking me out. It's not that I don't want to. I just like my routine. Is that weird?"

"Nothing you say at this point is that weird," I said. Drunk people said all kinds of weird stuff. I'd ask her to hang out when she was coherent enough to think about it.

"I've just had this routine since high school started and I don't like to change it," she said.

"Whatever you say."

"We could make out now," she said. "I finished my sandwich."

I laughed. "Let's wait a while, okay? You still seem..."

"What?" She panicked. "I'm doing something wrong."

"No, no, you're fine," I said. "I'm just... I'd rather talk to you right now."

"We can talk," she said. "I'm good at talking. I like talking. What should we talk about?"

"Whatever you want to talk about."

"I'm good with anything," she said.

"You can make a decision, you know," I said. "Once in a while, it's okay to want something specific, rather than being 'fine with whatever.' I'm not gonna stop liking you just because you want a ham sandwich instead of turkey."

"I like turkey, though," she said. "Not a big fan of ham, either. I just don't want to be more of a burden than I already am."

"You're not a burden," I said. "Why do you think that?"

"I can just tell," she said. "If my mom didn't have to pay for stuff for me, she could have a house like she wants. She could spend money on herself more. I know I'm a burden, at least financially. To her."

"Well, you're not a burden to me," I said.

"Maybe I will be, someday." She took a sip of water. "I always am. Unless someday I'm just... not."

"You won't be to me," I said again. "Now, how about you have some chips?"

Summer

WHAT HAPPENED at the party was a little fuzzy. I knew the fruit punch had alcohol in it, but I didn't know how much. I remembered talking to Nolan, but I didn't remember much about the specifics. He made me a sandwich, which was nice. He kept giving me chips and water after that while we talked. We kissed for a little while before he realized he had to get me home.

"Can you... smell it on me?" I asked.

He shook his head. "Just brush your teeth if you're worried. It smells more like chips than alcohol."

I still wasn't feeling one hundred percent when I got back to my house, but fortunately my mom didn't have too many questions.

I couldn't remember exactly what Nolan and I had talked about. I thought I mentioned feeling like a burden. I didn't usually voice those thoughts out loud. He told me I wouldn't be, but... he couldn't promise that. I *always* burdened the people I loved.

I thought Marta didn't *like* hanging out with me because I wasn't the person she wanted me to be, but she'd feel bad cutting me off because we'd known each other so long. She had a picture in her head of my potential, if I were normal, but I wasn't. I was a burden to her, and I'd be a burden to Nolan someday, too.

For now, I'd go to the bathroom and get a brand-new razor, and I'd sit on my bed and deal with this knowledge the only way I knew how.

But this was my last time.

7

Nolan

I COULD see what Summer meant when she said she'd never been to a "real" party before. When we got to Daisy's birthday party on Saturday, it was the school's handful of weird honor students crowded around a huge TV in the living room. It was definitely interesting, because I'd known this band of weird kids existed and I'd had many classes with them, but it never occurred to me that these were Summer's friends. I just knew Summer was friends with Marta and Daisy.

It was difficult to determine Daisy's financial situation, because the outside of her house was nicer than Summer's, but the inside could use a good cleaning, new carpet, and probably some new furniture—but the TV was bigger and nicer than what any of my friends had.

Once Daisy let us in the house, she took a seat on the couch next to a guy I'd never seen around campus, but they were sure friendly with each other. Summer looked at me as if to ask where I wanted to sit, and honestly—not on that leather couch that looked like it had been purchased before Daisy's parents were even married, and not on the crusty burnt orange carpet that probably hadn't been cleaned since the seventies. But I didn't want to be rude, so I sat on the edge and put my arm around Summer, keeping her between me and a girl with a black boyish haircut—if she hadn't been in my gym class last year, I probably would've assumed she was a guy based on the hair and how she dressed: baggy clothes, probably from the guys' section.

"What're we watching?" Summer asked Daisy.

"My favorite anime!"

I'd had a lot of assumptions about Summer way back when, but I'd never pegged her as one to hang out with the anime kids.

"Oh, that's cool," Summer said with a bit of disinterest.

"You all know each other, right?" Daisy asked, motioning across the couch. The only one I recognized by name was Lucia Torres from trigonometry. She had thick, braided hair and was wearing a baggy sweatshirt and jeans.

"Um... I think so," Summer said. She motioned to me. "This is Nolan; he's my boyfriend. Daisy said I could bring him, so here we are."

"I haven't actually met you." Another boyish-looking girl turned to face us; this one had a shaved head that was only a little grown out; the color was dark blonde, and her skin was pale like she'd never heard of the sun, much less seen it. She didn't introduce herself.

"I'm Summer," Summer said awkwardly. "I've seen you around."

"I'm Vanessa," the girl replied. "No nicknames."

So... these *weren't* all Summer's friends? That made me feel a little better—that and seeing her look down at her phone rather than watch whatever this anime was. There were a lot of things I was willing to try if someone I liked was into them, but watching anime had never been on that list.

"How do you all know each other?" I decided to ask.

Daisy motioned to the other three girls. "We all met in AP bio freshman year. Summer and I have known each other since elementary school, but I'm sure you knew that. And Ben and I met through mutual friends a few years ago. We've been dating since the summer, when we ended up at the same LARPing camp."

"How long have you and Summer been going out?" Ben asked me.

"A few weeks," I said.

"We've known each other for years, though," she said. "We just started talking this year."

"Yeah, the three of us have been at the same school for, like, ever," Daisy said.

The two boyish-looking girls exchanged a glance with Lucia. All three looked at us like they were trying to figure out how someone like me had ended up at their weird anime party. It occurred to me that Vanessa, who hadn't met Summer before, might be thinking the same thing about her—she didn't have a lot of makeup on today, but she was starting to look more like the types of girls my friends and I usually hung out with. Maybe she assumed Summer had always been part of my friend group—it wasn't like Summer was that well-known before.

The others I'd seen around campus. I'd seen them eat lunch by the band room. I'd seen them in the front rows of some of my AP and honors classes. I'd seen them walking around, always dressed in baggy hoodies and old jeans or cargo pants, off-brand athletic sneakers or outdoorsy sandals. Never any makeup, hair never really done—the ones who had enough hair to do anything with, anyway. Something just always seemed "off" about them. Not, like... I didn't think they belonged in the special education program or anything; they just never seemed to care what anyone thought of them. While Summer definitely didn't fit in before, at least she seemed to care about it and make some kind of an effort, even if it was a small one.

When Daisy asked for our pizza orders, neither Summer nor I had a preference, but the other three were giving Daisy and Ben what seemed like ridiculous pizza requests—one of them even asked for pizza with no cheese. What was the point?

Daisy and Ben left to pick up the pizzas, and I could tell Summer was uncomfortable with the host of the party—the person she knew best—out of the picture.

"Where's she getting the pizzas from again?" I asked.

"Round Table," Vanessa replied.

"Oh." A bit too greasy for my taste, but not the worst.

"Is that not good enough for you?" she asked me, confrontational to the point where I couldn't tell if she was joking.

"It's fine," I said. "I was just curious."

"It's the best place that will make it without cheese," she explained.

"What's even the point of pizza without cheese?" I asked, hoping it came across as a joke. "That's, like, one of the standard ingredients."

"We're lactose intolerant," she replied, pointing to the girl with the boyish haircut, who had introduced herself as Kim.

"Let it be known that she cares about it way more than I do," Kim said. "I don't fear death or pain."

Finally, Summer laughed, which I assumed was a sign that she felt more comfortable. "Not even a little bit?"

Kim shook her head. "Not even a little bit."

"I *do* fear death," Vanessa argued. "You should, too."

"What's there to be afraid of?" Summer asked. "We're all gonna die eventually."

"And eating pizza is more 'pain' than 'death' anyway," Kim said.

"Well, I'm not in the mood for either." Vanessa seemed genuinely offended.

"I'm in the mood to die," Kim said. "We've got another test in APUSH on Monday."

"I'll join you," Summer said. "I don't have a test; I just hate school. Except English."

The two of them laughed.

"Who do you have?" Kim asked her.

"Ms. Harris. She's the best. She's the only teacher who actually treats us like adults: lets us use our phones in class as long as we're not being distracting, stuff like that."

"Ah, I had her last year," Kim replied.

"But other than her class, I hate school," Summer explained. "Especially math."

"So you can die *after* English, but *before* math," Kim suggested.

"Won't work; I have math fifth period and English sixth."

I tried to meet Vanessa's gaze, wondering if someone else would be a little concerned about these "jokes." Finally, Lucia spoke up.

"You really shouldn't joke about that, you know," she said. "You know that girl across town hanged herself last year; one day it could be someone from our school or someone we know."

"Who said anything about suicide?" Kim asked. "I'm hoping my death will be a murder, one with a juicy story behind it. What about you, Summer? How would you like to die?"

I hoped she'd at least hesitate or look uncomfortable, but she just shrugged and said, "I'm open to suggestions. I'd prefer if it wasn't something painful, though. Instant would be nice."

"Like a car crash?" Kim asked.

"Would you two knock it off?" Lucia argued.

"Seriously," Vanessa seconded.

"You really shouldn't make jokes about that," I said.

Summer looked at me apologetically, almost panicked. "I'm sorry," she said. "I thought we were just kidding around—"

"Yeah, but some things you shouldn't kid about!" Lucia said.

"It's okay," I whispered to Summer. "Just don't do it again, okay?"

We didn't stay long after dinner, and Summer was quiet in the car on the way home.

"Were those all your friends?" I asked her.

She shook her head. "I know Daisy, and I've heard of Ben. I've seen the others around, but we're not that close."

"So you're not into anime?"

"Hell no. I watch sitcoms and some teen dramas, but that's it." She paused, and it got quiet again. "I'm sorry about those jokes," she said. "I guess I didn't realize... I don't know. Sometimes... it's just easier to laugh about things."

"Do you think about dying?" I asked.

She shook her head. "No. Not like that, no. I mean, I'm sure we all wonder how we're going to die—"

"You came up with your answer pretty fast," I said. "Instant, painless..."

"Well, you know, if I eventually have to die—be it sooner or when I'm old—I would like it to be as painless as possible. I'm sure everyone would."

"But that's not something everyone thinks about."

"Well, I think about a lot of stuff that nobody thinks about." She sighed. "I'm not going to kill myself, okay?"

I knew I needed to believe her, or at least act like I did. But knowing everything I knew... I just couldn't. So I said nothing.

"You think I'm going to kill myself," she said.

"Not necessarily," I replied.

What kind of response was that? *"Not necessarily?"*

"You're worried I'm going to."

"I just... don't want you to."

You could have said anything else, Nolan.

She turned to the window. "Well, you don't need to worry about me."

We were in her driveway, so I didn't press the issue. I kissed her goodnight and made sure she got in the house before I drove away.

Summer

I KEPT thinking about Nolan's comment: *"I don't want you to."* I knew it was bad to keep part of the truth from him—yes, I did think about dying sometimes; more than a normal, happy person would, which was one way I knew there was something wrong with me. But something about the way he'd worded that rubbed me the wrong way.

Dying, to me, was about not being a burden. The people in my life would miss me, but they'd get over it. My mom could afford the life she wanted. She wouldn't have to worry about me. Nolan would move on. My friends would move on. If I were to take my life, it would be for the benefit of those I cared about.

For Nolan to make *my* potential decision about *him* not wanting me to… I didn't like to think of it that way. I guess inevitably my death would affect those who cared about me, but I didn't want to think of it that way. And to have him make it so… apparent…

I decided not to think about it.

Instead, at school on Monday, I invited him to the church Christmas party my mom and I went to every December. It was about a week before Christmas, and it was pretty much the only time we went to church, but it was a holiday tradition.

"Hey." He greeted me at my locker with a brief kiss.

"Hey," I said. "So, what are you doing Sunday night?"

"Something with you?"

I smiled. "There's this church potluck my mom and I always go to."

"Oh. I didn't know you went to church."

"Do you?"

"Sometimes. The one up by the Olive Garden."

"Ours is by the Sonoma Chicken Coop," I said.

"Oh, nice, yeah, I've seen that one. Anyway, a potluck?"

"Sunday evening. There's, like, separate youth group stuff for teenagers, and we eat at a separate table from the adults."

He nodded. "Sounds fun."

I was excited because I didn't get to see the other students from church that often and I was usually the only single person at the table. There weren't very many of us, but those who attended church more often tended to pair off. It would be nice to be a part of that this year.

They weren't my *friends*, necessarily; we saw each other once or twice a year and kept in touch online. They were almost like distant cousins, except I saw them more often than my actual cousins who lived so far away.

Either way, I was excited to see them—and this time, I wouldn't be alone.

Nolan

SUMMER NEVER told me what to wear to her youth group thing, so I assumed a nice button-up shirt and some slacks would do. Her mother's car pulled up outside my house on Sunday evening, and I got in the backseat, surprised to see Summer sitting there instead of shotgun.

"Why are you in the back?" I asked.

"It's rude to make your guest ride in the back alone," she said as though she were reciting it—must be a family rule.

She looked nice; her hair was up and curled, and she had on a red blouse with a black skirt. She was even wearing red lipstick; I'd never seen her in red lipstick before. It was hot.

"Do they have mistletoe at these things?" I asked her.

She blushed. "Maybe." A pause. "Nice house, by the way."

"You've never seen my house?"

She shook her head.

"That's right; I guess you haven't." I handed her a Target bag. "Here's your sweater, by the way." Tomorrow would begin Winter Week at school, meaning Summer and I would get to dress up in matching outfits every day. Monday was "ugly Christmas sweater" day, and we both planned to wear these red sweatshirts with an "ugly" sweater print on them; I'd picked them up from Target yesterday and Summer had paid me back what she thought was the full price, but I'd only told her half the amount.

The ride to her church didn't take long. The hallways were lined with holiday garlands and other Christmas decorations, with a large manger scene displayed outside the multipurpose room. I followed her to the teens' table, where four couples were already sitting, holding hands under the table.

"Is it just couples?" I whispered to Summer.

"Not intentionally," she said. "The ones who come regularly kind of switch partners over the years. I don't recognize a couple of them, though; probably people from their school."

As we got closer, I immediately recognized one of the girls. At the edge of the table, cradling the hand of a tan-skinned girl with a green pixie cut, was a familiar girl with long, thick black hair in a braid with a green ribbon woven through.

"Esme?"

She glanced up at us. "Do I know you?"

No. Not yet. "Uh…" What could I possibly say? "Where do you work?"

"Starbucks on Peach and Layton."

"Didn't you make my drink a couple weeks ago?" I asked. "You have a memorable face."

She doesn't even live on this side of town, you idiot. Peach Avenue and Layton Road were a good half hour drive from here.

She shrugged. "Maybe. Well, I guess you know I'm Esme. Do you know Anjana?"

"Good to see you, Anjana," Summer said. "Nice to meet you, Esme. I'm Summer; this is my boyfriend, Nolan."

I waved. Summer introduced me to the rest of the table: Todd and Polina, Amy and Jin, and Barrett and Sonya. They were nice, but I couldn't help focusing on Esme. Had Esme met Summer here in the old timeline? Were they friends before the summer? Something told me that I needed to connect with Esme *now*, now that she was here—I wasn't sure why.

Then it hit me: Esme was the only one who'd talked to *me* after Tim's announcement. What if...? It seemed impossible, but if *I* could be thrown back in time to prevent Summer's death, maybe Esme had been, too. But how did I get her alone? Both of us were here with a date; going off alone with her wouldn't be a good look.

After dinner, we moved into another room to assemble pick-me-up kits for the church leaders to hand out to homeless people next week. Esme got up to use the restroom, and I told Summer I was going to get some water. I lingered by the fountain so I could make it look like I had just conveniently run into Esme on her way out.

"Hey," I said. "Um... are you sure we've never met before?"

"I thought we met at Starbucks," she said.

"And you never met Summer before tonight?"

"Nope."

I knew it was a long shot. I felt crazy enough for the whole timeline switch happening to *me*, but insinuating to Esme that she was also a part of it made me feel psychotic and creepy. But there was still something telling me that Esme was important.

"Do you and your girlfriend want to come over and watch a movie with me and Summer sometime?" I asked.

"Um, maybe," she said. "Why?"

"I just feel like you'd get along with her," I said. "She could use some more good friends."

"Well... I guess. I'll send you a friend request and we can set something up."

I smiled. "Awesome."

Summer

THIS WAS by far the most fun I'd ever had at the Christmas banquet. I felt like with Nolan there, it was so much easier to talk to everyone. Usually I just sat there and let them couple off, only speaking when someone asked me a question. I didn't mind just listening, but it was nice to be involved.

Nolan had something I didn't. I wasn't sure what it was, but it was so easy for him to start conversations with the other couples and make me feel included. It was like he knew all these secret passwords to normal social interactions that I didn't.

"Did you have fun?" I asked Nolan on the drive back to his place.

"Yeah, did you?"

"I really did," I said.

"I think Esme and Anjana are cool," he said. "We should double with them sometime."

My mother interjected from the front seat: "I keep trying to get Summer to hang out with Anjana. I've worked with her mother for years, but Summer's just so awkward every time we meet up."

"Thanks, Mom." I rolled my eyes. "I wouldn't mind double-dating with them. Do you think they'd be interested, though?"

"I think so," he said. "I'll reach out and set something up. Do you have any plans over break?"

"No, not really," I said. "You?"

"Well, we'll be down in Santa Clarita for a few days with my grandparents, but we'll be back by Christmas Eve," he replied. "Other than that, I'm free to hang out."

My mom pulled into Nolan's driveway, and I walked him to the door to say goodnight. He gave me a gentle kiss since my mom could still see us.

"See you tomorrow, Sum," he said.

"Yeah, see you."

Nolan

As SUMMER and her mother drove away, I started thinking about what I'd done for Christmas in the old timeline. I thought it was just the usual family stuff; I didn't have a girlfriend, and I wasn't seeing anyone even casually at that point.

Come to think of it, I didn't think I'd ever had a serious girlfriend for the holidays. I thought in seventh grade I'd been "with" someone, but we'd hardly talked outside of school. And then I realized: I hadn't gotten Summer a Christmas present.

Shouldn't I get her one? What if she couldn't afford anything for me and getting her a present made her feel bad? No, that was ridiculous. I just had to get her something cheap and meaningful. Or… would getting her something cheap when she *knew* I had money offend her?

I guess I'd forgotten how complicated relationships really were.

* * *

MONDAY'S "ugly sweater day" look got us a lot of "awww"s in the hallway. Tuesday was "white out" day so we both wore white T-shirts. Wednesday was "snow gear day," which was laughable considering we lived in California and only the kids who could afford to spend the holidays somewhere snowy had any snow gear—so while I had some stuff to choose from, Summer wasn't as stocked, and I let her borrow one of my fleece pullovers. It was a little big on her, but she still looked cute. We both had winter hats, since anything under fifty degrees here made our ears cold.

Thursday was "cozy day," which was a glorified pajama day—a little harder to match for, so we both just came in our own non-matching pajamas. Finally, Friday was "holiday hat day" and we showed up in matching Santa hats.

Summer was carrying a large dollar store bag when she met me by her locker. It held four boxes of mini candy canes; Summer always handed them out on the last day before break—to her friends and then some random assortment of people, the basis for which I had yet to determine because I wasn't sure what those classmates had in common. Every year, I was one of the recipients.

Well, this year I had something for her, too.

"Merry Christmas, Sum," I said, handing her a small gift-wrapped package.

She beamed, taking it from me. "What's this? I only have candy canes; I didn't know we were exchanging gifts today."

"There's no pressure to give me anything," I said. "Being with you is my gift this year." It was cheesy, but not entirely inaccurate considering how insane this do-over situation was.

She blushed. "Well, I'm going to get you *something*, so I guess we'll have to hang out before Christmas."

"I guess so."

She peeled back the paper to reveal a box of Ghirardelli chocolates. I figured they were *just* nice enough without making her feel bad if she couldn't afford something similar.

"These are my favorite!" she said. "How did you know?"

"They're my favorite, too," I said. "Well, the milk chocolate ones, anyway. I figured there's a good assortment there."

"Thank you so much!" She grinned. "I'll get you something before Christmas, I promise."

"No worries, Sum. I just wanted to get you something."

We kissed, a little more intense than a standard hallway kiss, but not intense enough to tip off any faculty that might be passing by.

As we broke away to head to class, I kept thinking back to the old timeline. It was rare that my memories of it were so vivid, but I could see it now: Summer had come to school on Friday in her Santa hat and an outfit not too different from what she had on today. She had boxes of dollar store candy canes that she was giving to a few people in the hallway.

"Nolan!" I remembered pretending not to hear her at first, and I kept walking to class, but she ran to catch up to me. *"Hey, I have a candy cane for you."* She'd given me one every year for as long as I could remember.

"Oh, thanks." I wasn't very appreciative. I never was; I usually threw them out when she wasn't looking, or once I think I'd regifted it to a girl I was into.

Thinking back to that exchange, it hit me that without this whole do-over, that would have been the last time Summer gave me a candy cane. And what did I do with it? I waited until she was out of sight and threw it away.

Things like that never seemed like such a big deal to me until now, knowing how different things could be. Knowing how lucky I was to get this do-over that I probably didn't deserve—but it wasn't about me. It was about Summer. The point wasn't for me to get to know her and see how much I actually liked her for *my* benefit; the point was to keep her alive.

Before, Summer was just some annoying girl I took for granted. Now, it was clear she had always been well-meaning. Maybe I was a jerk to her. I couldn't really remember how I'd acted before. I'd just tried to let her know subtly, without being rude, that I didn't want to be friends—but it got harder as time went on, as she kept pestering me, and maybe I lashed out a few times.

I wished I could remember what that last conversation had been. But it didn't matter now—none of that mattered now. All that mattered was how I treated Summer *now*.

I unwrapped her candy cane to eat and put the plastic wrapper in my chem binder to save. I wasn't going to take her for granted again.

Summer

NOLAN ASKED if I'd be interested in watching a movie with Esme and Anjana at his place on Sunday. He didn't know what movie; apparently Esme and Anjana wanted their pick to be a surprise. I'd never been on a double date before, but it did sound like fun.

When he came to pick me up, I remembered I'd never been inside his house. He'd seen the inside of mine, but I hadn't seen his. And I hadn't met his parents. If that had occurred to me sooner, I probably would've dressed nicer than what I had on: hair up, sweater, jeans, boots... At least I'd thought to put on makeup.

"Do I look okay?" I asked Nolan as I got in the car.

"You look great, Sum," he said without even looking at me.

"You're not even looking."

"I don't have to," he said. "I know you look great."

"For meeting your parents?"

He finally turned to face me. "Yes. You look great."

* * *

THE INSIDE of Nolan's house was just as nice as the outside. Artwork and professionally shot family photos on the pale brown walls, hardwood floors, matching furniture sets...

"My parents are upstairs," he said, "but I'm sure they'll come down to say hello before the afternoon is over. Esme just texted that they're almost here."

I followed him into the living room, where he took a seat on a pale blue couch with some grey-and-white throw pillows stacked neatly against the sides. I sat next to him and he put his arm around me.

"We could make out before they get here," he suggested.

I blushed. We hadn't done much more than light kissing; even at the party we'd just kissed for a while, but I wouldn't call it "making out." I wasn't going to turn his offer down, though, so I let him brush my hair out of my face and kiss me, gently at first, then harder, faster, and then he nudged me onto my back, the throw pillows pressing into my spine.

He moved his hand up my waist, and just as it was getting closer to my chest and I was trying to think of how to tell him I wasn't ready for that, the doorbell rang. He laughed and sat back up.

"I'll get that."

I nodded, and then I was alone in Nolan's living room, staring at his professional family portrait on the stand under the huge TV. All the media players and video games and fun-looking stuff were far more advanced than the Blu-ray player my mom got last year as a Christmas present from her sister.

"Hi, Summer!" Anjana's voice brought me back into the moment.

"Hey," I said as she and Esme sat in the adjacent loveseat. They were dressed far more casually in sweatshirts and leggings. I felt overdressed now.

"So, what movie are we watching?" Nolan asked, taking his seat next to me.

Esme proudly pulled a DVD case from her purse: *Camp Rock 2*.

"*Camp Rock*?" Nolan asked as if she'd held up a bag of rotting food.

"Actually, it's *Camp Rock 2*," Anjana said. "I told her I hadn't seen it yet and she told me I had to, and then we thought it would be funny to bring it here."

"We were originally going to bring a horror movie," Esme explained, "but then we realized we don't know either of you that well, and some people find horror movies... triggering."

"I love horror movies," I said. "They're so predictable. As long as you know it's fake, it's not scary."

"Exactly!" Esme cried. "Well, next time, we'll watch one. Now, however, we're watching *Camp Rock 2*."

"Did it occur to you that I'm a guy?" Nolan asked. "That's a girl movie. I haven't even seen the first one."

"Would you watch it for Summer?" Anjana asked.

I didn't bother mentioning that I hadn't seen the first movie either, or that I rarely watched Disney Channel. I didn't want to make this whole ordeal more complicated.

Nolan sighed. "Yes, I'll watch it for Summer. But this had better not be some sing-along version."

"I don't know the songs yet," Anjana assured him. "You'll be fine."

Nolan

IT BECAME obvious, fortunately, that Summer was no more invested in this stupid movie than I was. That meant we spent a good deal of the movie kissing—not so intensely that it would make Esme and Anjana uncomfortable, but it wasn't like they didn't have their share of mid-movie kisses before Esme would break away and shout, *"Wait, wait, this part is important!"* or *"Nobody talk during this song!"*

Esme and Anjana seemed so comfortable with each other, physically. The way they sat together, the way they kissed... Summer tended to be closed off. Even if I could tell she *wanted* to kiss me, it was like there was still something holding her back. Like on the couch earlier, when I'd tried to get on top of her, it was like she'd *wanted* to keep going, but she was so stiff and... Maybe she *didn't* want to keep going and I was just reading it wrong.

I thought about when Summer and I might take things a little further. I mean, we hadn't even gotten to second base, so it was presumptuous to think she'd be ready for sex. No doubt she was a virgin, so there was that to consider. I never knew the right way to bring that up with someone; with other girls I'd been with, we'd just sort of kept up with each other. We'd instinctively been on the same page.

Towards the end—or, what I hoped was the end—of the movie, I heard footsteps on the stairs, meaning one or both of my parents was coming to the living room.

"Hello," my mother said as I craned my neck back to see her and my father standing in the archway. "Sorry to interrupt."

"You're fine," Esme said.

"Summer," I said, nudging her to turn around. "These are my parents."

She waved. "Hi. I'm Summer." She cringed like it was somehow the wrong thing to say.

"Nice to meet you, Summer," my father said. "Well, enjoy your movie."

They walked through the front door, and Summer and I turned back to face the TV.

"That wasn't so dramatic, was it?" I asked her.

"I don't know what I expected," she said. "I guess I thought it would be a bigger deal."

"I'm sure they'll ask to have you over for dinner or something," I said. "They didn't want to interrupt our movie."

"How long have you two been dating again?" Anjana asked.

"Just over a month," Summer replied.

"And you're *just* meeting his parents?" Esme asked.

Way to make her even more nervous, Esme. "Well, my parents aren't usually that... involved in my dating life. They just remind me to be safe and use protection."

"Can't relate," Anjana replied. "Our parents have had each other over for dinner almost every weekend since we became official."

"They did tell us to use a condom once as a joke, though," Esme said. "You should've seen their faces when I asked what we were supposed to put it on."

"How soon did your parents meet your last girlfriend?" Anjana asked me.

I wasn't even sure when my last "serious" girlfriend was. Niamh wasn't serious per se, so my parents had never met her. Especially with the blurred timelines, I couldn't remember. "I haven't really *had* a serious girlfriend in a while. I don't remember."

"Well, I guess it's not a big deal," she replied. "You should get on those dinner plans, though. Summer deserves a proper introduction."

I nodded, and I couldn't bring myself to look at Summer and try to gauge her feelings about all of this. When Esme and Anjana left, she stood awkwardly with me in the entryway.

"You okay?" I asked.

She shrugged. "Um... do your parents think we're having sex?"

"I—well, they might assume, but I've never told them we are," I said. "In fact, I think at least once I've explicitly told them we *aren't*. They also probably notice the lack of charges to CVS on my credit card."

"CVS?"

"For condoms."

"Oh."

"Look, I—you're a virgin, right?" I asked her.

She nodded. "Are you?"

"No."

"Oh."

"Did you think I was?"

She shrugged. "I don't like to make assumptions." A pause. "How many...? Is that rude to ask?"

"I mean, it's a fair question, if you're thinking someday you might want to—"

"I'm not thinking about that right now," she said. "I'm just curious."

I tried to remember, due to the whole timeline shift. "Four." *Wait, Katie.* "Five. I mean five. But that's all."

"Oh."

"Were you expecting a smaller number?"

"I don't know."

"Is it a problem for you?"

"I don't know."

"Don't think I think of you any differently," I told her. "I mean... I like being with you. There's no rush to take that step. If somewhere down the road you feel like you want to, we'll talk about it."

"What if 'somewhere down the road' is, like, after graduation?" she asked.

I would be lying if I said it didn't annoy me a little that I'd have to wait that long, but on the other hand... "I'm just glad you think we'll still be together then. Like, that I'm not the only one who sees this lasting." *Or sees you living that long.*

"I just... I feel like there's so much uncertainty," she said. "So many risks, emotionally and physically, and... I just don't feel ready to... do that."

"And that's fine," I told her. "Don't worry about it."

But when I dropped her off at her house, I could tell she was still worried.

Summer

HAVING A boyfriend during the holidays was better than I could have imagined. The day before Christmas Eve, Nolan came back from his family trip to Santa Clarita and took me downtown to see all the lights and decorations. He bought us hot chocolate even though it was only sixty degrees because that was winter in California. It was the most fun I'd had in a long time. After lunch, we went ice skating.

"I'm glad we're doing this," he said.

"Ice skating?"

"Hanging out. I've never had a girlfriend during the holidays."

I blushed. "I've never—well, you knew that."

"It's nice."

"We should do this again next year," I said.

"Promise?" he asked.

"Can't think of anywhere I'd rather be. Well, except maybe somewhere with real snow."

He laughed. "Maybe that can be arranged next year. We'll have to see."

Nolan

WE HAD family over for Christmas, and I hid up in my room after a while. Socializing with relatives wasn't really my thing. Summer never told me what she did on Christmas, but I gave her a call. She answered pretty quick.

"Hey!"

"Merry Christmas," I said. "You busy?"

"No, not really."

"Cool, cool. I wasn't sure what you usually do on Christmas."

"It's just me and my mom," she said. "My dad will send me a present. We'll probably talk on the phone later. How about you?"

"Lots of family over," I said. "It gets boring after a while. I'd rather talk to you."

"Well, lucky for you, I'm free to talk. Did you get anything cool this year?"

I was about to answer her, but I wasn't sure if talking about everything I got would make her feel bad because I doubted her gifts were comparable. "I got a new phone," I said, trying to decide what else I wanted to mention. "Uh, some clothes from my relatives." A new laptop, a bigger TV for my room, some movies. "How about you?"

"Well, I passed all my classes this semester," she said, "and I did better in geometry than I was hoping for—a C+—and so I get to go on that Europe trip this summer! My mom put a deposit down. And I got a new phone."

"That's great!" My parents were planning to put the first deposit down; it wasn't due until the thirty-first. "That'll be fun, going on the trip together." Something I never would've imagined myself saying before.

"Yeah."

"Next Christmas, you should come over," I said. "You'll have met more of my family by then, anyway."

"I'd like that."

"Maybe... we could meet up later today," I said.

"You could come over."

"Yeah. Maybe I will."

Before I knew it, I was sneaking out the back door of the house and hoping the sound of my truck starting up wouldn't alert anyone to my disappearance; they were probably all too busy listening to Christmas music anyway. Once I was off the block, I turned the radio on.

Something about Summer making plans for a year from now was comforting. Like, maybe I'd done my job and I could relax now. I could just enjoy being with her and not worry so much about her going off the deep end.

Summer

I WASN'T so sure what to do when Nolan came over, because it wasn't like I had ever had a boyfriend—or even a friend—over on Christmas before. My mom made us hot chocolate and we watched *It's a Wonderful Life*.

"It's an interesting concept," Nolan said after the movie ended. "Thinking about if the world would be better or worse without you. Isn't it?"

"Yeah," I said, glad he seemed to understand that concept; maybe I could talk to him in more depth about it. "I mean, this was a movie, though. I'm sure for most of us, the difference wouldn't be *that* dramatic."

"I don't know about that," he said. "I think you make more of a difference than you realize. And that's the point."

I sighed. "If you say so." I wasn't going to take him down some depressing rabbit hole on Christmas.

When he had to get going, I walked him to his car.

"I had fun with you today," he said. "I—one of the best Christmases I can remember."

"Me, too."

We kissed each other goodbye and I watched him drive off. Maybe he had a point, though. Maybe I made more of a difference in people's lives than I realized. It was easy to see how much less of a burden I'd be on people if I wasn't around, but maybe the good I brought into people's lives outweighed that. Maybe my mom thought all the money it took to support me was worth it, even if I didn't live up to her social status at my age. Maybe there were things Marta valued about my friendship, and there were actual reasons she kept me around aside from the "we've been friends for this long so now we *have* to be friends forever" thing. Maybe my silly candy canes were the only gift some people got from a classmate. I wasn't *so* sure, but it was worth thinking about.

Nolan

As I pulled into my driveway, I realized I wasn't going to be able to sneak back in. My parents were going to want to know where I had been. They probably wouldn't be too happy that I'd just up and left the family gathering, even if it was to see Summer.

Maybe I could tell them I was just getting something out of the truck. I opened up the glove box to see if I could find anything believable. I realized what a mess the glove box was when a bunch of booklets fell out: road maps, the car manual, a workbook from last year, and a purple spiral-bound notebook covered in stickers.

Where had I seen that notebook before? It wasn't mine. I would never put glittery heart stickers, smiley faces, and other girly crap on a notebook. I didn't even think I'd own a purple notebook to begin with. I opened it up to see what it was.

September 7ᵗʰ—

First day of junior year. I know a couple people in my A-Day classes, we'll see how tomorrow goes I guess.

I dropped the notebook and gasped out loud, although there was nobody around to hear me. How was this possible? Was this the notebook Summer had left at the community center in the other timeline? How was it still here?

I flipped through and sure enough, the entries went all the way to June 24, a date which had yet to happen. I even checked to see if maybe some of the entries were consistent with the current timeline, but she mentioned not going to homecoming, and there were very few mentions of me from what I could see. I looked at the stickers on the front cover again and realized one of the hearts read "BE KIND ~ AP," the slogan of the anti-bullying assembly, which hadn't happened yet in this timeline, and probably the initials of the girl who the assembly was mainly about but I couldn't remember her name.

So this was it. This was Summer's notebook from the old timeline. In this notebook would be the key information I needed to know in order to save her.

Can anyone else see this? My mind wandered back to Esme. It was Christmas, so I doubted I'd be able to meet up with her today, but maybe this notebook would be my key to getting more information from her.

I hurried through the back door and up the stairs to my room; I didn't know if my parents noticed. I didn't have time to care about that right now. I had reading to do.

* * *

I COULDN'T finish the notebook. It was too much. I only made it to the end of November. There were far fewer mentions of me than I expected, but I'm not sure why I expected to be in it so much. I guess it's because *I* was the one sent back to stop her. Wouldn't I be more important in her notebook?

From what I could understand, her relationship with Marta was becoming strained because of Marta's new boyfriend. Summer got back together with Jonah because she was tired of being lonely and it was obvious he was the only one who would want to be with her. The few times I was mentioned, she'd tried to talk to me in the hallway but I'd seemed disinterested. She mentioned not being able to compare to the girls she usually saw me talking to. She said all she really wanted was to be friends because I was apparently so nice to everyone but her. I thought it was an exaggeration.

She had a list of "things to look forward to," but everything was crossed off except three items:

- Maybe getting my license
- Braces off (finally)
- Europe trip

She also had a list of goals for junior year:

- Get good enough grades to go to Europe
- Get a boyfriend who isn't Jonah
- Go to prom with a date (not Jonah)
- Driver's license
- Learn how to do makeup

I wasn't sure when or if she and Jonah had broken up again; I guess I'd learn if I kept reading. I remembered running into Marta and some guy at prom, but I didn't remember if Summer was there or not. I hardly had any memories of her because I'd tried to forget any interactions I had with her after they happened.

Why *was* I so closed off to her before? She was annoying, sure, but why did I find her so damn irritating? What was she doing that warranted shutting her out so wholeheartedly? It was all so fuzzy now.

What was I going to learn about myself if I kept reading that notebook?

Summer

NOLAN WANTED to come over for New Year's. I was excited, because that probably meant we would kiss at the turn of the year. I had never had a New Year's kiss before.

My mom put the countdown on the TV for us, but she stayed in her room until closer to midnight so we could have some privacy.

"Do you ever make New Year's resolutions?" Nolan asked.

I shook my head. "Not really. I never follow through with them, anyway."

"Well, what about... Where do you want to see yourself this time next year?"

I shrugged. "Passing all my classes? On track to graduate, I guess. You?"

"Both good things," he said. "I—hope we're like this, sitting together somewhere."

"Why wouldn't we be?"

"Sometimes I worry you'll just... see yourself somewhere else."

I laughed. "Where else would I see myself but with you? You're the first guy I—the first guy I've really liked."

He caressed my cheek with his thumb and said, "You're the first girl I've been in love with."

I grinned, almost unable to contain my excitement. "I—I love you, too."

"Well, good." He smirked. "I think that means this is gonna be a good year."

"The best."

My mother came back, gave us some party poppers, and poured three glasses of sparkling cider, and we watched the ball drop and the new year begin. Nolan kissed me at midnight, but only briefly since my mom was in the room.

"Happy new year, Summer," he said.

"Happy new year."

He had to go back home, but I couldn't stop smiling all night. I lay on my bed, staring up at the ceiling, thinking about our kiss and him telling me that he loved me.

A year ago, I never would've thought I was the kind of girl who could have something like this. But here I was...

Maybe I had deserved something like this all along.

8

Nolan

ESME SAID she'd meet me at the park on Sunday afternoon, but I could tell she was uncomfortable that it was just going to be the two of us. I wasn't sure how to frame it to make her feel any better. I told her I wanted to get Summer a present and needed another girl's opinion.

"So, what's so important that we couldn't just talk about it over text or on a phone call?" she asked as we took a seat on a bench.

"Can you just take a look at her notebook real quick?" I asked, tossing it to her. I hadn't touched it since Christmas. "Towards the back; the last page with writing on it."

"Why do you have Summer's notebook?"

"She left it at my place when we were studying," I lied. "Can you take a look at it?"

"Is this like a math notebook, or like a diary? I don't want to read—" She lifted the cover for just a second, then did a double-take and started flipping through. My heart pounded—what had she seen in that half a second that made her need to see the rest immediately?

"Uh, Nolan?" she asked. "This is blank."

"Blank?" I peered over her shoulder, but I could still see Summer's handwriting on all the pages. "Wait, are there stickers on the front cover?"

"No," she said. "I think you gave me the wrong notebook."

Frustrated, I took it from her and stared at it, trying to think of what to say next.

"I could've sworn Summer left her notebook in my room," I said. "But I guess this one is mine."

"Is that what you needed me for?" Esme asked.

"She had a list in the back of her notebook," I lied. "Stuff she wanted. I was gonna ask your opinion."

"And we couldn't talk about it over text?"

"...I'm more of a visual person when it comes to this kind of thing," I said, knowing it sounded stupid.

"I'm going to get going," she said. "This is weird. Please never invite me to hang out by myself again."

"Yeah, yeah, that's fine." I sighed. "I'm sorry."

"Are you *sure* there's nothing up?" she asked. "You're acting suspicious."

"I..." I had an idea. "I had a dream about Summer a couple nights ago," I lied. "Something happened to her. You were the only one with answers. I don't know why. And then when I saw the notebook, there was something written in it that worried me. Well, ideally, I would've actually had her notebook to show you, but I was hoping maybe you could give me some answers."

"I barely know Summer," she said. "But shoot: what was written in her notebook?"

"It was something about... dying." There wasn't anything like that—not that I had seen yet, at least, but I had to get to the subject.

"Dying how?"

"By... choice."

"By suicide?"

I nodded.

"If you think that's something she's thinking about," Esme said, "then it doesn't matter what kind of dream you think you had—you don't ask some random girl for help; you talk to *Summer* and get her to see a professional.

Maybe even talk to her parents. But never some random girl. Understand?"

"Yes."

"Are you asking me to talk to her?"

"No. Please, never tell her we had this conversation," I said. "If it's not something she's actually thinking about…"

"You don't want to give her ideas."

"Right."

"Or make her second-guess her behavior and why you misinterpreted it."

"Exactly."

"Okay, but consider this: if it *is* something she's thinking about, then she *needs* to talk to a professional," Esme said. "So do her a favor and figure out if she's thinking about it or not, because if she is and you just ignore this—"

"I won't," I said. "I can't. I have to help her, whatever it takes."

"Then talk to her, not me."

Summer

GOING BACK to school after a long break was never fun, but it was the start of a new semester and therefore the start of a fresh gradebook—meaning there was at least a brief window of hope for me.

I was doing well in English, though, so I wasn't worried about that class; Ms. Harris never gave me below a C+ on any assignment, and if I didn't earn a high enough grade, she'd talk to me after class, show me what I needed to fix, and give me a couple days to fix it. She'd always helped me out like that, ever since freshman English. I still remembered what she said the first time she pulled me aside freshman year:

"I know you can understand the material, Summer, and if you get stuck then it's my job as the teacher to help you. If learning the material was only about getting a passing grade on this assignment on a fixed due date with no exceptions, then why should I expect you to believe it's important enough

to learn? Now, let's take another look at question four."

I wished my other teachers were more like her. I might be in Algebra II if certain other teachers cared like she did. At least I'd passed the first semester of geometry, considering last year I'd ended first semester with a fifty-seven percent. With Nolan's help, I could probably pass this semester, too.

Nolan was acting weird around me, though. He barely spoke to me when we met at our lockers, and only kissed me lightly. It wasn't what I expected, considering he'd told me he loved me.

"Is everything okay?" I asked him, shutting my locker door.

"Yeah," he said absently. "Uh, did you leave a purple notebook at my house?"

I quickly rifled through my backpack to make sure it was still there. "No. It's right here," I said. "I don't remember ever bringing it to your house." I brought it to school to write in during class if I felt like it, but that was the only time it left my house, and I kept a close eye on it at all times when it wasn't in my backpack.

"Oh. Weird, I found one, but I don't recall owning a purple notebook," he said. "It was blank anyway."

"Alright."

"I *have* seen you write in that one before," he said. "I think, anyway. What's it for?"

"I'd rather not talk about it," I said. "It's personal."

"If it's personal, wouldn't you have a lock on it or something?"

"I just prefer regular notebooks," I said. "I have it with me at all times and I write personal things in it. Is that okay?"

"Yeah," he said. "Uh, I just had a weird dream about you. That's all."

"What kind of dream?"

"I don't remember," he said. "You had that notebook in it, though."

"Well, what happened?"

He shrugged. "I don't remember. I just know it wasn't a good ending. And it was something to do with your notebook. That's why I was just curious."

"Well, it's just a journal," I said. "No need to worry."

He nodded, hesitant. "If you say so."

Nolan

I HAD to get my hands on Summer's notebook somehow, see what kinds of things she was writing in it now, compare it to the other one. But she would notice if I tried to take it. I hadn't even finished reading the other one.

The thing I couldn't seem to place was *why* Summer's notebook had been in the lost and found in the first place. If she kept as close an eye on it as she implied, why was it somewhere for Tim to find and put in the lost and found? Did she leave it for someone to find?

Another memory from the old timeline resurfaced. That didn't happen often, and they weren't usually so vivid.

It was the very first informational meeting—one of the shorter, once-a-month ones that started back in March, not the all-day cultural seminars over the summer. It was a Saturday afternoon; I drove myself down to the community center, and Summer happened to be walking up the path to the entrance.

"Hi, Nolan!" She'd beamed, her smile lighting up her pale face. *"Are you coming on the Europe trip, too?"*

"I guess so." At that point, I had forgotten the trip was her suggestion in the first place, and I was disappointed to see her there.

She looked so different in that memory. She had no makeup on, and her hair was flat, worn down, and a little greasy; now she tied it up most of the time, and she put makeup on. She even dressed nicer now; that day she was wearing bright blue cropped sweatpants and a purple fitted T-shirt.

"Did you drive yourself here?" she asked.

"Yeah. You?"

"I took the bus," she explained. *"There's a stop a couple blocks from here,*

and it's a nice day, so it wasn't too bad to walk."

"Well, I'll see you around," I said, but she kept walking alongside me all the way into the multipurpose room, where she took a seat next to me.

"My best friend Marta is coming on the trip, too," she said, *"but something came up and she can't come to this meeting, so I'm supposed to take notes for her."*

That was when Esme came along. She took a seat on my other side, and I thought, *"Hey, at least a pretty girl is sitting near me now"*—I didn't realize she swung the other way until much later on.

"Summer, right?" she asked. *"From Anjana's youth group?"*

"Yeah." Summer couldn't seem to place her. *"Well, I only go on Christmas and sometimes Easter, but I know Anjana."*

"We met at Christmas; I'm Esme, remember?"

I sat between the two of them while they caught up and zoned out playing a game on my phone; I'm sure if I had been paying attention, I would've heard Esme mention how she knew Anjana and made that connection sooner, but I just couldn't stand the sound of Summer's voice shouting over me to Esme.

"I'm gonna go find this one guy I know," I lied; I didn't know anyone else on the trip at the time. *"I'll let you ladies catch up."*

I don't think I met Katie that day. I don't think she was there. The next thing I remembered was Summer catching up to me as I left the building.

"Are you so excited?" she asked me. *"I'm so excited."*

"I mean, it is a trip to Europe," I said.

"It's gonna be so great having someone else I know on the trip with me."

"Yeah, Esme seems nice."

"I meant you, silly," she said. *"I hardly know Esme. I just know her ex from youth group. But I think being on this trip together… we could finally get to know each other better. You and me, I mean. Like, we've known each other for so long, but we don't really hang out."*

"No, we don't, do we?" I tried not to roll my eyes. *"I don't know; you'll probably hang out with Marta, right? And I've got my buddy—"* I tried to remember the name of the guy I'd ended up talking to that day. I still don't remember; I think he pulled out of the trip before the summer meetings started.

"True. But we can still hang out sometimes," she said. *"Right?"*

"Sure. I'll see you at school." I waited until I was in my car with the windows rolled up to shout, *"Really, God? You had to send* her *on this trip, too?"*

I wondered if she was thinking about suicide then. Her journal had barely mentioned it up to where I'd read, and I was afraid to read more. When she did write about it, it came across like something she had thought of in the past, not something she was actively thinking of.

She also mentioned a friend named Bella who she knew in middle school but hadn't heard from in years, and being worried that Bella might have died by suicide. I vaguely remembered a girl named Bella in a couple of my classes, but I didn't think I'd ever talked to her.

I decided that the next step to get Summer to talk to me about her suicidal thoughts was to bring up Bella.

Summer

NOLAN WANTED to come over on Saturday to hang out. My mother would be home, which meant we could hang out in my room because she'd be able to hear any funny business from the kitchen.

"Mirrored closet doors, nice," he said.

"You don't have these?"

"Nope. I don't mind it, though. I've got a separate mirror."

I giggled to myself. "When I was little, I used to pretend that getting too close to the mirror could send you to a different universe."

"A different universe? Like, same people but different lives? Or, like, aliens?"

I shrugged. "I don't know. Just different. Like, maybe I was a princess, or...

maybe we were rich. Maybe I was popular. Maybe I had a boyfriend."

"Well, you've got at least one of those now," he said. "And—"

"If you call me 'your princess,' I'll make you go home."

"Okay, good to know." He laughed. "Do you still believe something like that could be possible? Like, a different universe where you have the opportunity to do things differently? But you're still the same person, and you have your same memories?"

"I don't know. I mean, it sounds impossible."

He put his hand up to the mirror. "How did it work? Do I push on it?"

I laughed. "If you push it off the runner, my mom will probably get even more mad than if we were actually doing anything in here."

"It's probably for the best." He took his hand away. "I like where we are now."

We kissed for a few seconds, then sat on the floor against my bed.

"Summer, do you remember a girl named Bella?" he asked. "From middle school?"

"Bella Montes?" I asked.

"Didn't you used to hang out with her?"

I smiled. "Yeah! She moved away, though. I don't know where she is now. Sometimes I wonder if she's even still alive."

"I'm sure she is," he said. "Some people just don't go online."

"Yeah, but she talked about—well, she never talked about suicide per se, but she talked about cutting. And people who cut are usually... well, you know."

He got quiet, but finally asked, "Have you ever...?"

"I don't." It was true. I hadn't in a while, not since the night of the party.

"You don't cut or you don't think about suicide?"

"Neither." Hadn't he asked me that before? Did it show somehow? How could he possibly know that I thought about it?

"That's good," he said. "If you do, though... you can tell me about it."

"I *don't*," I insisted.

"I know; I worded that badly," he said. "I just wanted to make sure you knew that you could talk to me about anything."

"Right now, I'd like to talk about anything else."

He nodded. "Sounds fair." He looked around the room. My walls weren't very decorated, just a few photos, birthday cards, and the occasional program from the conservatory's shows—I'd worked there over the past couple summers and always saw each play or musical at least once, since I got in for free once per show while I was working there.

"You've seen a lot of shows," he said.

"Not that many."

"More than me."

"Well, I *did* tell you that you were welcome to come see any of 'em while I was working there," I reminded him.

He sighed. "Yeah. I'm sorry I never took you up on that."

"It's no big deal," I said. "I get being busy and stuff."

"Yeah, but... I don't know. I just feel like I was rude about it."

"Well, I forgive you."

He half-smiled. "What's your favorite show that you've seen?"

"*Spring Awakening*," I said. "It was the first show they did last summer, and I actually paid to see it two more times after my free show. I bought the soundtrack, too."

"What's your favorite song from it?"

I opened my mouth to respond, but paused. My favorite song was called "And Then There Were None" because of the absolute *realness* of emotion it captured when it came to contemplating suicide. But if I told Nolan that, it would take us back to that conversation, and I didn't want to go back there—or give him reason to worry. It wasn't like that was something I was *actively* considering *now*.

"It's called 'The Mirror-Blue Night,'" I told him—my second favorite. "It's about struggling with coming-of-age, and, well, the guy who sang it at the conservatory was really good. And hot, not gonna lie."

"Do I have competition?" he asked playfully.

I laughed. "Well, considering he was nineteen and married, no," I said. "His husband isn't bad-looking, either, but somehow I think I have a better shot with you."

"Who says you have a shot with me?" he asked, sticking his tongue out.

"Let's not joke about that." I laughed uncomfortably. "How about we get some lunch?"

"Lunch sounds good."

Nolan

SUMMER'S FAVORITE musical was *Spring Awakening*. I'd seen it once— well, a bootleg of it that some chick I was seeing had. Technically, I hadn't seen it, because that was in the timeline that didn't exist anymore. But I remembered it well enough.

Having had her reassure me yet again that she didn't think about suicide... I needed to know, but I couldn't keep bringing it up with her. I wasn't going to get answers, and I was only going to upset her. So I turned to where I knew there might be answers: her old notebook.

As I kept reading, I learned that she and Jonah had broken up before Christmas. She'd dumped him because she realized he only wanted sex from her. And then she talked about *Spring Awakening*.

I don't feel bad about the breakup, but I don't feel good, either. It's like, one of those nights where I wonder if anything good can happen to me. I'm listening to music, and "And Then There Were None" comes on... and it just makes me think of how maybe one of these days I'll get tired of it. I'll get tired of waiting for something truly good to happen. I'll get tired of my life being like this, like some trial version of real life but I can't seem to find how to access the full version where good things happen. I'll get tired of being a burden to everyone. And I'll just… make it all stop.

I knew the entry was from the old timeline and she probably didn't feel that way anymore, but it was so eerie.

It was true that I didn't know how she'd died, but wasn't it obvious? And now it was less than six months from the day it'd happened, and I still didn't know how to stop it. I hoped I was doing the right things.

Summer

WE HAD a barricade drill in math class, which was the one class I had with Jonah. He had done a pretty good job of ignoring me since Nolan and I became official, but I suppose being stuck across from each other in a barricade of desks gave him a good opportunity to speak to me.

"So, Summer," he whispered. "You putting out for that guy you're with, or nah?"

I made the decision to not engage with him. This made him laugh.

"Oh, come on. I'm just joking," he said.

"Leave her alone, man," said Idris, a boy I'd known since middle school, seated a few people down from Jonah. His bright pink shirt popped against his dark skin and probably would've caught the attention of the hypothetical intruder we were barricading ourselves against.

It was nice of him to defend me. I wasn't sure he thought of me as a friend. We hadn't talked since middle school, and we usually just got into arguments over the best way to do a group assignment. I'd once had a crush on one of his friends who didn't like me back, which had caused some tension between us, too. It was surprising when I first saw him retaking geometry, though, because I'd always thought he was super smart.

"Since when do you care?" Jonah asked him. "Not like she's *your* girlfriend."

"No, but she's my friend," he said. "Right, Summer?"

"I—uh—right." *Were* we friends?

He nodded at me. "I got your back."

Jonah rolled his eyes, and I leaned back against the desk until the all-clear was given. We were dismissed for lunch shortly after, and Nolan met me at the door.

"Hey," he said. "How was your barricade?"

I shrugged. "Fine. Jonah tried to talk to me."

"Gross," he replied. "Do I need to take care of him for you?"

"No," I said. "Idris shut him up. You know him, right?"

"Yeah, we're buds," he said. "Well, we talk sometimes."

"He said we're friends, but we haven't talked since, like, eighth grade, and we weren't friends in middle school," I said.

He shrugged. "I don't know. Guys just tend to say that about girls they don't think negatively of. Like, if I don't dislike a chick, I'd say she's my friend, even if we aren't close."

"Oh." I paused. "Um, is that what you meant when you used to tell me *we* were friends? Like, before we started talking this year?"

He stopped in his tracks, like he was deep in thought about something. "Did—*did* I ever tell you we were friends?"

"I thought so. Well, maybe I just assumed, because we'd known each other so long and you were usually nice to me..."

"I was?"

"You said hi back and stuff, most of the time. I guess it doesn't matter now, though, right?"

He sighed. "I guess not, yeah. What matters is that now you're way more than my friend."

And he kissed me to prove it.

9

Nolan

My family didn't usually go anywhere for President's Week break, so that meant getting to spend more time with Summer, which was nice even if it was just watching movies at her place after her mother got home from work. Liam went somewhere snowy with his family, and Jake went to his grandparents' farm like he had over the summer. As always, he was sure glad to be back at school afterward.

Monday was Valentine's Day, which was exciting because I hadn't had a girlfriend on Valentine's Day since freshman year. I had already arranged to send Summer a singing valentine from the choir kids, along with whatever the GSA's "Valentine's grams" were, and I'd taped a red rose to her locker before she got to school.

As I waited by her locker, I saw a familiar dark-skinned woman heading into the main office. She was carrying a large box of equipment with her. I knew that woman... Who was she?

"Nolan!" Summer's voice startled me, and I realized she'd arrived at her locker. She beamed at the rose. "You so shouldn't have! You're too sweet!"

"Nothing's too sweet for you, Sum." I kissed her. "And speaking of sweet, how about we get some ice cream after school?"

"Okay." She smiled. "Um, can I pay for it, though? I feel like my present for you is going to be super underwhelming."

"I'll be the judge of that." I held my hand out.

She reached into her backpack and handed me a framed photograph. The frame was nice, some gold material that didn't look cheap, but the photo itself shocked me.

"Where did you get this picture?" I asked her.

In this photo, a young Summer and I sat on what looked like a red bounce castle. Was this fifth grade? It had to be; I had that stupid haircut.

"It's the last day of fifth grade," she said. "Do you remember? My dad took it."

I had no memory of this photo. And didn't Summer say her dad left? She never talked about him.

"He was in town for my fifth grade graduation," she explained after I didn't say anything. "And when he came to pick me up from school so my mom could work late, they had that carnival day for us, so he offered to wait for me so I could stay a bit longer. And he had his camera with him, so I asked him to take pictures of me with my friends. I thought I'd be brave and ask you if we could take a picture together. Do you remember that?"

If I thought really hard and looked at the picture, I could vaguely remember Summer asking if she could take a picture with me, because she was taking pictures with all of her friends—no, she'd said "classmates," but that wasn't true because I'd learned she didn't take any pictures with my friends when I asked them about it.

In the photo, it wasn't clear whether or not I wanted to be there—though I was sure I didn't. And then I remembered what Summer did with that picture— she had it up in her locker in sixth grade, and four different people asked me if Summer was my girlfriend during the first month of school, citing that our picture was in her locker, and I got tired of it.

I had Jake borrow his mother's stethoscope and had his older brother drop us off at the middle school on a Saturday, where we broke into Summer's locker and stole the picture, which Jake put through the paper shredder in his father's home office. I guess she'd never figured out I was the one who stole it.

"How long have you had this?" I asked her.

She shrugged. "My mom suggested I give you a framed picture of us, and when I was looking through our pictures, I remembered this one. I lost the copy I had all those years ago, so I asked my dad if he could send me the file so I could get it printed. Thankfully, he still had it."

"This is so cool," I told her. "Not underwhelming at all."

"Really?" She grinned. "You like it?"

"I love it," I assured her. "And I love you, Sum."

"I love you, too." She kissed me again.

"I'm gonna keep this in my room at home," I said, "where it's safe."

Summer

FOR MY second ever Valentine's Day with a boyfriend, today was better than I could have imagined. Jonah had just given me some cheap candy and called it a day, but Nolan sent me a singing Valentine's gram from the choir kids, *and* a couple of the GSA kids stopped by to give me a card and about half a jar of pink glitter that was probably still on my fingers from trying to get it off the desk.

Marta walked around all day with some stuffed animal Sutton had given her the night before, but I felt that my day was superior—not that it was a contest. Daisy and Ben had a dinner date planned.

Nolan drove me to the Baskin-Robbins, where we got a table and enjoyed our ice cream. I never wanted the day to end. It just felt so... perfect. Like this was all a dream.

But all good dreams must come to an end, because Marta called me at ten that night.

"Hello?" I answered. "I have to go to bed in, like, half an hour."

"I know, but Summer!" She giggled. "Guess what I did today! Guess!"

"Uh..."

"Sutton and I"—she lowered her voice to a whisper—"we had sex! We had sex!"

"What?" My eyes widened. "When?"

"In his car, like, two hours ago. My parents don't know, though, and don't tell your mom."

"You—you just—"

"I know!" She giggled some more. "I just feel so grown-up now, you know? Like, I am a woman now, and Sutton and I are for real. We're going to get married; I just know it!"

"So… was it good?"

"Of course it was good!" She seemed offended. "Why wouldn't it be good? Just because it was both of our first times doesn't mean we're automatically bad at it."

"So it didn't hurt, like my mom says it will?"

"Well, I mean, obviously it did at first, but it was still magical. Gosh, Summer, why can't you just be happy for me?"

"Sorry." I sighed. "Um, what did it feel like?"

"Words can't describe it," she said. "You just have to experience it for yourself. Hopefully Nolan will be as good as Sutton was. You really would have no idea it was his first time, too."

"Maybe it wasn't?" *Shit, no, don't say that!*

She gasped, obviously offended. "What? No, Summer! You just don't understand because you're a clueless virgin, but when two people love each other as much as Sutton and I do, it's good because of the magic that love creates! Obviously!"

"Sorry!" I said again. "You're right. I'm just a stupid virgin. What do I know?"

"Whatever. I'll see you tomorrow."

Nolan

I HAD almost forgotten about the woman in the front office yesterday morning until my APUSH teacher announced that we would be going to an assembly during class for Anti-Bully Week.

I remembered in the old timeline, when she'd told us that, a couple of the guys and I rolled our eyes and talked about how stupid this assembly was going to be.

Our school didn't have a bullying problem, so we didn't need this stupid assembly.

I had hated listening to Leah Browning talk about how her niece was bullied to the point of taking her own life because I didn't believe suicide was anyone's fault but the person doing it to themself. I felt I was a perfectly kind person and Leah Browning was just telling us all to walk on eggshells lest we offend someone and they decide to kill themselves about it.

Now I cringed remembering what I said to Liam and Jake at lunch: *"If that chick had just sucked it up a little longer, we could've used that chunk of time for something actually useful, like studying for the APUSH test."* They'd given me an uncomfortable look but hadn't told me how out of line I was.

Now, for Leah Browning's entire assembly, I couldn't help but think about Esme's implication that I had said or done something to Summer before she'd died. What if I *had*? I guess it didn't matter anymore, but it so easily could. I so easily could have *not* been sent back in time and had this chance to be a better person to her. I so easily could have had to live with knowing that I was at least part of the reason someone had died that way.

There were kids who'd told Leah Browning's niece to kill herself in text messages and spent years telling her she was a fat whore who would never have any real friends and would never be loved by anyone; those assholes had spray-painted the n-slur on her locker, and the principal had only suspended them for three days and made them wash it off. I hoped they had to live every day for the rest of their lives with the knowledge of what they'd done, if I didn't personally back them all over with my truck before today was over.

It could have been Summer, a voice kept echoing in my head. *It could have been Summer, and the asshole could have been you.*

But I'd never told her anything that horrible. I could take comfort in that much—the things people said to Leah Browning's niece were disgusting, but I'd never said anything like that to Summer. At least, I didn't think I had.

As everyone was claiming their free "be kind" wristbands and stickers, I approached Leah at the front table.

"Hi," I said.

"Hi!" she responded, awfully chipper considering the subject matter of her presentation.

"Uh, I just wanted to say thank you," I said. "For raising awareness and all. Some idiots just don't realize how their words and actions affect people."

She gave me a half-smile but didn't say anything right away. Then finally, she said, "Remember to be kind."

I nodded. "I will."

Summer

ANITA PRUNELL was seventeen years old last March when she died by suicide. She would've turned eighteen last June. She liked to dance, but quit dance classes in seventh grade because she was being bullied about her weight and her race. She'd never had a boyfriend or a girlfriend, but sometimes popular guys would flirt with her as a joke. She stopped getting her hopes up. She was very beautiful, but because she was a few sizes larger than the popular girls, they convinced her she was ugly. Some people wrote slurs on her locker because of her skin color. The other kids told her on a regular basis that she should kill herself, and they gave her what they perceived to be good reasons to do so. On March 14, almost a whole year ago, she listened.

I could've been friends with Anita Prunell. We probably had more in common than one would think. I couldn't stop thinking about her all day. At lunch, I stayed and talked to her aunt, Leah, who'd run the assembly. I wanted to know more about Anita. I wanted to know more about her life before she'd died. I wanted to feel like I knew her, because in some ways, it felt like I did.

But amidst thinking of all the ways I would try to help Anita Prunell if I could go back in time and find her, the worst thought I could possibly imagine popped into my head:

If it were me, would we be having an assembly?

Who thought like that?

Stupid, selfish Summer. You're a horrible, selfish person. You should've been the one to get hit by that car in eighth grade, and it should have killed you, and you would have deserved it because you're so selfish. And nobody would care because you're not a good person. You're not worth missing. You're not worth cancelling classes over, you're not worth an assembly, you're not worth—

"Hey, Sum."

I was at my locker. In front of me, Nolan was waiting.

"Hey," I said.

"Where were you at lunch?"

"Oh, uh, we had that assembly right before lunch, and I stayed and talked to Leah for a while," I said. "She told me more about what Anita was like growing up. It was nice."

"Do you ever think, like, I don't know..." Nolan hesitated. "If she could see how many people care about her, she wouldn't have done it? Like, the effect she's had?"

"I think that's the point," I said. "She didn't have that effect on anyone before she died, and then people realized, 'Oh, shit, my words and actions actually affect people.' Hell, half our school still doesn't care. The girls I sat behind were playing games on their phones through the whole assembly."

"Well, her aunt sure cared about her. Enough to do these assemblies to try and raise awareness."

"I don't think it's enough to know people care," I said. "It's about feeling like generally, people's lives would be better *without* you. She probably felt like she was burdening her loved ones in some way. I don't know. Her bullies told her she was worthless and the world would be better off without her, and she internalized it until she actually believed it. Like, 'My parents love me, but why would I burden them with my existence when I'm all these terrible things?'"

"But you know that's not true, right? You know all the things they said about her were—"

"I know," I said. "But I'm an outsider. Even if I had been friends with her, I don't know if I could've helped her. It takes so much work to undo that kind of damage. Once you start to believe you're a burden, I'm not sure you ever really stop. Not without, like, professional help. Like therapy or something."

"I just wish there was some way to let the people who think like that know how much they matter," he said. "You know? Show them how much their death would really affect people."

I nodded, but there was something he didn't get. Not everyone who died by suicide would get an assembly. Not because they didn't deserve it or because they didn't matter. But sometimes people just died, and life went on for most of the world. Even for their friends and families, life eventually went on.

Some people were Anita Prunells, who would end up leaving a bigger mark on the world, and some people were *"Wait, what was her name again?"* who everyone would either mourn or pretend to cry over for a few days before they realized they didn't actually care *that* much about her, and she was never *that* important, and nobody would think it was important to learn from her death, either.

I could guarantee more than half the people who'd taken a wristband or a sticker from Leah Browning today would be just as vile tomorrow. They wanted to help; they wanted suicides to stop, but they didn't want to change anything about themselves. They just wanted people like Anita Prunell to grow a thicker skin.

Nolan

SUMMER HAD mentioned feeling like a burden before, hadn't she? She definitely had in her notebook, but none of that was in this timeline.

I couldn't stop thinking about our conversation. She was talking about

Anita Prunell… or was she? Was she also talking about herself?

I tried to find an entry in her journal from today's date. Even if none of what was written mattered in terms of her current feelings, it would at least give me an idea of what she'd thought of the assembly, wouldn't it?

But she hadn't written anything. Her entries jumped from a Valentine's Day spent alone to March 14, and all that was written for that date was: *One day it could be me.*

The next entry was from two days later:

I haven't been able to write in this book for a while now. I don't want to get into it. I just keep thinking… No, I don't want to get into it.

What I do want to talk about is Marta. She and Sutton hooked up on Valentine's Day. They had sex. At least that's what she told me. And then he didn't talk to her for two weeks. She said it was so good or whatever, like I even know what makes sex "good." But then he didn't talk to her for two weeks. She didn't say why, but she posted a picture with him and so I assumed they were speaking again. She says their relationship is just more complex now, because they're having sex. She says they were each other's first, but I don't know if I believe that. Especially if he was "good" the first time. My mom says a guy won't be good the first time, and that even if it isn't his first time, my first time will hurt, at least somewhat.

I didn't tell my mom Marta's having sex. Marta would be so mad. She already got mad when I brought up that ~maybe~ she wasn't Sutton's first time. But he would never lie to her. I just don't know anything because I'm a dumb virgin who's never even had a good boyfriend—Jonah doesn't count, obviously. But I'm glad I never had sex with him, if sex changes everything about how you communicate with each other.

I guess that's part of why I don't want to have sex, at least not right now, even if I was dating someone I really liked. Besides being freaked out by the thought of it. I don't want everything to change. There's so much at stake, emotionally, not even counting the physical risks like STDs and pregnancy which could mostly be prevented with the right protection.

I don't know. I guess it's good that I don't have a boyfriend. I don't have to worry about any of this stuff.

So that was her deal with sex. Maybe I needed to talk to her about it, assure her I wasn't like Sutton—well, not entirely. I'd be lying if I said I'd never hooked up with a girl and then stopped talking to her. But Summer was different—I loved Summer, and I wouldn't do that to her.

I didn't want to wait a whole month to have that conversation with her, though. I decided I'd ask her about Marta tomorrow and see how much I could get her to talk about.

Summer

"WHAT'RE YOU doing after school today?" Marta asked when she came to my locker in the morning.

"I was just going to go home," I said. "Why?"

"So you don't have plans with Nolan?"

"No, we don't usually hang out after school," I said. I realized she might take that the wrong way. "Not because he doesn't want to; he's offered, I just like having the time to myself." *Please don't make me make unexpected changes to my routine; that's only okay when I initiate it.*

"Well, can I come over?" she asked.

I bit my lip—I didn't want to say no because I didn't want to be rude, but I *liked* my routine. "You don't have plans with Sutton? Don't you usually hang out after school?"

She shook her head, annoyed. "You just don't get it, Summer, because you've never had sex."

"Hey, say that louder next time." I cringed, shutting my locker door. "What don't I understand? That you can't hang out anymore?"

"Not every day!" She rolled her eyes. "After sex, guys tend to just… not talk to you for a while."

"A while?" My heart pounded. "That sounds awful. How long is 'a while?'"

"I don't know. He'll talk to me when he talks to me."

"Are you *sure* it was his first time, too?"

"Why wouldn't I be sure?"

Nolan's voice startled both of us. "Guy drama?"

I bit my lip again, because I knew Nolan had had sex before. But maybe he could help, then.

"How long do you wait to talk to a girl after you have sex for the first time?" I asked.

"Well, we usually talk for a little bit right after, before I go home or take her home," he said. "Then I'll probably text her the next morning if I'm not gonna see her at school. Why?"

Marta frowned. "Well, aren't guys supposed to wait a few days?"

"Why?" he asked.

"Because… well, you're a guy; you should know!"

He sighed. "To put it bluntly, if a guy doesn't talk to you for a few days after sex, either you were bad at it or he isn't looking for a relationship."

"Well, what if you're already *in* a relationship? And you were his first time, too? Huh? And don't tell me it was bad because trust me: it was good!"

"How do you know it was good?" Nolan asked. "I was terrible my first time; the girl didn't even fake it. She just asked me to stop."

"Did you talk to her after?" I asked.

"Yeah, it wasn't her fault I was bad," he said. "We'd been dating for a few months, too, so I wasn't gonna *not* talk to her."

"Forget it!" Marta folded her arms over her chest. "You've made your point!

You two are such the perfect couple and Sutton was only using me this whole time and lying to me. I get it! Well, you're wrong, and you know what else?" She looked right into my eyes, making me uncomfortable, and I glanced away. "You are a *horrible* friend for suggesting that!"

She stormed away, and Nolan put his arms on my shoulders. "She doesn't mean that," he said quietly. "She's just upset because she knows you're right."

"I never said that, though," I told him. "I just didn't understand why a guy wouldn't talk to a girl after doing that. And she said it was good, so I was just thinking maybe he was lying about it being *his* first time because my mom always said—"

"She's probably just saying it was good so you'll be jealous of her 'perfect' relationship," he assured me. "Trust me, chicks do that all the time. She's jealous that your boyfriend is obviously better than hers, so she's just trying to one-up you." He gave me a playful smirk. "Don't worry, Sum. She's just upset about *her* issues and she's taking it out on you."

I hesitated. "Listen, if we ever—if we ever *do it*—"

"I wouldn't stop talking to you," he said, then added with a smirk, "even if you're bad at it."

"There's just... so much uncertainty." I sighed. "I'm sorry if I'm making you wait longer than you want to. I'm just not ready."

"That's fine," he said. "The last thing I want is to make you feel pressured, you know?"

I nodded, and the bell rang. "Walk me to class?"

"Of course."

Nolan

"MARTA!"

I managed to catch her leaving the classroom across from mine, so it was a good chance to talk without Summer knowing. I felt weird getting involved in Summer's business, but since I was sure the whole point of being sent back in time was to be involved in Summer's business, I wanted to do my best to be there for her.

"What?" Marta asked. "Here to apologize? Or is Summer making you apologize for *her*?"

"Summer doesn't know I'm talking to you," I said. "I think *you* should apologize to *her*. You had no right to say that to her this morning."

"Like you know anything about our friendship!" She scoffed. "Summer's just jealous of me. She always has been. That's what you're dating, Nolan: a jealous wannabe who won't even put out for you. Isn't that sad?"

"Some friend you are."

"Shut up! Like I said, you know nothing about us! Did you know that when I got my first iPod in fourth grade, she told me she was going to get the same one? Huh? And did she tell you that when I got one of those custom look-alike dolls for Christmas, she told me she was saving up her allowance to buy one? Because she *always* has to copy me. I bet she only dated you because she was jealous of my relationship and she wanted to have what I had. Well, I'm sure you're a nice guy and all, but you two will *never* have what Sutton and I have."

I rolled my eyes. "Yeah, he hasn't talked to you since you had sex however many days ago; I'm *so* threatened by the stability of your relationship. God, I hope Summer and I never have a relationship like yours."

"It was two days ago, asshat!" she barked. "Stop acting like you know my business. Just know that Summer is the jealous type and if you keep dating her, she'll probably start copying everything you do, too."

"Well, while you're waiting for Sutton to call you, at least you'll have plenty of time to go fuck yourself."

I waved and kept walking towards Summer's classroom. How did Summer put up with her? Was this the first time Marta had gotten mad at her? Because if anyone had treated me like that, I would've cut them off before they ever had the chance to do it again.

Summer

I STARED at my ceiling, then checked the clock again: 2:58. And I hadn't fallen asleep yet.

Nolan didn't tell me what he'd said to Marta, but he warned me she might be upset because he tried to talk to her. It was weird, because Marta and I used to get in fights all the time when we were kids, but it had been years since she'd stopped speaking to me over something.

A part of me knew I needed to fight for our friendship and apologize for whatever it was I did. Usually I was the one who did something wrong. Even if I didn't realize what it was, I was always the one who needed to apologize. I'd gotten used to it.

But if we didn't make up, another part of me... would be sort of relieved. We did have a good friendship. But she had so many expectations for me, and the way that lately I couldn't even *suggest* something contrary to what she said without her flipping out—it wouldn't be so bad to have a break from that.

There were a few times in middle school when I could have stopped being friends with Marta. I always went back to her, though, after our fights. I had a hard time cutting people off, even toxic people. Not to say she was toxic, but... well, maybe she was. But she *had* been there for me... Physically, she'd been there, even if she never wanted to let me talk about my problems. I couldn't cut her off. I just couldn't.

Our fights were so stupid, back in the day. She once threatened to stop speaking to me "forever" in fourth grade because I'd told her I couldn't read one of the words she'd written in cursive in a note to me. She'd forgotten about it by the end of the day, but that was how most of our fights were.

She got an iPod for her birthday that year, a pink iPod like the one I'd kept showing my mom pictures of. Marta didn't even like pink back then. I told her it was so cool and that I'd been wanting one just like it, that I was hoping to get one for Christmas. She told me I would have to get a different brand because if

I got an iPod, I'd be copying her, even if I got a different color.

When my mom managed to save up enough money and surprised me with the pink iPod for Christmas, I hid it from Marta for months. I wasn't allowed to bring it to school, anyway, because it was so expensive, but I would hide it in my underwear drawer every time she came over and I told my mom not to mention it while Marta was over. She was confused, so I lied and said Marta might be jealous, and then hoped my mom never saw Marta's iPod, despite Marta practically waving it around in my face for months on end and telling me about all the cool things it did.

When Marta eventually found out that I did have an iPod, she said at least it was a different model than hers. Mine was actually a newer model, but apparently Marta's was still better because it was easier to hold on to and the battery lasted longer and it had better games on it. But I didn't care, and she got an even newer one a year later. I had a newer iPhone than her now—but we didn't talk about that.

In fifth grade, she got this custom-made just-like-you doll for Christmas. She brought it over to my house to show me, and I pulled out a mangled five-year-old catalog from the company that I had under my bed and showed her the order form I'd filled out when the catalog had come to our house. I told her I'd wanted one of those dolls so badly but it was too expensive for my mom, so I just looked at the catalog and hoped someday I could have one, but I was really excited that she'd gotten one.

She told me I couldn't get one of those dolls, because that would be copying her—even though she'd never expressed interest in having a doll like that before. She suggested I get another American Girl doll. Marta and I *did* used to bond over those catalogs when we were younger. But she stopped playing with them as much, and then suddenly she was all about this custom-made doll that only *she* could have.

So when my birthday was coming up and my mom asked if I still wanted one because she just might be able to afford it that year, I told her I was too old to be getting a doll. Instead, she got me a necklace-and-earrings set with my birthstone. I wore the necklace to Marta's house and she kept commenting on how ugly it was, even saying that she hoped it fell off in my sleep and her dog ate it so she'd never have to see it again.

But then a couple weeks later when she was at my house, she noticed the matching earrings still in their box. She asked me if I liked them, and I said I did but they weren't my favorite.

She then pointed out that I had a lot of earrings—and it was true: I had a ton of earrings from Claire's. But these ones were expensive, even if I didn't like them that much. I just wasn't a fan of the diamond shape, and I thought clear was kind of a boring color for earrings.

At school the next day, Marta told me that since I had so many earrings, I should give her the new pair because she didn't have a lot of earrings, and it wasn't like I even liked that pair. I thought that sounded fair, so I told her I would bring them tomorrow. She told me to make sure I didn't tell my mom I was giving them to her.

I was nervous, because my mom had spent a lot of money on those earrings for me, and what if she noticed they were gone? When I went to put the earring box into my backpack, my mom walked in and saw me. She asked what I was doing, and I told her that because I didn't like the earrings that much and I had so many other pairs, I was going to give them to Marta because she really liked them and she didn't have a lot of earrings.

My mom told me that those earrings were too expensive to give away, but I was more than welcome to give Marta one or two of my cheaper pairs. So I brought all the pairs I didn't like to school and told Marta she could pick any two pairs she wanted. When she asked why I didn't have the diamond earrings, I explained that my mom had caught me and told me they were too expensive, but I could give her any of my other pairs.

Of course, we got into a fight because the whole point was to give Marta the diamond earrings, and she didn't want any of my cheap ugly earrings, and not giving her the diamond earrings was selfish of me, and I wasn't supposed to tell my mom, and she said she was never going to speak to me again. She even sent another girl in our class over to explain to me that Marta was never going to speak to me again. The girl pointed across the playground to Marta, who was wishing on a dandelion: *"Right now, she's wishing that you die. That's how much she hates you."*

She tried a couple more times to convince me to give her the earrings before eventually letting it go. They were still at the bottom of my jewelry box and I'd never worn them, not because they were ugly, but because I would feel bad—Marta liked them so much more than I did, and she wanted them, but I wasn't allowed to give them to her.

I wondered if this fight about Sutton would go on long. I almost hoped it did, but then I felt bad, because a good friend wouldn't hope that.

Maybe Marta was right all those years ago—maybe I *had* been selfish. And maybe I *was* selfish. And maybe I *was* a horrible friend.

As quietly as I could, I went down the hall to my bathroom. When I flushed, I reached into the cabinet for a razor while the sound covered my tracks. When I finished washing my hands, I kept the water running for a little bit longer while I broke the plastic off the end.

When I got back to my room, I threw away the plastic bit under some tissues, pushed my "BE KIND ~ AP" wristband out of the way, and did the only thing I knew how to do when I didn't want to think about everything that was wrong with me.

10

DID I make things worse for Summer by talking to Marta? Marta was her best friend. They'd always been best friends, for as long as I could remember. If I saw Summer around, Marta was usually there with her. Whether or not she was a *good* friend was certainly up for debate, but they were close.

I reached under my bed and pulled out a stack of elementary school yearbooks. Right on top was fifth grade, so I opened it up to the group photo of our class. Sure enough, Summer and Marta were sitting next to each other—*man, they look different.* Marta's hair was in short pigtails and Summer had French braids. Summer was wearing an ugly dress; I remembered something about how her mother always handmade her dresses for picture day. The photo was in black and white, but I could tell the dress was some kind of floral print. It looked like the kinds of dresses girls on those extremist Christian cult reality shows wore: big, boxy sleeves, mid-calf length, high neckline. By contrast, Marta was wearing a T-shirt with a bunch of hearts on it and a knee-length denim skirt. Both of them had ugly sandals with huge fake flowers on them, paired with crew socks.

Underneath the class photo were some candids, and among those was a picture of Summer and Marta hugging in front of the classroom—this time, Summer was wearing a normal T-shirt. There was one of Liam and me on the playground; he was holding a soccer ball. In the middle of the book, there was a signature page—a special addition just for fifth graders' yearbooks—with lines for *"Name," "Phone Number,"* and *"Middle School"* so we could stay in touch with our friends who were going to different schools.

I remembered Summer asking me to sign hers, which had made me hopeful that maybe we were going to different middle schools, though we'd both ended up going to Elmont. I didn't remember what I'd written in her yearbook, but here in mine, in the middle of the list in bad cursive, she'd written:

Summer Madison | (408) 555-7026 | Elmont

Underneath her number in small, printed handwriting, she had also written, *"call anytime between 9 am/pm,"* but of course I'd never called her. I didn't remember asking her to sign my yearbook, but I must have grudgingly handed it over as a trade for hers.

Finally, in the back of the yearbook, I found what I was looking for: baby pictures. Much like eighth graders and seniors, fifth graders' parents had the option to send in baby pictures of their graduating students. Each person got a quarter of a page, and parents sent in however many pictures they could fit along with whatever note they wanted to write. They cost money to include.

Summer didn't have one, but Marta did, and one of the three pictures her parents had squeezed onto the page included Summer. It was a recent-at-the-time picture of both girls wearing matching shirts that, when they stood next to each other, read "best friends." Marta's shirt was the one that said "best."

Tomorrow, I would have to ask Summer if she wanted to stay friends with Marta. Maybe it wasn't too late to apologize—even if there was no way in hell I was going to mean it.

Summer

AT SCHOOL, Marta was waiting by my locker. I was surprised to see her there, but once she opened her mouth, I realized she wasn't here to make up.

"Your boyfriend is an asshole," she said. "You need to break up with him."

"What'd he do?" I asked.

"Does it matter? I said he's an asshole, so if you care about our friendship, you need to break up with him."

"Wait, so we're still friends?"

"Are you going to break up with Nolan?"

"I can't just break up with him if you don't give me a reason!" I didn't want to break up with Nolan, but if he'd done something *that* bad...

"I gave you a reason: he's an asshole."

I rolled my eyes. "What did he do specifically?"

"He acted like an asshole."

Before the conversation could go any further—or rather, anywhere at all—Nolan showed up.

"Hey, Sum," he said, greeting me with a quick kiss as usual. "You two friends again?"

"That's up to Summer," Marta said. "Summer, do you have anything you'd like to talk to Nolan about?"

"What did you do yesterday?" I asked him.

He sighed, like he didn't want to say anything. "Marta, I'm sorry I told you that you were a bad friend, and I'm sorry I wasn't as sensitive as I should have been about whatever's going on with you and Sutton."

I looked at Marta to see if that was what she was referring to. She kept her brows knit and her arms crossed.

"Would you want to date a guy who yells at your best friend?" Marta asked.

I glanced back at Nolan. I wished I knew more about what had happened between them.

"What did you do?" I asked him.

"I didn't like how she treated you," he said. "But I guess it wasn't my place to say anything."

I knew what I wanted to say, and my heart was pounding as I faced Marta.

Could I really say it? Could I really be so brave?

"I would rather date a guy who stands up for me," I said, "than a guy who doesn't call me after we have sex."

Her jaw dropped and her eyes practically popped out of her head; I hadn't seen her this genuinely shocked since Brad Carter had started his planet project presentation in fifth grade with, *"Let's talk about ur anus."* I didn't think she'd expected me to stand up for myself any more than I had. I was kind of glad Nolan was standing close enough to catch me should my legs give out.

Marta tried to mask her shock. She narrowed her gaze at me, like she was expecting me to take it back, to say I didn't mean it. But after all these years, I had finally said something assertive, and I wasn't ready to let go of that just yet.

"So you're choosing him over me?" she asked. "Your best friend since we were kids?"

I held firm, but my moment of bravery was gone. I couldn't say anything else. I couldn't even nod or shake my head. I just blinked at her while I tried to remember what words were.

"Are you going to say anything?" she asked after what felt like an hour. I just stared at her. She waved her hand in my face. "Hello? Are you retarded or something?"

I wasn't sure if it was from hearing my mother use that word so often—directed at me—or hearing Marta use it in passing so often over the years, but I was so desensitized to the term that Nolan's response almost scared me:

"What the fuck did you just say?" he yelled. "Don't you *ever* say that about her! Don't you *ever* say that about *anyone*!"

"Don't *you* tell me what to do!" she fired back. "I'm done. I'm gone. I'm out of here. Good luck with him, Summer. Or maybe I should wish Nolan good luck with you—a guy like that will never be happy dating a retard. Yeah, I said it again! What're you gonna do? Tell the dean? He's too busy enforcing the 'no hats and hoods' policy to care."

As she stormed away, Nolan shouted across the hall, "Go fuck yourself with a cactus, bitch."

The bell rang before anyone in the hall could react. Before I could run off to class, Nolan grabbed my hand until I looked up at him.

"It's not true, what she said," he told me. "You're not... that."

"I know," I said.

"Are you okay?"

I shrugged.

"I think you made a good choice," he said. "But I may be biased, since your choice benefits me a lot."

I laughed weakly. "We'll see how it goes. And who knows? She may come crawling back like she always does." *And convince me to apologize.*

Or maybe I was just telling myself that, because then I could ignore the possibility that this might really be the end for us.

Nolan

SUMMER LET me come over after school, but I could tell she was nervous about it because her mother wouldn't be home. I wondered if she thought I was going to try to have sex with her. I just didn't want her to be alone in case she was really upset about the Marta incident. I wondered if maybe, once we were alone, she'd talk about it more.

When I watched her turn the key in the front door, I noticed dark red lines on her arm.

"Your arm okay, Sum?" I asked, not sure *how* to ask her if they were what I thought they were.

She looked down at her wrist and paused for a second, totally silent. Then: "Oh, where'd that come from?"

There was enough confusion in her voice that I could probably believe her...

"Isn't that the same place you accidentally cut your arm in the shower a few months ago?"

She shook her head. "I don't think so. I don't know. It's not like I write down every little injury I get in my journal."

No, she definitely didn't.

"Alright." I'd drop it, for now.

She rubbed at her wrist. "So, uh... did you want to work on homework together or something?"

As we stepped into her entryway, I realized what I wanted to do, since we were at her house.

"Do you have any old yearbooks?" I asked her. "I was looking through some of mine last night."

Her eyes lit up. "Yeah! Come on. I'll show you."

I followed her down the hallway to her room, where she opened her closet door and reached for a stack of books.

"Any year you had in mind?" she asked, setting the stack down on her bed.

"How about..." I reached for fifth grade, trying to make it look random. "This one?"

I opened it up to the inner cover to see who had signed it:

Marta HAGS see you at Elmont!!

Texanah (408) 555-2509

ISABEL

Daisy Cabedo HAGS

"You were friends with Isabel?" I asked. That was such a weird dynamic; Isabel was very different from Summer. She'd been one of the biggest party girls in our grade before she'd dropped out last year to have a baby.

Summer shuddered. "No. She used to bully me, actually, in middle school.

I don't even know why she signed my yearbook. She just took it from me and wrote her name in it. She didn't even ask me to sign hers."

"Isabel bullied you?" I knew she was a party girl, but she'd never struck me as a bully.

"Oh, yeah, constantly. She'd yell that I was walking too slowly back to the locker room in gym. She'd come up to me at the library and ask me a bunch of rude questions like if I was even passing the class I was studying for. Once she accused me of copying her math homework and we had to have a whole meeting with the teacher and my mom. Oh, and in seventh grade, she pulled a chunk of hair out of my hair tie right before it was my turn to take my class picture, then pointed it out to me as if I didn't just feel her pull it out."

"Wow."

"She stopped in high school. Freshman year, she never even spoke to me. Last year she asked if she could have some pencil lead in math, then acted like giving it to her was the nicest thing anyone had ever done. It was weird. I heard she has a kid now, though."

"Yeah." I stared back at the sparse signature page. "Who else signed? This can't be everyone."

"That's fifth grade, right? There should be more on that insert thing they gave us."

"Oh, right."

I flipped to the middle, but there were hardly any signatures there either—

Marta | (408) 555-2764 | Elmont

Daisy | (408) 555-2339 | Elmont

Nolan | you | rock

Stephanie | (408) 555-7224 | Benton

"Did I really write this?" I asked.

She looked over my shoulder and laughed. "Yes. Oh, my gosh. I was *so* nervous to ask you to sign mine, and you didn't even write your phone number! And I was so worried you weren't going to Elmont because you didn't write it."

Now I remembered. I didn't want to give Summer my phone number, so I'd written that hoping she wouldn't read too much into it. Looking back, I probably could've just written my number wrong by "accident" or something to make her feel better, but it didn't matter now.

"You didn't have a lot of friends back then, did you?"

She shook her head. "I still don't."

"Well, you've got Daisy, right?"

"Yeah. We talk every other day in gym."

"And how about Anjana and Esme from your youth group?"

She shrugged. "We're friends online. I think they broke up, though. We don't really talk. They're nice."

"Well, if you want my opinion, they're better friends than Marta."

She chuckled. "Let's not talk about her."

"Alright. Did your parents get you one of those baby pages?"

"No, we couldn't really afford it. My mom said she'd get me one for senior year. I'm in one of Marta's pictures, though, because my mom asked her parents if they could put in a picture of both of us so I could be in the baby pages."

"That's sweet of her parents to do that."

"Would've been sweeter if she didn't throw it into an argument two years later about how she had to sacrifice her baby page because I was too poor to afford my own."

I shut the yearbook. "You know you're way better off without her, right?"

"I guess."

"Hey, pretty soon, the informational meetings for the Europe trip will start," I told her. "We'll probably meet some cool people there."

"Yeah."

She was going to be fine. I had to believe she would be.

* * *

WHEN I got home, I got Summer's old notebook out and flipped through looking for Marta's name so I could figure out what had happened to them in the old timeline. I had to know if Summer really needed her or not.

June 18th—

I saw something really bad today. My mom wanted to go to the mall together, but I convinced her to go to the one across town just in case everyone really was going to the mall and they just told me they decided not to—I didn't want to run into them and look pathetic.

Right. This was during the three weeks of intensive meetings right before the trip. Summer had overheard a few of us making plans to go to the mall that Saturday, and she'd asked if she could come, too. That had to be towards the beginning of the week. We'd said yes, but I told them we should tell her on Friday that we'd changed our minds and weren't going after all so we wouldn't have to hang out with her. Katie said it was mean, but she still went along with it. Summer probably wasn't a stranger to having that happen if she'd guessed it so spot-on. I kept reading.

My mom hates going to that mall because it's so expensive, but I told her I wanted lunch from the noodle place that our mall doesn't have. So she finally agreed. And what did I see while waiting in line at the noodle place? Who was in line in front of me?

SUTTON AND NOT MARTA!! As in, Sutton was very obviously on a date with someone else. Unless he puts his hand on all his friends' asses while waiting in line for noodles and makes out with them at the pickup area.

I don't think he even knows who I am. We've only met once, and he clearly saw me at the noodle place. I feel like if he remembered that I'm Marta's friend, he wouldn't have kept touching that other girl in front of me.

How do I tell her? Do I even tell her? Do I wait for her to find out? She wouldn't believe me. I should've gotten pictures as proof but I was afraid they'd see me. And then maybe she'd be like, "Why'd you just take pictures? Why didn't you yell at him for me? I would've yelled at a guy for you!" I doubt she would, though—yell at a guy for me. She'd probably just tell me that I was overreacting.

I don't know what to do. I'm a shitty friend. That's all I know.

I skipped to the next entry with Marta's name:

June 22nd—

Well, I told Marta. I went back and forth about it all week, but I finally told her. It went just about as well as I thought it would. She doesn't believe me. She thinks I'm just jealous of her and making shit up so she'll break up with Sutton and be a single loser like me. So we're not friends anymore. For now. Maybe for real this time.

Maybe she'll talk to me tomorrow. I don't even know who I'm going to hang out with on this trip now. Hopefully she forgives me before next week. Or apologizes, but that's a stretch. She never apologizes. I'm probably better off without her, but who am I going to hang out with in Europe if not Marta?

The next entry was two days later:

June 24th—

I don't know what to do. I can tell nobody else on the trip wants me there, even the few who are actually nice to me sometimes. And Marta... she's got her new, better friends now and doesn't need me. She never needed me. This fight was just a way out for her.

I couldn't keep reading. I realized that I was reading the *last* entry. My stomach was turning. That entry was the last thing Summer had written before she'd killed herself—well, before she'd died.

Summer needed Marta because Marta was all she had... but now, in this timeline, that wasn't true. She had Daisy, though Daisy wasn't going on the

Europe trip. By the time we were on that trip, I'd make sure she had Esme, and... she'd have me.

Summer

"MIDDLE COLLEGE?" I asked blankly.

Daisy nodded. "It's going to help my college apps so much," she said. "I just feel so *done* with the 'high school experience.' Middle college courses actually *mean* something to most universities, versus APs, which are pretty much just for show unless you get fives on the exams, and even then it's a coin toss."

I tried to process what this meant. "So you won't be around next year?"

She shook her head. "But we can still hang out on weekends and stuff, and there's social media."

"Yeah." *But it's not the same.* Daisy was the only friend I had left at school, even if we only talked in gym. But now she'd be off at West Valley while I was still stuck here. And if we didn't have classes together, we'd probably fall out of contact again like we did last year.

At least I had Nolan. At least I had someone left.

* * *

"ALRIGHT," the geometry sub said to the seating chart, "everyone who's not in their assigned seat is getting marked absent, so I'd suggest using the next thirty seconds to make necessary adjustments."

I looked up from my notebook to watch at least half the class get up and move.

"Wait, Brianna, you don't sit there?" Jonah asked.

"No," another girl called from across the room.

Jess, the girl who sat in front of me, turned around. "Hey, Sum. Are you and Nolan going to Sadies on Friday?"

The Sadie Hawkins dance was on Friday, and I knew I owed Nolan a dance since I'd skipped Black & White, but we hadn't talked about going. Friday evening was also the first parent informational meeting for the Europe trip, and Saturday afternoon was the first informational meeting for students.

It was already Wednesday, and I hadn't been dressing up for any of the theme days this week—Monday was "sports team" day, and I didn't even have a jersey because I'd never been all that interested in sports. My dad tried to take me to a baseball game once and I hated it—*and* my favorite lip balm that I'd gotten for Christmas months earlier melted in the car and got ruined.

Yesterday was "fake injury" day, which was weird anyway, and I didn't have anything to use except adhesive bandages, which I knew better than to waste on faking an injury. Most girls wore knee braces that they had for sports. Today was "fan" day, where we were supposed to wear merchandise for something we were a fan of. Jess was dressed like a *Harry Potter* character. I didn't know what to wear, so I'd just dressed normally.

"We might go," I told Jess.

"You totally should," she replied.

"I'll ask him about it at lunch."

"How are you going to ask him?" She leaned closer over her seat. "Do you have a poster?"

"Huh? I thought I'd just ask if he wants to go."

"Summer! You have to be creative. Like, haven't you seen all the cute proposals girls have been doing all week? Guys do it for prom and homecoming; we do it for Sadies. How did he ask you to homecoming?"

I blushed. "Um, I asked him, actually, and I just asked if he wanted to go while we were talking normally."

She sighed. "Girl, you've gotta let me help you. Follow me at lunch. I've got connections."

I sure hoped we weren't learning anything important in geometry today, since I couldn't jeopardize my C, but I also couldn't focus because I was so worried about what Jess meant by "connections."

Reluctantly, I followed her after class to find senior class president Neil at his locker.

"Babe," Jess said to him, "Summer's doing her Sadies proposal at lunch today, okay?"

"She can go after Teryn," he replied. "She came to me yesterday."

She nodded. "Fair enough. Sorry for the last-minute notice."

Now even more nervous, I followed the two of them to the center of the quad, where a microphone was already set up from Monday and Tuesday's lunchtime activities and "proposals."

Teryn, a curvy blonde girl who I thought was a sophomore, stood behind a wall with me and Jess while Neil introduced the day's activity—boys versus girls tug-of-war.

"But first," he said, "we have some other business to take care of. I believe a Miss Teryn Bee has something to say?"

My eyes widened as I watched Teryn step out from behind the wall and prance around the quad singing a Justin Bieber song until she got to the boy she was going to ask. She practically gave him a lap dance before ending with, "Sadies, Greg?"

"Sounds good to me," the guy said into the microphone.

They hugged while Neil collected the mic and returned to the center of the quad. I had no idea what I was going to do when he gave it to me. I couldn't sing, I wasn't about to give Nolan a lap dance, and I couldn't think of anything else creative.

"And one more announcement before the games begin," Neil said, "from a Miss Summer Madison."

Still unsure of what the hell I was going to do, I walked up to Neil and took the microphone. I wasn't going to hold everyone up while I panicked.

And then I realized that I had no idea where Nolan even was. We couldn't usually see the central quad from the lunch table where we ate with his friends, and even if he'd heard Neil, I wouldn't know where to look for him.

"Um…" I tried to scan the crowd. "Uh… if I could ask Nolan Alden to get up here really quick?"

"Louder," Neil said.

"Nolan?" I asked, trying to raise my voice. "Um, could you come up here for a minute, please?"

The good news was, waiting for him to show up gave me some time to think about what I was going to do next. The bad news was, the longer he took, the more I could feel everyone's eyes on me, wondering if Nolan was going to show up or not.

"Summer!"

I looked up to see Liam approaching me. I wasn't sure if that was good or bad.

"Where's Nolan?" I asked, trying to aim away from the microphone.

"He's retaking a chem test," Liam explained.

"He didn't tell me he was going to retake a chem test at lunch." I tried to stay smiling, like this was all part of my elaborate Sadies proposal plan.

"Last-minute schedule change from our teacher," he said.

"What the hell do I do now, then?" I asked a little more aggressively than I meant to.

Liam, however, nodded in understanding and took the microphone from me. "Summer's boyfriend is a dumbass who messed up section one of his last chem test, so it looks like you're all going to miss the show for now. Back to you, Neil."

I laughed as I handed Neil the mic, thankful that this mishap at least got me out of having to think of something creative.

"Aww," Neil said. "Well, hey, why don't you do whatever you had planned, and Liam can stand in for Nolan? That way we don't miss anything. Liam, do you have a date yet?"

"I do not," Liam said.

"Well, ladies, here's a look at what *could* be yours. Summer?"

Before I could even process Neil's suggestion, the crowd cheered and he pressed the mic back into my hands.

"Um... what?" I asked, accidentally right into the mic.

"Liam's gonna pretend to be Nolan, and you'll perform for him so we don't miss the show. Now, hop to it. We've got tug-of-war."

"Well, I wouldn't want to take up any—"

And then the crowd started chanting *my* name. I froze.

"What were you going to do?" Liam whispered.

"I don't know!" I whispered back. "This was very last-minute!"

"What's you and Nolan's song?" he asked. "Just sing that."

"We don't have a song and I can't sing!"

Liam turned to Neil. "Hey, buddy, put on a song. Any song."

With a confused expression, Neil walked over to the speaker setup and put on what I presumed was the background music for tug-of-war: "Holding Out for a Hero."

"You know this song?" Liam asked, and I nodded. "Sing along."

I looked at him and tried to sing along, but I did not feel better about this knowing that one, I was not good at singing, and two, I was singing directly into a microphone in front of the whole school. Fortunately, he seemed to have a backup plan: dancing exaggeratedly around me while I tried to sing. He would strike dramatic "buff" poses, pretend to be searching for something in the crowd, point to himself, and dance very poorly until the song finally ended. I was laughing so hard that I wasn't sure anyone could tell I was trying to sing.

"Liam," I said into the mic, "do you think Nolan wants to go to Sadies with me?"

He took the mic. "I'd say he'd be an idiot not to, but then again, he *is* retaking that chem test."

Everyone laughed as Neil took the mic back, and we bowed. As we headed back to our lunch spot, Nolan came bounding up to us.

"What the hell did I miss?" he asked. "I could hear from the science building. What the hell did you two end up doing?"

We caught up to Jake, who was laughing so hard he could barely speak. "Man—you missed—I can't believe—"

"I made love to her in the central quad," Liam said, slinging an arm around me. "She says it was an honor to be deflowered so publicly by your oldest friend."

"No, that didn't happen." I wiggled out from under his arm and grabbed Nolan's hand instead. "Wait, what do you mean, 'deflowered?'"

"Well, you're a virgin, right?" Liam asked. "Nolan said—"

"Liam said nothing and didn't get his legs broken after school," Nolan interrupted.

"You talk about that?" I asked.

"No!" all three of them said at once.

Nolan continued, "It came up, once, like, a long time ago. Months ago."

"Yeah, for all we know, you two could've done it since then," Jake said. "Not that it's any of our business."

"*Anyway*, Summer, I'd love to go to Sadies with you," Nolan said. "Unless you're already going with Liam."

"No, that—whatever the hell that was—was for you." I sighed. "So, great. We're going to Sadies."

"You guys go ahead," Nolan said to the others. "We'll catch up."

Once they were gone, he said, "We *don't* talk about stuff like that, Sum. I promise."

"Okay."

"So, is everything okay?"

I half-smiled. "It's been a long lunch."

The rest of the day was fairly normal, at least, but it took me a few hours to calm down from all the excitement—and sheer terror—of that proposal.

When Nolan met me at my locker at the end of the day, I asked him—

"What's our song?"

"Huh?" He seemed confused.

"Liam asked me what our song was. I wasn't sure."

He thought for a minute. "What was that song we both liked? When you asked me to homecoming, we were talking about music and there was an old song we both liked. I want to say it was by Fleetwood Mac."

"'Never Going Back Again?'" I asked.

He nodded. "That one. I always think of you when I hear it now."

"Perfect." I smiled. "My favorite song is our song."

"Well, it could also be the Bruno Mars song we kissed to, now that I think about it."

I shook my head. "I like this one better. Well, maybe we can just have two songs."

He grinned. "I think we deserve two songs."

"Perfect."

Nolan

I NOTICED Summer dressing up for the spirit days on Thursday and Friday— granted, they were easier than the first three days. Thursday's theme was to spell out a word with your friends, so Liam, Jake, and I came up with us and our Sadies dates spelling "COUGAR," our school mascot. Summer was the "G" and I was the "U."

Today was pink-and-blue day, so she wore a pink shirt and I wore a blue shirt. The theme of the dance was "glow in the dark," but we agreed to just wear normal outfits and get a bunch of glow sticks from the dollar store before the dance. It was a much more casual dance than homecoming or Black & White, which made things easier.

We met up with Liam and Jake and their dates beforehand to take some pictures, with everyone basically wearing the same outfits as we did at school.

Thanks to Liam and Summer's cutesy performance in the quad, Liam had found himself to be quite the eligible bachelor and snatched up a date with Tracy Choi, a cute girl in our grade. I didn't think he'd gone to Sadies in the old timeline, so it was nice to see him land someone nice for a date—maybe he'd actually get a serious girlfriend this time. Jake was going with his girlfriend of a few months, Caeley. They were still together when I'd gone back in time, and he'd taken her in the old timeline, too.

"I feel weird taking pictures," Summer said as we headed back to my car. "I mean, we're not all dressed up."

"Sure we are," I told her. "We're dressed up for the glow-in-the-dark pink-and-blue dance."

"I guess." She closed the door and buckled her seatbelt. "Hey, um, am I going to have to do that grinding thing again?"

"What do you mean?"

"At homecoming, you said that was how people danced. Um, I didn't like it all that much."

"What didn't you like about it?" I asked. "That's just how people dance at these things."

"I just feel weird basically rubbing my ass against your crotch for most of the dance," she said, blushing. "It feels wrong."

"Well, if you don't want to dance, we can sit and talk somewhere... or make out."

"I want to dance, but, like, are you sure there's not a way that doesn't involve a semi-orgy?"

"Yeah." I sighed. "We can just... go onto the main dance floor."

I was hesitant to agree, because the types of people who didn't stand in circles with their friends and grind on each other were... not necessarily *losers*, but everyone cool was in a circle. I just wasn't sure the right way to tell Summer that. Besides, I was probably overreacting. It wouldn't be that bad.

* * *

SOMETHING THAT hadn't occurred to me was that neither Summer nor I really knew how to dance, so we just stood facing each other and rocking to the beat of the song. We talked, somewhat, but it was hard to do with the loud music.

"Are you having fun?" I asked her.

"More fun than I would be if we were grinding," she said.

Two students came up to us, Grant Hayward and his best friend Jimmy Vogel, dancing with such exaggerated movements you'd think they were powering the DJ booth. Those two were practically joined at the hip; I'd never seen them without each other. I'd assume they were dating if they hadn't done an interview for the school paper freshman year explaining that Grant wasn't interested in dating at all, and Jimmy said his ideal girlfriend would be any one of the cheerleaders. I think one of the cheerleaders had taken him to homecoming last year.

"Hey, Nolan! Hey, Summer!" Grant said excitedly—he was far more outgoing than Jimmy, who usually didn't talk much in crowded spaces like this. Not that I'd ever talked to them at a dance, because I was always in a circle with my friends in a back corner, not on the main dance floor.

Summer smiled at them. "Hey, guys! Having fun?"

"You bet!" Jimmy said, almost too quiet for us to hear. I realized both of them were wearing tuxedos—guess they didn't get the memo that it was a casual dance.

"How come you two aren't dancing?" Grant asked. "You gotta *move!*"

"I don't have any moves, Grant," I told him. "You have fun, though!"

"Just follow our lead!" he insisted.

"Oh, I'm not much of a dancer," I said again. "You two seem like you're on a level far more advanced than I could learn in one night."

Usually when they started talking to me in class, I tried to streamline the conversation or silently catch the gaze of a special education attendant, who would divert their attention to someone who was more interested in talking to them. But I wasn't sure if the attendants were even at this dance. Were they off-duty after classes?

It wasn't that I didn't like Grant and Jimmy. It was just that talking to them was... unpleasant. I never knew what to say, I was never interested in what either of them wanted to talk about—usually a video game I didn't play or a comic series I didn't read—and if I *did* have something to say, it was always wrong somehow and required a lengthy explanation as to why. Some people were good at communicating with the special education students, but I wasn't.

"You can show me how to dance," Summer said to them. "Well, you can try, anyway."

The two of them kept dancing, and Summer laughed as she tried to emulate their movements, mostly unsuccessfully.

"I give up," she said. "You two are much better dancers than me."

"At least you tried!" Grant said. "Looks like Nolan isn't manly enough to dance!"

"Does that mean I'm manly enough?" Summer asked playfully.

"Yes!" Jimmy said, and both boys laughed.

"Hey, Nolan, guess I'm manlier than you," she said, sticking her tongue out.

Before I could come up with a witty response, Grant got Summer's attention again. "Summer, do you play Minecraft?"

"No, sorry," she replied.

"You should play it! It's, like—so you have this world, right? And—"

"Hey, why don't you two go dance with some of your other friends?" I asked, not wanting to hear him explain what Minecraft was for the tenth time. "Are any of your other friends here?"

"I'm telling Summer about Minecraft!" he explained.

"Why don't you tell her at school on Monday?" I tried.

"But if I tell her *now* then maybe she'll want to download it and we can play it together over the weekend."

"You can play with us, too!" Jimmy said. "Do you have Minecraft?"

"That reminds me," I said. "Summer, we have to go find Liam. We're supposed to meet up with him now."

"Liam's in that boring circle dancing inappropriately," Jimmy said, pointing.

"Thanks for the help!" I told him, dragging Summer away.

"Why do we need to talk to Liam?" she asked.

"Because if I hear Grant explain what Minecraft is one more time, I'm going to personally hack into the server and delete the whole game."

She laughed, but there was something off about it.

"They're nice guys," she said.

"I know they are," I assured her. "I just... don't know how to talk to people like that."

"People with autism?" she asked as we sat down on the mostly-folded-up gym bleachers.

"Yeah, that. I think that's what they have."

"It is," she said. "I still remember when I met them. It was seventh grade, in art class. The teacher had the special education attendant come in and explain that there were going to be three students from the program joining our class. She said, 'They have autism, which just means they're a little different, but you can still talk to them and be their friends.'"

"Three? Who was the third one? I only ever see them with each other."

"Jean Dyer. I don't know if they're friends; she's just in the special education program with them. I doubt all those kids are friends with each other."

"Why not?"

"Are we friends with all the people in our grade?"

"True, but there can't be more than thirty of 'em. They're, like, a little family.

Well, I guess that's still big for a family, but you know what I mean."

"I just feel bad for them," she said. "I mean, most of the kids I've met from the program hardly talk, but Grant and Jimmy and a few others just want to fit in with people like us."

"Then someone should've told them this was a casual dance," I said, smirking. She sighed, like I'd missed her point. "That was a joke; I'm sure they're perfectly happy in their tuxedos."

"I just meant, like, they want to fit in like us. But it seems we can barely even hold a conversation with them."

Oh. "We can go back and talk about Minecraft, if you want."

"No, no, I mean, I *get it*; I can hardly have meaningful conversations with them, either. I try, but, like, it's hard. I just wish I knew how, because I know what it's like to want to fit in and to feel like you can't no matter how hard you try. Who knows if they're even worried about that, though? I'm probably just projecting."

"They're probably not as worried about it as you think," I assured her. "I mean, look at them out there, dancing like that and wearing tuxedos to a casual dance. They're probably happy just being themselves. They don't need to fit in with us."

"That doesn't mean I can't be nice to them," she said.

"We *should* be nice to them," I said. "They're different, sure, but that doesn't mean we have to treat them like they're weird or anything like that."

"I guess I just feel bad because... I used to be mean like that," she said. "To Jean Dyer. She started going to my day camp the summer before third grade, and my friends and I were, like, scared of her because she doesn't talk. She just, like, stares at you and sometimes tries to grab your arm or your stuff. Up until, like, eighth grade, Marta and I would scream and run away if she ever tried to interact with us. I guess it didn't occur to us back then that she had feelings and could understand what we were doing."

"You didn't know how to communicate with her," I told her. "And you were just kids. You learn from stuff like that. It doesn't mean you're a bad person."

She shook her head. "I don't want to talk about it anymore. Can we go back to dancing?"

"I'd like that."

We managed to avoid running into Grant and Jimmy again, and we had fun dancing until a slow song finally came on. I held her waist, and she slung her arms around my neck.

"Summer?" I asked.

"Yeah?"

"I think the world needs more people like you," I said. "You have a good heart. That's not exactly common these days."

She blushed. "You have a good heart, too."

"No, not like you," I said.

"Sure. For as long as I've known you, you've been so nice to everyone," she explained. "You always say hi to everyone in the halls, you hold doors for people, you wave back when people wave to you... You used to be one of the only guys who was actually nice to me growing up. Then for a while it seemed like you were annoyed by me, but then we started talking this year, and, well, since you've been nice to me recently, so many other people are, too."

"I'm sorry if I was ever not nice to you," I said. "You're an amazing girl, Sum. I should've gotten to know you sooner than I did."

"Oh, this one memory of you always sticks out," she said. "In fourth grade, on Valentine's Day, when Liam gave everyone Nerds and Megan Sanders dropped hers. You gave her yours, even though that meant you wouldn't have any. I thought that was so nice of you, and I wanted to be nice like that. I kept thinking back to that day, and in sixth grade I decided I was going to bring candy canes to school at Christmas to make people feel appreciated. So, you say I have a good heart, but you inspire me to be good. You have since we were kids."

I held her closer to me. It was all I could bring myself to do. I'd inspired Summer to be nice when I'd hardly been nice to her.

Well, I used to be nice to her. She was right. I was nice to everyone, I guess; if someone hadn't pissed me off, then I didn't see a reason to be rude to them. But most people didn't read too much into it. Summer, on the other hand, seemed to think that me *not* being an asshole to her meant that I wanted to be friends, as in, the kind of friends who actually hung out and talked regularly, not just people who waved at each other in the halls.

And even *that* wouldn't have been so bad—Summer was awkward, yes, and I hadn't wanted to be friends with her, but I could've kept being nice to her if I hadn't known she had a crush on me. I was so worried she'd misinterpret my friendliness even further because she already seemed to act like she had a shot with me and I didn't want to lead her on. So I became colder to her, but she kept acting like we were friendly, and I was annoyed by it.

She used to ask me if we were friends, and in the beginning, I would say, *"Yeah, sure,"* because to me, anyone who hadn't pissed me off was a friend. I just, I don't know, expected her to know the difference between "yeah, I don't hate you, we're friends" and "yeah, we're friends, let's hang out." But she *kept* asking, and it took everything in me to not outright be an asshole and say, *"No, we're actually not."* I don't know why I couldn't just say that; it would've saved us a lot of trouble in the old timeline. It just felt too mean. I guess in retrospect, I'd still been leading her on in a way.

Her words echoed in my head: *"I know what it's like to want to fit in and to feel like you can't no matter how hard you try."* Summer might not have had a social disorder like Grant and Jimmy, but she was an awkward girl who just wanted to fit in, and I'd spent years pushing her away.

If I'd gotten to know Summer as a friend back then, I would've saved us both so much trouble. I could've found out I liked her sooner. I would've actually been nice to her and could've saved myself this whole do-over year—not that I wasn't grateful for it now. Most of the things that were "awkward" about her all those years, I found endearing now. *Most* of them—I would still rather be in that circle with our friends rather than out here on the main dance floor, for instance. But the past was the past, and all I could do now was enjoy our second chance, because I was so lucky to have it. I didn't deserve it, that was for sure, but Summer did.

Summer deserved better, and I was grateful I'd gotten the chance to be better to her.

Summer

NOLAN DROPPED me off after the dance—he didn't try to fool around this time. I guess he figured I'd let him know when I wanted to do that.

I had a nice time at Sadies, but I still felt bad about the way we'd blown off Grant and Jimmy. That wasn't entirely Nolan's fault; I'd blown them off before because I didn't know how to get out of a conversation about something like Minecraft—something I had no interest in but they seemed dead set on having a lengthy conversation about.

I knew they deserved better; I just didn't know how to be better. I wished there was some sort of class on how to communicate with people like that—or just people in general, for that matter. A class that taught things like how to act at a school dance, or how relationships worked and when it was the right time to move forward with stuff like making out and sex. There were so many things I felt like I was supposed to know, because everyone else seemed to know, but I just... didn't.

Sometimes I wondered if there *was* something wrong with me. But I'd spent enough time around Grant and Jimmy to know that I wasn't like them. It wasn't *that*.

At least with Grant and Jimmy, I could kind of talk to them. Well, I could make them think we were having a conversation, even if I was just listening to them talk and saying, *"Oh, wow, that sounds cool,"* every so often. I still felt horrible about the way Marta and I used to act around Jean. Even now, Marta still said things like, *"Oh, fuck, there's Jean; let's get out of here"* under her breath when we saw her across the hall.

One time I'd tried to stand up for Jean. It was last year, when I was with Jonah. He, Marta, and I were standing at my locker when Marta said, *"Ugh, Jean's coming. Let's go before she tries to molest us."*

"That's a little extreme," I said, closing my locker.

"She grabs my arm and pulls on it. What would you call that?"

"Bothering, maybe?"

"You know, in Spanish, the word for 'to bother' is 'molestar,'" Jonah said. *"Maybe Marta was just trying to be cultural."*

"Well, Jean can't talk," I said. *"She's just trying to communicate in the way she knows how."*

"Well, the way I know how to communicate with her is getting the fuck away from her before she can 'molestar' me," Marta replied.

"Maybe she just wants to fit in like the rest of us. Maybe she just hopes people like us will be nice to her."

"She's never going to fit in; she's retrasada," Jonah said with a dramatic fake-Spanish accent.

"In English?" Marta asked.

"Retarded."

She'd laughed, and Jonah had laughed, and I'd managed an uncomfortable laugh, but I hated when people used that word against the special education students. I may have been desensitized to hearing it thrown at me by my mother or Marta—even Bella, back in middle school, used to refer to her closest friends as "retards" as a term of endearment—but I hated hearing it used against the very people it was supposed to hurt.

And while I had so many good memories of Nolan being so friendly to everyone over the years, there was one memory of him that I wished I could forget.

In sixth grade, everyone who turned in all their completed reading logs by the end of April would get to ditch school for the day and go to an Oakland A's game for being "all-star readers." I thought for sure I had only missed one, and there was a grace to allow for one missing log, but the day before the game, our English teacher informed me that I had missed four. I didn't argue. After all, I didn't even *like* sports, and the only appeal of going to the game was getting out of classes—well, and Nolan would be there, and maybe he would talk to me—but I let it go.

When everyone else was getting ready to go, the teacher announced that a few students from the special education program would also be going to the game as a reward for some separate thing in their class, and they'd be taking the same bus.

Nolan, who sat at the desk clump next to mine, turned to Jake. *"Are you kidding me? I don't want to take the same bus as the retarded kids."*

I didn't remember what Jake said or if anyone else overheard, but I remembered that moment vividly. For a while, it made me not like him—even if I was still as much of an asshole to Jean Dyer. Simply not outright calling her the r-slur was hardly better, but I didn't see that back then. Eventually, that typical Nolan charm reeled me back in, but for the rest of sixth grade, I saw him differently because of that moment.

I didn't hold it against him now—it was the only memory I had of him being an asshole, amidst *so* many memories to the contrary—but it crossed my mind from time to time. I wished I could forget about it, because like he said, we learn and grow from those experiences. He did try to be nice to Grant and Jimmy tonight. He yelled at Marta when she used that word against me, and he told her not to say that about anyone. He wasn't the same boy who'd made that one comment that day.

Just like I wasn't the same girl who let out dramatic, bloodcurdling screams with Marta at the sight of Jean Dyer.

Maybe I'd feel less shitty about my past if I could apologize for it—but if I could hardly communicate with Grant and Jimmy, then I didn't have the slightest clue where to start with Jean. All I could do was be a better person and hope it was enough.

* * *

Nolan picked me up at lunchtime on Saturday so we could get something to eat before heading to the community center for the first informational meeting for the Europe trip. Everyone's parents had their first meeting last night, and students would have a meeting today. I wasn't sure why they couldn't just have the meetings on the same day, especially because if Nolan couldn't take me, I would've had to take the bus so my mom wouldn't have to drive down there *again* just to sit in the car for an hour, but supposedly the rest of the initial informational meetings would be for parents *and* students.

Then, for the first few weeks of summer, the students would have "cultural enrichment workshops" every weekday morning until the trip started. They sounded boring, but I was also kind of excited for them. If nothing else, it provided a chance to get to know more people on the trip besides Nolan—and Marta, who I was already dreading seeing at the meeting tonight.

"Hey, Sum." Nolan greeted me with a kiss. "You ready?"

I nodded. "I'm excited to see who else will be on the trip."

"Me, too. Not that spending the whole time with just the two of us wouldn't be incredible."

I laughed. "Hey, maybe they'll all suck and we can do that anyway."

"We already know *one* person on the trip sucks," he said.

"Yes, thanks for reminding me."

We ran into Esme on our way into the auditorium. I was surprised to see her there, but it was nice to see a familiar face.

"Hey, guys," she said. "How've you two been since the holidays?"

"Great, and you?" Nolan replied.

"Hanging in there," she said. "Let's go sit down."

We caught up with Esme for a bit, but Nolan kept glancing around the room like he was waiting for someone. I wondered if he was worried about running into Marta, too.

By the time the program coordinator, Tim, stepped onto the stage, she hadn't shown up. I wondered if maybe she'd decided not to go after all.

At least, I could hope.

Nolan

I DIDN'T see Katie at the meeting. I couldn't remember if she'd been there in the old timeline; I remembered Summer saying Marta couldn't make it, and a few of the other kids I'd made friends with weren't at the first meeting, either. I probably couldn't avoid seeing Katie again, but I wasn't ready for Summer to find out about what had happened between us on homecoming, and I wasn't sure if Katie would say anything if she saw us.

I zoned out for most of the meeting itself, since I'd already been through just about every informational meeting there was for this trip. There had only been four left when the timeline switch had happened.

Back in the old timeline, I'd had my solid group of friends—and Katie. Sometimes Esme was a part of that group, and sometimes we'd say something about someone else that she thought was "too mean" and she wouldn't talk to us for a couple of days—like when we made those plans to go to the mall without Summer. Then there was the group we called the "wannabes," who were this bunch of gossipy "mean girls" who would sell out their closest friends to gain social status. I thought I remembered Marta hanging around with them sometimes when she wasn't with Summer. Those girls would try to hang out with us sometimes, but they were so annoying. Not as annoying as Summer at the time, though.

At home, I looked through Summer's notebook again. I was curious if there was anyone else on the trip that she'd specifically mentioned. Maybe there were people we should try to avoid or something like that.

June 16th—

I slept over at Marta's last night so her mom could give us both a ride to the meeting today. Apparently, the other people on the trip don't like me. I don't know what I could have done so far. They're nice to me, or at least I thought they were. Esme's nice to me but then she goes and hangs out with the people who make fun of me. Marta didn't say what specifically they said, just that they make fun of me. This girl Katie's talked to me a couple times and she seemed nice, but apparently she and her friends talk crap about me behind my back. Marta says that Katie and Nolan are the worst when it comes to that. I knew Nolan didn't really like me, but I didn't know he talked crap about me.

Katie didn't talk crap about Summer. I vented to her occasionally, but she'd usually just nod along or say something noncommittal like, *"I'm sorry you had to deal with that."* She never contributed or initiated it. She was the one who'd told us the mall thing was too mean. Why did Marta tell Summer that Katie was the worst? I kept reading.

Nolan's really popular with this group, like at school. I guess the gist is that if the popular kids don't like me, I'm gonna have a bad time. So he talks crap about me and I guess they join in because they'd rather fit in than stick up for me. I get it. I've been there, with people like Jean. The other kids on the trip will have a much nicer time if they befriend Nolan's popular group than if they're nice to someone like me who apparently nobody likes except Marta.

Well, even that's debatable, because apparently she goes along with them when they say I'm annoying, because they like her and she wants to be in with them, too. I wish she'd stick up for me. I know they're her friends, but I've been her best friend for years. Why can't she stick up for me?

I had noticed Marta hanging around the wannabe crowd, but I guess in my mind I'd assumed she was still best friends with Summer. Knowing what I knew now, I stood by my suggestion that Marta could go fuck herself. I hadn't realized how bad it was before witnessing it myself. And it only got worse:

It's like the summer after sixth grade, when we went to the same day camp. A few weeks in, we went out to dinner together after, and it was just us while her mom had to take her brother somewhere. Marta told me that the girls who were being nice to me had a bunch of inside jokes about me. Like about how I have trouble making eye contact—I guess I accidentally stared at their chests when talking to them or something, and so they'd "be Summer" and look at each other's chests and talk to each other. And they'd mimic stories I'd told them that they thought were stupid, because apparently nothing I told them was actually funny or interesting. They would ask me questions and use my answers as fuel for more jokes, not because they were actually interested in where I got my clothes or why I didn't shave my legs yet.

At first, I was just upset that people I thought were my friends were actually being mean to me. But a few weeks later, it occurred to me that when Marta told me all those things, she didn't once mention that she stood up for me. In fact, it wasn't "THEY do these things." It was "WE do these things," as in she was doing them too. She would "be Summer" with them, and she'd even tell them more things about me. But by the time I realized that, day camp was over entirely.

I never knew how to bring it up to her, so I let it go, but I still think about it sometimes. I get it, really. When you just want to fit in and people with a higher social status are giving you positive attention, you'll do anything. Even sell out your best friend.

Today she told me that she might hang out with her new friends more on the trip than with me. So I guess I have to figure out who I'm going to hang out with, which will be hard considering apparently nobody likes me. Maybe I can figure out why Nolan talks crap about me, and fix this. It's wishful thinking, but it's all I have left.

Maybe I didn't fully realize the effect I had back then, talking crap about her like I did. Because my friend group was the "popular" group, I was sending the message that to be popular, you needed to diss Summer. That wasn't my intention at all, but... it wasn't like I would have minded back then if I'd realized what I was doing. I didn't care about her. In that timeline, I was a dick to Summer; in a way, I wasn't *expected* to stand up for her, anyway.

Marta, on the other hand, was Summer's best friend. Of all people, *she* should have stood up for her. And if she was going on the trip in this timeline, I was going to make sure everyone knew what kind of a friend she was.

Or should I? Would intentionally turning everyone against Marta be as bad as unintentionally turning everyone against Summer? Summer didn't do anything to really deserve it. Marta was an even bigger asshole than I used to be.

I supposed it wasn't my score to settle; it was Summer's. She should be the one to make the decision. And besides, Marta hadn't technically done half the things Summer mentioned in the journal entry yet, though I wouldn't put it past her to do them in this timeline.

In this timeline, Summer probably didn't need to worry too much about Marta getting hers. But that didn't mean I wasn't going to give her the opportunity.

11

MARCH FLEW by, and before I knew it, it was my seventeenth birthday: April 8, the last day of school before spring break.

The timing made it convenient to have a party, but my two friends were now down to one, and I felt weird calling Nolan's friends *my* friends even though I ate lunch with them every day—and a "party" with just Daisy and Nolan just didn't sound like it would be that much fun. He told me I should invite Esme, but I didn't feel like I knew her all that well.

So instead, he said he'd take me to get smoothies after school. But first I had to get through the school day.

"Happy birthday, Summer!" Daisy said when she passed me in the hall that morning. We didn't have gym today, so I hadn't been sure I'd even see her today.

I beamed. "Thank you!"

When I turned around, Nolan was approaching with a mylar balloon. As he got closer, I realized the balloon was tied to a gift bag and he was carrying a baking tray covered with foil.

"Happy birthday, Sum." He kissed me and then held out the gift bag and the tray. "You like chocolate cake, right?"

I blushed, grinning as I took everything from him. "Yes! Did you make this?"

"Well, my mom did," he explained. "The cake, I mean. The present is store-bought."

"Thank you!" I tried to balance the cake while I opened the tape on the gift bag, and he offered to hold on to the cake for a second. Inside the bag was a makeup palette—it looked like the expensive one everyone was obsessed with back on Black Friday.

"I figured you'd want some nice makeup for Europe," he said. "Uh, you can thank Caeley for the suggestion; she said you'd like that one."

I'd met Jake's girlfriend a few times, but she didn't usually eat lunch with us. She seemed nice. She wore a *lot* of makeup, so I trusted her opinion. It meant a lot that Nolan would get me something so nice.

"Thank you," I said again. "You didn't have to get me this."

"Well, I didn't have any old pictures of us to frame for you," he said. "I'm not good at cute gifts like that, so I went with practical. There's a card in there, too, by the way."

I felt around and sure enough, the envelope had blended in with the side of the bag. I took out the card—the front had a drawing of a cake with a bunch of hearts and read *"Happy Birthday"* in cursive font.

Inside, under the default inscription—*"To the most special girl I know, hope your day is full of lots of love—and lots of cake,"* he had written:

Summer,

I feel so grateful to be able to spend your birthday with you. You've changed my life in ways you could never know, and I hope you have the best birthday ever. Can't wait to spend many more birthdays with you.

Love,

Nolan

I hugged him. "Thank you so much!"

"Of course, Sum. You deserve it."

"I can safely say this is already a better birthday than last year," I told him as we broke apart.

"What happened last year?"

"Well, practically everyone got cars for their sixteenth birthday, but I still don't know how to drive, and even if I had gotten my license back then, my mom told me we'd have to share a car until I could save up for my own. So I felt kind of left out, especially when everyone who wished me a happy birthday asked me what kind of car I was getting."

"Oh. Yeah, that would suck."

"That wasn't the worst part, though," I went on. "That was the day Jonah told me his gift to me was going to be birthday sex, so we got in a pretty big argument that led to us breaking up a few days later. And he didn't even get me an actual present. Not that I needed one, but like, he just assumed I'd want to have sex."

"Well, Jonah's a dick," Nolan replied. "Good thing you upgraded. Of course, if you *want* to have birthday sex, the offer's on the table."

I rolled my eyes playfully. "No, thank you." I paused. "Sorry."

"Nah, it's fine," he said. "I don't get my hopes up too much about that."

"Someday I'll be ready," I assured him. "Just... not today."

"Don't worry about it, Sum." He smirked. "I've got two perfectly good hands."

It took me a second to realize what he meant. "Oh." I didn't really want to think about him doing that. "Thanks for sharing."

"Well, how about we change the subject?" he asked. "Do you want to get your license?"

I shrugged. "I just... don't have time. I'm going to be gone most of the summer, and I can't take Drivers Ed right now because I need to focus on school. But maybe next summer."

"I could take you out practice driving," he said. "I'm turning eighteen in August. I'll have to check the rules for that, but, like, as long as we don't get pulled over, nobody needs to know."

I laughed. "I wouldn't feel comfortable risking your life like that."

"Hey, I wouldn't take you on the freeway, just an empty parking lot." He laughed, too. "But I appreciate your concern for my safety."

Nolan

IN SUMMER'S notebook, she mentioned having some "party" with just Marta and Daisy, who didn't particularly like each other, and her birthday being uneventful. She mentioned that back in December, some girl in her English class had gotten three separate homemade cakes from her friends for her birthday. She also talked about how everyone walked around with balloons from their friends on their birthdays, and nobody ever did anything like that for her, so she always felt left out. So I made sure I brought her a cake, a balloon, and a present to make her feel special.

After school, I took her across the street to get smoothies. I remembered us getting smoothies on the second day of school, back when I still wanted to get out of this timeline. That was the day I'd noticed her braces for the first time. They were magenta then, but she'd switched them out for light blue at some point. I thought they might have been orange for a while.

"When do you get your braces off again?" I asked.

"July," she said. "Well, it was supposed to be July, but we'll be in Europe, so my orthodontist said we'd have to postpone until, like, right after we get back."

"Couldn't take 'em off the week before so you can enjoy Europe without them?" I asked. "Or chew gum on the plane?"

She laughed. "Nope, my mom checked." She took a sip of her drink. "You had braces before, right?"

"Yeah, fifth and sixth grade."

"That's right; you had them in the picture of us." She blushed. "I was looking at it the other day. I, well, I printed off a copy for myself, too, since I lost the original one I had."

"That's cute; where do you keep yours?"

"On my dresser," she said. "I still can't believe the old one just, like, vanished out of my locker over the weekend. It bothered me for so long wondering what happened to it."

I sighed. "Uh, Summer?"

"Yeah?"

"I—might have been the one who took it."

She raised an eyebrow. "What do you mean?"

"It's entirely possible that Jake and I went down to the school one weekend and broke into your locker and took it."

"What? Why? How?"

"We used his mother's stethoscope," I explained. "I swear we didn't do anything else to your locker. We just took the picture."

"But *why*?" She laughed, but I could tell she was still confused. "If you wanted a copy, I could've made you one."

"That—wasn't exactly why I took it." I took a deep breath. "People kept asking me if you and I were dating, since you had that picture in your locker."

"Oh, they asked me, too," she said. "I always said no. You were dating some girl you met over the summer, right? I think I would tell people that you were dating someone else, too, when they asked. I think I even started telling them I liked someone who went to another school—which was true; I had a crush on this guy in my youth group at the time—so they hopefully wouldn't bother *you* about it. I mean, it felt good that people assumed I was with someone like you, but I didn't want to cross any boundaries."

"Then why'd you hang a picture of us in your locker?" I asked.

"We were friends," she said. "Or, well, I wanted to believe we were. Everyone had pictures with their friends in their lockers, so I put some of Marta and Daisy, and... You were popular, and I thought maybe if people saw a picture of us, they'd think I was cool enough to talk to, and I could be popular, too."

"So, you just wanted people to assume we were... friends?"

"Kind of. I mean, I also wanted to believe that. But why'd you take the picture? Just because people thought we were dating?"

"Well, back then I didn't want them to think that," I said.

She stared at the table, uncomfortable.

"I'm fine with people thinking that *now*," I said. "That was years ago. I *hope* people know we're dating now."

She didn't respond for a while. "You could have just asked me to take it down. I would've just kept it at home if you had asked me. You didn't have to steal it."

"I know. I was just a stupid kid back then. I guess I didn't know how."

"I didn't think it would be a big deal," she said. "I mean, you said we could take the picture. You were smiling in it. And, like, you never told me I couldn't show it to anyone."

"Yeah, but a straight girl having a picture with a straight guy in her locker usually implies... I guess I just didn't think you would put it there."

"Whatever." She sighed. "That was years ago. I guess it doesn't matter now."

"Yeah. I'm sorry I was such a dick to you before," I told her.

"It's okay," she said, managing a smile. "Things are different now."

"And thank God they are."

Summer

ALL THINGS considered, today was a good birthday. Not the best; I doubted anything would top the party I had in second grade back when my parents were still together and we could afford things like pizza and cake and drinks for everyone in my class and the neighborhood. That was back when I used to hang out with the neighbors, before the ones close to my age all eventually moved away. Back when we could afford a top-tier magician, and I got a CD player that everyone thought was so cool, and people talked about my party for weeks after because it was such a big hit...

Who knew how much things would change over the summer, how that would be my last big party, how the other moms would start avoiding mine as if divorce were contagious? The number of kids who were nice to me grew smaller and smaller. Daisy and Marta were always my only real friends, but other people used to be friendly to me. Bella was my friend in middle school before she moved, and that was around the time I started getting bullied anyway.

And I couldn't help but feel *sad* knowing that Nolan was the one who stole the picture out of my locker—that he disliked me so much back then that the idea of me having a picture to imply we were friends was too much for him. Well, his issue was the implication that we were dating, but I'd always denied that, so I didn't see how it was such a big deal.

I guess it didn't matter now, since we were dating and he'd apologized for the way he'd acted back then, but... I was upset that I hadn't realized I was doing anything wrong at the time. Here I was, violating someone's boundaries without even realizing it, and rather than ask me to change what I was doing, he'd broken into my locker and stolen the picture.

It was like when I started getting bullied the following summer, and I didn't even realize it until Marta told me. For weeks, I had no idea I was doing anything wrong, and rather than point things out to me so I could correct myself, people made fun of me.

I guess that was just how kids were; I couldn't expect everyone to explain all these hidden social rules that they just naturally seemed to understand. I still didn't understand how everyone else just *knew* these things and I didn't. Where did they learn them? Was there something missing in my brain?

But I didn't want to think about that. I wanted to think about how I'd had a good birthday, and how I'd gotten a nice present and a homemade cake from Nolan, and how so many classmates had wished me a happy birthday this year, and how my mom had taken me to dinner at my favorite restaurant and gotten me a nice new suitcase, locks, and a carry-on bag as presents since I'd need them for the Europe trip, as well as a nice travel pillow. "Practicality" seemed to be the theme of my presents this year, but I didn't mind.

My dad even called me, and since we both had iPhones now, we got to FaceTime. He sent me a hundred dollar gift card in the mail. He also told me he'd bought his plane ticket for his annual "spend a week with Summer" trip, this year for a week after I'd get back from Europe. It was a good birthday.

So, I thought, looking at my reflection before I got ready for bed, *this is seventeen.*

Maybe seventeen would be a good year. After all, sixteen wasn't too bad—the second half, anyway.

Nolan

SPRING BREAK was great, but it was hard being away from Summer. I hoped next year I could convince my parents to let her come with us to our beach house in Newport—we had a guest room, and it wasn't like even if we—knock on wood—*were* having sex at that point, we'd do it in the room next door to my parents.

I did keep up with her over texts; she didn't go anywhere, but she said she enjoyed the time to herself while her mother was at work.

But now that spring break was over, prom was the next big thing on everyone's minds. In the old timeline, I'd taken this girl on the volleyball team who I'd been hooking up with on-and-off, and according to Summer's notebook, she hadn't gone at all. She said it was probably for the best, because if she got a dress for junior prom, her mother would make her reuse it for senior prom, and that was the prom that "really" mattered, so she'd just hold out hope for next year. It was eerie thinking how she never would have made it to senior prom before.

So, of course, I wanted to give her a promposal that would make her feel special—and make up for the Sadies incident.

"Hey, Sum." I greeted her at her locker with a kiss on Monday morning. "It's good to do that again."

She blushed. "I missed you."

"I missed you, too. I'm hoping next year maybe you can come with us."

She laughed. "My mom would never go for that."

"Well, maybe we can convince our parents to let it happen."

"We'll see. We've still got a whole year, anyway."

In APUSH, I tapped Liam on the shoulder.

"What's up?" he asked.

"I need your help with something tomorrow."

Summer

WHEN I got to school on Tuesday, Nolan wasn't at my locker, but there was a note taped to it. I opened it up and read:

Break. Back gate. Got a surprise for you ;)

I wasn't sure what it meant, but it was Nolan's handwriting, so I was excited. However, when I got to the back gate, only Liam and Jake were there.

"Uh, am I supposed to meet Nolan here?" I asked.

Jake nodded. "Look higher."

"Higher?"

He and Liam pointed to the tree they were standing under. I looked up, and Nolan was sitting on one of the branches.

"Hey!" I smiled, nervous. "Um, I'm not supposed to climb up there with you, am I?"

He laughed. "No. But I could use your help getting down."

"Wait, have you been up there all morning?"

"No," he said. "We left chem a few minutes early. Here, take my hand."

He reached down, but before I could grab his hand, a long strip of paper unfurled. It read "PROM?" in big block letters.

"Summer Madison, will you go to prom with me?" he asked, as a chorus of "awww"s echoed from the students around us.

I blushed. "Of course!"

He dropped the paper, climbed down from the tree, and kissed me.

I didn't know if I'd ever believed I'd actually get asked to prom, especially not by Nolan. Well, I suppose once we started going out, it'd felt like a possibility, but Nolan had always been my "dream date," my unattainable celebrity-esque crush. To think that a year ago, being asked to prom felt out of reach, but now I was going with *Nolan Alden*, my boyfriend, and he loved me... It was almost too good to be true.

Of course, when I mentioned prom over dinner, my mom also seemed to think that me having a decent prom experience would be out of reach.

"Why are tickets so expensive?" she asked. "When I was in high school, they were twenty bucks. You need *a hundred* dollars for the ticket?"

"Well, the school provides dinner," I explained.

"So did mine! Well, can you skip the dinner and just go somewhere with Nolan before?"

I shook my head. "For safety reasons or something, they won't let us skip the dinner part. I checked."

"Well, if the ticket is a hundred dollars, that's going to cut into your budget for a dress. Do you understand?"

"I know."

"And I'm assuming you're going to need another hundred dollars next year?"

"Probably. If Nolan and I are still together."

Why did I say that? Why wouldn't we be? He always mentions wanting to be together a year from now. I have no reason to be insecure about that. Except that it already feels too good to be true to be with him, and I guess I figure sooner or later he'll realize I'm not worth—

"Well, I'll give you two options for the dress, then," she said. "First is we can find a new dress. It can't be too expensive, but if we get you a new dress, you have to wear it for senior prom next year, too."

"That's fine." It wasn't ideal, but it was definitely better than trying to fish something out of my closet; I didn't even *have* a long dress, and my homecoming dress was definitely not formal enough, even if I wanted to wear a short dress to prom. Some girls did, but I'd been dreaming of a long dress for as long as I could remember.

"The second option," my mother said, "would be to look at Goodwill for a dress, and you could get a new one next year."

I cringed. It wasn't like my mother had taught me to look down on people who had to shop at Goodwill, but the girls in my grade had certainly made some implications over the years. Even if I didn't necessarily agree with them, the idea was still embarrassing. Besides, the lack of luck we'd had finding a homecoming dress at *discount* stores didn't give me a lot of hope for finding a prom dress at a thrift store.

"What if we can't find one at Goodwill?" I asked.

"Well, then we'll have to hope we can find one under two hundred dollars. We can try T.J.Maxx this weekend—"

My phone started vibrating against the table.

"It's Nolan," I said, confused. "Should I answer it?"

"Go ahead."

"Hey," I said. "What's up?"

"Hey, Sum. Can my mom talk to your mom?"

"Um... sure? We're eating dinner right now, though."

"Oh, right, you eat dinner earlier. Uh, well, if you text me her number, I could just have my mom call her later."

"Okay. Yeah, sounds good."

I was nervous, because our parents had never actually met. They'd said hello briefly at the first parent informational meeting for the Europe trip, but there wasn't a lot of time for them to talk. My mother had mentioned that it was weird they hadn't asked to connect with her—for whatever reason, *she* couldn't ask to connect with *them*—but I wasn't sure what his mother wanted to talk to her about, and it was stressing me out.

It stressed me out more when I could overhear my mother on the phone later—not the words she was saying, but the tone she used. It was her "customer service" voice, which she usually used when talking to someone from work before hanging up and venting to me about what an idiot that person was.

However, when the call ended, she didn't say anything to me. I was afraid to ask questions, so I didn't.

I just hoped everything was okay.

Nolan

"HEY, SUM." I greeted her with a kiss, but she seemed closed off today. "Everything okay?"

"What did our mothers talk about last night?"

"Oh, my mom just wanted to know if you two needed help paying for a prom dress," I explained. "I know they're expensive and all. She was also supposed to offer to pay for your ticket, since I asked you. Chivalry, you know."

Her eyes widened. "Oh. You don't have to do that. We'll be fine—"

"It's no big deal, Sum. She said your mother turned the offer down, anyway."

She bit her lip. "Okay. Well, good to know, I guess."

"They also talked about meeting for pictures," I said. "I think the plan is to go to the rose garden and meet up with Liam, Jake, Caeley, and whoever Liam goes with. That's where people usually take pictures. Our parents are going to meet there and probably have dinner together while we're at prom. My mom said it was our treat."

"Well, that's good that they're finally meeting." She sighed. "Is it weird that they haven't met yet? Or that you spend time at my place when my mom's home, but I don't spend much time with your parents?"

"I don't think it's weird," I assured her. "I mean, I haven't had many serious relationships. I guess I don't know how it's all supposed to work."

She raised an eyebrow, confused. "But you said you've had sex with five girls."

"Yeah?"

"Were you... not in serious relationships with those girls?"

"Not... all of them."

She kept staring at me, like she wanted a further explanation.

"The first one I'd been seeing for a while, and it didn't last much longer. The third one was a longer relationship. One was... consistent hookups, but we didn't define it as a relationship, and she was seeing other people. And... two were... one-time things." I watched her eyes widen the longer I went on.

"One-time things?"

"We were on the same page about everything. It wasn't like I hooked up with someone and left her when she was looking for a relationship or something like that."

She made a face, taking it all in. I wasn't sure what I was expecting her to say next, but it definitely *wasn't*—

"Maybe after prom... you can make it six." She looked up at me, then at the ground again. "Maybe."

"What? Are you—are you *sure*?"

She nodded. "I... You love me, right?"

"Of course, Sum. I'd never do anything to hurt you. That's why I want to make sure you're sure."

"Well, I'm sure." She sighed. "I think."

"There's no pressure. Like... why don't we talk about it closer to prom? It's still two and a half weeks away."

"Okay. Just... you might want to, um, get some... protection, because I can't—I don't—"

"Yeah, sure, I can get some just-in-case condoms. And I can try to convince my parents to stay out late." In the old timeline, I'd managed to convince them to stay out until midnight. The dance ended at eleven, so I'd had enough time to bring my date home, fool around, and get dressed so it wasn't obvious, even though my parents definitely knew what we were doing. As long as I used protection, they didn't care that much.

"Great. So, you'll get that done… Is there anything I need to do?" she asked.

"Well—Summer, are you *sure* you want to do this?"

"We're just making preparations, just in case. But I'm pretty sure."

"Okay."

"So, *just in case*, is there anything I need to do?"

I tried to think. "Um, do you—well, do you shave?"

"…My legs?" she asked. "Yeah. Legs and underarms, since eighth grade. Why? Does it look like I don't? My mom says I can't shave past my knees but that you can barely see that hair anyway. Do I need to shave my thighs for this?"

"No," I said. "Uh… I wasn't talking about your legs."

"My arms? My mom said I should never shave my arms."

I shook my head. "Your arms are fine. Uh, you know the expression 'mowing the lawn?'"

"No."

She wasn't going to make this easy. "Well, I'm going to assume you probably *don't* shave if you don't know what I'm talking about, so… if you wouldn't mind, I, uh, like it better when a girl… doesn't have a whole forest… there." I motioned to my own lower body so she'd hopefully get the hint. With the way her eyes widened, I was sure she got it now.

"I—can't do that," she said. "I'm not allowed to, and my mom buys razors from the dollar store which already cut up my legs pretty often, so I'd really rather not—"

"Okay." I sighed. "Okay. Forget I said anything. It's fine."

"Are you sure?"

"Summer, the fact that you're even offering sex is huge for us. I shouldn't be too greedy."

She nodded. "Okay. Well, I'm sorry."

"No, it's fine. It's just my preference; I'm not gonna love you any less."

The bell rang, but we just stood there staring at each other.

"So... you get protection and a place for us, and... I'll see what I can do about the forest situation."

Summer

I WAS surprised when my mom drove past the shopping center with the T.J.Maxx and the Ross and drove straight to the mall. I was still under the assumption that we were trying Goodwill first. But she took me to Macy's—the clearance section, but still Macy's.

"Are you sure?" I asked. "I'm really fine with Goodwill—"

"We're not *poor*, Summer. You can get a new dress for prom."

Something about her tone was off-putting. "So, I'm just picking a dress for both years, then?"

"We'll see. Just pick one you like—under two hundred dollars—and maybe we'll find it in our budget to get a new dress next year, too."

Nolan said my mom had turned down the offer for his mother to pay for my dress and the ticket, so how else did we magically have the money for a dress now?

"I'm really okay with something from T.J.Maxx," I said. "I mean, it's only junior prom; maybe next year I'll want something from Macy's, but—"

"We're not *poor*, and I don't need anyone assuming we are," she said again. "I can afford to buy my daughter her own prom dress. And shoes, but we'll look at Payless for those."

Still unsure, I began my search for a dress. Macy's seemed to have a decent selection of dresses under two hundred dollars, even outside of the clearance rack, and I found two in my size to try on.

The first was a peachy orange, and the part below my waist was pleated. It was sectioned off by a fabric belt wrapped around my waist with a fabric flower towards one side. It was strapless, so it was a little hard to hold up, but there were clear straps included in a little baggie attached to the tag. The clearance price left it at seventy-five dollars.

The second was more expensive, at a sale price of $133, and it was also strapless with optional clear straps. It was pink with rhinestones around the waist.

"I like the pink one," I said nervously, because it was the more expensive one.

"Okay," my mother said. "We'll get the pink one."

"Are you sure?"

"You want the pink one."

"And I can wear it for two years—"

"Don't worry about that right now. You like the pink one. We'll get the pink one."

Once we got the dress, we stopped at Payless to buy a pair of silver three-inch pumps that weren't too hard to walk in. They happened to have a cute silver clutch purse for a decent price on a stand while we were waiting in line, and it had an optional chain so I could wear it on my shoulder.

Finally, we went to Target to get makeup and look at hair accessories. My nice eyeshadow palette from Nolan was mostly neutrals, and the darker magenta colors in my homecoming palette wouldn't really work with the light pink of this new dress, so my mom wanted to get a small quad with glitter and fun lighter colors. She also let me pick out a new lipstick; I went with a shiny soft pink color that came in bright packaging.

On our way to look at hair stuff, we went down the fragrance aisle and she let me pick out a small size of any perfume I wanted. I went with one called "Fancy" because the tester smelled nice. I would use it for more than just prom, of course. The nearly two-ounce bottle of it cost twenty dollars.

"Do you think we could get a new curling iron?" I asked, since the one she had was probably as old as me. "My hair fell pretty quickly at homecoming."

"Maybe." She sighed. "Or what if we did a braid instead? Or braided part of it? That way we wouldn't need to curl it."

"I like that idea better," I said, remembering how gross the hairspray felt. So we picked out some cheap rhinestone pins and some elastics.

Before we could leave, my eye caught on the razor aisle, and I thought about what Nolan had said at school.

I wasn't even sure I *wanted* to have sex, but hearing him talk about those other girls... I was sure if I didn't at least *try* to seem more open to it, it would cause problems for us. Maybe it was time we took this step. Maybe I could be brave.

But even if I did... there was the matter of my "forest," as he'd so eloquently put it.

"Um, I was thinking," I said. "Maybe I could get a nice razor to shave my legs with, since the dollar store ones usually leave scrapes and little cuts that just wouldn't look good."

"Your legs are covered by the dress," my mom reminded me.

"That's right. Never mind." *Wasn't like I wanted to shave there anyway.*

With prom now two weeks away, I was having second thoughts about telling Nolan I was ready. I either had to *get* ready in two weeks, and I wasn't sure how to do that, or tell him I'd changed my mind, and I doubted he'd be happy about that.

It was stupid. He loved me, right? He'd still love me if I wasn't ready for sex. But what if he needed that? What if that was something he just *needed*, and if he couldn't get it from me...? I had to at least try.

Nolan

WEDNESDAY NIGHT was the next informational meeting for the Europe trip. This one we'd be attending with our parents, but we'd break off from the adults for half. If I remembered correctly, this was the meeting where they gave us our packing lists and a general itinerary, and our parents got more detailed flight information with phone numbers of who to contact in various situations. We'd also briefly meet the Europe-based trip guides via prerecorded videos. There would be a Q&A where Tim answered questions, and then we'd split up.

What I didn't count on was running into Summer and her mother in the parking lot.

"Great to see you two!" my mother said. "Is Summer getting excited for the trip?"

"Yeah," her mother replied. Summer gave me a polite smile. "How about you, Nolan?" her mother asked me.

"I've definitely been looking forward to it," I said—for longer than she'd ever understand.

"Oh, while we're here, do you know what color Summer's prom dress is going to be?" my father asked. "We're looking at tuxes this weekend. Might as well get a tie, too, if we need one."

"It's pink," her mother replied.

"Like your homecoming dress?" I asked Summer.

"No, it's like a light pink," she said to me.

"Baby pink," her mother said.

"I think I have that color," I said. "I'll check tonight." I thought the girl I'd taken to homecoming last year wore light pink.

Inside the auditorium, I saw Marta and her parents sitting together—so she *was* still going on the trip.

"Oh, should we sit with Marta?" Summer's mother asked her.

"That's okay," she said quickly.

Does her mother not know?

"We can all sit with them," my mother insisted before turning to Summer's mom. "Is Marta one of Summer's friends from school?"

238

"Yes, they've been inseparable since kindergarten."

Summer cringed, but I wasn't sure what to do. I grabbed her hand and followed our parents to the row behind Marta and her parents. My parents went first, then me and Summer, and then Summer's mom.

"Hi!" Summer's mother said to Marta's parents in front of us. "How's everything going?"

They seemed just as out of the loop. "Great, getting excited for the prom! They grow up so fast, don't they?"

Marta shot Summer and me a dirty look, but I decided to take this one. "Marta, are you going with Sutton?" I asked.

"Yes, actually. He asked me on Saturday," she said. "We went to the pool where he spelled it out with pool noodles. It's lucky his senior prom is the weekend after so we can go to both."

"That's so sweet," Summer replied. She was clearly trying to pretend everything was normal, but I could still hear something off in her voice.

"Are the four of you planning to take pictures together?" Summer's mother asked us.

"Jake's parents are talking about getting a limo; there should be room to add two more to the group," my father said.

"No, we're meeting up with Sutton's friends," Marta replied.

"Doesn't he go to a different school?" I asked.

She ignored the question. "Where are you getting your dress from, Summer?"

"I got it at Macy's on Sunday, actually," she said.

"Oh, good. I'm getting mine from David's Bridal, so we won't have to worry about having the same one." Marta gave Summer another dirty look while our parents weren't watching. "I mean, I didn't think we would be, anyway; I assumed you'd get yours from Marshalls like your eighth grade graduation dress. Remember when we were supposed to get those matching ones in different colors from Nordstrom, but your mom said it was too expensive?"

"I never said that!" Summer's mother said, defensive.

"Didn't you, though?" Marta's father asked. "You said it didn't make sense to spend so much money on something Summer would probably grow out of over the summer."

"There's a funny joke: it still fits," Summer whispered to me. "Barely, but it does."

"Well, whatever. I don't see what that has to do with Summer's prom dress," her mother said. "I can afford to buy my daughter her own dress, thank you very much."

"I hope I didn't offend you in offering to help," my mother said. "I just know those things can run hundreds of dollars, so with your financial situation—"

"What financial situation?" Summer's mother asked. She glared at her daughter as if Summer had said something wrong.

Summer had never said her financial situation was supposed to be a secret, but even if she'd never said anything… I'd been to her house. I could tell they weren't as well-off as we were, not even close.

My mother seemed to realize she'd said something wrong and tried to salvage it. "Well, being a single parent—"

"I make enough for me and Summer, thank you," she said.

Before things could get more intense, Tim announced that the meeting was beginning. I only hoped this wouldn't get taken out on Summer later.

"To start off today, we have some videos sent to us from the trip guides who will be working with us in Europe—just in case anyone thought the local trip leaders and I were going to be the only ones responsible for seventy teenagers," Tim said.

Most of the audience laughed, but Summer's mother whispered to Summer just loud enough for me to hear: "What did you tell them about our financial situation?"

"Nothing!" Summer whispered back. "It was probably just an assumption. I swear."

Her mother didn't say anything else.

* * *

WHEN WE split between adults and students, I tried to find Esme so Summer and I could hopefully talk with her some more. Then, a familiar voice sent shivers down my spine—

"Nolan?"

I could feel my heartbeat skyrocketing. "Katie. You're... on this trip."

Summer glanced between the two of us.

"Yeah, I am," Katie said. "Didn't expect to see you here. Or ever again."

"This is my girlfriend, Summer," I said quickly, then immediately wondered if that would make everything worse.

"Hi," Summer said. "Uh, nice to meet you."

Katie stared at her for a second, then smirked at me. "So *that's* Summer."

"What do you mean?" I asked nervously.

"You're the one who called me Summer when we hooked up," she said.

Oh, gross, that's right. I had nearly forgotten her creepy *"I can be Summer, if you need me to be"* comment that had essentially killed any feelings I'd still had for her.

"What?" Summer asked. She dropped her voice to a whisper. "You two... you two have had sex?"

"Don't worry, Summer. He's all yours," Katie said. "It was a one-night stand, and his mind was obviously on you, anyway." She turned back to me. "You know, I *really* hoped I'd never run into any of the guys I hooked up with that month again, but you—you never even texted me after. It was like you just—*poof*—disappeared. So since you don't want to talk, how about we continue on our separate ways during this trip?"

She didn't say anything else. She just took a seat all the way across the room.

Summer looked horrified. "I—I have so many questions," she managed.

"I have answers," I assured her. "First things first, it was *not* when you and I were together. It was before that."

"When?"

"September."

"Before or after homecoming?"

"Why does that matter?" I asked. "We weren't going out then."

"Just answer the question, please."

"After," I said. "It was very soon after."

"How soon?"

"...Hours." Better to be honest.

"Was it the same *night*?"

"Yes." I sighed. Her eyes widened, and I could tell I'd just lost a great deal of her trust with that one admission. "I—we had been texting, and I thought things with you weren't going to work out, so I texted her to see if she wanted to hang out. She offered to hook up, and I told her I was fine hanging out, but she's the one who insisted we hook up. I wasn't into it; I accidentally called her Summer once because I couldn't stop thinking of you. And that's when I decided to come talk to you the next morning, because I couldn't get my mind off you."

"So you were texting another girl when you went to homecoming with me?"

"*You* said it was just a casual, see-where-things-go type of date."

She nodded slowly. "Okay. That's true, I guess. I did say that. I—just don't really like that."

"I'm sorry," I said. "Believe me, I'd take it back if I could."

"Is that why you didn't call her after?"

I sighed. "I had a lot on my mind, and... she didn't seem like the type who would mind. It felt like we both very much agreed it was a one-time thing. In retrospect, I should have clarified or at least messaged her after to say I felt we shouldn't continue anything. That's my bad. My mistake."

She nodded, taking it all in. I could tell she was upset, and I didn't blame her. It was a relief when two of the trip leaders finally entered the room to start the students' meeting.

"Even if I'm not good," Summer whispered to me, "you'll call me after, right?"

Wait, did I somehow not blow any possibility of that happening out the window?

"Absolutely," I said. "With us, something like that could hardly ruin things. I promise you, Summer, I would never do that to you."

"But you did it to Katie."

"Katie's not you," I said. "I love you. And you're my girlfriend; she was just... a one-time thing."

She nodded. "I still have to think about it."

"I understand," I said with a sigh.

She didn't say anything else. We had packets to go over with the trip leaders, anyway.

12

Summer

THE WEEK leading up to prom, the girls in my classes kept asking me questions, like where I'd gotten my dress from, if we were getting a limo, or where I was getting my hair and makeup done—they seemed to think it was "so sweet" that my mother was doing my hair and makeup.

Nolan, Liam, and Jake kept me updated with their plans for renting a limo and taking pictures at the rose garden, and I heard my mother on the phone with Nolan's parents a few times, so they were probably discussing details. She seemed to have gotten over her issue with Nolan's mother assuming she didn't make a lot—she didn't, but she seemed to not want his parents to know about that. At the very least, she wasn't using her customer service voice with them anymore.

I asked Daisy if she and Ben were going to prom, but neither of them were particularly into dances, so they wouldn't be there. I wished she'd come—not that I didn't like Nolan's friends, but it would be nice to spend some time with someone I'd been friends with since childhood—besides Nolan, of course.

And then, the big day finally came. It was a Saturday, so my mom was off work to help me get ready. I took a shower and shaved—my legs and underarms— and then we went to the florist to get a boutonniere. My mom gave me an at-home manicure with silver nail polish from the dollar store—and even though my shoes covered my toes, she gave me a pedicure, too, just because it was prom.

She also gave me a steam facial in the kitchen sink before doing my makeup. My hair had mostly dried, but despite my protests she finished up with the blow-dryer before working on a side-braid, weaving in some baby's breath flowers from the florist.

So then it was just my dress, which she helped me put on and fix the clear straps for. I put my things in the clutch purse and slipped on my shoes, and before we left for the rose garden, my mom let me borrow a modest pearl necklace from when she was in high school.

On the car ride to meet Nolan at the rose garden, I kept thinking about how tonight might really be the night that we had sex for the first time—that *I* had sex for the first time. I was so nervous. I still didn't know what I was supposed to do, and it wasn't like I could just ask my mother how sex worked. Hopefully Nolan would be patient with me.

If I didn't chicken out, anyway.

Nolan

THE ROSE garden was just as crowded as it had been in the old timeline. Jake and Caeley and their mothers were the first to meet me and my parents there. Liam showed up shortly after with his mother, and then his date, Sofia—I thought he'd gone with her before, too—and her father showed up, so I was just waiting for Summer.

"Maybe she's standing you up," Liam said with a chuckle.

I rolled my eyes. "Keep it up, man, and I won't share the goods with you." He'd asked to borrow a couple condoms from the pack I'd bought since he hadn't been able to replenish the stash in his sock drawer after his mother had found it last month.

"Where are they, anyway?" he asked.

I tapped the suit pocket against my chest. "I'll give 'em to you when the limo gets here."

He nodded. "Just don't let Summer pin a hole in them when she gives you your flower thing."

Summer and her mother finally pulled into the parking lot, and I watched her get out of the passenger seat. The closer Summer got, the wider my eyes got. A year ago, I wouldn't have even recognized this girl. If someone told me *that* was Summer Madison, I would have laughed. But she *was* Summer, and she was beautiful, and she was mine.

Her dress swished around her ankles as she walked; she held part of it up to keep from tripping, and she was looking up at me rather than at her feet. There was something different about her tonight, like... like she *knew* she was beautiful, and she wasn't waiting for me to let her know. She already knew. And how could she *not*? Her eyes sparkled, her smile shone, and as she got closer, I could smell some kind of sweet perfume, a fruity scent but mostly sweet, like caramel and vanilla.

"Hey," she said, giving me a shy smile. "Um, this is for you." She held up a box from the florist.

"Summer, you look..." *Beautiful* couldn't do her justice in that moment. Her hair was braided to the side with flowers, her eyeshadow brought out the pale pink in her dress, her lips were shiny and soft... "You look amazing, Sum."

She blushed, or maybe it was her makeup. "Thank you," she said. "You, too."

"Oh, uh, I got you a wrist corsage," I said, holding up the box. "I figured it'd be easier than a pin." I wasn't sure what the flowers were called—my mom had picked it out—but they were light pink like her dress, with some of the same little white ones she had in her hair.

"Yours is a pin, sorry."

"No, that's fine. I don't think they make 'em any other way for us guys," I said. "Just, uh... be careful with it, because I have things in that pocket that you don't want to poke a hole in."

I wondered if our parents had coordinated, because my flowers looked similar to hers. Once we got that ordeal straightened out, it was time to take pictures. Out of the corner of my eye, I could see Marta with some guy who I assumed was Sutton, posing by themselves with some adult as their photographer. I hoped Summer's mother didn't see them and insist we take pictures together, but fortunately, we made it to a nice area before anyone could notice.

We took some group pictures, then individual couple shots, and the entire time I couldn't believe how lucky I was. I never wanted to let go of Summer.

"Have a good time," her mother said to us as everyone's parents got ready to leave.

"We will," I assured her, still holding Summer's hand. "I'll have her home by midnight."

Her mother laughed. "The dance ends at eleven. You'll have her home by eleven-thirty."

"Okay. Eleven-thirty." Well, that put a wrench in our plans.

The six of us got in the limo, and before we knew it, we were off to the hotel where we'd have dinner and then prom.

I wasn't sure how Summer and I were going to have time to have sex—unless it was a quickie in my car, which I doubted she wanted for her first time—if I had to have her home by eleven-thirty. Unless we could leave the dance early?

My parents were having dinner with Summer's mother, but maybe I could convince them to bring my car to the hotel so Summer and I could leave early. As long as they were there, they could give the staff permission to let us leave. I'd make something up, like the dance was boring and we wanted to go get Taco Bell or something not *too* obvious…

"Sum," I whispered. "Do you want to leave around ten? I can get my parents to sign us out and bring my car."

"Why would we leave early?" she asked.

"Your mom wants you home at eleven-thirty. That's… not really enough time to… you know."

"Oh. Well, would we miss anything?"

"They crown the king and queen at nine-thirty, if you care about that stuff."

"I don't know the seniors all that well," she said. "I guess we can leave early."

"If you change your mind, let me know," I told her.

Just for kicks, I bet Jake ten dollars that the same seniors who'd won in the old timeline would win in this one. I didn't want to stake too much on it, just in case the do-over had caused a rift in anyone else's timeline.

Summer

I NEVER knew a school dance could feel so magical. Rather than the gym, we were in a big hotel ballroom with better lighting and better acoustics for the music and more intricate decorations. The room was decorated to match some pirate theme, and there was a photo booth with pirate props where Nolan and his friends and I took pictures together.

The dinner was alright; it was just some salad, a dinner roll, and a pasta dish from the hotel. It wasn't very filling, but it tasted good, at least.

I was having so much fun that I didn't even mind the grinding circle all that much when we got to the dance floor. Nolan asked me if I was okay with it, and to my surprise, I felt like I could say yes. Maybe because *that* was easier than thinking about the plans we had later tonight.

We slow-danced during the slow songs, and we had some pretty fun conversations with his friends in the circle. I found out that Liam's date, Sofia, was a sophomore on the badminton team who wanted to major in disability education in college, and that she volunteered with a local youth theater group for performers with special needs. She talked a lot about her plans to pitch an upscale "Best Buddies Prom" to the president of the Best Buddies club for next year, since the special education students always had their own version of prom in the school gym every year instead of getting a nice hotel like us for some liability reason. She mentioned they would probably have to fundraise for it, and Nolan said she could count on a generous donation from him. I wanted to promise the same, but I doubted my mother would give me more than a few dollars for that.

"Are you having fun?" Nolan asked me when we stepped away to get some water.

"I actually am," I said. "Thanks for taking me."

"Gotta make sure you get your money's worth," he said playfully.

"On that note, my mom can't find out we left early," I said, "or I'll never hear the end of her paying a hundred dollars for me to not stay the entire time."

"Really?" He smirked. "I thought she'd be pissed if she found out we left early to have sex."

"Well, she can't find out about that, either."

"Don't worry. She won't."

Another slow song started to play.

"Wanna dance?" he asked.

"Sure."

Nolan

LOOKING INTO Summer's eyes while we danced, I still couldn't believe how good I had it. Not just being with her tonight, but having her at all. I was lucky to have this second chance with her. I would have missed so much.

"This feels like a fairytale," she said. "Well, a very piratey fairytale."

We danced, we laughed, we talked, we enjoyed the refreshments... and then my parents sent a text to let me know they were in the parking lot.

"It's time to head out," I whispered to Summer. "You ready?"

She nodded. "Let's do this."

My father signed us out with the security staff, and we went to where he'd parked my truck: next to my mother's car, which she'd driven so they'd have a way back home later.

"We'll be home around midnight," my father said. "Be safe."

I nodded. "We will."

Summer got in the passenger seat, and I got in the driver's side.

"Do they... know?" she asked.

"They're probably assuming," I said, "but I told them we were bored and wanted to go to Taco Bell instead of staying longer."

"Now that you mention it, food sounds good," she said. "That portion size at dinner was way off."

"Oh, we'll both be hungry later; I'll swing us through a drive-through on the way back to your house."

"Perfect."

As I pulled out of the parking lot, I glanced over at her. I just never wanted to stop looking at Summer; she was so beautiful tonight. I had to keep my eyes on the road, though; I wasn't trying to kill us both. *Maybe I should use different phrasing...*

And just then, rain started pattering against the windshield.

It was raining that day I gave her a ride home.

Why was I thinking about that day *now*? That day didn't matter anymore; it had never happened. Summer was here, in my passenger seat.

Just like she was that day.

We hit a red light. The rain made everything kind of blurred. Suddenly, that day was all I could think about. It was the last time I'd seen her before she'd died.

It was raining then, just like now. She was wearing blue shorts, bright blue, kind of like the kind cheerleaders wore to practice, and this white tank top. Her hair was down like it always was back then. She didn't have any makeup on. I found her after the trip meeting when I was looking for Katie.

"Hey, did you see Katie?" I asked her. *"I was hoping to give her a ride to swim."*

She nodded. *"She just left with Noemi. I don't have a ride home, though, if you're not busy."*

"Well, I do have some last-minute stuff to grab for the trip—"

"I'll get you coffee when we pass the Starbucks," she said. *"As a thanks. I just need a ride. I hate waiting for the bus in the rain."*

"What about Esme? You're friends, right? Can't she drive you?"

"She lives half an hour away. Her mom said no."

"Can't you drive?"

"I haven't had time to get my license. Please? I live really close to school."

"That's out of my way."

"Pleeeease?"

I rolled my eyes. *"Fine."*

"I can't believe we're actually doing this." Her voice snapped me back into the current timeline. "But I'm glad we are. You know? I'm glad it's *you*."

"Uh... yeah."

"I never thought I'd actually do this, not for a long time."

"We don't have to."

"No, I want to."

The light changed, and I took my foot off the brake.

She was quiet in the car, when I gave her the ride that day. I remembered putting the radio on just to hear *something*—and I realized it was the same song that was playing faintly out of my speakers *now*, making me remember even more vividly. I had turned the radio on, hoping to zone out and forget she was even there. She didn't say much until we got to a red light.

"I'm really glad you're coming on the trip, too," she said. *"I know we don't talk much at school, but when you showed up to the first meeting... I was just really excited to have someone else I knew there. And I think it'll be a good chance to get to know each other better."*

"Well, I mean, you'll probably hang out with Marta, and I'll have my group... There's a lot of people going on the trip. We probably won't see each other that much."

"It'd be nice to spend some time together, though," she said. *"Besides, Marta*

doesn't really... Well, I don't know how much we'll hang out."

"Isn't she your best friend?"

"It's complicated."

"Esme's nice to you; you can hang out with her."

"Why don't you want to hang out with me? I thought we were friends. You've said we're friends."

"Because you won't—" I shook my head. *"Sure. We'll hang out at some point, if we have time. Whatever."*

"I don't want you to spend time with me out of pity." She sighed. *"I just thought we were friends, that's all. Whatever. We don't have to hang out. Just don't lie to me."*

"What does it take with you?" I demanded. *"No matter what I say, you're not happy."*

"Because I know there's something wrong with me," she said. *"In an ideal world, we'd be friends, and you'd want to be friends. Maybe more than that, but I'm not stupid. I know you like Katie and that's fine. I just wanted to be friends, like you said we were. But what I don't want is your pity and your lies just because you think that's what I want. You've never listened to me, have you?"*

"Just tell me what you want from me," I said. I looked up and saw the long drive-through line ahead of us. *"Forget this. I'll just park. We'll order inside; I'll pay for my own."*

"No, I promised."

"Fine."

"Are you okay?" Summer's voice brought me back to the present again as I pulled into my driveway.

"Yeah," I said. "I—yeah. I'm fine."

"Are you sure?"

"Summer... are you sure I'm the one you want to do this with?"

"Of course."

"But what about everything you said before, about all the uncertainty—?"

"There will always be uncertainty," she said, "but you... you've shown me that you care about me. I've fallen in love with you, and that's what makes this feel right."

I put my hand on hers. "I love you, Summer. Thank you, for... everything."

She smiled for a second, but then got that nervous expression.

"Do you want to go inside?" I asked.

She nodded. "Could I... just get myself ready, before we... get started?"

"Yeah. Do whatever you need to. There's a bathroom just off my room; I'll wait for you."

She followed me upstairs, and I went into my room and sat on the bed while she stepped into the bathroom across the hall.

I closed my eyes and went back to that day again, in the Starbucks parking lot. We'd both gotten our drinks, and she'd paid like she'd said she would. We stayed under the awning for a few minutes since it was raining.

"Can I just ask you something?" she said.

"I guess."

"Why am I not good enough for you?" she asked. *"We've known each other for years, but you won't acknowledge me. You hate me."*

"I don't hate you. You just—"

"Don't lie to me. Stop lying; I don't need you to lie."

"I'm not—"

"Just tell me what's wrong with me! I know there's something wrong! I know you talk shit about me with everyone, and I want to know what I ever did to you!"

"Fine!" I should've known it was too far. *"You want the truth, Summer? You really want to know what I think of you? I think you're annoying as hell*

and that you can't take a hint to save your life. I tried to be nice to you, but it was never enough, and you always have to come looking for more. We're not friends, okay? I don't like you. You're annoying and clingy and you don't know when to quit. And then you try to talk to my friends, too, like we're all friends, like we want *you to hang out with us. You think you fit in with us; like we'd care if you didn't show up at the airport next week. And you think for some reason I want to be friends with you, despite every evidence to the contrary I've given you, and you won't give up. I don't care about you, Summer, not even as a friend. You're not my friend, and you never were. You're nothing to me."*

She didn't say anything. She just stared at me, like she was waiting for more. She didn't look fazed by what I'd said, not in the slightest.

"You really wouldn't miss me, then. If you never saw me again?"

"Honestly? I'd be relieved."

"And you don't think anyone else would miss me?"

"I don't know. Maybe Marta, or your other friends. But I can't speak for anyone else."

"You can only speak for yourself. And you wouldn't miss me."

"I have no reason to."

She nodded. Then, she turned to walk away.

"Where are you going?" I asked.

"I'll take the bus home," she said.

"Summer, come on. It's raining. I said I'd give you a ride."

"No, it's fine. You're free of me. I won't bother you anymore."

"Fine, whatever." I rolled my eyes. *"See you Monday."*

"Maybe you will, maybe you won't." She turned back one last time to face me. *"Have a good weekend, have fun in Europe, and if I never see you again, have a nice life!"*

I watched her storm to the bus stop and stand there in the rain. I made sure she got on a bus and then went back to my car and drove home. I remembered thinking she was being so dramatic in the moment, but how could I not have seen it before? I'd practically killed her myself. How could I have said that to her?

I laid back on the bed and stared up at the ceiling. I didn't deserve this do-over. The only reason I was here was because Summer didn't deserve to die.

The door opened.

"Nolan?" Summer asked.

I sat up and looked at her. She was still in her prom dress, but her arms were covering her chest like she was nervous.

"You okay?" I asked her.

She nodded. "Can you unzip my dress?"

"Already?"

"Well, I don't want to rip it or anything."

I stood up and she turned her back to me. I put one hand on the zipper and one hand on her shoulder, but hesitated.

"Are you sure?" I asked her.

"Yes," she said. "I promise."

My hand shook. I stared at the zipper, but all I could see was Summer getting on that bus, never to be seen again. The last thing I'd ever said to her was that I wouldn't care if she died. She was practically screaming for help and I pushed her away, right to her death. And now she was going to trust me with something that meant so much to her.

I don't deserve her.

I couldn't do it. "I can't," I said. "I don't deserve this... you. You trust me so much, but I was horrible to you before. How could you trust me enough to do this?"

She shook her head, facing me. "You weren't nice to me, but I don't think you were horrible. But, Nolan, however you were before... you've changed. You're different now."

She could say that because she didn't know just how terrible I was. She'd never heard me say those horrible words to her in her moment of weakness. She had no idea what a monster I was.

"*You* changed me," I told her. "I needed to be better for you."

"And that's how I can trust you. You've shown me the better you."

I looked into her eyes.

"I love you, Summer," I told her, and I meant it. "You're everything to me."

"I love you, too."

Summer

NOLAN UNZIPPED my dress. I couldn't wear a bra with it because of the neckline; even my skin-colored one couldn't be hidden. So as the long dress fell to the ground, I stood in nothing but a pair of plain grey underwear because I didn't have anything nice. I hoped it was enough.

He took a step back from me, like he was guilty of something.

"This is okay, right?" I asked him. "I—didn't have anything nice to wear."

"You're beautiful, Summer," he said. "You're perfect."

I blushed. "Thank you. Um... so, what do we do next?"

He slipped off his suit jacket and took my hand, and we sat down on his bed. Something caught my eye: on his nightstand, next to the framed picture of us in fifth grade, was the pink stuffed animal I gave him that he'd won for me all those years ago. That helped me relax—this was Nolan, and he really loved me, and I loved him, too.

He kissed me, and we kept kissing, and our hands moved: his to my waist, mine to his shoulders, like we were slow-dancing, and then we almost naturally moved so we were lying down on the bed, him on top of me. He pulled away for a second to undo his tie and the buttons on his shirt so he could throw it all aside. We kissed some more, and he gently grabbed my breasts. It felt weird, but good. I let it happen, wondering if there was something similar I was supposed to do to him. Then he pulled away again, and suddenly we were both in our underwear.

The kissing felt good, but it was in that moment that I realized: if we were going to do this, I was going to have to see him naked. I had never seen *anyone* naked before. I mean, I had a general idea of what to expect, but... I didn't *want* to see him naked. I... didn't want to have sex. I wasn't ready. Everything felt nice, and I loved him, but deep down I wasn't ready.

"Stop!" I said, covering my eyes. I felt so pathetic, but I couldn't do this.

"You okay?" he asked, sitting back from me.

I shook my head. "I can't do it. I'm not ready."

"Okay," he said. "That's okay."

"No, it's not. I—I told you we'd do this, but I'm sorry. I just can't. And I don't know when I *am* going to be ready. I'm sorry. Don't be mad."

"I'm not mad," he said, squeezing my shoulders. "You're not ready; that's fine. I was skeptical in the first place. I'm not going to be mad at you, Summer." He sighed. "To be honest... I'm not sure I feel right about this tonight, anyway."

"You don't?"

He shook his head. "Not tonight."

"I don't know how long it'll take me to be ready," I said.

"That's okay," he said. "You're worth waiting for."

We sat there in silence for a few minutes. I didn't think either of us knew what to do next.

"Do you want to get dressed and go to Taco Bell?" Nolan asked. "We still have almost an hour."

"Can we... just lay here for a few minutes?" I asked. "Together?"

"Okay."

He wrapped his arms around me. It was nice, just feeling his chest rise and fall with each breath... but I felt terrible for chickening out. I was seventeen; shouldn't I be able to do this? *What is wrong with me?*

One day, Nolan would probably realize that I couldn't give him what he wanted and that I wasn't enough for him. But until that day came, I was going to enjoy being with him, because it was nice to pretend something this good could happen to me.

13

Nolan

I CALLED Summer on Sunday afternoon just to talk. Just so she'd know I wasn't mad. I didn't *love* the idea that she probably wouldn't be ready to have sex for a long time, but having to entertain myself in that department and getting to be with Summer was better than being without her. I just hoped she could believe me.

And I was being honest when I'd told her I didn't feel right about it on Saturday—I didn't. Not when I could so freshly remember the last thing I'd said to her in the old timeline. Even if that timeline didn't matter anymore... it just didn't feel right.

"Maybe next time," Liam said at lunch on Monday while we waited for Summer. "Sofia didn't want to, either; apparently she's 'saving herself.'"

"Are you gonna go out with her again?" I asked.

He shrugged. "That would be up to her."

Summer came and sat down next to me. "Hey," she said.

"Hey. How was geometry?"

"Well, I got a C+ on last week's test," she said. "Seventy-eight percent— the second-highest score I've gotten in that class."

"Proud of you," I said. "Hey, wanna hang out after school?"

"Today?"

"Sure."

"Um... how about tomorrow?" she asked.

"Okay. Are you doing something after school today?"

"No, I—I just was looking forward to my routine. That's all."

Liam and Jake looked at me questioningly. I shrugged.

"Alright. Well, we can hang out tomorrow."

"Perfect."

Summer

"YOU *DON'T* have to have sex in high school," Daisy assured me. "That doesn't make you weird. Honestly, it makes you smart."

"Smart?"

"Ben and I have talked about it a lot. We both agree there's just so much risk with doing that in high school," she said. "Besides, we're still kids. We're not really *adult* enough to be doing that yet."

"Nolan's already done it, though."

"So? It's never too late to start making better life choices," she said.

* * *

"YOU STILL have a CD player in your room?" Nolan asked.

"Yeah." I'd told him we could hang out in my room, and he'd assured me he wasn't going to try anything. I still felt bad, even if Daisy thought we'd done the right thing. "It was my eighth birthday present."

"Does it still work?" he asked.

"Probably," I said. "Did you want to listen to music?"

"Sure," he said. "Do you have *Rumours*?"

I smiled. "My mom does. I don't know where her CDs are, though. But if you want to listen to our song, I have it on my phone."

"What CDs do you have?" he asked. "I'm curious."

"I have a few in my nightstand drawer," I said. "You can look—"

Do I have a razor in there? When was the last time I cut myself?

"This drawer?" He slid it open. "Ooh, I see a good one." He laughed, holding up the album for me to see: "*Kidz Bop 6*. A girl with taste, finally."

I laughed, too. "I hate that CD so much. My aunt gave it to me for my birthday one year thinking it'd be something I'd enjoy. The cover of 'Come Clean' alone makes me wish I didn't have ears."

"Let's see what else you've got." He opened the drawer, and I watched nervously.

The last time I cut myself was... months ago? But did I ever throw away the razor? Or did I leave it—?

"Why do you have a razor in your drawer?" he asked, holding it up. "Do you shave your legs in your sleep?"

"Why *is* that in there?" I tried to seem confused. "That's weird."

"Want me to toss it?"

"Please."

That was a close one.

"You've gotta have more than *Kidz Bop*, the *Ice Princess* soundtrack, and *Spring Awakening*."

"They're probably in storage, since I uploaded them all to my computer," I said. "I just have a bunch of random crap in that drawer now."

He sat down next to me by the closet door. "Well, I trust that you have good taste in music. We both like *our* song."

I half-smiled. "Everything's gonna be okay with us, right?"

"Of course, Sum," he said. "Don't worry."

"Well, it's what I do best." I tried to make it sound like a joke.

"I know," he said, "and that's why I want to make sure you know: you don't have to worry. I want to be with you, Summer. I love you."

"Are you sure it's okay? If it doesn't happen for us for a long time?"

He nodded. "Let's not worry about the future so much, alright? Let's just enjoy being together now."

"Sounds good to me."

Nolan

AFTER PROM, school went by fast. Summer and I seemed to be back to normal, which was nice, because I tended to worry about her worrying. We had another informational meeting and got the schedules for our three-week workshop program that would take place during the first weeks of summer. And then at school, we got our yearbooks.

I handed mine to Summer at lunch. "Sign, please."

She smiled. "Only if you sign mine."

I never knew what to write in my close friends' yearbooks, since we were just going to see each other and talk all the time anyway. Maybe next year would be different, since we would be graduating.

I thought about it and wrote:

Summer,

Thank you for an amazing year. I wasn't looking forward to this year at all, but being with you made it all worth it. Can't wait to spend our summer together!

Love, Nolan

She giggled when she handed hers back to me.

"What's funny?" I asked.

"You'll see." She giggled again.

I opened it up to see what she had written:

Nolan—

You rock

Love, Summer

I laughed, putting my arm around her and kissing the top of her head. "Amazing," I told her. "Most romantic signature you could've come up with."

We passed our yearbooks around the table with Liam's and Jake's, and then we started looking for how many pictures we were in throughout the yearbook.

"Why aren't you looking?" I asked Summer.

She shrugged. "I'm never in any."

"Well, maybe this year will be different." She had to be in *some* pictures, right? My friends and I always ended up in a few candids, at least. But she was right—I didn't see her in any.

"I told you." She sighed. "It's okay, though. I'm used to it."

"Hey, next year we'll make sure you're all over this thing," I said. "Jake's taking yearbook next year, anyway, so he'd better make sure of it."

Grant and Jimmy approached our table excitedly. Someone else was with them—Jean Dyer, with her usual blank expression, hunched over, breathing through her mouth, eyes darting around until they fixated on something or someone...

"Hey, pals!" Grant said. "Will you sign our yearbooks?"

Had this happened in the old timeline? Yes, it definitely had. I remembered because it had turned into a conversation about Minecraft that lasted the rest of lunch.

"Sure," I said. "Pass 'em down."

Grant, Jimmy, and Jean were easy—I just had to write *"Have a great summer! —Nolan"* three times and that was that. Summer seemed to be taking a while with Jean's yearbook, though. By the time she passed it to me, I was curious enough to read what she'd written:

Hi Jean,

I hope you have a great summer! You're awesome!

Your friend,

Summer Madison

Curious as to why it had taken her so long to come up with that, I wrote my standard line and handed it back to Jean. The three of them waved and kept walking to find more people.

"What'd you write to Jean?" I asked Summer, pretending I hadn't read it. "You had her book for a while."

She shrugged. "I don't know. I wanted to tell her she's cool, but, like, I felt like I was being too patronizing. Even what I ended up writing... I guess I wanted to apologize for all the years Marta and I were mean to her, but I don't know how."

"Summer, you're not friends with Marta anymore, right?" Liam asked.

"That's why I eat with you guys every day now." She laughed but sounded nervous.

He laughed, too. "Good, so now I can finally say it: Marta's an ass. She's in my cooking class and she's so rude to the special ed kids."

"Last year when they had that 'pledge to end the r-slur' banner for everyone to sign, I heard her say that the banner *was* the slur," Jake said. "Almost drop-kicked her right there, but I didn't want to hit a girl."

"At least you two won't be stuck in Europe with her for a month." I shuddered, then slung my arm around Summer. "At least we've got each other, though."

"Hey, a trip to Europe for school credit—I'd want to go even if Mrs. Garth was supervising the trip," Jake said, referring to our terrible APUSH teacher who'd nearly convinced him to transfer out of the class. "You two are so lucky."

"Luckier than you'll ever know," I said, squeezing Summer tight.

Summer

THE LAST week of school was finally upon us. Then it would be three weeks of cultural enrichment workshops, thirty-five days in Europe, getting my braces off, a week of my dad in town, and then senior year.

I couldn't believe the school year was almost over. It seemed like just yesterday I was sitting in homeroom wondering if this year was even going to be any good. But it was better than good—it was the best school year I could remember since... well, ever, probably.

Daisy signed my yearbook in the locker room on our last day of gym, but she hadn't ordered one, so I couldn't sign hers.

"I can't believe you're not going to be here next year," I said. "I feel like we finally got the chance to catch up after two years of not having any classes together."

"Hey, we can still talk," she reminded me. "West Valley isn't that far away. And with social media, it'll be like I never left."

"Yeah, but it's not the same." I sighed. "I miss middle school sometimes. You and me and Bella... and Marta when she wasn't being a jerk to you two."

"Oh, yeah, I forgot about Bella," Daisy said. "I wonder how she's doing."

Me, too, more than you know. "I'm sure she's doing great in Reno."

"I'm actually thinking of going to a school in Reno after West Valley," she replied. "They've got a great engineering program. I'll let you know if I run into her."

"Please do." I laughed so it would seem playful, not deathly serious.

* * *

MY LAST class of this year was English, which was my favorite class and the class I was doing the best in. Ms. Harris gave everyone cute little award certificates for random things; for instance, mine was "best vocab sentences" for the vocab quizzes. I thought it was so sweet, and I put it in my binder to keep.

As everyone was leaving, I stayed behind to talk to Ms. Harris.

"Hi, Summer," she said. "Any big vacation plans?"

"Yeah, actually. I'm going to Europe for a month," I said.

"Oh, the student trip? Congratulations. You'll enjoy it!"

"I hope so." I smiled. "Um, I just wanted to tell you that you were my favorite teacher this year. And the other two years I've had you. So thank you."

"Aww, you're sweet," she said. "I enjoyed having you in my class. Are you taking honors next year, too?"

I nodded. "That's the plan."

"Well, you'll do great," she said. "Just remember to come back and visit me."

"I will," I said. I wished she taught senior English; I was worried my new teacher wouldn't be as nice as her. "I'm actually hoping to have a TA period next year, and hopefully I can be your TA."

"I would love that!" she said. "I hope that works out. Have a great summer and enjoy your trip!"

"Thank you. I will." There was something more I wanted to say, like... *Thank you for believing in me, because I didn't believe I could actually get an A- in any class this year.* But I kept walking to my locker. Nolan caught up to me there.

"It's summertime!" he cheered. "Three weeks 'til Europe!"

"Three weeks doesn't even sound that long," I said. "It's going to feel like a long time, though."

"Longer than you know." He laughed, then stuck something into my locker through one of the vent slats.

"What's that?" I asked.

"It's for you to read on the first day of senior year," he explained.

"You realize I'm going to need to know what that says right now, right?" I laughed, turning the dial.

He put his hand on the locker. "Nope. It's a surprise. But it's a good surprise. Don't worry."

"Ha—you know me." I took my hand off the lock. "But fine. You win."

"Want to get dinner tonight?" he asked. "To celebrate the end of junior year?"

"I'll have to ask my mom, but sure," I told him.

This was going to be a great summer to finish off a great year.

Nolan

SUMMER'S MOTHER agreed to let her go out for frozen yogurt after dinner, so I picked her up and took her to Yogurtland.

"So, we both like 'original' flavor," I observed, watching her pass up most of the toppings. She put chocolate chips on hers, but that was it. "You gotta have more toppings than that, though. I'm buying."

She laughed. "This is all I like."

"No strawberries?" I asked, shaking my head. "You're missing out."

"I don't like fruit in my desserts," she said. "Well, I like chocolate-covered strawberries, but that's about it. I just... don't like mixing flavors."

"But fruit is meant to be a part of dessert," I insisted, adding some sliced bananas. "You're crazy, Sum."

She bit her lip. "Sorry."

"Hey, I was just kidding around," I told her. "You do you. Not like I'm the one eating it."

The bells on the door jingled, and I turned to see who had walked in—to my surprise, it was Jean Dyer and an older woman, possibly her mother. Jean's face lit up—I didn't think I had seen her smile before—and she pointed at us.

"Are those your friends?" the older woman asked.

Jean nodded excitedly.

"Hi," the woman said to us. "Do you know Jean from school?"

"Yeah," I said. "Nice to see you both. I'm Nolan."

Summer waved. "I'm Summer."

"I'm Jean's mother, Melinda," she said. "Nice to meet you. Come on, Jean. Let's get some yogurt."

Jean waved at us, and we waved back.

"I'm glad I'm here with you," Summer said. "Marta would've been rude to her."

"Even in front of her mother?"

"You'd be surprised."

I put my arm around her. "I'll make sure she doesn't have any friends on this trip."

"Don't do that," she said. "As long as she leaves me alone, I'm fine."

So there it was: Summer didn't want revenge. Disappointing, but I had to respect her for it.

"You don't always have to be the bigger person, you know," I told her. "If you want to take her down for everything she's done—to you and to others—I'm right there with you."

"I'm okay. But thanks."

I sighed, but smiled. "Alright, that's probably the better decision anyway."

"I'll let you know if she pushes me over the edge," she assured me.

"Excellent. I'll have a plan on standby."

She laughed. "Of course you will."

"It's what I'm here for."

"For revenge on girls you barely know?"

"No." I put my hand on top of hers. "For you."

14

Summer

"TODAY, WE will be learning all about Spain, since that's our first stop," Tim announced. "We'll have a presentation here, a break, then some alternating group workshops, lunch, and then we'll meet back together in here to wrap up."

This whole Europe thing was finally starting to feel real. I was really going to go to Europe! My mom had gone when she was in college, so she was excited to tell me all the places I should go when we had free time.

The workshops started out fun, but I started to feel intimidated by how much Nolan seemed to know about Spain—it was only the first day, but it was like he'd taken the workshop before or something.

"Have you been to Spain before?" I asked as we walked across the street to a shopping center for lunch.

He shook his head. "Never left the country. Not even to Canada or Mexico. Can you believe that?"

"No," I said, "because you seem like you know so much in the workshops."

"Oh, I just did a little research on the side when I was bored," he said. "Guess I got carried away. How about you? Where's the farthest you've ever traveled?"

"I've only left California to go to Florida and visit my dad or go to Disney World with extended family, but we haven't done that since elementary school. And my dad usually comes here since his place isn't exactly guest-friendly."

"That's so crazy," he replied. "So you've never been to New York, or Las Vegas, or the Grand Canyon? You've never gone skiing in Colorado?"

"Nope."

"Tell me you've been camping in Yosemite, at least. Or Tahoe."

I shook my head. "Not really a camping kind of person."

"What about the DC trip in eighth grade?"

"My mom's work days were cut back that year, so we couldn't afford it."

He shook his head. "Summer, you still have so much of the world to see. After graduation, I'm taking you on a road trip."

I laughed. "Where?"

"Anywhere but here," he said. "We'll make a list of all the places you have to see, and we'll go to as many as we can. Sound good?"

"Like a bucket list?" I asked.

He nodded. "Yeah. But you don't die at the end. Got it?"

"Got it."

Nolan

I GUESS I had to tone down my knowledge from taking the workshops in the old timeline. I could tell Summer was intimidated by what I knew.

The idea of a road trip made me excited, though, so I pulled out my laptop and started typing up a list of places to go:

```
San Diego

Los Angeles

Disneyland

Universal Studios

Joshua Tree

Santa Monica

Newport

Grand Canyon

Las Vegas

Tahoe
```

```
Yosemite

Big Sur

Crater Lake

Oregon Coast

Mount Rainier

Seattle

Yellowstone

Rocky Mountains

Washington, DC

Chicago

NYC
```

I smiled as I kept typing. I was going to put so many places on this list that Summer would have no choice but to stick around long enough for me to take her to all of them.

Not that I was still worried; she actually seemed perfectly fine, and I'd probably done my job right in keeping her alive, but I suppose a part of me would always worry because of what I knew could have happened.

I reached under my bed for her notebook and decided to finish it tonight—get it over with so I could focus on the present.

As I read the last entry over and over, I thought about what I'd learned:

June 24th—

I don't know what to do. I can tell nobody else on the trip wants me there, even the few who are actually nice to me sometimes. And Marta... she's got her new, better friends now and doesn't need me. She never needed me. This fight was just a way out for her.

Marta and Summer had gotten in a fight because Summer had caught Sutton cheating on her and Marta didn't believe her. Marta was also generally an asshole who would trade Summer for social status at the snap of someone's fingers. So because I had inadvertently convinced the "cool" kids on the trip—and those who wanted to be cool—to avoid Summer, she'd felt like she had nobody. Maybe Esme, but even she was passively mean to Summer sometimes. I still needed to get to know her better in this timeline.

Something's wrong with me but I don't know what. I guess I've never written that out before, but I've always known. My mom won't let me see a psychiatrist, she says I don't need one and it's a waste of money. But there has to be something wrong with me.

I still wasn't sure what she meant by that. Did she mean depression? Did she want to see a psychiatrist? Maybe I needed to talk to her about that.

Do I even want to go on this Europe trip anymore? Is it worth it? It's too late to pull out of the trip, though. I guess I screwed everything up. I could've saved everyone so much trouble. All of this is my fault. I'll never learn how to just be normal.

And that was the last thing she'd ever written. If I *really* thought about it, I could see her sitting backstage in the auditorium, waiting for the rain to pass, setting the notebook down when we'd started talking that day… and I could see her standing up without looking back. She'd probably forgotten the notebook because she was so caught up in getting that ride from me; she probably hadn't intended to leave it behind on purpose. She wouldn't have wanted anyone to find it.

I put the notebook back under my bed. I wasn't going to look at it again. That timeline was gone. *Summer is alive, and she's going to stay that way for a long time.*

Summer

"WHICH OVER-THE-COUNTER medications did they say you needed?" my mother asked as we turned into the pharmacy section. She'd decided to take me to Target after dinner to start picking up things for the trip.

"It says that since I'm under eighteen, we have to put them all in a box or bag with my name on them and give them to Tim at the airport," I said.

"I asked you which medications, not whether or not we needed a box," my mother replied. "We'll get a box later. Right now we're getting the medications."

"Right, sorry." I sighed. "Non-aspirin pain reliever, cold medicine, cough drops, allergy medicine, eye drops, decongestant—"

"Slow down."

"Sorry."

"We're in the allergy aisle. So, eye drops." She picked something off the shelf. "Go get your regular allergy medicine. I'm going to get some extra stuff since we don't know how you'll react to the climates there."

I headed over to get off-brand Claritin and happened to see nasal decongestants on the way, so I picked up a box.

"I got the decongestants, too," I explained, putting them in the cart. "Cheapest brand. I mean, store brand. You know."

"Right. I got you a nasal spray," she replied. "I'm also getting you this." She held up a pink box. "This is very intense allergy medication, and it will make you drowsy, so only ask Tim for it if you're having a severe reaction to something. This isn't the kind of stuff I want you just taking for the heck of it."

"Got it."

"It says to take up to two, but I'm going to write a note to Tim saying to only give you one unless you're having a *severe* reaction because too much of this stuff could kill you."

I nodded. We checked off everything on the "first aid and medications" section of the packing list and decided to start on the toiletry section.

"Any chance I could get a nice razor for this trip?" I asked. "You know, so I'm not walking around Europe with scrapes on my legs?"

I picked one up off the shelf to show her. It was seventeen dollars and came with a refill cartridge. The razor had five blades instead of two, and I couldn't see a way to easily break off the ends—not that I'd felt the need recently, but it would be nice to have more of an obstacle if those thoughts came back.

"Just shave more slowly, like I keep telling you, and you won't nick yourself as often," my mother said. "Those razors are a cash grab. The dollar ones work just fine. What's next on the list?"

I watched her toss a pack of dollar-brand razors into the cart. I wondered if she ever wished *she* could have nicer things for herself, if she didn't have to pay for things for me. If she didn't have to feed and clothe and house me, and send me to college someday, and buy me things like a new prom dress... would she still shave her legs with the dollar razors? Would she travel, like she had when she was younger? Would she have a nice house like she wanted?

I knew I was a financial burden to her, but she would never admit it.

"Summer? Hello? What's next on the list?"

"Oh, sorry—"

"You can't just stand there staring into space like you're retarded," she said. "We have to get the stuff on your list."

"Well, we don't have to get it all *today*—"

"Do you not want to go shopping? I thought you *wanted* to get some items checked off the list today. Are you just done now that I said no to the expensive razors?"

"Excuse me?" a voice interrupted us.

We both turned to face a large dark-haired woman standing at the end of the aisle. She had her arms crossed, a prescription bag hanging from one hand.

"Can I help you?" my mother asked in her customer service voice.

"I couldn't help but overhear your conversation, and I just wanted to say that you *really* shouldn't be using the r-slur like that. What if someone with a real mental challenge was nearby and heard you talking like that? And how do you think it makes your daughter feel?"

Leave me out of this, please. I'm used to it, I wanted to say.

"I'm sorry if I made you uncomfortable," my mother said to her in that fake polite tone. "In the future, though, you should probably stay out of others' private conversations. Thank you for your concern; have a nice day."

She didn't wait for the woman to respond. She just walked out of the aisle. I stayed frozen, unsure of how to make this better.

"Does she always talk to you like that?" the woman asked me.

"Summer, let's go!" my mother called. "We're checking out now."

"But what about the rest of the—?"

"You wanted to be done shopping. We're done shopping. Now don't just stand there like a 'person with mental challenges.' Let's go."

I mouthed *"sorry"* to the woman as I followed my mother to the checkout. The walk back to the car was completely silent, but once the doors shut—

"Who did that bitch think she was, policing other people's private conversations? I'm an adult and I can talk however I want. If you're going to stand in the middle of the aisle and stare into space like a retard, then I'm going to say that. I don't like how every little thing has to be 'politically correct' now, because what's 'correct' seems to change every single day. That's what we called it when I was growing up, and that's what I'm going to call it now."

And then I said something I'd never dared to say to her before: "Do you ever think there's actually something mentally wrong with me?"

"When you act like that, sure."

"I'm being serious. Is there something wrong with me?"

"No, Summer, you just need to stop acting like an idiot."

"But what if I don't know how?" I asked. "Sometimes I just freeze up and I can't help it."

"You're not retarded, Summer."

"I know, I just—I want to see a psychiatrist," I said. "I know you don't believe in them, but I *know* there's something wrong with me. I think I might be depressed or something, because even when things are going well for me, I can't help but feel like—like I don't deserve it, and I'm not meant to be happy."

"Did I not give you a good enough life?" she asked. "I go without so I can always make sure you have a roof over your head, food to eat, new clothes to wear every year—I bought you a brand-new prom dress—"

"No, that's it," I said. "I have all these good things, but I feel like I don't deserve them and I don't deserve to be happy."

"Why don't you deserve to be happy?"

"I don't know! That's why I want to see a psychiatrist!"

She didn't say anything else, and we just drove home in silence. I took my stuff to my room and started organizing it all in my suitcase, but it was moot because I still needed so much stuff and the trip wasn't for another couple of weeks, so I couldn't start packing clothes yet.

Eventually, I fell into a fitful sleep. At six the next morning, when my mom was getting ready to leave for work, she came into my room.

"You have an appointment Wednesday evening," she said. "Supposedly it's covered by insurance. You'll have to take the bus to my office and I'll drive you."

Nolan

"WEREN'T SUMMER and Marta friends at some point?" Esme asked on Friday morning. We were sitting in the auditorium waiting for today's meeting to start.

"Barely." I rolled my eyes. "Well, they were, but Marta hardly acted like it. Why?"

"Because Marta's trying to make friends with me, and I swear if I even *think* about Summer, she senses it and jumps down my throat, like, 'Did you know Summer is a horrible friend for this reason?'"

"Don't waste your time with her," I said. "Stick with me and Summer, trust me."

"On that note, what did you do to Katie? She *hates* you."

I shook my head. "Regrettable one-time hookup for both of us. It was mostly my mistake; based on how she acted, I assumed she didn't want anything more, but I still should've texted her the next day or something."

"At least you admit you screwed up," she said. "Some guys never do."

"Is that why you're gay?" I was hoping it came across as a playful joke.

She laughed. "No, I'm gay because I'm attracted to girls and not boys. I never experimented with boys; I was just speaking generally."

Summer came in and took a seat next to me like usual. I could tell there was something on her mind.

"Hey, Sum." I put my arm around her. "You okay?"

She nodded. "I—need to talk to you later. Just you."

"Oh, okay."

"Everything okay, Summer?" Esme asked.

"Yeah, it's just personal stuff."

"Well, if you ever need to talk about anything, I'm a good listener."

Summer smiled at her, but there was something off, like she was uncomfortable. "Thanks."

* * *

"SO, WHAT do you need to talk about?" I asked Summer at lunch.

She sighed. "I'm... going to the doctor on Wednesday."

"Is something wrong?"

"No." She shook her head. "Well, not like that. I don't know, I guess. That's why I'm going. It's a psychiatrist."

"Your mom's letting you see a psychiatrist?" I asked.

"Apparently her insurance covers this one." She shrugged. "I'm skeptical, but she said I could."

"And... why now?" I asked, suddenly worried.

"I'm just tired of feeling like there's something wrong with me," she said. "I've always felt that way, for as long as I can remember. I just don't know how to put it into words. So I'm hoping the doctor will know."

I wrapped my arms around her before I even realized I was doing it. But I guess it hit me in that moment that Summer was getting help. I wasn't sure whether that meant she was having suicidal thoughts *now*, but no matter what she was going through, she was finally getting help.

"I'm so happy for you, Summer," I told her. "I'm really glad you're getting this help. I want you to be healthy and to be around for a long time."

She laughed. "That's the plan. I'm just glad you're not freaked out by it."

"Why would I be freaked out?"

She shrugged. "I don't know. 'Psychiatrist' is a scary word."

"A psychiatrist is a mental health doctor. If you're struggling with mental health, that's where you should be."

"But so many people get freaked out by mental illnesses. There's horror movies about personality disorders and stuff. Not that I think I have one of those—well, not that it would be bad if I did—well—you know what I'm saying."

"I just want you to be healthy, Sum. I'm along for the ride."

"Speaking of rides," she said, "I won't need a ride home Wednesday because I have to take the bus to my mom's work downtown."

"Nonsense," I told her. "I'll give you a ride. I could even drop you off at the doctor and your mother could meet you there if that's easier."

"You don't have to."

"I know. But I want to, Sum," I said. "I want to be there for you in whatever way you need me."

She smiled but then looked at the ground. "Maybe this psychiatrist will help me believe that I deserve someone like you."

I put my arm back around her. There was so much I wanted to tell her—that it was *me* who didn't deserve *her*, this second chance, her admiration, her desire to be friends all these years—but it was moot now.

"I hope so," I said. "Because you do. More than you'll ever know."

Summer

OVER THE weekend, my mother took me to get some more of the things on the packing list. We almost had the whole thing checked off; we just needed travel adapters and a travel alarm clock, along with some other miscellaneous items.

I hung out with Nolan and Esme at the meetings. Esme was nice; she always knew how to make a good joke and she made the effort to include me in conversations. I was just wary about trusting her because so many popular girls over the years had used similar tactics to lure me into traps.

Wednesday rolled around, and my mother declined Nolan's offer to drive me to the doctor's office but agreed to let him drop me off at her office.

"Should I wait with you until she comes out?" he asked. "I don't feel right leaving you alone downtown."

"It's not as sketchy as it looks," I assured him. "I've waited for her by myself plenty of times. The homeless people are actually really nice, and believe me, nobody's willing to share their drugs for free around here."

He stared at me for a moment and said, "I'm going to wait with you."

Eventually my mom came out of the building, and we waved to Nolan as he drove off. At the doctor's office, we each filled out our own paperwork—I wasn't sure if my mom would see mine or not, so I lied about whether or not I had self-harmed or had suicidal thoughts—and then waited for the psychiatrist, Dr. Leven, to call us both in.

The first portion of the appointment was spent answering some basic questions about my home life while we were all in the room together, and then the doctor wanted to talk to me alone, and then she'd talk separately to my mom.

"So, Summer," Dr. Leven said once it was just the two of us, "what concerns can I help you with?"

I took a deep breath. "I don't really know where to start. I guess... I think I have depression. Or something. Something's wrong with me; I know that much. I'm not normal."

"Why don't you feel like you're normal?"

I shrugged. "I mean, I know happy people don't have the kinds of thoughts I have…"

"What kinds of thoughts?"

"Like I don't deserve to be happy. Like I'm a burden to everyone I love, and they'll all realize someday that they're better off without me in their lives. Like I'm a bad person and everyone *would* be better off without me."

"Tell me a little bit more about that."

I sighed. "There's… I guess it all goes back to the fact that I don't *feel* normal. I never have. It's like, for as long as I can remember, I've felt like there's some kind of paywall between me and normal life. And if I can't get past it, then I'm never going to be worth anything. Why would anyone want me around if I'm just going to be a bad friend, and never know the right way to act, and… freeze up in stressful situations and stand in the middle of an aisle in Target staring into space, or leave my cousin sitting on the ground at Disneyland because I'm too frozen to help him up, and then my mom will ask me if I'm re—" *I can't say that word. She's a psychiatrist; she knows what it means.* "Well, you know. And I'm always going to be a bad friend because I don't know how to act in social situations a lot of the time; it's like there's this secret code that everyone else in the world just naturally knows, but I need them to explain it to me, and then they get mad about it."

Dr. Leven took some notes and flipped through the questions my mother and I had filled out.

"Have you been tested for autism?" she asked.

"What? No, I don't have that," I said.

"So you were tested, and you don't have it?"

"I wasn't tested for it; I just know I don't have it."

"How do you know?"

"Because I've seen the kids at school who do, and I'm not like them."

She wrote something else down. "Autism is a spectrum, Summer. No two people with autism are exactly alike. Some may be nonverbal, and some may be more talkative than non-autistic people. Some may have a special interest they love to talk about for hours. Some struggle with eye contact—it's worth noting that you haven't once made eye contact with me."

"I'm sorry." I tried to meet her eyes, but it felt awkward, so I looked at the space behind her. "I just feel so weird about making eye contact with people I've just met."

"And that's common in autistic people," she replied. "Though there could be other explanations; it's a very common trait. It's not a bad thing, no matter the cause. You can find ways to work around it, like looking at something directly behind someone to give the illusion that you're making eye contact."

"I really don't think that's what I have."

Grant and Jimmy had... a kind of voice, I guess. The way they talked. Jean always walked hunched over and carried herself a very specific, closed off way. Grant leaned back more than most people when he walked, and always kept his arms up like he was marching. And there wasn't anything I talked about the way those boys talked about Minecraft.

"Well, you described having trouble with understanding social cues," Dr. Leven continued. "Many autistic people struggle with social cues and need someone to explain to them what feel like 'basic' social rules that everyone else knows."

I didn't say anything.

"You also mentioned freezing up in stressful situations—when you're overstimulated, you may go into sensory overload. That's a common autistic trait."

Still nothing.

"I'm not saying you *do* have it, but I would like to arrange a time to have you tested," she said. "I'll discuss that with your mother."

"I just—" *How do I say this?* "I don't want to be…"

"You said your mother calls you the r-slur when you experience sensory overload?"

"If that's what it's called, then yes."

"And you don't want to be that."

"No, I don't." I sighed. "And I *know* that's not what autism is, but… that's what everyone at school would see me as."

"Nobody at school has to know. Your diagnosis is between you, your mother, your doctor, and whoever you decide needs to know."

"Would I have to take special education classes?" I asked.

"It depends. Many people with autism are capable of succeeding in mainstream classes, but your school may offer one or two classes that work on social skills that could be beneficial to you, to help you learn those hidden social rules and, as you worded it, get past the paywall."

"I already picked my classes for next year; I'm going to be a senior."

If I had to take some social skills class, I wouldn't get to be a TA for Ms. Harris…

"Again, these are all recommendations," Dr. Leven said, "based on a *potential* diagnosis. The biggest thing to remember is that you can still live a 'normal' life. You just might need some help with some things, like social rules." She pulled a pamphlet out of one of the acrylic holders on her wall. "This pamphlet talks about some common autistic traits; it might be beneficial to look over. None of them mean you're 'abnormal,' and they *certainly* don't mean you're the r-slur. You're a teenage girl, and the struggles you face are unique to you. Some teenagers struggle with acne, some have abusive home lives, and some have social processing disorders."

I took the pamphlet, but as I did, I suddenly remembered all those years ago sitting at my desk in sixth grade, and I heard Nolan's voice as clearly as if he were in the room with us: *"Are you kidding me? I don't want to take the same bus as the retarded kids."*

And Marta: *"A guy like that will never be happy dating a retard."*

I knew that I wasn't *that*. Whether or not these tests came back positive or whatever—however autism tests worked—I *knew* that slur was irrelevant. But I couldn't stop thinking about what it might mean.

"Do you feel like a better understanding of social rules would help you feel like less of a burden?" Dr. Leven asked.

I shrugged. "Maybe."

"Are there other reasons you feel like a burden?"

"I guess... financially, to my mother."

She nodded. "Why?"

"She could have so much if she didn't have to support me."

"But don't you think she wouldn't trade you for any of that?"

"I guess." *But it doesn't help.*

"What do you do when you feel like you're burdening the ones you love? Do you talk to them about it?"

I shook my head. "No. I never know what to say or how to say it."

"So you just bottle all those thoughts up?"

"Pretty much."

"Do you ever hit a breaking point?"

"After a while."

"What does that look like?"

If I tell her, she has to tell my mom. "Just... wanting to disappear. Not *die* per se, but... cease to exist."

"Do you have suicidal thoughts?"

"No," I lied. Maybe next session I would tell her. I was still preoccupied thinking about this whole potential autism diagnosis.

"Do you harm yourself, physically?"

"No." *What's the point of being here if you're going to lie about everything, Summer?* "Well, not for a long time."

"How long?"

How long? Good question. "Years." *Back to the lies, I see, you worthless waste of everyone's time.*

"When did you self-harm?"

"In seventh grade, when my friend at the time showed me how. She moved away after eighth grade, and I haven't seen or heard from her since."

"And you haven't self-harmed since then?"

"Right." *You lying piece of shit.*

"Okay." She nodded. "So, you don't want to die. You just wish you could disappear and stop burdening everyone, correct?"

"Ideally, yes."

She wrote something down. "We're running short on time, so I'd like to continue our discussion about this next session, if that's alright."

"Okay," I said. *This is your last chance to be honest. Last chance to make this meeting matter.*

"The important thing is that you can control your intrusive thoughts enough that you aren't self-harming or having suicidal thoughts."

"Right." *You are so fucking messed up, Summer, and you're never going to get better.*

"I'd like to speak to your mother now," she said. "You can wait in the lobby. Please look over that pamphlet, and we can discuss a day for you to come in and get tested when I'm done speaking with your mother."

I nodded.

"I just want to make sure you understand—if you *do* have autism, it doesn't mean you're 'broken' or 'abnormal' or that there's something wrong with you. It's just something different, and everyone in the world has differences. An autistic person is not broken, and they do not need to be cured—there *is* no cure, and there doesn't need to be one. You can get help for things like social cognition and sensory overload, and you can learn how to accommodate those things and adapt your life to them. Don't look at this like there's something wrong with you, okay? Just something different."

I nodded again, and she walked me to the waiting room, where I switched places with my mother.

I looked through the pamphlet. There were a lot of traits I identified with, like finding comfort in routines and feeling stressed—*sensory overload*—when those routines were interrupted. I *hated* spontaneous plans after school that I didn't have time to prepare for. They messed with my routine. It was incredibly rare when I felt comfortable initiating plans with someone that interrupted my routine; even rarer did I feel comfortable accepting an invitation to do so from someone else.

Sensory issues—hating the feeling of hairspray in my hair or the air from the blow-dryer in my face. Never being able to wear turtlenecks or sweaters with itchy fabric even briefly because I felt like I was suffocating. Or during idle time in class, I'd rub erasers against my nails and I'd specifically buy pencils based on which erasers felt best.

There was the way my memory worked; I could remember what day it was when Nolan and I had talked at his birthday party in third grade and what I was wearing and what song was stuck in my head at the time, but I could not for the life of me remember what I'd learned in math class. And aversion to or general disinterest in sex—while not *all* people with autism experienced that, it was common enough to be mentioned in the pamphlet.

Dr. Leven had mentioned being able to get help with learning social rules, so I could potentially be able to function more normally and fit in better. Maybe if the diagnosis came back positive, that would be a good thing. It would mean an actual explanation for what had been wrong with me this entire time—well, one part of it, at least. I knew I eventually had to get into my suicidal thoughts and self-harm as well, which weren't mentioned anywhere in the pamphlet as autistic traits.

But being able to put it into words, into a diagnosis, sounded... nice.

There was just the matter of what other people would say if they found out—the other kids at school, my teachers, even Nolan. Would he really be able to look at me the same, knowing I was one of the—?

My mother stormed out of the other room. *Has it been half an hour already?*

"We're leaving," she said. "Let's go."

"Wait, aren't we supposed to make an appointment to—?"

"I'm not paying that woman another cent," she said.

"What happened?"

"That braindead 'psychiatrist' is trying to tell me you're retarded," she said. "More like she just wants to milk more money out of us and pump you full of drugs before your brain is fully developed."

"Isn't this covered by insurance?" I asked. *Are there even drugs to treat autism?*

"I highly doubt everything *she* suggests will be covered."

"What was she suggesting?"

"She wants to get you tested to see if you're retarded," she said again. "I'm not wasting my time with that. I've known you for seventeen years; you're *not* retarded."

"But the things in this pamphlet make sense!" I said. "It doesn't mean I'm... *that*. It just means I have trouble with social stuff, and I can get help for it."

"You're *not* retarded, Summer," she said again, "and I'm not paying some money-hungry woman to convince you that you are!"

"But—"

"*Are* you?" she asked. "If you are, tell me now, because if you're *so* fucking stupid that you need all these special therapies and classes and medications, then we'll have to pull you out of school because obviously you need to be in a special school, and you're definitely too stupid to go on this trip to Europe."

"I—"

"And you can kiss Nolan goodbye; you even *mention* that you *might* have a mental disorder to him, and he'll be gone. I can't believe you even told him you were seeing a psychiatrist!"

"Well—"

"So what is it?"

I shoved the pamphlet to the bottom of my bag. "No, I'm fine," I said. "She probably just wants money."

"Did she at least solve your problem with feeling like you don't deserve to be happy?" my mother asked.

"Well, she mentioned the next session would—"

"No, you see, she just wants our money," she said. "I brought you to this session to solve your problems and she couldn't even do that."

Aren't the sessions covered by insurance? "I guess not."

"You just need to remember that you *do* deserve to be happy," she said. "You haven't done anything so horrible or unforgivable that you don't deserve happiness. Right?"

"Right." *Wow, I'm cured. Thanks, Mom.*

"Good. Now, let's get some dinner. Taco Bell sound good to you? I think they still have those five-dollar meal deal boxes."

"Perfect." *Apparently as perfect as things are ever going to get.*

Nolan

SUMMER DIDN'T mention her appointment the next day, but Esme was sitting with us, so she probably just didn't want to talk about something so personal. Esme also wanted to eat lunch as a group, so I had to wait until after the meeting to finally talk to Summer.

"How was your doctor's appointment?" I asked as we got in my car.

She started crying, almost out of nowhere. I couldn't remember her ever crying in front of me before—certainly not in this timeline.

"Summer?" I tried putting an arm around her.

"I'm never going to figure out what's wrong with me!" she said.

"Sure you will. Obviously *one* session isn't going to—"

"No, that's the *only* session my mom is going to take me to," she explained. "The doctor wanted to get me tested for—something, and my mom freaked out and left and said we could never go back."

"Tested for what?"

She took several deep breaths before speaking. "The doctor thinks I might have autism."

"What?" Summer couldn't have *that*, could she? She was nothing like—

"It's because I'm not good at social rules and stuff," she said. "I've always felt like there's this secret code that everyone else just *knows* and I don't. It's why I act so awkward all the time. It's why you had to teach me how to act at dances and stuff."

Well, that did explain that, but... "But you're not—"

"It's a spectrum," she continued. "Everyone's different. Some are like Grant and Jimmy, some are like Jean, and some are like... Well, I'll never know if I have it or not, because my mom won't let me get tested for it."

"Why not?"

"Because I'm 'not retarded.'" She rolled her eyes, tears still falling. "If my mother would just *listen* to the psychiatrist and understand that's not what it means—"

"Of course that's not what it means," I said. "Only assholes still throw that word around."

She shook her head but didn't say anything right away. Finally, she said, "You used to."

I wasn't sure what to say to that. It wasn't like she was wrong.

"I know that's totally unfair to bring up," she continued, "because I'm sure there was a time where I used to, too, and we're not the same people we used to be, but—"

"No, you're right," I told her. "I did used to say it. I have no defense for that."

The last time I remembered saying it was around sixth grade. A bunch of us were going to an Oakland A's game as a treat for completing all our reading logs, and we were told the special education students were also going to the game for their own reason. We were going to take the same bus, and I'd told Jake that I didn't want to ride in the same bus as "the retarded kids." I guess Lucia Torres overheard, because she told the teacher before the busses left and I was promptly escorted off the bus and made to sit in the office until my dad came to pick me up.

Before I could launch into some defense about how unfair it all was, he had a lecture prepared, and it was one of the few times I could remember him actually being disappointed in me—*angry* with me. At first I was just *scared* to say the word again, but eventually I understood why it was wrong. I even ended up explaining to my friends why it was wrong a few weeks later when we were hanging out at my place, and my dad helped me do so.

"You wouldn't look at me differently, would you?" Summer asked. "I mean... I'm still me."

"You are," I told her. "You're Summer, and you're my girlfriend, and I'm not going anywhere. I promise."

"Even if I ever do find out I have it?"

I shook my head. "Nothing at this point could make me not want to be with you," I told her. "You're Summer. I want *you*. I love *you*. Just promise me you won't go anywhere, too, okay?"

She nodded. "Okay."

I drove her home, like usual, but stopped in the driveway.

"Are you going to be okay?" I asked her. "Like... if you're not allowed to get help for whatever's going on with you?"

She nodded. "I've made it this far, haven't I?"

"Call me if you need to talk."

"I will."

"See you tomorrow?"

"Definitely."

* * *

"Hey, Nolan?"

At the sound of my father's voice, I quickly shut my laptop. "Yeah?"

He raised an eyebrow; I wasn't fast enough. "We don't need to have another talk about pornography and sex trafficking, do we?" he asked.

I shook my head. "I promise that's not what I was doing."

He nodded but opened up my laptop and turned it to face him anyway. "Oh. Okay." He gave it back to me. "But can I ask why you're on the Autistic Self Advocacy Network?"

I sighed. "It's not my place to say anything, but... Summer might have autism. Her doctor wanted to get her tested, but her mother wouldn't let it happen, and... if she *does* have it, I just want to know how to be there for her."

He smiled. "You're a good guy, son. I guess we did alright with you." He patted my shoulder. "You know, one of the secretaries at the law firm has autism. Wouldn't have known if it wasn't in her file for her accommodations."

"Accommodations?"

"Yeah. She needs a noise-cancelling headset because sometimes if the lobby gets crowded, she gets overwhelmed by the noise. She can answer phone calls on it, too, so she doesn't fall behind. She's actually the most efficient secretary I've ever had. Very organized, precise... It's not a bad thing like some people make it out to be."

"Like Summer's mother."

"I don't know the full situation, so I can't judge," he said. "But if she's interested, I could arrange for Summer to meet with Valeria and talk with her sometime."

"I'll let her know."

"Anyway," he said, "your mother made brownies downstairs if you'd like one. I'll let you get back to your research."

"Thanks."

Summer's going to be okay. I know it.

Summer

IT WAS an interesting feeling: to be *this close* to knowing what was "wrong" with me and how to get help, and then being hit with the reality that I'd never know and I'd never get help for it.

Maybe I should've told Dr. Leven about my cutting. She'd have to tell my mother... Maybe if she'd led with that, my mother would've seen that I needed help. Maybe she would have let me go back. Then again, she might just throw me into a mental hospital. Whenever a suicide story came on the news, she'd say something like, *"Their parents should've put them in a mental hospital before it got that far."*

Maybe that was where I *needed* to go—but not until after the Europe trip. I wasn't going to miss that.

Nolan was so unreasonably cool with everything; there was no way he could *actually* not look at me any differently, was there? Maybe he thought everything would be okay now, but the realization would hit him later on. Especially if I had to go to a mental hospital—he'd never look at me the same after something like that, would he?

I turned the volume up on my headphones—I was listening to my favorite song from *Spring Awakening*: "And Then There Were None." It was about one of the characters' last pleas for help before he took his life.

Sometimes I wondered how much longer I could convince myself to keep going, knowing that I was never going to get better. I was never going to get help or even know for sure what I needed help *for*.

I sat up on the bed and stared at my suitcase on the floor. I could open the pack of razors and cut myself again. But... if I had impulsive thoughts like that *and* could control them well enough to resist the temptation to listen, then... that was good, right? According to Dr. Leven?

As long as I could control those impulses, I would be fine.

Besides, it was less effort to stay in bed than to open up a new pack of razors and break off the end of one.

15

Nolan

"ONE MORE week," I said to Summer at lunch. We were eating under an awning to stay out of the rain. "This time a week from now, we'll be on a plane to Barcelona."

She nodded. "A long-ass flight, but it'll be worth it."

Esme got up to use the restroom, so I decided to bring up Valeria.

"I learned something yesterday," I said. "My dad's favorite secretary at work has autism, apparently."

"What?" Summer asked. "How did that come up?"

"Oh, uh, I was looking at the Autistic Self Advocacy Network on my laptop and he caught me," I explained. "I told him it was for an extra credit project. And he told me about Valeria, his secretary. Apparently she's the best he's ever had. Her autistic traits actually help her with the work she has to do, I guess."

"Oh. Cool."

"Um... maybe, if you wanted to talk to her—"

"Well, we don't even know if I have it."

"Right." I nodded. "But it might be nice just to talk to someone who does. Just in case. Someone who might understand what you're going through."

"Well, everyone who has it has different traits."

"But I'm sure there's some overlap."

"Nolan, please just drop it." She sighed. "We don't know if I have it, so let's just pretend that conversation never happened, okay? As far as you know, I'm perfectly normal."

"It doesn't make you 'not normal'—"

"Nolan."

"Alright, fine," I said. "I'll drop it."

Summer

I COULDN'T concentrate in the workshop after lunch, so I just wrote in my journal and hoped it looked like I was taking notes. I couldn't imagine what would happen if Tim confiscated my notebook and read it—out loud or to himself. I wouldn't be going to Europe. I'd be going to a mental hospital for sure.

June 24th—

It's an interesting feeling: knowing for sure that I'll never have answers. There's still college, I guess, but if I test positive for autism then my mom will probably pull my tuition saying that I'm "too retarded to go to college" or some bullshit like that.

A year is so far away, too. The soonest I'd be able to get help for whatever my problems are is a whole year from now. Can I really keep this up another whole year?

And even so, if I find out that's what it is... I'll have a word to describe the problem, but at what cost? Getting social skills classes and stuff probably costs money that I don't have. And despite how understanding Nolan is acting, there's no way he could be cool with it. At the end of the day, he'd still look at me like one of the special education kids at school. He'd be nice to me, but he wouldn't want to date me anymore. Especially not if other people at school found out. Marta would have a field day: she'd make sure everyone called me the r-slur, behind my back and to my face. I guess it's what I deserve for treating Jean Dyer like shit for all those years. This would be my retribution, and I deserve it.

How long am I expected to keep doing this? To keep living like this *knowing I'm never going to be able to get help? Knowing I'm always going to be a burden to everyone I love?*

Maybe it's time I just… set them all free.

I shut the notebook and stuffed it in my bag as everyone else began packing up their stuff.

"Hey, Summer!" Esme called. "I went to Tim's office to get a bandage and happened to catch a glimpse of the hotel assignments for Barcelona." She grinned. "We're roomies! Us and Katie."

"Oh. I don't think Katie likes me very much," I told her.

She laughed. "No worries. I'll have your back. One more week!"

"One more week," I echoed.

Nolan caught up to us and slung his arm around me. "Someone's excited."

"Duh!" Esme laughed. "Hey, I'm Summer's roomie in Barcelona, so if you ever wanna sneak over—"

"Our third roommate is Katie," I said, "so probably not."

"I'll take care of Katie," Esme promised.

"Only if Summer wants me to come over," Nolan replied.

I nodded. "We'll see." Maybe I *would* finally sleep with him on this trip, just to prove to myself that I could do it. To prove to *him* that I could do it. That we could do that, and I wasn't a coward or immature… that it wasn't something he needed to worry about.

One more week, and we'd be in Europe.

One more week.

Nolan

"ARE YOU alright?" I asked Summer as we got in my truck. "You've been distant today."

She shrugged. "I'm fine. Next Friday just can't come soon enough."

"You're telling me." I grabbed her hand. "I'm so glad this all worked out,

Sum. I can't wait to travel the world with you."

She smiled but didn't say anything. I let go of her hand and pulled out of the parking lot.

"I've been working on our US Travel Bucket List, too," I told her. "We're gonna take the sickest road trip after graduation."

She nodded. "Can't wait."

"Are you *sure* everything's okay?" Maybe I was being paranoid, but... it was June 24. That was the last day I'd seen her in the old timeline. Possibly the last day she was alive.

Today. Tomorrow. Or the next day.

"Of course," she said. "Sorry. I'm just tired."

"Ah, yeah. Not looking forward to the jetlag, but we'll get through it."

"Definitely."

"Well, if you want to stop at Starbucks, I could get you a drink," I said. "I know it's a little late in the day for coffee, but if you want some, it's on me."

"I'm okay, but thank you," she said. "I'll just take a nap when I get home."

"Do you want to do something this weekend?" I asked her.

"Maybe," she said. "What were you thinking?"

"I have to help out in the yard all day tomorrow, but we could go see a movie after?"

"That's okay," she said. "How about Sunday?"

"Sure. Movie? Or maybe get lunch?"

"Actually... I think my mom wanted to go shopping for trip stuff on Sunday," she said.

"I can come along."

"No, she'd just get frustrated." She sighed. "I'll just see you Monday."

"You sure?"

She nodded. "Yeah. It's okay. We've got thirty-five days to hang out all we want."

"That's true."

When I pulled into her driveway, I didn't want to let her get out of the car. I didn't want her to go off somewhere I couldn't see her. Not today. But I knew I was just being paranoid. Everything was going to be okay.

"I love you, Summer," I said. "I don't know if I say that enough."

She smiled. "You do," she assured me. "And I love you, too."

"I couldn't have gotten through this year without you," I told her. "So thank you."

"Thank *you*," she replied.

We kissed in the front seat, my hand in her hair.

"Here, I'll be a gentleman today," I said. "Let me walk you to the door."

She laughed but went along with it. I hugged her on the porch, as tightly as I could. And then I watched the front door close behind her.

Summer

ONE MORE week.

I couldn't keep doing this. What was going to Europe going to accomplish? It would be fun, but... it wouldn't solve my problems. I'd still have to live with those for the rest of my life.

But it was too late to pull out of the trip and get my mother her money back. I just felt bad going on the trip and spending her money on me because... was I even worth it? Who knew how much longer I could keep going? If I were going to do something... it would make sense to do it before the trip. Maybe in extenuating circumstances, my mother could get a refund and use the money to travel herself, or get the house fixed up how she wanted, or buy herself some new clothes for the first time since I'd been born.

No, I was being ridiculous. That wouldn't solve anything. There was no harm in going on this trip. I just had to try and make the best of my life despite my undiagnosed... whatever it was. Whatever was wrong with me. Or, not "wrong," but "different." I was sure there had to be a separate diagnosis to explain why I felt worthless and cut to deal with that. But whatever it was, I could still make the best of it. I'd been doing it for seventeen years; I could make it for a few more.

And then after college, I'd have my own job with my own insurance, and *I* could decide what services were worth paying for.

What was five or six more years, right? Five or six more years of...

Feeling like I wasn't worth the space I took up in this world...

Feeling that I didn't deserve the good things that happened to me...

Knowing that I burdened everyone I loved...

Not understanding how to act in social situations and annoying everyone because of it...

Cutting myself when it was all too much to deal with...

Yeah. I suppose I could do that for five or six more years.

Nolan

I HATED doing yard work when it was more than ninety degrees outside, but I hated it even more when it meant that I *could* be spending time with Summer but I *wasn't*. Especially today.

Pull weeds, dispose of weeds, trim the bushes, throw away the bush trimmings, mow the lawn, clean out the pool... The pool was my least favorite. We hardly even used it anymore—it would be nice on a day like today when it was almost a hundred degrees, but alas, the water was green under the tarp and would be until I got around to cleaning it.

I *could* be at the movies with Summer, but I was stuck cleaning the stupid yard.

I wondered what she was up to. Shopping with her mother, maybe, or was that tomorrow? I wanted to talk to her at some point *today*, just to make sure she was still... I'd have to call her when I got to a good break point in the list.

Between doing the bushes and the pool, I'd give her a call.

Summer

"CAN WE make bread today?"

My mother looked up from her book. "We don't have yeast to make bread. Why do you want to make bread?"

"I just thought it could be fun," I said. "Never mind."

"Well, we can get yeast, I guess, if you want to make bread."

I nodded, and we headed for the garage. The drive to the grocery store was only a few minutes. I pulled out my phone to message Daisy on the way.

Hey, I just wanted to say you're a great friend. I know we tend to fall out of touch from time to time, but I always appreciate our conversations and you've been there for me for years. I think you're going to do great at middle college, even if I'll miss you.

By the time we got to the baking aisle, she'd responded.

Thank you, Summer, that's so nice of you to say! I'll miss you, too. Have fun in Europe!

I sent her back a smiley face while my mom grabbed the yeast.

"Is there anything else you need while we're here?" she asked.

"No," I said. "Just the yeast, I guess." We'd exhausted everything on the packing list that could be picked up at a grocery store, anyway.

"Are you sure? Nothing for your last week in America?"

"I'm good," I said.

When we got back to the car, I went into the notes app on my phone and backspaced through Daisy's name.

"You'd better eat this bread," my mom said. "Last time we made bread, you only had a couple slices before it went bad. I can't eat the whole thing by myself, you know."

"I know. I'm sorry."

"Don't be sorry. Just eat the bread."

Making the bread was nice. We didn't argue. We talked about Europe, and where I should go in London, and what I needed to send her pictures of in some of the other places.

While the bread was rising on the counter, I went to my room and called my father. It went to voicemail, which was what I was halfway hoping for anyway.

"Hey, it's Summer," I said. "I was just thinking about... Almaden Lake. How we used to take walks there on Saturdays, when we lived in the old house. Well, I guess those are some of my favorite memories from when you were here. Maybe we'll talk soon. I just wanted to say that I love you and, well, thank you for those memories. Goodbye."

I hovered over my phone for a few minutes, debating if I wanted to call Nolan right now or not, or just text him. I wasn't sure what I wanted to say.

I called him, and he answered on the fourth ring.

"Hey, Sum," he said. "I was just thinking of calling you."

"Oh?"

"Yard work sucks," he said. "I don't know how my parents are gonna keep up the lawn while we're in Europe. I need a break, and what better excuse than talking to you?"

I smiled. "Glad I could help."

"So, what's the occasion? Or did you just miss me?"

"I... actually have some good news," I said. I felt so bad for lying to him, but I hoped he'd realize I was only doing it to set him free.

"Oh, yeah? Let me hear it."

"I talked to my mother," I went on, "and she agreed to let me see a different psychiatrist. I have an appointment Monday morning, so I won't need a ride to the meeting, and I'll also be there late."

"Summer, that's amazing! I'm so happy for you," he said. "Really, I—

that's so great to hear. I'm really glad you're getting the help you feel like you need."

"Well, I also need to say thank you to you," I said. "This past year has been the best year of my life. I think a lot of things got better when we became friends. You mean a lot to me, and I want to make sure you never question that, or that I love you. No matter what happens... with this diagnosis or lack thereof, or the trip, or whatever. You're one of the best things that ever happened to me, and I couldn't have gotten this far without you."

"I love you, too, Summer," he said. "You've changed my life for the better, too. I think I'd be lost without you."

It was quiet. I wasn't sure what to say.

"You still there?" he asked.

"Yeah. Um... also the reason I called... I broke my phone charger and I'm on... twenty-seven percent. So, like, I'm going to get a new one, but I'm not going to be able to use my phone tomorrow. So I wanted to talk to you now and also let you know that."

"Oh, that sucks," he said. "I could bring over a spare charger—"

"It's fine. I could use some time away from the digital world, anyway," I said. "Don't worry about me."

"Are you sure?"

"Positive."

"Okay. Well, I'll see you Monday, right?"

"Where else would I be?"

He laughed. "I love you, Sum."

"I love you, too."

I went back into the kitchen, then backspaced "Dad" and "Nolan" out of the notes app.

"I just put the bread in the oven," my mom said. "Should be half an hour."

When it was ready, she served us each two slices with butter.

"We could start doing this every week again," I said, "when I get back. We could just do it on Saturdays or Sundays instead of Mondays, since we have school and work now."

"Only if you eat it," she reminded me.

"I know."

I tried to think of what else to say.

"You know I think you're a good mom, right?" I asked.

"I try," she said. "I just don't think you need some doctor who wants to pump you full of drugs telling you that you're mentally challenged."

"You know autism isn't medicated, right?"

"Well, whatever, I've raised you for seventeen years and I know you're not retarded. I don't want anyone making you believe that you are."

"I don't think that," I said. "That's not what autism is."

"You're fine, Summer," she said. "You've been fine for seventeen years. The doctors just want money."

I nodded. "I guess. Well, you are a good mom. I'm sorry I'm not a good daughter."

"I never said that," she replied. "I just don't like to see you not put in the effort I know you're capable of. Your grades have been going up—that's good. I'm excited for you to go on this trip. Wherever you want to go to college, we'll figure it out. There's financial aid."

"I know. I'm going to be fine," I said. "It's been a rough road, but things are good now. It's all going to be fine."

"Right."

After I put my plate in the sink, I gave her a hug.

"I love you," I said.

"I love you, too, Summer. Just remember, you have to help me finish the bread."

"I know. Thanks for making it with me."

"You're welcome."

"And thanks for always trying to do what's best," I said, "even if we don't see eye to eye on everything. I've never doubted your sacrifices for me. Anyway. I love you."

"I love you, too," she said again.

I took my phone into my room. I backspaced "Mom" out of the notes app, and then turned it off. She would let me know that dinner was ready after a while. I was sure it would involve the bread somehow. I felt guilty about the bread, but that was all. It was a small price to pay for her freedom.

Daisy would excel in middle college without the "high school experience" and go off to Berkeley or Stanford like she wanted. My father would check his voicemail tomorrow, I was sure. Maybe he could get his plane tickets for August refunded. Nolan would have a great time in Europe. Everyone would do just fine. They'd get over it.

I opened my suitcase, found what I was looking for, and tore open the packaging. I was going to be one less inconvenience, one less awkward person people were nice to out of pity, one less annual plane trip, one less burden.

My wristband from the Be Kind assembly slid down my wrist. I pushed it back out of the way. Sometimes being kind wasn't enough.

I loved them all, but I couldn't do it anymore. I would never even get to know what was really wrong with me, and I would never be able to get help for it. If I couldn't fix myself, I would be a burden to the people I cared about. I guess I simply wasn't worth it.

I closed my eyes and laid back on my bed as I finally made my decision: the one that couldn't be undone. I could already smell the soup Mom was making for dinner. It smelled good; maybe I would've liked it. It'd go great with bread. But that didn't matter now.

I opened my eyes one more time and stared at my ceiling until it blurred, then closed them again. I thought of all the times my mom had yelled at me because my room wasn't clean enough; I thought of sleepovers here with Daisy and Marta and Bella; I thought of Jonah trying to sneak in and the time we threw some dirty clothes out into the hallway as a joke, then got yelled at by my mother; I thought of the times I'd asked to redecorate my room to be more to my liking but it was never in the budget; I thought of rainy days spent in bed studying—or trying to—or sneaking on my laptop when I was supposed to be grounded, getting caught; I thought of as many memories in this room as I could until I couldn't think of anything anymore. Because none of it mattered now. Nothing mattered now.

And then, suddenly, I was having second thoughts. What if this was a mistake? I had to fix this, before it was too late. Was there still time?

"Mom!"

But I could hear her doing dishes, meaning she couldn't hear me, and I didn't have the energy to make my voice any louder. And even if I did get her attention, what was I supposed to tell her? I couldn't make this look like an accident. I'd have to be hospitalized. I wouldn't get to go to Europe. Maybe I'd even be institutionalized—but that might mean finding out what was wrong with me—but no, then Nolan would worry about me; everyone would always be too worried about me and I'd be even more of a burden.

Maybe I could call for help myself? But my phone was too far for me to reach; I could barely see anymore. It wouldn't turn back on in time, anyway; that phone always took ten years to power back on.

It was too late. There was nothing I could do about it now but let it happen, and even if I could do something about it, everything would be worse. I had finally managed to screw up so badly that it couldn't be undone. But maybe I was right all along, and this really would be for the best.

One less burden in everyone's lives. Everything would be okay.

Nolan

NO STUDENT, and I mean *no* student should be expected to wake up before ten in the morning during summer vacation. Save me all your crap about summer jobs, camps, activities, whatever—this is the one time a year when kids are allowed to be kids, or in my case, teenagers are allowed to be teenagers. No deadlines, homework, study sessions, or anything holding us back—unless, of course, you want to go on a thirty-five day excursion to Europe the summer before your senior year, and then the program decides you need to meet every weekday from nine to two-thirty for three entire weeks.

But this was the last week. The last Monday I had to be awake at this hour, and come Friday evening I'd be on a plane to Barcelona with Summer by my side, and all of this will have been worth it: the weeks of early mornings and this whole year.

I shut off my alarm, jumped in the shower, threw some clothes on, and hopped in my truck, just like any other morning, except Summer was at her doctor's appointment, so I wouldn't be picking her up. It was sunny today, bright and beautiful like a summer day should be.

I pulled through the Starbucks drive-through for a double-shot espresso, parked in the community center's visitor lot, and headed into the auditorium.

Summer obviously wasn't here yet, and I took my usual seat up by the front so I could save hers—she never did say what time she'd be back from her appointment—and took out my phone to pass the time.

"Morning," Esme greeted me, taking a seat. "Where's Summer?"

"Doctor's appointment," I explained. "She'll be here late."

"Ah."

We both sat with our phones, waiting for the meeting to start. Mine started ringing with a call from my mother—but it was also almost a quarter past nine. The meeting was supposed to start at nine, and Tim was always right on time... wasn't he? I let the call go to voicemail.

Up front, Tim cleared his throat, meaning it was time to put our phones away and pay attention. He usually came in clapping or talking loudly; this time he was so quiet I wouldn't have noticed he was onstage if I hadn't been sitting so close. My phone vibrated.

MOM: CALL ME BACK ASAP!!!

"Everyone, listen up." Tim was serious, like something was wrong. "Everyone, eyes and ears up here." He wasn't being as loud as usual, so it took a little bit longer for everyone to quiet down.

Something about this felt so familiar. When was the last time Tim was *this* serious? Suddenly, a horrible feeling washed over me, because I remembered the last time Tim was acting like this. I hadn't heard from Summer since Saturday. She'd told me her phone was dead, her charger was broken, and she had a doctor's appointment—*and I am a fucking idiot. I am such a fucking idiot!*

"Everyone, I... I don't know how to say this, but it's very serious, so I need everyone to *really* listen this morning, okay?"

No, please, God, no! Please, please, no, this can't be happening.

Everyone got quiet, finally. And then he said it:

"I—truly regret to inform you all... Summer Madison passed away over the weekend."

This isn't real. This isn't happening. I'm in the wrong timeline. I was hyperventilating. Esme was looking at me, but all I could focus on was the lack of explanation for why Tim would say those words. *This is not the right timeline.*

Hands shaking, I opened up my phone to check my call history. Our call from Saturday was still there. This *was* the new timeline. And that was the moment my body must've gone into shock. My chest tightened, my eyes were burning, I felt like I couldn't breathe—no, I really couldn't breathe. I couldn't move. Tim's voice was so muffled I could barely make it out. I was frozen. How could Summer be dead? After everything?

You should've just brought her a fucking phone charger, you imbecile!

I didn't wait for Tim to finish. I couldn't feel myself moving, but I must have gotten up and run out of the room because I was outside.

"Summer!" I shouted, as if she were outside the community center just waiting to come in for the meeting. There was no response. "Summer!" I shouted again, and still nothing.

I took my phone out and called her. It went straight to voicemail.

"Hey, it's Summer. Leave a message!"

"Summer," I whispered one more time.

This wasn't real. This couldn't be real. How did I screw this up? I'd gone back and redone an entire year just to end up back where I'd started? With Summer's blood on my hands? But it felt different this time. This time it was real. This time I really loved her. This time, I had no idea *why.*

Amidst everything, I realized why my mother had called—she knew. Summer's mother had called to tell her so she could tell me. I couldn't speak, so I replied to her text as best I could with my vision blurred from tears:

`I know about Summer. I'll call back when I get the chance, I promise`

Just so she wouldn't worry about me. *If I had only worried about Summer. I shouldn't have just believed her about her stupid broken phone charger—the one time I decide not to worry—*

The fountain. I had to get back to that fountain; I'd wish to go back, just to Saturday this time so I could bring her a phone charger, and she'd see that I cared about her. I could talk to her and stay with her and make sure she didn't do anything. I should've known it was too suspicious to be true. I was just so excited she was getting to see a psychiatrist after all... *Which also wasn't true, because of course it wasn't, you stupid fucking idiot.*

I couldn't breathe. This wasn't happening. I shut my eyes and concentrated on Summer: in the passenger seat of my car on Friday, on the phone on Saturday afternoon—how could she be dead this time too? It made no sense!

I need to go back! I need to fix it!

I felt a hand on my shoulder, and I jumped.

"Summer?" I turned around—it was Esme.

"This doesn't feel real," she said.

"Why did she do it?" I asked, furious. "Why?"

"What do you mean, 'did it?' Do you think...? You don't think she—?"

"I *know* she did!" I shouted. "She needed help and her mother wouldn't let her get it. She lied to me so I wouldn't try to call her yesterday or try to pick her up this morning, and I believed her and now she's gone! How the fuck could I let it happen *again*?"

"What are you talking about?"

I tried to get my breathing under control. My legs were shaking and I collapsed onto the grass. Esme sat beside me, silent.

"I treated Summer horribly," I said quietly. "She just wanted to be friends, and I blew her off every time, for no good reason. It got worse, though, and I yelled at her and told her she was nothing, that she would never be worth anything; she was just a hopeless loser. I got other people to bully her; you were one of them. I just wanted her to leave me alone. I told her nobody would miss her. It was my fault."

"What—what the hell are you talking about?" Esme demanded.

"She killed herself, and... I didn't realize how badly I treated her until... I woke up on the first day of school, and it was like I had this chance to redo the whole year, treat her better and prevent this. But I screwed it up *again*!"

"Slow down! *What?*"

I told Esme everything—from the fight in the Starbucks parking lot to making a wish in the fountain to waking up on the first day of school, to falling for Summer and doing everything I could to try and prevent this.

"I tried so hard," I said. "I don't understand how I could screw up this time, too."

"I—don't know if I quite believe you, but I also don't really know why you'd make all that up," she said. "But do you really think *you're* the reason she killed herself? Regardless of, uh, alternate universes?"

"I told her she was nothing to me! That was the last thing I said to her, before I got this second chance: I said I wouldn't care if I never saw her again. But now... if I had just gone to her house and brought her a fucking phone charger, she'd still be here. It was my responsibility to save her. To make her feel like she mattered. That she was worth it. And I failed."

"You 'failed' because you didn't bring her a phone charger? What the hell was going to happen after you brought her that phone charger?" Esme demanded. "Maybe she would have made it another day, or another month, or another year—but if she killed herself, she had *deep* problems that needed professional help. There's only so much you could have done."

"But I could have—"

"How could you be so selfish?" Esme asked. "How could you possibly think that you were the only thing negatively impacting her life? It was so much deeper than that; it had to be. You can't fix people, and you can't save them. You're not a mental health professional."

"Then what was the point of all this?" I asked. "Redoing everything?"

"What do you mean?"

"If she was going to kill herself either way, then why did I have to redo everything? Why couldn't I have just lived my normal life where she was nothing to me? Why did I have to love her and feel like this now?"

"I bet you learned a lot from getting to know Summer as a person. I bet you're a better person for it." She exhaled. "Nolan, it wasn't *your* fault. There were so many other things going on with her. Her death could have been prevented, but not by you, at least not you alone."

In the timeline where I was cruel to Summer, I didn't feel much when she died. A little guilt, maybe, but I wouldn't have dwelled on it, and it would've gone away.

Now I felt loss. Grief. Anger. Everything. I wanted answers. I wanted to know why she'd done this, but I wouldn't get any answers from her. Not anymore.

"We need to go to the fountain," I said. "It's in the new Peach Avenue shopping center... some town over from here. I need to at least *try* to undo this."

"The Anita Prunell fountain?" Esme asked.

"Anita Prunell... She's the girl from the Be Kind assembly, right? Who died last year?"

She nodded. "She went to my school. I live by that shopping center."

I realized Esme had on a teal wristband, just like the one Summer always wore from the assembly.

"Did—did you know her?"

"Not really, but I saw the shit everyone put her through," she said. "I talked to her once, when I was helping her scrub the n-slur off her locker the third time it happened. I told her she should report it, and she said she'd done that before and the principal hardly cared. Sometimes I wished I would've talked to her more, because... it's so easy to feel like *you* could have done something."

She sat back, pressing her palms into the grass. "And maybe you could have," she went on. "Maybe you could have brought Summer a phone charger and talked to her and stopped her from doing whatever she did. Maybe someone could've found her a few minutes earlier and stopped her. Maybe I could've called her just to talk or something. None of it changes the fact that she was sick. She was sick and she couldn't get help. There wasn't anything you could have done. Summer couldn't get the treatment she needed. That's not on you."

"But… if the fountain worked before—"

"We can go to the fountain if it'll give you closure," she said, "but I wouldn't put too much stock in another miracle."

I nodded. "Do you want to drive? I don't think I'm in the best state of mind to."

"Okay." She hesitated. "I might need some gas money, though, if I'm going to be making this trip four times today."

"Got it."

She drove me to the shopping center once we let Tim know we were leaving and got permission from our parents, and I found a penny at the bottom of my bag and stared at it for a second.

"Would it be too weird if I went inside and bought something to try and replicate *exactly* how this happened before?" I asked.

"Not any weirder than you being a time traveler from an alternate universe."

She gave me half a smile, seemingly unsure if I was ready to smile about anything, but I did my best to return it.

She waited in the car. I went to the card aisle and tried to remember which sympathy card I'd bought in the old timeline—it wasn't like I'd been paying attention. It wouldn't hurt to buy a sympathy card, anyway; I hadn't even thought about what facing Summer's mother would be like, but surely I would need to talk to her at some point about this.

I wondered how she was taking this, if she blamed herself at all or wondered what would've happened if she'd listened to her daughter. A surge of anger rushed through me as I thought about how this could have been prevented if her mother had just—

But I stopped myself. I had no idea what that woman was feeling, or what she'd been taught growing up, or any of that, and being angry with her wouldn't bring Summer back to life. The only thing that *might* was making this wish, which meant I needed to pick out a sympathy card to try and get my lucky penny from the cashier.

I picked one that felt right; it was one of the cheapest ones, and I was certain that I wouldn't have paid more than I'd had to. I took it to the cashier and opened up my wallet while she rang me up.

"That's gonna be $1.71," the woman said.

I looked in my wallet for singles—didn't I pay with singles before?—but I only had a five. *That's fine. That can still give me change.* As I handed her the bill, I realized I was pretty sure the cashier was a guy before. This was the only register open, so it wasn't like I'd gone to the wrong one…

"Was there, uh, a guy that used to work here?" I asked the woman, feeling so stupid because I couldn't even remember any identifying features *about* that guy to help place him in her memory.

"We just opened last month," she explained. "There are a couple guy cashiers, but I took this extra shift today, so you get me."

She offered a warm smile as she handed me my change. I tried to subtly knock some of it off the counter when I picked it up.

"Oops," I said, trying to sound casual. "I've got it."

I checked each piece of change that had fallen—there was a penny in the midst, heads up. *Thank God.*

"Landed heads up," I said, showing the cashier the penny. "That's lucky, right?"

She shrugged. "I guess so."

This was all wrong—but I had the lucky penny. That was the important part. The rest probably didn't matter as much.

As I was leaving, I thought about how little I even understood about the timeline shift I'd been living in for a year now. I knew how the new timeline had affected me, and Summer for the most part, but what had happened to everyone else? To the guy Jake had sold his Bruno Mars ticket to before? To the girl I'd taken to prom in the previous timeline? To Katie, besides the obvious? To Marta—would she find out Sutton was cheating on her from someone else? *Was* he even cheating on her in this timeline? Something had definitely happened that put the wrong Walgreens cashier in my path, even if the penny itself was the most important piece of the puzzle—or, at least, I hoped it was. Maybe the only reason the wish had worked before was because of some extremely specific circumstance that I had somehow undone without realizing it in my attempts to save—

That was when I bumped into a woman on my way towards the fountain, causing her to drop her wallet.

"I am so sorry—" I began helping pick up her change, and then I realized: this was Leah Browning. I *knew* I'd run into her in the old timeline, too.

"Leah," I said, meeting her eyes. "Anita's aunt. Right?"

She nodded. "Did you know Anita?"

"You did an assembly at my school in February." I wished I was wearing the wristband. "My—my, uh, girlfriend and I were really touched by Anita's story."

"That fountain over there—we put it up in her memory," Leah explained. "There's a placard with the suicide hotline on it at the base beside her name. And, of course, a reminder to be kind."

Being kind wasn't enough. She needed help. Summer needed help. But I wasn't going to say that to her.

"I should get going," I said. "I... have something to take care of. But thank you, you know, for everything you do... for suicide prevention."

"Of course," she replied, turning to leave. "Have a great day, and remember to be kind."

I carefully made my wish and tossed the penny in the fountain, and then I got back in Esme's car.

"Where do we go from here?" I asked. "If it doesn't work? How do we move on from this?"

She shrugged. "I think that's what the grief counselors are for."

"I don't want to talk to counselors," I said. "I want to talk to Summer."

"I think that if Summer had had the chance to meet with counselors, there's a good chance she'd still be here. If I were you, I wouldn't take that for granted."

She had a point. I took a deep breath, trying to process everything.

"She's really gone, isn't she?"

"I don't see why Tim would lie about something like that."

"And there's nothing anyone can do about it this time, is there, if the fountain doesn't work again?"

"No, there isn't."

She put her arm around me, and we both cried. I wasn't ready to talk to the counselors today, but I wouldn't refrain from getting professional help to process this. In thinking about Summer, I wondered how many other kids out there would still be alive if they'd been able to access professional mental health resources.

Summer had mentioned something one time, months ago—something about wanting to start some type of organization that helped kids get access to those kinds of resources. She would have helped so many people, if only there had been someone to help her.

"Esme?" I asked.

"Yeah?"

"I need you to help me with something."

* * *

THE FIRST day of senior year. I straightened my tie; I had to look good for the assembly. I tried looking at my news feed before I left for school, but seeing everyone's pictures from the Europe trip wasn't what I needed. I took the weird pink stuffed animal from my bed and gave it a squeeze before putting it in my backpack and heading out the door.

Homeroom. We got our schedules, but instead of first period, we went to the multipurpose room. The rest of my class sat in the audience, but I joined

Leah Browning onstage. I took a seat behind her podium with Esme and Daisy.

"Last February, I came to talk to you all about my niece's suicide," Leah said, "and the last thing I wanted was to come back here on these terms. I spoke with Summer Madison after my presentation last winter. She was very caring and sweet. It breaks my heart to hear what happened. It truly does. I want to turn my time over to a few of Summer's friends, who spent the last two months working on a project they'd like to share."

Leah sat down, and Daisy took her place at the podium. She was the most eloquent speaker out of the three of us, and I wasn't sure I could speak in front of the whole school about Summer's death today.

"Two months ago, Nolan and Esme approached me with an idea," she said, "of something we could do in the wake of Summer's passing. They were supposed to go with Summer on a trip to Europe, but instead stayed behind to help launch this, with Ms. Browning's assistance." She clicked a button on the remote clicker in her hand. "The Prunell-Madison Foundation for Mental Health."

A picture of Summer appeared on the screen, as well as a picture of Anita Prunell. I kept my eyes on the audience so I wouldn't have to look at the photos.

"Donations to the Prunell-Madison Foundation go directly to teens and college students struggling to pay for medications like antidepressants, or to pay for therapy sessions, inpatient holds, rehabilitation centers, or transportation to and from any of the above. Donations also go towards educating teens, young adults, and parents about mental illnesses. It's important to be informed, especially in the case of parents choosing treatment options for minor-aged children. Throughout this school year, we'll be giving assemblies about the Prunell-Madison Foundation at various middle schools, high schools, and even colleges and universities. Nothing we do or say can bring Summer back, but we *can* work to inform others about mental illness and prevent tragedies like this from happening in the future."

The crowd clapped solemnly.

"I also wanted to say a few words about Summer," Daisy continued. "She was one of my best friends. I've known her since kindergarten. When I first heard the news... it didn't feel real. It still doesn't, most days. I'll still have passing thoughts to message her when something reminds me of her, or just to say hello. Think about your best friend, or someone close to you. Think about how you'd feel if you could never see or speak to that person again. If you think that person is worth saving, remember that everyone who dies by suicide meant something to someone, and help us spread awareness about this foundation."

Daisy sat down, and the principal introduced a tribute video we'd made for Summer. There was a moment of silence afterward—seventeen seconds, because Summer would forever be seventeen. Leah handed out pamphlets with information about Summer and Anita's foundation and how to donate or spread the word. Then everyone went back to class, Daisy and Esme went back to their own schools, and it was just another school day.

Esme was right—nothing any of us did or said, now or in some alternate timeline, could have stopped Summer's death. She was sick and she needed treatment, but she didn't get it and now she was gone.

It was never up to me to save her. I couldn't have saved her, and I knew that now. Because of her, I knew a lot more than I would have if I hadn't lived it all over again. Because of her, others were going to be able to get help. So it wasn't all for nothing.

At break, I saw Lucia, Kim, and Vanessa from Daisy's birthday party talking to Leah outside the auditorium. Each of them was taking a handful of pamphlets. Ms. Harris, one of the English teachers—Summer's favorite teacher—was also talking to Leah. She was blotting her eyes with a tissue. I was watching her take out her checkbook when someone's voice startled me.

"Hi, Nolan."

It was Jess Romano; I'd had a few classes with her, but I didn't know her well.

"Hey," I said.

She gave me a tight hug, and I gave her a light, awkward one back. "I know I wasn't close with Summer," she said, "but she was such a sweet girl. I wish I'd known how to help her. I never would've known she was depressed; she never acted like it."

"Thanks." I wasn't sure what else to say to her.

"I'm going to donate to your foundation," she said.

"Summer's foundation," I corrected her. "Summer's and Anita's."

"Right. Well, I'm going to ask my parents after school today."

"I appreciate it."

She hugged me again and kept walking. Then I noticed Ms. Harris approaching from the other direction.

"Hi, Nolan," she said. "I wanted to say thank you for all the work you're doing to raise awareness."

"Oh. Uh, thank you." I paused. "You were Summer's favorite teacher. She raved about your class all the time."

She nodded. "I was very lucky to get to know her."

"Me, too."

"Good luck with the foundation," she told me. "It's going to be a lot of work, but if you can save even one life, it will be worth it."

"Thank you."

I just wish that life could've been Summer's.

She walked away, and just when I thought I was done with the attention—

"Nolan?"

I looked up. Grant, Jimmy, Jean, and one of the special education teachers had come up to my side.

"Oh, hey, guys," I said.

"We just wanted to say that we're really sorry to hear about Summer," Grant said.

"She was always really nice to us," Jimmy added.

The special education teacher put a hand on Jean's shoulder and said, "Jean thought Summer was a very nice friend and she's sorry for your loss."

"Thank you," I said.

"And we wanted to give you some money for her foundation," Grant said. He reached into his pocket. "The three of us came up with seven dollars and fifty-four cents, but we're going to ask our parents for more tonight."

"Oh, uh, you really don't have to," I said. "Besides, I can't take donations. Only Leah can."

"We'll bring it to Leah, then," the teacher assured me.

"We don't want anyone else to die like this," Grant explained. "So if we can help, we want to help."

"I appreciate it," I said. "Really."

"Well, we should get going," the teacher said. "Let us know if you need anything."

"Thank you," I told her. "Uh... Grant, Jimmy? Maybe this weekend you guys can come over and show me how Minecraft works?"

Their faces lit up. "Yeah! I'll ask my mom!" Jimmy said.

"Me, too," Grant replied. "We're here for you, buddy! And we'll give you so much stuff—"

"Jean, you can come, too," I offered. I didn't want to exclude her.

Jean shook her head, frowning.

"Oh, Jean doesn't like Minecraft," Grant explained. "She always reminds us not to talk about it around her."

"Yeah, we get a little carried away sometimes," Jimmy said. "You'll have to let us know if we're talking about it too much, 'cause sometimes it's hard for us to tell when people aren't interested in what we're saying."

"But as long as you remind us, we'll shut up," Grant assured me. "See you this weekend?"

"See you this weekend."

Their teacher escorted them down the hall, and I took a step towards the lockers. I wasn't ready to look at Summer's locker—with that stupid note I gave her probably still sitting in it. She was supposed to open it today. It said, *"We made it,"* but she'd never see it, because she didn't.

Marta was in the locker bay, though, blocking the view. She was standing at her own locker. I couldn't believe she'd had the audacity to still go on that trip.

Summer's own mother had refused to help with the foundation; she was probably still in denial. She hadn't even had a funeral for Summer, just a private gathering for family only. She would come around in her own time, though. Esme, Daisy, and I had checked in with her from time to time and brought her food for a while in the beginning, until she told us to stop. I didn't get the chance to speak with her father, but he'd sent Leah a check for $1,700 after she'd called to tell him about the foundation. He assured her he'd send more over time—something about the cost of plane tickets every year. My parents had signed up to be recurring donors.

"Take a picture. It'll last longer," Marta snapped. I suppose I'd been staring.

"Sorry," I told her. "Uh... how was the trip?"

"Amazing," she replied, adjusting her hair so I could see she was wearing a pair of diamond earrings. "Shame you and Esme pulled out of it."

"Well, we had more important things to do," I reminded her. "Speaking of... how are you?"

"Great," she said. "I just spent thirty-five days in Europe, Sutton's moving in with some friends this weekend so I'll be able to spend more time with him, and I got all the classes I wanted for this year."

"You know what I meant."

She tossed her hair. "No, I don't, actually."

"Summer."

"Summer's over."

"*Summer*, your former best friend who we just had an entire fucking assembly about."

She shrugged. "I don't know what to tell you, Nolan. Summer's gone, and she was dead to me long before anyone else."

I couldn't hold back. "You're a heartless bitch, Marta, and losing your friendship was one of the best things that could've happened to Summer."

"You tell yourself that, but she's still dead, isn't she?"

I wanted to yell at her. I wanted to go off and make her regret it, but in that smirk, I could see the corners of her lips trembling. She was grieving, too, even if she didn't want to admit it. So I walked away.

Across the hall, I saw Jonah. He glanced at me for a second but didn't say anything. I didn't want to talk to him, anyway. So I went to my own locker.

Liam's voice startled me. "Hey, man."

I looked up. "Oh, hey."

"What you're doing is great, you know," he said. "You're gonna help a lot of people."

"Yeah." I sighed. "Yeah."

"I know it doesn't change the fact that Summer—well, you know. And I don't want to say some cheesy 'if she was still here, you wouldn't be helping all these people' kind of thing, either, because it doesn't make her death okay."

"No, it doesn't."

"But you know what? At least you can move forward knowing that you were a good person to her," he said. "The girls who bullied Leah's niece— they have to spend the rest of their lives wondering if they contributed to her suicide. Probably knowing that, at least to some degree, they did. But you? You were great for Summer. She just needed treatment, and that's all there is to it."

I nodded. "Yeah. I guess there's that."

Maybe what I'd said to Summer in the other timeline was what pushed her over the edge. Maybe it was just her inability to get help for her depression, or whatever else she might have been dealing with. I'd never know the answer to that. But in this timeline, I didn't have to wonder.

"If you ever need to talk about it, though," Liam said, "I got you. Jake, too."

"Thanks, man. I appreciate it."

We hugged, and he went on his way to class. I stared at Summer's locker—unclaimed this year.

I didn't have to accept Summer's death—not yet, at least. I didn't have to believe it was okay that she'd killed herself, or that in some twisted way it would end up being a good thing.

The only thing I had to do was fight for people like her, until they could fight for themselves.

If you are looking for a sign to keep going,
this is it!

National Suicide Prevention Lifeline:

988

or

1-800-273-8255

Acknowledgements:

To my friends and family who have supported me from the beginning, or at least for as long as we've known each other.

To everyone who beta read this book (or critiqued an early edition as part of a class assignment for Fiction Writing in fall 2020)

To Dr. Lewis for making us read that AWFUL book that inspired me to write better representation for autistic characters--believe me, there are more to come!

To Mrs. Sarringhaus for inspiring my love of writing from a young age.

To all the teachers who supported me from elementary school through college, especially the ones who never took my notebooks away when I was writing during class ;)

To my therapist for helping me survive the journey of writing and publishing this book.

To Michelle, my talented artist friend.

To Kelsey, my editor.

To and in memory of my sweet Sugar baby, because the chapters of this book that I wrote with you in my lap are the best ones.

Author's Note

** * **

"SAVING SUMMER" started buzzing around in my head as an idea for a short story in late 2017. Many different versions popped in and out of my head from then until November 6, 2019, when everything suddenly came together for me in the middle of a British literature class I was taking at the University of Delaware. I remember thinking in that moment that I knew exactly what I wanted to do, and then trying my best to pay attention for the remainder of class until I could run back home and start outlining this novel in the small window of time I had before I needed to get ready to meet a friend later that evening. If that professor happens to be reading this, I do confess that I *might* have started typing up part of the outline during class.

It's been so surreal to see this novel come together, and to think of all the changes it's been through along the way, and the setbacks I endured both with actual writing and with the steps in the publication process. This was a hard novel for me to write at times, emotionally—the first draft of Summer's final scene took ages to get through. But if you're reading this, that means "Saving Summer" has officially gone from an idea that popped into my head almost seven years ago to a completed, published novel.

Thank you for taking the time to read this novel. Your support means more to me than I can put into words. The only thing I have ever consistently wanted to be for as long as I can remember is a writer, and your support allows me to fulfill that dream.

When I was a teenager myself struggling with my own mental health, I remember developing this desire that the right person would come along to "save" me. Most of the media that I consumed pointed to the idea that true love could save you from yourself in the end. Of course as I grew up, I learned that that isn't how the world works. Depression is a lot deeper than just needing the right person to love you back to life.

As I crafted Summer's story and Nolan's journey with her, I wanted to tell a story that told the brutal truth. It was hard to commit to that ending with how much I grew to love these characters, their flaws, their growth, and their histories... I wondered if letting Summer die was the right choice in the end. Of course, I knew what I had to do.

Along the way, however, I realized there was another story I wanted to tell.

When I was diagnosed with autism in the summer of 2010, the world was—or at least, it felt like—a much different place. I was fourteen years old and my biggest fear was that people from school would find out and would treat me differently. Now, either there is less of a stigma surrounding autism, or most people in my life have just grown up, but either way I am able to feel comfortable with sharing this part of myself. I am able to embrace this part of myself and know it was never something to be ashamed of.

In the spring of 2020, I took a class that focused on YA literature, and we had to read a book featuring an autistic protagonist. The book was not written by an autistic person, and as a result, the way the character was written made me uncomfortable and the whole book left a bad taste in my mouth. Some of my classmates also seemed to feel a similar way when we were discussing the book, and it made me realize that I had the power to create autistic characters written by an autistic author.

Almost immediately, I started drafting a new story with an openly autistic protagonist and her experiences and struggles and triumphs and growth, and her ultimate happy ending... Well, when I went back to my draft of "Saving Summer," I realized that making Summer's character autistic-coded would make sense. The story could not have the same happy ending as the other project coming together in my head, but it could tell another important story: the story that's an unfortunate reality for too many people.

I could show how harmful the stigma against autism was to people: how it could prevent them from receiving a diagnosis, or from embracing that part of themselves the way I was eventually able to. I could show the growth some of the characters experienced–and the lack thereof for others–when it came to that stigma. However, I had to decide: did I really want my first autistic protagonist, my *only* autistic protagonist for some length of time until I could finish and publish another story, to be a character who dies before she's even able to get an official diagnosis, let alone come to terms with it and embrace herself for who she is, and be loved by those around her for who she is?

While the harmful effects of stigmatization are an unfortunate reality for too many people, I want people like my fourteen year old self to be able to read about people like them who grow up to be loved and celebrated for who they are. But I didn't want to waste the opportunity to tell Summer's story, either.

I hope you'll look forward to autistic representation that comes with a happier story in my next novel, which is in the beta reading stage as you read this. In the meantime, I'm thankful to share this story with you and the many important messages embedded within.

Thank you again for your support and for reading this novel. Hope to see you again soon!

Olivia Linder

About the Author

Photo by Opal + Hannah Photography

Olivia Linder is an independently published author. She was born in San Jose, California in 1996, where she lived until age nineteen. She graduated from the University of Delaware in 2021 with a bachelor's degree in English education. She now resides in Delaware. At fourteen, she was diagnosed with autism. She has always been passionate about reading and writing, and her stories come from the heart.

Follow Me on Social Media!

www.OliviaLinderBooks.com

@OliviaLinderAuthor

Facebook | Instagram | YouTube

Olivia Linder Books logo by Michelle Winks